W9-DJA-395

PENGUIN CLASSICS

THE TURN OF THE SCREW
AND OTHER GHOST STORIES

SERIES ADVISOR: PHILIP HORNE

HENRY JAMES was born in 1843 in Washington Place, New York, of Scottish and Irish ancestry. His father was a prominent theologian and philosopher and his elder brother, William, also became famous as a philosopher. James attended schools in New York and later in London, Paris and Geneva, before briefly entering the Law School at Harvard in 1862. In 1864 he began to contribute reviews and short stories to American journals. He visited Europe twice as an adult before moving to Paris in 1875, where he met Flaubert, Turgenev and other literary figures. However, after a year he moved to London, where he met with such success in society that he confessed to accepting 107 invitations in the winter of 1878–9 alone. In 1898 he left London and went to live at Lamb House, Rye, Sussex. Henry James became a naturalized British citizen in 1915, and was awarded the Order of Merit in 1916, shortly before his death in February of that year.

In addition to many short stories, plays, books of criticism, biography and autobiography, and much travel writing, he wrote some twenty novels, the first of which, *Watch and Ward*, appeared serially in the *Atlantic Monthly* in 1871. His novella 'Daisy Miller' (1878) established him as a literary figure on both sides of the Atlantic. Other novels include *Roderick Hudson* (1875), *The American* (1877), *The Europeans* (1878), *Washington Square* (1880), *The Portrait of a Lady* (1881), *The Bostonians* (1886), *The Princess Casamassima* (1886), *The Tragic Muse* (1890), *The Spoils of Poynton* (1897), *What Maisie Knew* (1897), *The Awkward Age* (1899), *The Wings of the Dove* (1902), *The Ambassadors* (1903) and *The Golden Bowl* (1904).

SUSIE BOYT was educated at St Catherine's College, Oxford, and University College London, where she studied Anglo-American literary relations. She is the author of six novels and a memoir. She writes regularly for the Arts and Life section of the *Financial Times* and is a director at the Hampstead Theatre in London.

PHILIP HORNE is a Professor of English at University College London. He is the author of *Henry James and Revision: The New York Edition* (1990); editor of *Henry James: A Life in Letters* (1999); and co-editor of *Thorold Dickinson: A World of Film* (2008). He has also edited *Henry James, A London Life & The Reverberator*; and for Penguin, Henry James, *The Tragic Muse* and *The Portrait of a Lady*, and Charles Dickens, *Oliver Twist*. He has written articles on Henry James, and on a wide range of other subjects, including telephones and literature, zombies and consumer culture, the films of Powell and Pressburger and Martin Scorsese, the texts of Emily Dickinson, the criticism of F. R. Leavis, poetic allusion in Victorian fiction, and Bob Dylan and the Mississippi Blues. He is a General Editor of the Cambridge University Press edition of the Complete Fiction of Henry James.

HENRY JAMES

The Turn of the Screw and Other Ghost Stories

Edited and with an Introduction and Notes by
SUSIE BOYT

PENGUIN BOOKS

PENGUIN CLASSICS

UK | USA | Canada | Ireland | Australia
India | New Zealand | South Africa

Penguin Books is part of the Penguin Random House group of companies
whose addresses can be found at global.penguinrandomhouse.com

This edition first published in Penguin Classics 2017
002

Introduction and editorial material © Susie Boyt, 2017
Chronology copyright © Philip Horne, 2008, revised 2017
All rights reserved

The moral right of the editors has been asserted

Set in 10.25/12.25 pt Sabon
Typeset by Jouve (UK), Milton Keynes
Printed in Great Britain by Clays Ltd, St Ives plc

ISBN: 978-0-141-38975-2

www.greenpenguin.co.uk

MIX
Paper from
responsible sources
FSC® C018179

Penguin Random House is committed to a
sustainable future for our business, our readers
and our planet. This book is made from Forest
Stewardship Council® certified paper.

Contents

THE TURN OF THE SCREW AND OTHER GHOST STORIES

Chronology

1843 *15 April*: Henry James born at 21 Washington Place in New York City, second of five children of Henry James (1811–82), speculative theologian and social thinker, whose strict entrepreneur father had amassed wealth estimated at $3 million, one of the top ten American fortunes of his time, and his wife Mary (1810–82), daughter of James Walsh, a New York cotton merchant of Scottish origin.

1843–5 Accompanies parents to Paris and London.

1845–7 James family returns to USA and settles in Albany, New York.

1847–55 Family settles in New York City; HJ taught by tutors and in private schools.

1855–8 Family travels in Europe: Geneva, London, Paris, Boulogne-sur-Mer. Returns to USA and settles in Newport, Rhode Island.

1859–60 Family in Europe again: HJ attends scientific school, then the Academy (later the University) in Geneva. Learns German in Bonn.

September 1860: Family returns to Newport. HJ makes friends with future critic T. S. Perry (who records that HJ 'was continually writing stories, mainly of a romantic kind') and artist John La Farge.

1861–3 Injures his back helping to extinguish a fire in Newport and is exempted from military service in American Civil War (1861–5).

Autumn 1862: Enters Harvard Law School for a term. Begins to send stories to magazines.

1864 *February*: First short story, 'A Tragedy of Error', published anonymously in *Continental Monthly*.

    May: Family moves to 13 Ashburton Place, Boston, Massachusetts.

    October: Unsigned review published in *North American Review*.

1865 *March*: First signed tale, 'The Story of a Year', appears in *Atlantic Monthly*. HJ's criticism published in first number of the *Nation* (New York).

1866–8 Continues reviewing and writing stories.

    Summer 1866: W. D. Howells, novelist, critic and influential editor, becomes a friend.

    November 1866: Family moves to 20 Quincy Street, beside Harvard Yard, in Cambridge, Massachusetts.

1869 Travels for his health to England, where he meets John Ruskin, William Morris, Charles Darwin and George Eliot; also visits Switzerland and Italy.

1870 *March*: Death in USA of his much-loved cousin Minny Temple.

    May: HJ, still unwell, is reluctantly back in Cambridge.

1871 *August–December*: First short novel, *Watch and Ward*, serialized in *Atlantic Monthly*.

1872–4 Accompanies invalid sister Alice and aunt Catherine Walsh ('Aunt Kate') to Europe in May. Writes travel pieces for the *Nation*. Between October 1872 and September 1874 spends periods of time in Paris, Rome, Switzerland, Homburg and Italy without his family.

    Spring 1874: Begins first long novel, *Roderick Hudson*, in Florence.

    September 1874: Returns to USA.

1875 *January*: Publishes *A Passionate Pilgrim, and Other Tales*, his first work to appear in book form. It is followed by *Transatlantic Sketches* (travel pieces) and then by *Roderick Hudson* in November. Spends six months in New York City (111 East 25th Street), then three in Cambridge.

    11 November: Arrives at 29 rue de Luxembourg, Paris, as correspondent for the *New York Tribune*.

    December: Begins new novel, *The American*.

1876 Meets Gustave Flaubert, Ivan Turgenev, Edmond de Goncourt, Alphonse Daudet, Guy de Maupassant and Émile Zola.

December: Moves to London and settles at 3 Bolton Street, just off Piccadilly.

1877 Visits Paris, Florence and Rome.

May: *The American* is published.

1878 Meets William Gladstone, Alfred Tennyson and Robert Browning.

February: *French Poets and Novelists* (collection of essays), is the first book HJ publishes in London.

July: 'Daisy Miller' (novella) serialized in *The Cornhill Magazine*; in November *Harper's* publish it in the USA, establishing HJ's reputation on both sides of the Atlantic.

September: Publishes *The Europeans* (novel).

1879 *December*: Publishes *Confidence* (novel) and *Hawthorne* (critical study).

1880 *December*: Publishes *Washington Square* (novel).

1881 *October*: Returns to USA; visits Cambridge.

November: Publishes *The Portrait of a Lady* (novel).

1882 *January*: Death of mother. Visits New York and Washington, DC.

May: Travels back to England but returns to USA on death of father in December.

1883 *Summer*: Returns to London.

November: Fourteen-volume collected edition of fiction published by Macmillan.

December: Publishes *Portraits of Places* (travel writings).

1884 Sister Alice moves to London and settles near HJ.

September: Publishes *A Little Tour in France* (travel writings) and *Tales of Three Cities*; his important artistic statement 'The Art of Fiction' appears in *Longman's Magazine*. Becomes a friend of R. L. Stevenson and Edmund Gosse. Writes to his American friend Grace Norton: 'I shall never marry ... I am both happy enough and miserable enough, as it is.'

1885–6 Publishes two serial novels, *The Bostonians* and *The Princess Casamassima*.

6 March 1886: Moves into flat at 34 De Vere Gardens.

1887 *Spring and summer*: Visits Florence and Venice. Continues friendship (begun in 1880) with American novelist Constance Fenimore Woolson.

1888 Publishes *The Reverberator* (novel), 'The Aspern Papers' (novella) and *Partial Portraits* (criticism).

1889 *A London Life* (collection of tales) published.

1890 *The Tragic Muse* (novel) published.

1891 HJ's dramatization of *The American* has a short run in the provinces and London.

1892 *February*: Publishes *The Lesson of the Master* (story collection).

March: Death of Alice James in London.

1893 Three volumes of tales published: *The Real Thing* (March), *The Private Life* (June), *The Wheel of Time* (September).

1894 Deaths of Constance Fenimore Woolson and R. L. Stevenson.

1895 *5 January*: *Guy Domville* (play) is greeted by boos and applause on its premiere at St James's Theatre; HJ abandons playwriting for many years. Visits Ireland. Takes up cycling. Publishes two volumes of tales, *Terminations* (May) and *Embarrassments* (June).

1896 Publishes *The Other House* (novel).

1897 Two novels, *The Spoils of Poynton* and *What Maisie Knew*, published.

February: Starts dictating, due to wrist problems.

September: Takes lease on Lamb House, Rye, Sussex.

1898 *June*: Moves into Lamb House. Sussex neighbours include the writers Joseph Conrad, H. G. Wells and Ford Madox Hueffer (Ford).

August: Publishes *In the Cage* (short novel).

October: 'The Turn of the Screw', ghost story included in *The Two Magics*, proves his most popular work since 'Daisy Miller'.

1899 *April*: *The Awkward Age* (novel) published.

August: Buys the freehold of Lamb House.

1900 Shaves off his beard.

August: Publishes *The Soft Side* (collection of tales). Friendship with American novelist Edith Wharton develops.

1901 *February*: Publishes *The Sacred Fount* (novel).

1902 *August*: Publishes *The Wings of the Dove* (novel).

1903 *February*: Publishes *The Better Sort* (collection of tales).

September: Publishes *The Ambassadors* (novel).

October: Publishes *William Wetmore Story and his Friends* (biography).

1904 *August*: Sails to USA, his first visit for twenty-one years. Travels to New England, New York, Philadelphia, Washington, the South, St Louis, Chicago, Los Angeles and San Francisco.

November: Publishes *The Golden Bowl* (novel).

1905 *January*: Is President Theodore Roosevelt's guest at the White House. Elected to the American Academy of Arts and Letters.

July: Back in Lamb House, begins revising works for the New York Edition of *The Novels and Tales of Henry James*.

October: Publishes *English Hours* (travel essays).

1906–8 Selects, arranges, writes prefaces and has illustrations made for New York Edition (published 1907–9, twenty-four volumes).

1907 *January*: Publishes *The American Scene* (travel essays).

1908 *March*: *The High Bid* (play) produced at Edinburgh.

1909 *October*: Publishes *Italian Hours* (travel essays). Health problems.

1910 *August*: Travels to USA with brother William, who dies a week after their return.

October: Publishes *The Finer Grain* (collection of tales).

1911 *August*: Returns to England.

October: Publishes *The Outcry* (novel adapted from play). Begins work on autobiography.

1912 *June*: Receives honorary doctorate from Oxford University.

October: Takes flat at 21 Carlyle Mansions, Cheyne Walk, Chelsea; suffers from shingles.

1913 *March*: Publishes *A Small Boy and Others* (first volume of autobiography). Portrait painted by John Singer Sargent for seventieth birthday.

1914 *March*: Publishes *Notes of a Son and Brother* (second volume of autobiography).

August: Outbreak of First World War; HJ becomes passionately engaged with the British cause and helps Belgian refugees and wounded soldiers.

October: Publishes *Notes on Novelists* (criticism).

1915 Is made honorary president of the American Volunteer Motor Ambulance Corps.

July: Becomes a British citizen. Writes essays about the war (collected in *Within the Rim* (1919)) and the Preface to *Letters from America* (1916) by the poet Rupert Brooke, who had died the previous year.

2 December: Suffers a stroke.

1916 Awarded the Order of Merit in New Year Honours.

28 February: Dies. After his funeral in Chelsea Old Church, his ashes are smuggled back to America by sister-in-law and buried in the family plot in Cambridge.

Philip Horne, 2017

Introduction

First-time readers should be aware that details of the plots are revealed in this Introduction.

Was Henry James really interested in ghosts? In ghosts, simply and purely, as and for themselves? Ghosts seem too crude a matter for a writer whose reputation is founded on a commitment to rendering, with truth and subtlety, the complete landscape of human consciousness. James's genius for encompassing the fine detail of being makes him seem more acute-minded, more attached to scrutiny and scruples than supernatural concerns and sensational occurrences could ever bear. He might be thought both too worldly and too innocent for ghosts. For there is a crassness and bluntness to the supernatural and to horror; ghosts can lend an ugly, unearned swagger to a story, and the vagueness of spirits and their simple motivation or lack of agency may seem wholly at odds with the rigour and the conscientiousness of James's versions of consciousness.

Besides, what sectors of James's sphere of interest do ghosts occupy or pass through? Are ghosts clever? Do they care about fine feelings and fine furniture? Does money mean a great deal to them? Did any ghost ever mind how bad the shops of Venice are, or suffer dreadfully with its digestion, or gaze out in a Piccadilly direction and see an evening six parties deep? Are ghosts' motives – misery, revenge, heart-break – too low and crass for a writer of James's stature?

Do ghosts exercise themselves over how to exist fully in the world without taking on any of the taint that the word 'worldly' carries? Can ghosts be ground in the very mill of the conventional? Are ghosts only really of interest to James because of the stimuli and provocation they present to the human nervous system?

'The supernatural story, the subject wrought in fantasy, is not the *class* of fiction I myself most cherish,'[1] James wrote, as if to break the news to ghosts gently. 'Shameless pot-boiler',[2] '*jeu d'esprit*'[3] and 'that wanton little Tale',[4] was how James variously described 'The Turn of the Screw', as well as 'a poor little pot-boiling study of nothing at all.'[5] It was as though at times he felt bashful in relation to his best ghost-work, or felt he ought to appear so. In the mid-twentieth century, F. R. Leavis's final verdict on 'The Turn of the Screw', that it was a 'non-significant thriller, done, nevertheless, with the subtlety of the great master', stemmed from a belief that there was nothing 'ponderable' about the tale, nothing deeper than the 'reek' of 'Evil' that James refers to in his Preface.[6] Yet in a letter to Hendrik Andersen in 1906, James thickened the plot by writing that the expression 'pot-boiler' could represent 'in the lives of all artists, some of the most beautiful things ever done by them.'[7] Oh!

Certainly, supernatural concerns and sensational content figured in James's writing throughout his career. He was committed to the 'dear old sacred terror', returning to it frequently. He maintained a lifelong interest in paranormal phenomena, attending meetings at the Society for Psychical Research, where his brother William held high office. James was friendly with, and corresponded with, its more prominent members, such as F. W. H. Myers and Edmund Gurney, and there are references to the Society and its work in his letters and notebooks. 'I see ghosts everywhere,' James wrote in a letter to Francis Boott on 11 October 1895,[8] and it cannot be denied. James is haunted by them. It is true to say, however, that the ghosts in his ghost stories are not always the best things about them. It is sometimes hard for ghosts to match the calibre of the scenes they haunt. In tales such as 'The Romance of Certain Old Clothes', 'The Last of the Valerii' or 'Owen Wingrave', the supernatural elements occasionally seem beneath James.

'Owen Wingrave' is a small masterpiece in which the beliefs and traditions of a proud and brutal military family harden in the face of the complete lack of desire in its most able son for a career as a soldier. The characters are complex and the crisis of Owen's pacifist principles is richly drawn and deeply felt. Spencer Coyle, the man in charge of preparing young Owen for Sandhurst, is shocked and disappointed by Owen's turn of mind, but he also cannot help looking at the Wingrave family and thinking 'that the boy was the best of them'. Yet the impact of discovering that Owen's great-great-grandfather once killed his own child in anger, or that Owen's living relatives talk of his pacifist scruples 'as you wouldn't talk of a cannibal's god', even the sternly disapproving atmosphere of the family portraits on the stair, all these moments are graver, stranger and more profound than the passages concerning the vengeful ghost. Like the elements of revenge in Jacobean revenge tragedy, the ghostly parts of James's stories now and then seem their least appealing aspect. Virginia Woolf said of 'Owen Wingrave', 'The catastrophe has not the right relations to what has gone before', and I think there is something in that.[9] The ghosts aren't necessarily needed, or rather, they're already there.

In the eight stories that form this volume, the range of ghosts, the play and the menace of ghosts and their meaning, is broad and varying. Ghosts can provide companionship and excitement, they can punish and terrify. They can provoke bouts of rivalry, they can murder, they can push a fellow to the brink of madness, and they can also embody the complexities of a path not taken. They can be courtly. They can serve as a premonition of an imminent death. They can judge, convict and condemn.

Ghosts in James's stories and wider fiction are often catalysts, appearing at transitional times. Returning to his former home after a third of a century 'ready to climb ladders, to walk the plank, to handle materials and look wise about them', the hero of 'The Jolly Corner', Spencer Brydon, might well have felt dismayed *not* to have met with some kind of ghostly visitation, for the situation absolutely requires one. Looking back over the life he might have led he almost psychoanalyses an alternative ghost-self into being. He sees 'the impalpable ashes of his long-extinct youth, afloat in the air like microscopic motes' and later he 'found all things come back to the question of what he personally might have been, how he might have led his life and "turned out"'.

The shadowy figure of a ghost, incomprehensible and blurred at its edges, helps some of James's more untried characters spring sharply into focus. Ghosts can be a spur to heroism. If happiness comes from difficulties overcome, ghosts can provide these difficulties in spades. In 'The Turn of the Screw', the spectral figures provide opportunities for kindness, professional conscientiousness, gallantry followed by sainthood if not deification, as the fraught governess rouses herself to rescue the children she believes are morally and physically endangered. Looking after children and all the 'grey prose' that might involve would never have been enough for this young woman.

Ghosts can be a mark of distinction for those who experience them, evidence of fine-grained sensibility. In 'Sir Edmund Orme', seeing the ghost is a proof of being in love. In 'The Friends of the Friends', the lady and gentleman who both separately see ghostly visions of a parent at the time these parents die are held to inhabit a higher plane than the rest of their circle. It is a sign of their refined consciousness. According to Ralph Touchett in *The Portrait of a Lady* (1881), the Gardencourt ghost appears to those who have lived to 'suffer enough'.

More prosaically and humorously in 'The Third Person', the Frush cousins' ghost brings excitement and the promise of adventure, glamour even, lifting otherwise monochrome lives:

'He's young,' she added.
'But he's *bad*!' said Miss Susan.
'He's handsome! . . . Splendidly.'
' "Splendidly"!'

Neither lady, we feel, has ever quite had a conversation like that before about a man.

Ghosts, and the meanings that they have, can also change during the course of a story. Later in 'The Third Person', the ghost of the cousins' long-lost convicted smuggling ancestor inhabits many different personas as the pair get to know him. Initially he frightens as an intruder would, but jealousy, for

Miss Amy, follows swiftly in fear's wake: 'Why, she [Miss Amy] afterwards asked herself in secret, should the restless spirit of a dead adventurer have addressed itself, in its trouble, to such a person as her queer, quaint, inefficient housemate?' Yet despite setting these cousins up as rivals for his attention, the ghost of Cuthbert Frush brings his kinsfolk closer. He gives them a joint interest in the way a charming niece might in a Jane Austen novel; he is their weather, their politics, their news. When the cousins decide that the ghost has outstayed his welcome, is beginning to be a headache and a bore, something to be well rid of, they enjoy a game of working out what that 'well' might signify. For a brief spell the tale becomes a detective story – the ghost has given them intrepid work to fill their days. The ghost of Cuthbert Frush casts a flattering light on the old cousins, allowing them to appear to each other as characters from a book or, better still, a play. 'There had been something hitherto wanting, they felt, to their small state and importance; it was present now, and they were as handsomely conscious of it as if they had previously missed it.' The dead man brings the cousins something valuable in the extreme – more life. He turns these two kinsfolk who keep different hours and have little in common into something they weren't quite before his arrival – a family. They will be talking about him for the rest of their lives.

The more you look for ghosts or hints of ghosts – ghosts of ghosts – in James's body of work, the larger, the more essential, the more over-arching they appear. In his 1910 essay 'Is There a Life After Death?' James linked the thoroughness of his artistic methods to the sublime, to something spiritual and unknowable. 'I deal with being, I invoke and evoke, I figure and represent, I seize and fix, as many phases and aspects and conceptions of it as my infirm hand allows me strength for; and in so doing I find myself – I can't express it otherwise – in communication with *sources* . . .' Later he continues, 'in proportion as we do curiously and lovingly, yearningly and irrepressibly, interrogate and liberate, try and test and explore, our general productive and, as we like conveniently to say, creative awareness of things . . . in that proportion does our function strike us as establishing sublime relations.'[10] In fiction that is partly devoted to uncovering, monitoring and weighing the starts and false starts, the pathways and hiding places of being, what due is to be paid to the sides of consciousness that resist or retreat from being known? How can one best represent this other side, which may refuse to be prised open, for it contains the unknowable, the secret, the bewildering? Is one answer to this question ghosts?

And if actual ghosts make one recoil slightly, not necessarily from fear but for artistic reasons or matters of taste, if you take a sidestep and ask what is more interesting to James (and to me) than the things that haunt people, the answer comes back 'Nothing!' The mute call from the past, acutely felt; loss made vivid in the present; words unuttered striking another character with full force; the smarting of old or freshly realized error . . . If we allow the ghostliness of these typical Jamesian experiences – of health shot through, of grief, of entrenched family history; of regret – then we, like James, must see ghosts everywhere too.

Before looking at James's ghostly masterpiece 'The Turn of the Screw' in detail, I want to draw attention to broader ideas of hauntings in two short novels James wrote about the same time: *What Maisie Knew*, which appeared the year before 'The Turn of the Screw', in 1897, and *The Spoils of Poynton*, which first appeared in serial form as *The Old Things* the year before that. There is a moving passage in *What Maisie Knew* when Maisie is walking in Kensington Gardens with her stepfather Sir Claude and unexpectedly happens upon her mother Ida. Ida is meant to be playing in a billiards tournament 'at Brussels', but here she is in the park very much 'with' a man, a man unknown to Maisie and her stepfather.

> 'My own child,' Ida murmured in a voice – a voice of sudden confused tenderness – that it seemed to her she heard for the first time. She wavered but an instant, thrilled with the first direct appeal, as distinguished from the mere maternal pull, she had

ever had from lips that, even in the old vociferous years, had always been sharp. The next moment she was on her mother's breast, where, amid a wilderness of trinkets, she felt as if she had suddenly been thrust, with a smash of glass, into a jeweller's shop-front, but only to be as suddenly ejected with a push and the brisk injunction: 'Now go to the Captain!'[11]

This scene, perhaps the most memorable in the book, achieves its power through the temporary collapse of Ida's habitual 'violent splendour'. The resultant 'sudden confused tenderness' conjures for a second Maisie's mother's near-opposite – a soft maternal spirit, much-missed. The oddness of the situation – Maisie's mother's being caught out, wholly unexpectedly – has allowed something uncanny to peep through her mother's fierce brilliance, by accident. There is a wildly hopeful aspect to this accident which suggests that such unprecedented softness is Maisie's mother at her most sincere, when all her defences are down. This is a child's idealized view, naturally. Still, a traditionally maternal note has found its way into her mother's tone at last, and this ghost of a tender mother makes all Ida's harshness, for an instant, look like a veneer. Is it possible her mother might want her or better still need her? This is cause for high celebration. Maisie, briefly, is overjoyed. The vision is sustaining – only then to be forcibly knocked out of Maisie almost as soon as it has arisen. She is punished for seeing the ghost of what a mother might be, what a mother might mean. One senses, however, that the vision will remain in the memory and the imagination where Maisie's generous nature will cherish it . . .

In *The Spoils of Poynton*, towards the end of the novel, there is speculation about an actual ghost at Poynton, the house that widowed aesthete Mrs Gereth has now passed down to her son Owen:

'Somehow there were no ghosts at Poynton,' Fleda went on. 'That was the only fault.'

Mrs. Gereth, considering, appeared to fall in with this fine humour. 'Poynton was too splendidly happy.'

'Poynton was too splendidly happy,' Fleda promptly echoed.

'But it's cured of that now,' her companion added.

'Yes, henceforth there'll be a ghost or two.'

Mrs. Gereth thought again: she found her young friend suggestive. 'Only *she* won't see them.'[12]

The implication here is that Owen will be haunted, as he lives his life, by the fact that he has married the monstrous Mona Brigstock when he might have had the superior Fleda Vetch for his wife: haunted by regret, haunted by the ghosts of lost kindness and sensitivity and fellow feeling.

Yet it is the hazy remembrance of the 'maiden-aunt' who used to live at Mrs Gereth's new home, Ricks, which provides the most haunted section of the book. Fleda Vetch senses the ghost of this aunt, powerfully, in Ricks' atmosphere and it delights and sustains her, opening out the possibilities of the sort of life generally viewed as closed.

> The more she looked about the surer she felt of the character of the maiden-aunt, the sense of whose dim presence urged her to pacification: the maiden-aunt had been a dear; she should have adored the maiden-aunt. The poor lady had passed shyly, yet with some bruises, through life; had been sensitive and ignorant and exquisite: that too was a sort of origin, a sort of atmosphere for relics and rarities . . .

It is this scene from *The Spoils of Poynton* that I return to in thought more than any other – to the extent that I put something of the aunt's brave, delicate, suffering atmosphere into a small flat in my own first novel. The ghost of a good mother for Maisie also continues to haunt my imagination, where I sometimes find myself, on an ordinary Tuesday, wishing Maisie good things, better things.

'The Turn of the Screw' has been written about more than any other work by Henry James. There is something about its dark heart, its obsessive heroine and its invitations and refusals to be pinned down that renders it irresistible to critics. And yet it is knowing in the extreme. Almost everything you might say of it, the tale says first about itself. 'The story *won't* tell . . . not in any literal, vulgar way,' Douglas warns us in the framing narrative. Well, you can say that again. Any ghost worth its salt will make you yourself feel like an interloper on account of its prior claim, and the story gives us that remark also: 'While these instants lasted indeed I had the extraordinary chill of a feeling that it was I who was the intruder,' says the governess.

'The Turn of the Screw' is a tale in which facts and sensations of wildly differing importance frequently carry the same amount of emphasis, are indeed so mixed and merged that it can be bewildering; but then we are alerted to this in the governess's first line: 'I remember the whole beginning as a succession of flights and drops, a little see-saw of the right throbs and the wrong.' This sentence hints that the difference between good and bad is uncertain from the start and that any attempt to distinguish between the two can take on the arbitrary quality of a child's game. 'The Turn of the Screw' examines what it means for a highly strung young woman to see herself fully, or to try to, for the first time. What novelty do we find in pride of place in the governess's bedroom? Why, full-length mirrors, in which she will be able to observe herself 'from head to foot', which we are told her previous 'scant home' lacked.

'The Turn of the Screw' is a complex, rich text that can withstand the most forensic levels of analysis, even those based on psychological theories devised decades after it was conceived.[13] You can approach it as a ghost story of unparalleled subtlety and skill – where the ambiguity itself stands as a sort of third ghost – or, equally, it can be read as an intricate portrait of an inexperienced young woman with a surfeit of consciousness and a youngest daughter's natural desire for heroism, who gains her first taste of romance and straight away steps into a world of overwhelming responsibility and loss.

'The Turn of the Screw' made a strong impression from its initial appearance in *Collier's Weekly* magazine, where it ran in twelve episodes from January to April 1898. It was published in book form in October of the same year, alongside the tale

'Covering End', in a volume called *The Two Magics*. Most contemporary critics were enjoyably horrified by 'The Turn of the Screw'; they took both pleasure and satisfaction in the suffering it portrays, as well as a delight in the way it achieved its effects. On 15 October 1898, *The New York Times Saturday Review of Books and Art* described it as 'a deliberate, powerful, and horribly successful study of the magic of evil, of the subtle influence over human hearts and minds of the sin with which this world is accursed'.[14] *Literature* on the same day termed it 'so astonishing a piece of art that it cannot be described'. A week later *The New York Tribune* claimed that the story 'crystallizes an original and fascinating idea in absolutely appropriate form' and the *Detroit Free Press* called the work a 'horribly successful study' of depravity. In December of that year *The American Monthly Review of Reviews* termed it 'the finest work . . . [James] has ever done – for the foul breath of the bottomless pit itself, which strikes the reader full in the face as he follows the plot, puts to shame by its penetrating force and quiet ghastliness the commonplace, unreal "horrors" of the ordinary ghost-story; it does indeed give an extra "turn of the screw" beyond anything of the sort that fiction has yet provided.' In March 1899 the reviewer in *Chautauquan* went even further, writing that James's technique was 'a skill little short of the supernatural', as though James himself were a phantom of talent: inexplicable, other-worldly, beyond compare. These reviewers saw the novella as a work of art with a definitive, even transcendent quality – echoing the view of the story that Douglas himself puts forward in its framing device: 'Nothing at all that I know touches it . . . For dreadful – dreadfulness! . . . For general uncanny ugliness and horror and pain.'

A smaller band of the novella's early critics found the story made for compromising reading, forcing the reader to collude with the horror on the page. It was wrong to be entertained by such misery, was the view, and to do so indicated a moral insufficiency on the part of the reader. In October 1898 *The Outlook* proclaimed that 'The story itself is distinctly repulsive.' In November *The Bookman* stated that 'We have never read a more sickening, a more gratuitously melancholy tale.' In

January 1899 *The Independent* went as far as to suggest that in reading the tale 'one has been assisting in an outrage upon the holiest and sweetest fountain of human innocence'. These critics considered the work itself morally reprehensible. They thought it cynical and written 'down' for a breathless magazine audience, for money and for popularity, perhaps in response to James's recent wounding failure with his play *Guy Domville*, which had been painfully mauled at its premiere on the London stage in 1985.

Some twenty-five years later, commentators began to condemn the children's governess. F. L. Pattee, in 1923, suggested that the story might be about her psychological disturbance; Edna Kenton pointed out the following year that it was possible to doubt the 'young governess's word'. These views gained strong currency in 1934 in Edmund Wilson's famous study, 'The Ambiguity of Henry James', in which he pronounced that 'the young governess who tells the story is a neurotic case of sex repression, and the ghosts are not real ghosts at all but merely the governess's hallucinations.' Thirty years later comparisons were drawn by Oscar Cargill between the heroine in 'The Turn of the Screw' and the subject of Sigmund Freud's 'The Case of Miss Lucy R.'. Lucy R. was a patient Freud treated in 1892–3, a governess from Glasgow working for a wealthy Viennese widower, with whom she had fallen in love. There are more recent essays too, which speak of rescuing the children from the Freudians, and studies condemning the Freudians for just not being Freudian enough. James's own life is brought to bear by some of these critics, who see in the ghosts, real or imagined, images of the author's own 'struggles with his sexuality', as one might term it today.

The attempt to ascertain whether the ghosts the governess sees are real or figments of her taxed imagination seems doomed to failure. Such clamouring after certainty hinges partly on something that isn't relevant at all – whether you yourself think there are such things as ghosts. More importantly, even the critics who doubt the existence of the ghosts, believing that the governess has conjured them out of her own neurosis, from the stress and pressures of her situation and her ardent desire

for her employer or as a vehicle for childish heroism, all agree
that the governess herself believes the ghosts are real. I have
never heard an argument made that the ghosts are a deliberate
ruse on her part, a wilful deception to further her own ends. It
is interesting to note that in no other ghost story by Henry
James is the appearance of ghosts presented as the false invention of an overwrought mind.

Of course, if the ghosts are real within the action rather
than imagined, the story holds a different kind of horror. Actual
ghosts bring a universal distressing element of terror into what
otherwise would be a harsh and specific domestic tragedy.
James himself found the story terrifying. When he had finished
correcting the proofs, he told his friend Edmund Gosse: 'I was
so frightened that I was afraid to go upstairs to bed!'[15] It is true
that the ghosts are consummately vivid on the page: Miss Jessel's terrible, miserable figure in the schoolroom, usurping our
heroine at the writing table; Quint roaming the grounds in a
scene 'stricken with death'. Yet it is worth pointing out that
even if Miss Jessel and Quint had both left in disgrace, died
and had the decency to vanish from the scene for ever, not
deigning to haunt at all, the scant facts of their sad histories
would have hung heavy in the air at Bly. Our governess could
have been jealous of the fact that they had spent so much time
with 'her' children. She could still have been shocked and curious about the 'freedoms' they had taken with Flora and Miles.
She could have wanted to solve the mysteries of their exist-
ences. This might well, in the absence of firmer things to dwell
upon, have turned into an obsession . . .

I view the ambiguity in 'The Turn of the Screw' not as an
obstacle to understanding but almost as a character in itself,
for it is carefully built and has strong properties and currents.
Ambiguity is central to the tale and although it invites readers
to reach for resolution and interpretation, the novella is at its
best, by which I mean yields the most, when the ambiguity is
held as a sort of beacon of inspiration and fine intelligence,
rather than interpreted away. Besides, when the dangers of
overinterpretation actually pierce the plot of a story as they do
in 'The Turn of the Screw', where the governess and her charges

materially suffer as a result of her mania for locating meaning in whatever she sees, it is wise to be wary in one's reading. Deliberating whether the ghosts are real or unreal seems to have become a way of not attending to the story. David Lodge captures this best when he writes 'James's later fiction constantly aspired to the condition of ambiguity – that the impossibility of arriving at a single, simple version of the "truth" about any human action or experience is, in the broadest sense, what that fiction is about.'[16] As with all works of art where ambiguity is a dominant feature, it feels more useful to investigate how this condition is achieved and what it means rather than attempting to resolve or do away with it.

'The Turn of the Screw' gains its mystery and power from the way Henry James sets distinct opposing currents running forcefully against each other. These currents destabilize, confuse and subvert the way information is related to the reader, creating an atmosphere that is fraught and taxed. James invites us to have a less complex set of responses to the governess's tale than the tale itself merits, to go along with things despite our mounting sense of unease and, in this way, we are seduced into a breathless version of events that may sit uncomfortably with us, but which we are reluctant to challenge. We are carried away by the governess's impressions, just as she herself is, yet even as we feel the force of her strength of feeling, which is mesmerizing, our awareness that her rendering of the situation is partial, and may be skewed, grows and brims.

This first occurs when we receive Douglas's fine character reference for the young governess – even though they only meet ten years after the events in the story, it still stands as a prism through which her history is to be read. 'She was the most agreeable woman I've ever known in her position; she'd have been worthy of any whatever.' We are told that she was 'awfully clever and nice' and that he 'liked her extremely'. We are also given a picture of her methods: 'we had, in her off-hours, some strolls and talks in the garden . . . I remember the time and the place [of her telling him her story] – the corner of the lawn, the shade of the great beeches and the long hot summer afternoon.' Should a governess spend her time off strolling about with the young gentleman of the house, regaling him with the adventures she has passed? It does not seem ideal. This early example of behaviour that could scarcely be called immaculate framed by high praise sets a pattern for many more moments in the tale where occurrences or phrases of an opposing nature are set next to each other as though they carry the same meaning.

Once the governess's narrative begins, we are frequently invited to take consciousness for conscientiousness and anxiety for loving care. Many of the unsettling aspects of 'The Turn of the Screw' stem from the governess's mania for self-analysis. She monitors herself as a doctor might hover over a favourite patient. Her every step and breath is entered into extravagantly, her feelings reported as facts. The fuller the governess's descriptions and impressions are, the more precise and reliable we may expect them to be, but this is not the case. She purports to offer us a narrative of openness and full accounting but the more information we are given, the more confusing and claustrophobic things become. Yet how else are we to make sense of events, except through her words? Her rendering of the fine detail of every drop or soaring of her spirits does not result in self-knowledge or action or even caution, but in opaqueness and paralysis. Furthermore, her obsessive thinking sometimes limits feelings of sympathy or empathy. (Her utter disdain for Miss Jessel's suffering always surprises me.) In addition, the governess's emphasis is often misleading, for she can be playful and slapdash in relation to the things that matter most and serious-hearted and analytical towards situations that you would associate with pleasure and ease. At times her routine sensory perceptions are presented with the kind of thoroughness one would only require if one did not already know what an eye did, or of what an ear was capable. This all adds up to a novella with a central nervous system that is tense, fraught, alarming, brimming and highly strung.

None of this, of course, is remotely surprising considering the baffling ways in which events in the governess's own life have unfolded. Her recent past has been crammed with the most bewildering push and pull between girlhood and adulthood, between reality, expectation and fantasy. First she has reached the (perhaps painful) decision to leave home and seek work. Next she is greatly moved by a meeting with the sort of man she has only dreamed of or read about in novels, a childish sensation, certainly, but one with a troubling grown-up sexual undertow. She has been asked to do this man a great favour for a handsome sum, which makes her feel like a heroine of worth, perhaps a rare feeling for the youngest daughter of a poor country parson. She has the experience of having profound gratitude shown to her, a sense of a solid and admirable man being in her debt, very likely the first time this has happened. He expresses this by taking her hand, almost certainly the first time *that* has happened. She is then told that he never wants to hear from her, let alone see her again. This is perhaps as dizzying as Maisie's smash into the jewellery shop that is her mother's breast, where for a brief second there was the ghost of softness and rescue.

To confuse things further, the governess arrives at the man's country house expecting gloom and drear, and it isn't anything like as bad as she has anticipated. She is allocated one of Bly's best rooms, given the run of the house and grounds, handed 'her' children, set up as an adult with power and responsibility. She has many of the accoutrements of the mistress of the house. There is a set of sums before her with wrong answers that she is being asked to pronounce correct. Is it any wonder she feels bolts of triumph and uncertainty?

We can sense the governess's struggle to understand and frame her situation while experiencing overriding feelings of bewilderment, in her patterns of speech. Throughout the tale she has a strange conversational tic of presenting us with pairs of words that go against the grain of each other as though they are almost synonyms. She refers to the children's 'false little lovely eyes' and sees Miles as living 'in a setting of beauty and misery', as though false and lovely, and misery and beauty, are well-known bedfellows. She sees 'repulsion' and 'compassion' at once in Mrs Grose. She qualifies the word 'happiest' with the word 'grotesque' in describing the night Flora spends with the housekeeper, after the crisis in Chapter XX. She attempts to convey the strength of her vision by saying it was 'as definite as a picture in a frame', as though this were an example of maximum reality. These speech patterns are unsettling, as they strive to assert or resolve something outside their reach. Her tripped-up phrases, her synonyms that are closer to opposites, add to the precariousness of the atmosphere.

Despite the governess's lavish chronicling, we gain a growing awareness as the story progresses that there is much we are not being told. We hear in Chapter IV that she has had 'disturbing letters from home', to which the children provide a valuable antidote, but she does not tell us what the troubles are. Illness, financial problems, bereavement? She says that she understands how little girls idolize boys, for she 'had had' brothers. Does she not still? As with many a good literary heroine before her, no mention is made of her mother. Does she share a vista on the world of grief that the children inhabit? We don't know. We learn that Miles has been expelled from school and there is much speculation as to why, yet she does not make any enquiries for days and days, and even congratulates herself on this ('I had made up my mind . . . I was incisive . . . I was wonderful'). Meanwhile, a stroll on a pleasant afternoon is rendered with a level of detail designed to stun:

> This moment dated from an afternoon hour that I happened to spend in the grounds with the younger of my pupils alone. We had left Miles indoors, on the red cushion of a deep window-seat; he had wished to finish a book, and I had been glad to encourage a purpose so laudable in a young man whose only defect was a certain ingenuity of restlessness. His sister, on the contrary, had been alert to come out, and I strolled with her half an hour, seeking the shade, for the sun was still high and the day exceptionally warm. I was aware afresh with her, as we went, of how, like her brother, she contrived – it was the charming thing in both children – to let me alone without appearing to drop me and to accompany me without appearing to oppress. They were never importunate and yet never listless. My attention to them all really went to seeing them amuse themselves immensely without me: this was a spectacle they seemed actively to prepare and that employed me as an active admirer. I walked in a world of their

invention – they had no occasion whatever to draw upon mine; so that my time was taken only with being for them some remarkable person or thing that the game of the moment required and that was merely, thanks to my superior, my exalted stamp, a happy and highly distinguished sinecure. I forget what I was on the present occasion; I only remember that I was something very important and very quiet and that Flora was playing very hard.

Of course the full-blown intricacies of this sort of observation are familiar to us from other Henry James characters of this period. We might think of the obsessive tendencies of the heroine of *In the Cage* (1898), who lives her life vicariously through the comings and goings of the clientele of the Mayfair post office where she is in charge of telegrams. We might think of *The Sacred Fount* (1901), where the hero's dedication to uncovering the carryings-on of the other weekend guests results in an orgy of interpretation, the vast majority of which proves hollow. Similarly, in *The Spoils of Poynton*, Fleda Vetch's fidelity to living by a set of principles that soar above those required by the challenges that face her (she adopts a sacrificial moral code more suited to sainthood than romance in the country) reflects an equally obsessive character. In these cases we are aware early on that we are witnessing distortions of temperament, of situation. These characters may behave as though they are caught up in 'matters of life and death', but we know it is not true. The governess's narrative in 'The Turn of the Screw', however, is so intense and tightly focussed that we believe from the start that matters of life and death genuinely lie at the heart of the story.

This sense of obsessiveness is given even more power when James occasionally relaxes the tension, spiking the governess's overwrought thoughts with calm observations natural to the world of adults and children. These moments are surprisingly arresting and unnerving, perhaps because they mean we can no longer confidently say that things are *not* as they seem. When the governess mentions that her favourite hour of the day is the 'small interval alone' when the children are asleep, you have to read the statement twice. It is almost impossible to countenance, such is her wild preoccupation with their beauty, their heart-stirring play, their delicate instincts and high moral standing. The moment delivers a gust of fresh air, as when someone who always lies suddenly delivers a straight answer. It is also disconcerting, because it contrasts so strongly with the governess's general outlook. The smash of normality takes on the appearance of something untoward.

The governess sometimes appears to make the standard banal observations that parents and carers of children routinely make, yet her comments distort the familiar even as they suggest it. She says of her youngest charge, at the end of Chapter I, that she wants to 'win the child into the sense of knowing me', which sounds perfectly straightforward until you reflect that a new governess in a new job ought to be exercised about getting to know her charges, not the other way round. Later, she tells us 'I used to speculate . . . as to how the rough future (for all futures are rough!) would handle them and might bruise them.' On the face of it this is an ordinary parental concern. You gaze at your perfect infant with its almost impossible-to-believe tiny toes and tight fists and tangle of hair (if you're lucky) and you think of its going out into the world. You imagine a child tackling the strains of adulthood with a child's limited strength and resources, a baby going to work on a train, or queuing for lunch or getting the sack; and it all seems dangerous and alarming. But this attempt at sharing in conventional adult fellow-feeling doesn't quite work. These concerns don't apply to Flora and Miles, because they have not known the mythical peace of early childhood. Their past is already fallen and broken, their young lives, from the start, blighted by dreadful hurts, bereavement, loss and neglect. It is a brilliant and brilliantly subtle distortion.

For these children, of course, are orphans, par excellence. They've been orphaned and orphaned and orphaned. They are little monuments to loss, for the five people closest to them have all died in the last few years. They occupy that strange emotional territory that is usually the reserve of the very elderly: they know more people who are dead than are alive. Their father, a soldier, has died. Their grandparents are also recently dead. Their two companions, Quint and Miss Jessel, are gone. So steeped in loss are they that the loss of their mother does not even merit a mention, but Miles, the older child, might well remember her, and her death makes six. These children of loss are mysterious and unfathomable. Their thorough acquaintance with disaster gives them a certain status and power. The one living relative we know of, their dashing uncle in Harley Street, is determined not even to hear their news. Is there anything else the world can throw at them? Of course, the fiction of Henry James is never a safe place to be a child. One only has to think of little Effie in *The Other House*, Pansy Osmond in *Portrait of a Lady*, even Maisie Farange, but in 'The Turn of the Screw' James has surpassed himself in this regard. In a letter to F. W. H. Myers in 1898, James said he had intended the children to be 'as *exposed* as we can humanly conceive children to be'.[17] They are.

This wall of grief makes our heroine's appointment even more intimidating and her responsibility all the greater. The very best thing she can do for the children is to stay alive herself. There are not many jobs for young women where this requirement tops the list ... The eagerness of the children to attach themselves to the governess may strike us as the conduct of small bereaved people who feel they've nothing to their name. They might well have the joy that the terminally ill sometimes possess, where everything before them is a sort of gift, the spring blossom viscerally beautiful and so on. Is that how they receive their new governess? Is that why they engage with so much verve and brio in her lessons and games? Why they love to hear about the funny turns of phrase of the women in her village? We are told that following the death of Miles and Flora's grandparents in India, their eldest son, the children's uncle, became their guardian. So it seems these children have also moved continents, from warmth to cold, from the grandparents' home to boarding school, the care of strangers, the formality of a staffed English household. Of course they would turn in on each other, for comfort and for understanding, these children with an embarrassment of loss. Does this make them unreachable to their governess, despite their apparent ardour for her? She calls them 'almost impersonal'. Does this further frustrate her desire for control? No adults in their lives have proved themselves to be dependable, thus far. Why should they put their happiness in her hands?

Grief in the house plays a large part in the governess's narrative method. The more mysterious and closed-off the children become, the more she tries to prise herself open, for answers. The governess exhibits a sort of girlish greed in this regard: the more unequal she feels to the task of protecting her charges, the more she endeavours to prove herself a heroine. She states her desire for recognition at the start: 'I daresay I fancied myself in short a remarkable young woman and took comfort in the faith that this would more publicly appear.' Is she a governess who wants to achieve the status of a governess-heroine like Jane Eyre? For our governess is certainly schooled in the adventures of the governess-heroines who have gone before. It is scarcely surprising that one of her earliest concerns appears to be with what exactly a heroine is: how do you become one, which is the best sort? What sort of character is she and in what story? The children's story, alongside Flora, with her 'hair of gold and her frock of blue' inside the 'castle of romance inhabited by a rosy sprite'? The darker tale of madness and attics and ruin?

A heroine's trajectory might typically be: accept the job in the most becoming and modest way; win the children over, and help compensate them for some of their grief and suffering; earn their trust; shape them in a way that is pleasing; make great strides with their lessons and characters and, through this diligent work, win the heart of the master. She has come 'to be carried away', she announces to Mrs Grose on her first day, as she was 'carried away in London'. To a certain extent it is she who carries both the children and Mrs Grose away. At times she carries us. Her hopes are not without precedent, of course. We might think again of Jane Eyre, who of course marries her employer, although not until he is brought low by tragedy. Even when Mr Rochester meets Jane for the first time and pretends not to know who she is, he has a broken ankle, he needs her support. Yet who needs *this* woman? The master does not need her, and nor do the children. They like her, but it is hard for her presence to register as fully with them, it seems, as all the things they have lost. Miles and Flora never truly meet the feelings of love she conceives for them, almost at first sight, and the governess's romantic hopes with her employer have even less substance. 'Never trouble me again', 'let me alone' is what people say after an argument, or an acknowledged estrangement. Even if it is said with a good deal of charm and hand-holding and gratitude, in a grand house filled with beautiful things, it might make a good ending between a man and a woman, but it is a terrible beginning. It is almost a curse. Of course, it is scarcely the master's fault if his prospective employee has constructed a romance built around their two brief meetings. But demanding she 'never, never' contact him? How does it occur to him that she will manage? He doesn't think. It doesn't occur. Her gradual realization of this truth prompts a crisis. There is something starving about the governess's imagination and her paucity of experience that necessitates the ghosts. They will force the children to need her at the deepest level. They lend her life meaning. Why be Jane Eyre when you could trump her brave and noble spirit as a saint, 'fighting with a demon for a human soul'?

All the opposing currents in the story serve to prepare us for the most uneasy pairing of all, the contract between the governess and the reader. For all her neuroses and unreliable narration, there is a deep, essential bond between the heroine of 'The Turn of the Screw' and those who read her story. While Mrs Grose and Miles and Flora do not see the ghosts, which may well have been conjured from the governess's inability to stretch to the requirements of her situation, the reader sees them unequivocally. Peter Quint and Miss Jessel are made marvellously vivid to us. They loom and terrify from the page. They frighten both the governess and ourselves. If she has made them up then so have we.

In 'The Turn of the Screw' and the other stories in this collection, ghosts furnish James with opportunities to examine the more troubling, mysterious and disarming aspects of consciousness. James's ghosts excavate, reveal and illumine. They may terrify, they may amuse, but they also serve as ambassadors of knowledge and understanding, showing us things we otherwise would not see, or recognize, or could not bear to entertain. Whether shedding light on the more dreadful aspects of family life and the complexities of late adolescence, or negotiating disappointment and the thinning out of great expectations, ghosts that would be simple and uncouth in the hands of others can lend themselves to the deepest and most subtle investigations in the works of Henry James.

James's obsession with ghosts may at times seem hard to fathom but what work he puts them to . . .

NOTES

1. From a letter to Violet Paget, 27 April 1890, *Henry James Letters*, vol. 3, ed. Leon Edel (Cambridge, MA: Harvard University Press, 1974–1984; 1980), pp. 276–78.

2. From a letter to F. W. H. Myers, 19 December 1898, *Henry James Letters*, vol. 4, ed. Leon Edel (Cambridge, MA: Harvard University Press, 1974–1984), pp. 87–88.

3. From a letter to H. G. Wells, 9 December 1898, *Henry James Letters*, vol. 4, ed. Leon Edel (Cambridge, MA: Harvard University Press, 1984), pp. 85–87.

4. From a letter to the psychiatrist Dr Louis Waldstein, 21 October 1898, *Henry James Letters*, vol. 4, ed. Leon Edel (Cambridge, MA: Harvard University Press, 1984), p. 84.

5. From a letter to Paul Bourget, 19 August 1898, *The Letters of Henry James*, vol. 1, ed. Percy Lubbock (London: Macmillan, 1920), pp. 286–90

6. F. R. Leavis, 'James's "What Maisie Knew": A Disagreement', *SCRUTINY*, vol. 17, no. 2 (Summer 1950), pp. 117, 116.

7. From a letter to Hendrik Anderson, 25 November 1906, *Dearly Beloved Friends: Henry James's Letters to Younger Men*, ed. Susan E. Gunter and Steven H. Jobe (Ann Arbor, MI: University of Michigan Press, 2004), p. 61.

8. From a letter to Francis Boott, 11 October 1895, *Henry James Letters*, vol. 4, ed. Leon Edel (Cambridge, MA: Harvard University Press, 1974–1984), pp. 23–24.

9. Virginia Woolf, *Granite and Rainbow* (New York: Harcourt, Brace, 1958), p. 70.

10. William Dean Howells, *In After Days: Thoughts on the Future Life* (New York: Harper, 1910), p. 193–233.

11. Henry James, *What Maisie Knew* (London: Penguin, 1985), p. 108.

12. Henry James, *The Spoils of Poynton* (London: Penguin, 1987), p. 203.

13. In a 1942 radio programme, the American poet and critic Allen Tate said 'James knew substantially all that Freud knew before Freud came on the scene'. Mark van Doren (ed.), *The New Invitation to Learning* (New York: Random House, 1942), p.231.

14. Quotations from contemporary reviewers and later commentators are taken from *The Turn of the Screw: Authoritative Text, Contexts, Criticism*, ed. Deborah Esch and Jonathan Warren (New York: W. W. Norton & Company, 1999) and Edward J. Parkinson, ' "The Turn of the Screw": A History of Its Critical Interpretations, 1898–1979', (PhD dissertation, Saint Louis University, 1991).

15. Edmund Gosse, *Aspects and Impressions* (London: Cassell and Company, 1922), p. 38.

16. See David Lodge's introduction, *The Spoils of Poynton* (London: Penguin, 1987), p. 6.

17. From a letter to F. W. H Myers, 19 December 1898, *Henry James Letters*, vol. 4, ed. Leon Edel (Cambridge, MA: Harvard University Press, 1974–1984), pp. 87–88.

Further Reading

BY HENRY JAMES

Beidler, Peter G. (ed.), *The Collier's Weekly Version of Henry James's The Turn of the Screw as It First Appeared in Serial Format in 1898* (Seattle, WA: Coffeetown Press, 2010).

Bromwich, David (ed.), *The Turn of the Screw* (London: Penguin Classics, 2011).

Edel, Leon (ed.), *Henry James Letters*, 4 vols (Cambridge, MA: Harvard University Press, 1974–1984).

Fender, Stephen (ed.), *Daisy Miller and Other Tales* (London: Penguin, 2016).

Gorra, Michael (ed.), *The Aspern Papers and Other Tales* (London: Penguin Classics, 2014).

Gunter, Susan E., and Steven H. Jobe, (eds), *Dearly Beloved Friends: Henry James's Letters to Younger Men* (Ann Arbor, MI: University of Michigan Press, 2004).

Horne, Phillip (ed.), *Henry James: A Life in Letters* (London: Penguin Classics, 1999).

Lodge, David (ed.), *The Spoils of Poynton* (London: Penguin, 1987).

Lubbock, Percy, (ed.), *The Letters of Henry James*, 2 vols (London: Macmillan, 1920).

GENERAL

Bayley, John, *The Characters of Love: A Study in the Literature of Personality* (London: Constable, 1960).

Cargill, Oscar, 'Henry James as Freudian Pioneer', *Chicago Review*, vol. 10, no. 2 (Summer 1956), pp. 13–29.

—— 'The Turn of the Screw and Alice James', *PMLA*, vol. 78, no. 3 (June 1963), pp. 238–49.

Despotopoulou, Anna, and Kimberly C. Reed, (eds), *Henry James and the Supernatural* (Basingstoke: Palgrave Macmillan, 2011).

El-Rayess, Miranda, *Henry James and the Culture of Consumption* (Cambridge: Cambridge University Press, 2014).

Felman, Shoshana, 'Turning the Screw of Interpretation', *Yale French Studies*, no. 55/56 (1977), pp. 94–207.

Gosse, Edmund, *Aspects and Impressions* (London: Cassell and Company, 1922).

Hadley, Tessa, *Henry James and the Imagination of Pleasure* (Cambridge: Cambridge University Press, 2009).

Hughes, Clair, *Henry James and the Art of Dress* (Basingstoke: Palgrave, 2001).

James, Alice, *The Diary of Alice James*, ed. Leon Edel (Lebanon, NH: Northeastern University Press, 1999).

Kaplan, Fred, *Henry James: The Imagination of Genius. A Biography* (London: Hodder & Stoughton, 1992).

Leavis, F. R., 'James's "What Maisie Knew: A Disagreement"', *SCRUTINY*, vol. 17, no. 2 (Summer 1950), pp. 115–27.

Lustig, T. J., *Henry James and the Ghostly* (Cambridge: Cambridge University Press, 1994).

Parkinson, Edward J., '"The Turn of the Screw" A History of Its Critical Interpretations, 1898–1979', Saint Louis University PhD thesis, 1991. Turnofthescrew.com.

Tóibín, Colm, 'Pure Evil – Colm Tóibín on The Turn of the Screw', *The Guardian*, 3 June 2006.

Wilson, Edmund, 'The Ambiguity of Henry James', *Hound & Horn*, vol. 7 (April–June 1934), pp. 385–406.

A Note on the Texts

'The Romance of Certain Old Clothes', James's first ghost story, first appeared in *The Atlantic Monthly* magazine, in February 1868. 'The Last of the Valerii' also first appeared in *The Atlantic Monthly*, in January 1874. 'Sir Edmund Orme' was first published in the Christmas edition of *Black and White*, in November 1891. 'Owen Wingrave' was first published in *The Graphic*, in November 1892, the Christmas issue. 'The Friends of the Friends' was first published, under the title 'The Way It Came', in *Chapman's Magazine of Fiction*, in May 1896. 'The Turn of the Screw' was first published, as a serial, in *Collier's Weekly*, between January and April 1898, as a result of a commission for a twelve-part ghost story. 'The Third Person' was first published in James's collection of stories *The Soft Side* (1900). 'The Jolly Corner' first appeared, in December 1908, in *The English Review*.

James was an inveterate reviser, and there are usually changes between serial and book publication of his writings; when he returned to earlier works to prepare them for inclusion in *The Novels and Tales of Henry James*, 24 vols (New York: Charles Scribner's Sons, 1907–9), commonly known as the New York Edition, they often underwent significant alteration. The texts of 'The Romance of Certain Old Clothes' and 'The Last of the Valerii', which were not included in that edition, are those of the first book publication, in *A Passionate Pilgrim, and Other Tales* (Boston: James R. Osgood and Company, 1875). The text of 'The Third Person', also omitted from the New York Edition, is from its first publication, in *The Soft Side* (London: Methven & Co., 1900). All the other texts are from the New York Edition: 'Sir

Edmund Orme', 'Owen Wingrave', 'The Friends of the Friends' and 'The Jolly Corner' in Vol. XVII (1909); 'The Turn of the Screw' in Vol. XII (1908).

Since the stories come from various sources and are somewhat inconsistent in spelling and punctuation, these have been standardized throughout this volume. In addition some errors, mostly the printers', have been corrected by reference to earlier and later texts; some minor adjustments have been made to punctuation, including the substitution of n-rule dashes for m-rule except for broken-off speech and sentences; contractions opened up by James (e.g. could n't) are closed up (couldn't). Single quotation marks replace double ones, and for a single word or phrase in quotation marks, the closing mark is placed before a comma or full stop; and 'ise' spellings have been standardized throughout as 'ize', in accordance with Penguin Classics style. There has been no attempt to regularize James's use of italics for foreign words and expressions.

The Turn of the Screw
and Other Ghost Stories

THE ROMANCE OF
CERTAIN OLD CLOTHES

Toward the middle of the eighteenth century there lived in the
Province of Massachusetts a widowed gentlewoman, the
mother of three children. Her name is of little account: I shall
take the liberty of calling her Mrs Willoughby, – a name, like
her own, of a highly respectable sound. She had been left a
widow after some six years of marriage, and had devoted herself to the care of her progeny. These young persons grew up in
a manner to reward her zeal and to gratify her fondest hopes.
The first-born was a son, whom she had called Bernard, after
his father. The others were daughters, – born at an interval of
three years apart. Good looks were traditional in the family,
and this youthful trio were not likely to allow the tradition to
perish. The boy was of that fair and ruddy complexion and of
that athletic mould which in those days (as in these) were the
sign of genuine English blood, – a frank, affectionate young
fellow, a deferential son, a patronizing brother, and a steadfast
friend. Clever, however, he was not; the wit of the family had
been apportioned chiefly to his sisters. Mr Willoughby had
been a great reader of Shakespeare, at a time when this pursuit
implied more liberality of taste than at the present day, and in
a community where it required much courage to patronize the
drama even in the closet; and he had wished to record his
admiration of the great poet by calling his daughters out of his
favourite plays. Upon the elder he had bestowed the romantic
name of Viola; and upon the younger, the more serious one of
Perdita,[1] in memory of a little girl born between them, who
had lived but a few weeks.

When Bernard Willoughby came to his sixteenth year, his

mother put a brave face upon it, and prepared to execute her husband's last request. This had been an earnest entreaty that, at the proper age, his son should be sent out to England, to complete his education at the University of Oxford, which had been the seat of his own studies. Mrs Willoughby fancied that the lad's equal was not to be found in the two hemispheres, but she had the antique wifely submissiveness. She swallowed her sobs, and made up her boy's trunk and his simple provincial outfit, and sent him on his way across the seas. Bernard was entered at his father's college, and spent five years in England, without great honour, indeed, but with a vast deal of pleasure and no discredit. On leaving the University he made the journey to France. In his twenty-third year he took ship for home, prepared to find poor little New England (New England was very small in those days) an utterly intolerable place of abode. But there had been changes at home, as well as in Mr Bernard's opinions. He found his mother's house quite habitable, and his sisters grown into two very charming young ladies, with all the accomplishments and graces of the young women of Britain, and a certain native-grown gentle *brusquerie*[2] and wildness, which, if it was not an accomplishment, was certainly a grace the more. Bernard privately assured his mother that his sisters were fully a match for the most genteel young women in England; whereupon poor Mrs Willoughby, you may be sure, bade them hold up their heads. Such was Bernard's opinion, and such, in a tenfold higher degree, was the opinion of Mr Arthur Lloyd. This gentleman, I hasten to add, was a college-mate of Mr Bernard, a young man of reputable family, of a good person[3] and a handsome inheritance; which latter appurtenance he proposed to invest in trade in this country. He and Bernard were warm friends; they had crossed the ocean together, and the young American had lost no time in presenting him at his mother's house, where he had made quite as good an impression as that which he had received, and of which I have just given a hint.

The two sisters were at this time in all the freshness of their youthful bloom; each wearing, of course, this natural brilliancy in the manner that became her best. They were equally dissimilar in appearance and character. Viola, the elder, – now in her twenty-second year, – was tall and fair, with calm grey eyes and auburn tresses; a very faint likeness to the Viola of Shakespeare's comedy, whom I imagine as a brunette (if you will), but a slender, airy creature, full of the softest and finest emotions. Miss Willoughby, with her candid complexion, her fine arms, her majestic height, and her slow utterance, was not cut out for adventures. She would never have put on a man's jacket and hose; and, indeed, being a very plump beauty, it is perhaps as well that she would not. Perdita, too, might very well have exchanged the sweet melancholy of her name against something more in consonance with her aspect and disposition. She was a positive brunette, short of stature, light of foot, with a vivid dark brown eye. She had been from her childhood a creature of smiles and gaiety; and so far from making you wait for an answer to your speech, as her handsome sister was wont to do (while she gazed at you with her somewhat cold grey eyes), she had given you the choice of half a dozen, suggested by the successive clauses of your proposition, before you had got to the end of it.

The young girls were very glad to see their brother once more; but they found themselves quite able to maintain a reserve of good-will for their brother's friend. Among the young men their friends and neighbours, the *belle jeunesse* of the Colony, there were many excellent fellows, several devoted swains, and some two or three who enjoyed the reputation of universal charmers and conquerors. But the home-bred arts and the somewhat boisterous gallantry of those honest young colonists were completely eclipsed by the good looks, the fine clothes, the punctilious courtesy, the perfect elegance, the immense information, of Mr Arthur Lloyd. He was in reality no paragon; he was an honest, resolute, intelligent young man, rich in pounds sterling, in his health and comfortable hopes, and his little capital of uninvested affections. But he was a gentleman; he had a handsome face; he had studied and travelled; he spoke French, he played on the flute, and he read verses aloud with very great taste. There were a dozen reasons why Miss Willoughby and her sister should forthwith have

been rendered fastidious in the choice of their male acquaintance. The imagination of woman is especially adapted to the
various small conventions and mysteries of polite society. Mr
Lloyd's talk told our little New England maidens a vast deal
more of the ways and means of people of fashion in European
capitals than he had any idea of doing. It was delightful to sit
by and hear him and Bernard discourse upon the fine people
and fine things they had seen. They would all gather round the
fire after tea, in the little wainscoted parlour,[4] – quite innocent
then of any intention of being picturesque or of being anything
else, indeed, than economical, and saving an outlay in stamped
papers and tapestries, – and the two young men would remind
each other, across the rug, of this, that, and the other adventure. Viola and Perdita would often have given their ears to
know exactly what adventure it was, and where it happened,
and who was there, and what the ladies had on; but in those
days a well-bred young woman was not expected to break into
the conversation of her own movement or to ask too many
questions; and the poor girls used therefore to sit fluttering
behind the more languid – or more discreet – curiosity of their
mother.

That they were both very fine girls Arthur Lloyd was not
slow to discover; but it took him some time to satisfy himself
as to the apportionment of their charms. He had a strong
presentiment – an emotion of a nature entirely too cheerful to
be called a foreboding – that he was destined to marry one of
them; yet he was unable to arrive at a preference, and for such
a consummation a preference was certainly indispensable,
inasmuch as Lloyd was quite too gallant a fellow to make a
choice by lot and be cheated of the heavenly delight of falling
in love. He resolved to take things easily, and to let his heart
speak. Meanwhile, he was on a very pleasant footing. Mrs
Willoughby showed a dignified indifference to his 'intentions',
equally remote from a carelessness of her daughters' honour
and from that odious alacrity to make him commit himself,
which, in his quality of a young man of property, he had but
too often encountered in the venerable dames of his native
islands. As for Bernard, all that he asked was that his friend

should take his sisters as his own; and as for the poor girls themselves, however each may have secretly longed for the monopoly of Mr Lloyd's attentions, they observed a very decent and modest and contented demeanour.

Towards each other, however, they were somewhat more on the offensive. They were good sisterly friends, betwixt whom it would take more than a day for the seeds of jealousy to sprout and bear fruit; but the young girls felt that the seeds had been sown on the day that Mr Lloyd came into the house. Each made up her mind that, if she should be slighted, she would bear her grief in silence, and that no one should be any the wiser; for if they had a great deal of love, they had also a great deal of pride. But each prayed in secret, nevertheless, that upon *her* the glory might fall. They had need of a vast deal of patience, of self-control, and of dissimulation. In those days a young girl of decent breeding could make no advances whatever, and barely respond, indeed, to those that were made. She was expected to sit still in her chair with her eyes on the carpet, watching the spot where the mystic handkerchief should fall. Poor Arthur Lloyd was obliged to undertake his wooing in the little wainscoted parlour, before the eyes of Mrs Willoughby, her son, and his prospective sister-in-law. But youth and love are so cunning that a hundred signs and tokens might travel to and fro, and not one of these three pair of eyes detect them in their passage. The young girls had but one chamber and one bed between them, and for long hours together they were under each other's direct inspection. That each knew that she was being watched, however, made not a grain of difference in those little offices which they mutually rendered, or in the various household tasks which they performed in common. Neither flinched nor fluttered beneath the silent batteries of her sister's eyes. The only apparent change in their habits was that they had less to say to each other. It was impossible to talk about Mr Lloyd, and it was ridiculous to talk about anything else. By tacit agreement they began to wear all their choice finery, and to devise such little implements of coquetry, in the way of ribbons and topknots and furbelows as were sanctioned by indubitable modesty. They executed in the same inarticulate fashion an agreement of sincerity on these delicate matters. 'Is it better so?' Viola would ask, tying a bunch of ribbons on her bosom, and turning about from her glass to her sister. Perdita would look up gravely from her work and examine the decoration. 'I think you had better give it another loop,' she would say, with great solemnity, looking hard at her sister with eyes that added, 'upon my honour!' So they were forever stitching and trimming their petticoats, and pressing out their muslins, and contriving washes and ointments and cosmetics, like the ladies in the household of the Vicar of Wakefield.[5] Some three or four months went by; it grew to be mid-winter, and as yet Viola knew that if Perdita had nothing more to boast of than she, there was not much to be feared from her rivalry. But Perdita by this time, the charming Perdita, felt that her secret had grown to be tenfold more precious than her sister's.

One afternoon Miss Willoughby sat alone before her toilet-glass combing out her long hair. It was getting too dark to see; she lit the two candles in their sockets on the frame of her mirror, and then went to the window to draw her curtains. It was a grey December evening; the landscape was bare and bleak, and the sky heavy with snow-clouds. At the end of the long garden into which her window looked was a wall with a little postern door,[6] opening into a lane. The door stood ajar, as she could vaguely see in the gathering darkness, and moved slowly to and fro, as if some one were swaying it from the lane without. It was doubtless a servant-maid. But as she was about to drop her curtain, Viola saw her sister step within the garden, and hurry along the path toward the house. She dropped the curtain, all save a little crevice for her eyes. As Perdita came up the path, she seemed to be examining something in her hand, holding it close to her eyes. When she reached the house she stopped a moment, looked intently at the object, and pressed it to her lips.

Poor Viola slowly came back to her chair, and sat down before her glass, where, if she had looked at it less abstractedly, she would have seen her handsome features sadly disfigured by jealousy. A moment afterwards the door opened behind her, and her sister came into the room, out of breath, and her cheeks aglow with the chilly air.

Perdita started. 'Ah,' said she, 'I thought you were with our mother.' The ladies were to go to a tea-party, and on such occasions it was the habit of one of the young girls to help their mother to dress. Instead of coming in, Perdita lingered at the door.

'Come in, come in,' said Viola. 'We've more than an hour yet. I should like you very much to give a few strokes to my hair.' She knew that her sister wished to retreat, and that she could see in the glass all her movements in the room. 'Nay, just help me with my hair,' she said, 'and I'll go to mamma.'

Perdita came reluctantly, and took the brush. She saw her sister's eyes, in the glass, fastened hard upon her hands. She had not made three passes, when Viola clapped her own right hand upon her sister's left, and started out of her chair. 'Whose ring is that?' she cried passionately, drawing her towards the light.

On the young girl's third finger glistened a little gold ring, adorned with a couple of small rubies. Perdita felt that she need no longer keep her secret, yet that she must put a bold face on her avowal. 'It's mine,' she said proudly.

'Who gave it to you?' cried the other.

Perdita hesitated a moment. 'Mr Lloyd.'

'Mr Lloyd is generous, all of a sudden.'

'Ah no,' cried Perdita, with spirit, 'not all of a sudden. He offered it to me a month ago.'

'And you needed a month's begging to take it?' said Viola, looking at the little trinket; which indeed was not especially elegant, although it was the best that the jeweller of the Province could furnish. 'I shouldn't have taken it in less than two.'

'It isn't the ring,' said Perdita, 'it's what it means!'

'It means that you're not a modest girl,' cried Viola. 'Pray does your mother know of your conduct? does Bernard?'

'My mother has approved my "conduct", as you call it. Mr Lloyd has asked my hand, and mamma has given it. Would you have had him apply to you, sister?'

Viola gave her sister a long look, full of passionate envy and sorrow. Then she dropped her lashes on her pale cheeks and turned away. Perdita felt that it had not been a pretty scene; but it was her sister's fault. But the elder girl rapidly called back her pride, and turned herself about again. 'You have my very best wishes,' she said, with a low curtsey. 'I wish you every happiness, and a very long life.'

Perdita gave a bitter laugh. 'Don't speak in that tone,' she cried. 'I'd rather you cursed me outright. Come, sister,' she added, 'he couldn't marry both of us.'

'I wish you very great joy,' Viola repeated mechanically, sitting down to her glass again, 'and a very long life, and plenty of children.'

There was something in the sound of these words not at all to Perdita's taste. 'Will you give me a year, at least?' she said. 'In a year I can have one little boy, – or one little girl at least. If you'll give me your brush again I'll do your hair.'

'Thank you,' said Viola. 'You had better go to mamma. It isn't becoming that a young lady with a promised husband should wait on a girl with none.'

'Nay,' said Perdita, good-humouredly, 'I have Arthur to wait upon me. You need my service more than I need yours.'

But her sister motioned her away, and she left the room. When she had gone poor Viola fell on her knees before her dressing-table, buried her head in her arms, and poured out a flood of tears and sobs. She felt very much the better for this effusion of sorrow. When her sister came back, she insisted upon helping her to dress, and upon her wearing her prettiest things. She forced upon her acceptance a bit of lace of her own, and declared that now that she was to be married she should do her best to appear worthy of her lover's choice. She discharged these offices in stern silence; but, such as they were, they had to do duty as an apology and an atonement; she never made any other.

Now that Lloyd was received by the family as an accepted suitor, nothing remained but to fix the wedding-day. It was appointed for the following April, and in the interval preparations were diligently made for the marriage. Lloyd, on his side, was busy with his commercial arrangements, and with establishing a correspondence with the great mercantile house to which he had attached himself in England. He was therefore not so frequent a visitor at Mrs Willoughby's as during the months of his diffidence and irresolution, and poor Viola had less to suffer than she had feared from the sight of the mutual endearments of the young lovers. Touching his future sister-in-law, Lloyd had a perfectly clear conscience. There had not been a particle of sentiment uttered between them, and he had not the slightest suspicion that she coveted anything more than his fraternal regard. He was quite at his ease; life promised so well, both domestically and financially. The lurid clouds of revolution were as yet twenty years beneath the horizon, and that his connubial felicity should take a tragic turn it was absurd, it was blasphemous, to apprehend. Meanwhile at Mrs Willoughby's there was a greater rustling of silks, a more rapid clicking of scissors and flying of needles, than ever. Mrs Willoughby had determined that her daughter should carry from home the most elegant outfit that her money could buy, or that the country could furnish. All the sage women in the county were convened, and their united taste was brought to bear on Perdita's wardrobe. Viola's situation, at this moment, was assuredly not to be envied. The poor girl had an inordinate love of dress, and the very best taste in the world, as her sister perfectly well knew. Viola was tall, she was stately and sweeping, she was made to carry stiff brocade and masses of heavy lace, such as belong to the toilet of a rich man's wife. But Viola sat aloof, with her beautiful arms folded and her head averted, while her mother and sister and the venerable women aforesaid worried and wondered over their materials, oppressed by the multitude of their resources. One day there came in a beautiful piece of white silk, brocaded with celestial blue and silver, sent by the bridegroom himself, – it not being thought amiss in those days that the husband elect should contribute to the bride's trousseau. Perdita was quite at loss to imagine a fashion which should do sufficient honour to the splendour of the material.

'Blue's your colour, sister, more than mine,' she said, with appealing eyes. 'It's a pity it's not for you. You'd know what to do with it.'

Viola got up from her place and looked at the great shining fabric as it lay spread over the back of a chair. Then she took it up in her hands and felt it, – lovingly, as Perdita could see, – and turned about toward the mirror with it. She let it roll down to her feet, and flung the other end over her shoulder, gathering it in about her waist with her white arm bare to the elbow. She threw back her head, and looked at her image, and a hanging tress of her auburn hair fell upon the gorgeous surface of the silk. It made a dazzling picture. The women standing about uttered a little 'Ah!' of admiration. 'Yes, indeed,' said Viola, quietly, 'blue is my colour.' But Perdita could see that her fancy had been stirred, and that she would now fall to work and solve all their silken riddles. And indeed she behaved very well, as Perdita, knowing her insatiable love of millinery, was quite ready to declare. Innumerable yards of lustrous silk and satin, of muslin, velvet, and lace, passed through her cunning hands, without a word of envy coming from her lips. Thanks to her industry, when the wedding-day came Perdita was prepared to espouse more of the vanities of life than any fluttering young bride who had yet challenged the sacramental blessing of a New England divine.

It had been arranged that the young couple should go out and spend the first days of their wedded life at the country house of an English gentleman, – a man of rank and a very kind friend to Lloyd. He was an unmarried man; he professed himself delighted to withdraw and leave them for a week to their billing and cooing. After the ceremony at church, – it had been performed by an English parson, – young Mrs Lloyd hastened back to her mother's house to change her wedding gear for a riding-dress. Viola helped her to effect the change, in the little old room in which they had been fond sisters together. Perdita then hurried off to bid farewell to her mother, leaving Viola to follow. The parting was short; the horses were at the door and Arthur impatient to start. But Viola had not followed, and Perdita hastened back to her room, opening the door abruptly. Viola, as usual, was before the glass, but in a position which caused the other to stand still, amazed. She had dressed herself in Perdita's cast-off wedding veil and wreath, and on her neck she had hung the heavy string of pearls which the young girl had received from her husband as a wedding-gift. These things had been hastily laid aside, to await their possessor's disposal on her return from the country. Bedizened in this unnatural garb, Viola stood at the mirror, plunging a long look into its depths, and reading Heaven knows what audacious visions. Perdita was horrified. It was a hideous image of their old rivalry come to life again. She made a step toward her sister, as if to pull off the veil and the flowers. But catching her eyes in the glass, she stopped.

'Farewell, Viola,' she said. 'You might at least have waited till I had got out of the house.' And she hurried away from the room.

Mr Lloyd had purchased in Boston a house which, in the taste of those days, was considered a marvel of elegance and comfort; and here he very soon established himself with his young wife. He was thus separated by a distance of twenty miles from the residence of his mother-in-law. Twenty miles, in that primitive era of roads and conveyances, were as serious a matter as a hundred at the present day, and Mrs Willoughby saw but little of her daughter during the first twelvemonth of her marriage. She suffered in no small degree from her absence; and her affliction was not diminished by the fact that Viola had fallen into terribly low spirits and was not to be roused or cheered but by change of air and circumstances. The real cause of the young girl's dejection the reader will not be slow to suspect. Mrs Willoughby and her gossips, however, deemed her complaint a purely physical one, and doubted not that she would obtain relief from the remedy just mentioned. Her mother accordingly proposed on her behalf a visit to certain relatives on the paternal side, established in New York, who had long complained that they were able to see so little of their New England cousins. Viola was despatched to these good people, under a suitable escort, and remained with them for several months. In the interval her brother Bernard, who had begun the practice of the law, made up his mind to take a wife. Viola came home to the wedding, apparently cured of her heartache, with honest roses and lilies in her face, and a proud smile on her lips. Arthur Lloyd came over from Boston to see his brother-in-law married, but without his wife, who was expecting shortly to present him with an heir. It was nearly a year since Viola had seen him. She was glad – she hardly knew why – that Perdita had stayed at home. Arthur looked happy, but he was more grave and solemn than before his marriage. She thought he looked 'interesting',[7] – for although the word in its modern sense was not then invented, we may be sure that the idea was. The truth is, he was simply preoccupied with his wife's condition. Nevertheless, he by no means failed to observe Viola's beauty and splendour, and how she quite effaced the poor little bride. The allowance that Perdita had enjoyed for her dress had now been transferred to her sister, who turned it to prodigious account. On the morning after the wedding, he had a lady's saddle put on the horse of the servant who had come with him from town, and went out with the young girl for a ride. It was a keen, clear morning in January; the ground was bare and hard, and the horses in good condition, – to say nothing of Viola, who was charming in her hat and plume, and her dark blue riding-coat, trimmed with fur. They rode all the morning, they lost their way, and were obliged to stop for dinner at a farm-house. The early winter dusk had fallen when they got home. Mrs Willoughby met them with a long face. A messenger had arrived at noon from Mrs Lloyd; she was beginning to be ill, and desired her husband's immediate return. The young man, at the thought that he had lost several hours, and that by hard riding he might already have been with his wife, uttered a passionate oath. He barely consented to stop for a mouthful of supper, but mounted the messenger's horse and started off at a gallop.

He reached home at midnight. His wife had been delivered of a little girl. 'Ah, why weren't you with me?' she said, as he came to her bedside.

'I was out of the house when the man came. I was with Viola,' said Lloyd, innocently.

Mrs Lloyd made a little moan, and turned about. But she continued to do very well, and for a week her improvement was uninterrupted. Finally, however, through some indiscretion in the way of diet or of exposure, it was checked, and the poor lady grew rapidly worse. Lloyd was in despair. It very soon became evident that she was breathing her last. Mrs Lloyd came to a sense of her approaching end, and declared that she was reconciled with death. On the third evening after the change took place she told her husband that she felt she would not outlast the night. She dismissed her servants, and also requested her mother to withdraw, – Mrs Willoughby having arrived on the preceding day. She had had her infant placed on the bed beside her, and she lay on her side, with the child against her breast, holding her husband's hands. The night-lamp was hidden behind the heavy curtains of the bed, but the room was illumined with a red glow from the immense fire of logs on the hearth.

'It seems strange to die by such a fire as that,' the young woman said, feebly trying to smile. 'If I had but a little of such fire in my veins! But I've given it all to this little spark of mortality.' And she dropped her eyes on her child. Then raising them she looked at her husband with a long penetrating gaze. The last feeling which lingered in her heart was one of mistrust. She had not recovered from the shock which Arthur had given her by telling her that in the hour of her agony he had been with Viola. She trusted her husband very nearly as well as she loved him; but now that she was called away for ever, she felt a cold horror of her sister. She felt in her soul that Viola had never ceased to envy her good fortune; and a year of happy security had not effaced the young girl's image, dressed in her wedding garments, and smiling with coveted triumph. Now that Arthur was to be alone, what might not Viola do? She was beautiful, she was engaging; what arts might she not use, what impression might she not make upon the young man's melancholy heart? Mrs Lloyd looked at her husband in silence. It seemed hard, after all, to doubt of his constancy. His fine eyes were filled with tears; his face was convulsed with weeping; the clasp of his hands was warm and passionate. How noble he looked, how tender, how faithful and devoted! 'Nay,' thought Perdita, 'he's not for such as Viola. He'll never forget me. Nor does Viola truly care for him; she cares only for vanities and finery and jewels.' And she dropped her eyes on her white hands, which her husband's liberality had covered with rings, and on the lace ruffles which trimmed the edge of her nightdress. 'She covets my rings and my laces more than she covets my husband.'

At this moment the thought of her sister's rapacity seemed to cast a dark shadow between her and the helpless figure of her little girl. 'Arthur,' she said, 'you must take off my rings. I shall not be buried in them. One of these days my daughter shall wear them, – my rings and my laces and silks. I had them all brought out and shown me to-day. It's a great wardrobe, – there's not such another in the Province; I can say it without vanity now that I've done with it. It will be a great inheritance for my daughter, when she grows into a young woman. There are things there that a man never buys twice, and if they're lost you'll never again see the like. So you'll watch them well. Some dozen things I've left to Viola; I've named them to my mother. I've given her that blue and silver; it was meant for her; I wore it only once, I looked ill in it. But the rest are to be sacredly kept for this little innocent. It's such a providence that she should be my colour; she can wear my gowns; she has her mother's eyes. You know the same fashions come back every twenty years. She can wear my gowns as they are. They'll lie there quietly waiting till she grows into them, – wrapped in camphor and rose-leaves, and keeping their colours in the sweet-scented darkness. She shall have black hair, she shall wear my carnation satin. Do you promise me, Arthur?'

'Promise you what, dearest?'

'Promise me to keep your poor little wife's old gowns.'

'Are you afraid I'll sell them?'

'No, but that they may get scattered. My mother will have them properly wrapped up, and you shall lay them away under a double-lock. Do you know the great chest in the attic, with the iron bands? There's no end to what it will hold. You can lay them all there. My mother and the housekeeper will do it, and give you the key. And you'll keep the key in your secretary, and never give it to any one but your child. Do you promise me?'

'Ah, yes, I promise you,' said Lloyd, puzzled at the intensity with which his wife appeared to cling to this idea.

'Will you swear?' repeated Perdita.

'Yes, I swear.'

'Well – I trust you – I trust you,' said the poor lady, looking into his eyes with eyes in which, if he had suspected her vague apprehensions, he might have read an appeal quite as much as an assurance.

Lloyd bore his bereavement soberly and manfully. A month after his wife's death, in the course of commerce, circumstances arose which offered him an opportunity of going to England. He embraced it as a diversion from gloomy thoughts. He was absent nearly a year, during which his little girl was tenderly nursed and cherished by her grandmother. On his return he had his house again thrown open, and announced his intention of keeping the same state as during his wife's lifetime. It very soon came to be predicted that he would marry again, and there were at least a dozen young women of whom one may say that it was by no fault of theirs that, for six months after his return, the prediction did not come true. During this interval he still left his little daughter in Mrs Willoughby's hands, the latter assuring him that a change of residence at so tender an age was perilous to her health. Finally, however, he declared that his heart longed for his daughter's presence, and that she must be brought up to town. He sent his coach and his housekeeper to fetch her home. Mrs Willoughby was in terror lest something should befall her on the road; and, in accordance with this feeling, Viola offered to ride along with her. She could return the next day. So she went up to town with her little niece, and Mr Lloyd met her on the threshold of his house, overcome with her kindness and with gratitude. Instead of returning the next day, Viola stayed out the week; and when at last she reappeared, she had only come for her clothes. Arthur would not hear of her coming home, nor would the baby. She cried and moaned if Viola left her; and at the sight of her grief Arthur lost his wits, and swore that she was going to die. In fine, nothing would suit them but that Viola should remain until the poor child had grown used to strange faces.

It took two months to bring this consummation about; for it was not until this period had elapsed that Viola took leave of her brother-in-law. Mrs Willoughby had shaken her head over her daughter's absence; she had declared that it was not becoming, and that it was the talk of the town. She had reconciled herself to it only because, during the young girl's visit, the household enjoyed an unwonted term of peace. Bernard Willoughby had brought his wife home to live, between whom and her sister-in-law there existed a bitter hostility. Viola was perhaps no angel; but in the daily practice of life she was a sufficiently good-natured girl, and if she quarrelled with Mrs Bernard, it was not without provocation. Quarrel, however, she did, to the great annoyance not only of her antagonist, but of the two spectators of these constant altercations. Her stay in the household of her brother-in-law, therefore, would have been delightful, if only because it removed her from contact with the object of her antipathy at home. It was doubly – it was ten times – delightful, in that it kept her near the object of her old passion. Mrs Lloyd's poignant mistrust had fallen very far short of the truth. Viola's sentiment had been a passion at first, and a passion it remained, – a passion of whose radiant heat, tempered to the delicate state of his feelings, Mr Lloyd very soon felt the influence. Lloyd, as I have hinted, was not a modern Petrarch;[8] it was not in his nature to practise an ideal constancy. He had not been many days in the house with his sister-in-law before he began to assure himself that she was, in the language of that day, a devilish fine woman. Whether Viola really practised those insidious arts that her sister had been tempted to impute to her it is needless to enquire. It is enough to say that she found means to appear to the very best advantage. She used to seat herself every morning before the great fireplace in the dining-room, at work upon a piece of tapestry, with her little niece disporting herself on the carpet at her feet, or on the train of her dress, and playing with her woollen balls. Lloyd would have been a very stupid fellow if he had remained insensible to the rich suggestions of this charming picture. He was prodigiously fond of his little girl, and was never weary of taking her in his arms and tossing her up and down, and making her crow with delight. Very often, however, he would venture upon greater liberties than the young lady was yet prepared to allow, and she would suddenly vociferate her displeasure. Viola would then drop her tapestry, and put out her handsome hands with the serious smile of the young girl whose virgin fancy has revealed to her all a mother's healing arts. Lloyd would give up the child, their eyes would meet, their hands would touch, and Viola would extinguish the little girl's sobs upon the snowy folds of the kerchief that crossed her bosom. Her dignity was perfect, and nothing could be more discreet than the manner in which she accepted her brother-in-law's hospitality. It may be almost said, perhaps, that there was something harsh in her reserve. Lloyd had a provoking feeling that she was in the house, and yet that she was unapproachable. Half an hour after supper, at the very outset of the long winter evenings, she would light her candle, and make the young man a most respectful curtsey, and march off to bed. If these were arts, Viola was a great artist. But their effect was so gentle, so gradual, they were calculated to work upon the young widower's fancy with such a finely shaded *crescendo*, that, as the reader has seen, several weeks elapsed before Viola began to feel sure that her return would cover her outlay. When this became morally certain, she packed up her trunk, and returned to her mother's house. For three days she waited; on the fourth Mr Lloyd made his appearance, – a respectful but ardent suitor. Viola heard him out with great humility, and accepted him with infinite modesty. It is hard to imagine that Mrs Lloyd should have forgiven her husband; but if anything might have disarmed her resentment, it would have been the ceremonious continence of this interview. Viola imposed upon her lover but a short probation. They were married, as was becoming, with great privacy, – almost with secrecy, – in the hope perhaps, as was waggishly remarked at the time, that the late Mrs Lloyd wouldn't hear of it.

The marriage was to all appearance a happy one, and each party obtained what each had desired – Lloyd 'a devilish fine woman', and Viola – but Viola's desires, as the reader will have observed, have remained a good deal of a mystery. There were, indeed, two blots upon their felicity; but time would, perhaps, efface them. During the first three years of her marriage Mrs Lloyd failed to become a mother, and her husband on his side suffered heavy losses of money. This latter circumstance compelled a material retrenchment in his expenditure, and Viola was perforce less of a great lady than her sister had been. She contrived, however, to sustain with unbroken consistency the part of an elegant woman, although it must be confessed that

it required the exercise of more ingenuity than belongs to your
real aristocratic repose. She had long since ascertained that her
sister's immense wardrobe had been sequestrated for the benefit
of her daughter, and that it lay languishing in thankless gloom
in the dusty attic. It was a revolting thought that these exquisite
fabrics should await the commands of a little girl who sat in a
high chair and ate bread-and-milk with a wooden spoon. Viola
had the good taste, however, to say nothing about the matter
until several months had expired. Then, at last, she timidly
broached it to her husband. Was it not a pity that so much
finery should be lost? – for lost it would be, what with colours
fading, and moths eating it up, and the change of fashions. But
Lloyd gave so abrupt and peremptory a negative to her enquiry,
that she saw that for the present her attempt was vain. Six
months went by, however, and brought with them new needs
and new fancies. Viola's thoughts hovered lovingly about her
sister's relics.[9] She went up and looked at the chest in which
they lay imprisoned. There was a sullen defiance in its three
great padlocks and its iron bands, which only quickened her
desires. There was something exasperating in its incorruptible
immobility. It was like a grim and grizzled old household servant, who locks his jaws over a family secret. And then there
was a look of capacity in its vast extent, and a sound as of
dense fulness, when Viola knocked its side with the toe of her
little slipper, which caused her to flush with baffled longing.
'It's absurd,' she cried; 'it's improper, it's wicked'; and she
forthwith resolved upon another attack upon her husband. On
the following day, after dinner, when he had had his wine, she
bravely began it. But he cut her short with great sternness.

'Once for all, Viola,' said he, 'it's out of the question. I shall
be gravely displeased if you return to the matter.'

'Very good,' said Viola. 'I'm glad to learn the value at which
I'm held. Great Heaven!' she cried, 'I'm a happy woman. It's an
agreeable thing to feel one's self sacrificed to a caprice!' And
her eyes filled with tears of anger and disappointment.

Lloyd had a good-natured man's horror of a woman's sobs,
and he attempted – I may say he condescended – to explain.
'It's not a caprice, dear, it's a promise,' he said, – 'an oath.'

'An oath? It's a pretty matter for oaths! and to whom, pray?'

'To Perdita,' said the young man, raising his eyes for an instant, but immediately dropping them.

'Perdita, – ah, Perdita!' and Viola's tears broke forth. Her bosom heaved with stormy sobs, – sobs which were the long-deferred counterpart of the violent fit of weeping in which she had indulged herself on the night when she discovered her sister's betrothal. She had hoped, in her better moments, that she had done with her jealousy; but her temper, on that occasion, had taken an ineffaceable fold. 'And pray, what right,' she cried, 'had Perdita to dispose of my future? What right had she to bind you to meanness and cruelty? Ah, I occupy a dignified place, and I make a very fine figure! I'm welcome to what Perdita has left! And what has she left? I never knew till now how little! Nothing, nothing, nothing.'

This was very poor logic, but it was very good passion. Lloyd put his arm around his wife's waist and tried to kiss her, but she shook him off with magnificent scorn. Poor fellow! he had coveted a 'devilish fine woman', and he had got one. Her scorn was intolerable. He walked away with his ears tingling, – irresolute, distracted. Before him was his secretary, and in it the sacred key which with his own hand he had turned in the triple lock. He marched up and opened it, and took the key from a secret drawer, wrapped in a little packet which he had sealed with his own honest bit of blazonry. *Teneo*, said the motto, – 'I hold'. But he was ashamed to put it back. He flung it upon the table beside his wife.

'Keep it!' she cried. 'I want it not. I hate it!'

'I wash my hands of it,' cried her husband. 'God forgive me!'

Mrs Lloyd gave an indignant shrug of her shoulders, and swept out of the room, while the young man retreated by another door. Ten minutes later Mrs Lloyd returned, and found the room occupied by her little step-daughter and the nursery-maid. The key was not on the table. She glanced at the child. The child was perched on a chair with the packet in her hands. She had broken the seal with her own little fingers. Mrs Lloyd hastily took possession of the key.

At the habitual supper-hour Arthur Lloyd came back from

his counting-room. It was the month of June, and supper was served by daylight. The meal was placed on the table, but Mrs Lloyd failed to make her appearance. The servant whom his master sent to call her came back with the assurance that her room was empty, and that the women informed him that she had not been seen since dinner. They had in truth observed her to have been in tears, and, supposing her to be shut up in her chamber, had not disturbed her. Her husband called her name in various parts of the house, but without response. At last it occurred to him that he might find her by taking the way to the attic. The thought gave him a strange feeling of discomfort, and he bade his servants remain behind, wishing no witness in his quest. He reached the foot of the staircase leading to the topmost flat, and stood with his hand on the banisters, pronouncing his wife's name. His voice trembled. He called again, louder and more firmly. The only sound which disturbed the absolute silence was a faint echo of his own tones, repeating his question under the great eaves. He nevertheless felt irresistibly moved to ascend the staircase. It opened upon a wide hall, lined with wooden closets, and terminating in a window which looked westward, and admitted the last rays of the sun. Before the window stood the great chest. Before the chest, on her knees, the young man saw with amazement and horror the figure of his wife. In an instant he crossed the interval between them, bereft of utterance. The lid of the chest stood open, exposing, amid their perfumed napkins, its treasure of stuffs[10] and jewels. Viola had fallen backward from a kneeling posture, with one hand supporting her on the floor and the other pressed to her heart. On her limbs was the stiffness of death, and on her face, in the fading light of the sun, the terror of something more than death. Her lips were parted in entreaty, in dismay, in agony; and on her bloodless brow and cheeks there glowed the marks of ten hideous wounds from two vengeful ghostly hands.

THE LAST OF THE VALERII

I had had occasion to declare more than once that if my god-daughter married a foreigner I should refuse to give her away. And yet when the young Conte Valerio was presented to me, in Rome, as her accepted and plighted lover, I found myself look-ing at the happy fellow, after a momentary stare of amazement, with a certain paternal benevolence; thinking, indeed, that from the picturesque point of view (she with her yellow locks and he with his dusky ones), they were a strikingly well-assorted pair. She brought him up to me half proudly, half timidly, pushing him before her, and begging me with one of her dovelike glances to be very polite. I don't know that I am particularly addicted to rudeness; but she was so deeply impressed with his grandeur that she thought it impossible to do him honour enough. The Conte Valerio's grandeur was doubtless nothing for a young American girl, who had the air and almost the habits of a princess, to sound her trumpet about; but she was desperately in love with him, and not only her heart, but her imagination, was touched. He was extremely handsome, and with a more significant sort of beauty than is common in the handsome Roman race. He had a sort of sunken depth of expression, and a grave, slow smile, suggesting no great quickness of wit, but an unimpassioned intensity of feel-ing which promised well for Martha's happiness. He had little of the light, inexpensive urbanity of his countrymen, and more of a sort of heavy sincerity in his gaze which seemed to sus-pend response until he was sure he understood you. He was perhaps a little stupid, and I fancied that to a political or æsthetic question the response would be particularly slow. 'He is good, and strong, and brave,' the young girl however assured me; and I easily believed her. Strong the Conte Valerio certainly was; he had a head and throat like some of the busts in the Vatican. To my eye, which has looked at things now so long with the painter's purpose, it was a real perplexity to see such a throat rising out of the white cravat of the period. It sustained a head as massively round as that of the familiar bust of the Emperor Caracalla,[1] and covered with the same dense sculptural crop of curls. The young man's hair grew superbly; it was such hair as the old Romans must have had when they walked bareheaded and bronzed about the world. It made a perfect arch over his low, clear forehead, and prolonged itself on cheek and chin in a close, crisp beard, strong with its own strength and unstiffened by the razor. Neither his nose nor his mouth was delicate; but they were powerful, shapely, and manly. His complexion was of a deep glowing brown which no emotion would alter, and his large, lucid eyes seemed to stare at you like a pair of polished agates. He was of middle stature, and his chest was of so generous a girth that you half expected to hear his linen crack with its even respirations. And yet, with his simple human smile, he looked neither like a young bullock nor a gladiator. His powerful voice was the least bit harsh, and his large, ceremonious reply to my compliment had the massive sonority with which civil speeches must have been uttered in the age of Augustus. I had always considered my god-daughter a very American little person, in all delightful meanings of the word, and I doubted if this sturdy young Latin would understand the transatlantic element in her nature; but, evidently, he would make her a loyal and ardent lover. She seemed to me, in her blond prettiness, so tender, so appealing, so bewitching, that it was impossible to believe he had not more thoughts for all this than for the pretty fortune which it yet bothered me to believe that he must, like a good Italian, have taken the exact measure of. His own worldly goods consisted of the paternal estate, a villa within the walls of Rome, which his scanty funds had suffered to fall into sombre disrepair. 'It's the Villa she's in love with, quite as much as the Count,' said her mother. 'She dreams of converting the Count; that's all very well. But she dreams of refurnishing the Villa!'

The upholsterers were turned into it,[2] I believe, before the wedding, and there was a great scrubbing and sweeping of saloons and raking and weeding of alleys and avenues. Martha made frequent visits of inspection while these ceremonies were taking place; but one day, on her return, she came into my little studio with an air of amusing horror. She had found them *scraping* the sarcophagus in the great ilex-walk;[3] divesting it of its mossy coat, disincrusting it of the sacred green mould of the ages! This was their idea of making the Villa comfortable. She had made them transport it to the dampest place they could find; for, next after that slow-coming, slow-going smile of her lover, it was the rusty complexion of his patrimonial marbles that she most prized. The young Count's conversion proceeded less rapidly, and indeed I believe that his betrothed brought little zeal to the affair. She loved him so devoutly that she believed no change of faith could better him, and she would have been willing for his sake to say her prayers to the sacred Bambino at Epiphany.[4] But he had the good taste to demand no such sacrifice, and I was struck with the happy promise of a scene of which I was an accidental observer. It was at St Peter's,[5] one Friday afternoon, during the vesper service which takes place in the chapel of the Choir. I met my god-daughter wandering happily on her lover's arm, her mother being established on her camp-stool near the chapel door. The crowd was collected thereabouts, and the body of the church was empty. Now and then the high voices of the singers escaped into the outer vastness and melted slowly away in the incense-thickened air. Something in the young girl's step and the clasp of her arm in her lover's told me that her contentment was perfect. As she threw back her head and gazed into the magnificent immensity of vault and dome, I felt that she was in that enviable mood in which all consciousness revolves on a single centre, and that her sense of the splendours around her was one with the ecstasy of her trust. They stopped before that sombre group of confessionals which proclaims so portentously the world's sinfulness, and Martha seemed to make some almost passionate protest-ation. A few minutes later I overtook them.

'Don't you agree with me, dear friend,' said the Count, who always addressed me with the most affectionate deference, 'that before I marry so pure and sweet a creature as this, I ought to go into one of those places and confess every sin I ever was guilty of, – every evil thought and impulse and desire of my grossly evil nature?'

Martha looked at him, half in deprecation, half in homage, with a look which seemed at once to insist that her lover could have no vices, and to plead that, if he had, there would be something magnificent in them. 'Listen to him!' she said, smil-ing. 'The list would be long, and if you waited to finish it, you would be late for the wedding! But if you confess your sins for me, it's only fair I should confess mine for you. Do you know what I have been saying to Camillo?' she added, turning to me with the half-filial confidence she had always shown me and with a rosy glow in her cheeks; 'that I want to do something more for him than girls commonly do for their lovers, – to take some step, to run some risk, to break some law, even! I'm will-ing to change my religion, if he bids me. There are moments when I'm terribly tired of simply staring at Catholicism; it will be a relief to come into a church to kneel. That's, after all, what they are meant for! Therefore, Camillo mio, if it casts a shade across your heart to think that I'm a heretic, I'll go and kneel down to that good old priest who has just entered the confessional yonder and say to him, "My father, I repent, I abjure, I believe. Baptize me in the only faith."'

'If it's as a compliment to the Count,' I said, 'it seems to me he ought to anticipate it by turning Protestant.'

She had spoken lightly and with a smile, and yet with an undertone of girlish ardour. The young man looked at her with a solemn, puzzled face and shook his head. 'Keep your reli-gion,' he said. 'Every one his own. If you should attempt to embrace mine, I'm afraid you would close your arms about a shadow. I'm a poor Catholic! I don't understand all these chants and ceremonies and splendours. When I was a child I never could learn my catechism. My poor old confessor long ago gave me up; he told me I was a good boy but a *pagan*! You must not be a better Catholic than your husband. I don't understand your religion any better, but I beg you not to change it for mine. If it has helped to make you what you are, it must be good.' And taking the young girl's hand, he was about to raise it affectionately to his lips; but suddenly remembering that they were in a place unaccordant with profane passions, he lowered it with a comical smile. 'Let us go!' he murmured, passing his hand over his forehead. 'This heavy atmosphere of St Peter's always stupefies me.'

They were married in the month of May, and we separated for the summer, the Contessa's mamma going to illuminate the domestic circle in New York with her reflected dignity. When I returned to Rome in the autumn, I found the young couple established at the Villa Valerio, which was being gradually reclaimed from its antique decay. I begged that the hand of improvement might be lightly laid on it, for as an unscrupulous old *genre* painter, with an eye to 'subjects', I preferred that ruin should accumulate. My god-daughter was quite of my way of thinking, and she had a capital sense of the picturesque. Advising with me often as to projected changes, she was sometimes more conservative than myself; and I more than once smiled at her archæological zeal, and declared that I believed she had married the Count because he was like a statue of the Decadence. I had a constant invitation to spend my days at the Villa, and my easel was always planted in one of the garden-walks. I grew to have a painter's passion for the place, and to be intimate with every tangled shrub and twisted tree, every moss-coated vase and mouldy sarcophagus and sad, disfeatured bust of those grim old Romans who could so ill afford to become more meagre-visaged. The place was of small extent; but though there were many other villas more pretentious and splendid, none seemed to me more deeply picturesque, more romantically idle and untrimmed, more encumbered with precious antique rubbish, and haunted with half-historic echoes. It contained an old ilex-walk in which I used religiously to spend half an hour every day, – half an hour being, I confess, just as long as I could stay without beginning to sneeze. The trees arched and intertwisted here along their dusky vista in the quaintest symmetry; and as it was exposed uninterruptedly to the west, the low evening sun used to transfuse it with a sort of golden mist and play through it – over leaves and knotty boughs and mossy marbles – with a thousand crimson fingers. It was filled with disinterred fragments of sculpture, – nameless statues and noseless heads and rough-hewn sarcophagi, which made it deliciously solemn. The statues used to stand there in the perpetual twilight like conscious things, brooding on their gathered memories. I used to linger about them, half expecting they would speak and tell me their stony secrets, – whisper heavily the whereabouts of their mouldering fellows, still unrecovered from the soil.

My god-daughter was idyllically happy and absolutely in love. I was obliged to confess that even rigid rules have their exceptions, and that now and then an Italian count is an honest fellow. Camillo was one to the core, and seemed quite content to be adored. Their life was a childlike interchange of caresses, as candid and unmeasured as those of a shepherd and shepherdess in a bucolic poem. To stroll in the ilex-walk and feel her husband's arm about her waist and his shoulder against her cheek; to roll cigarettes for him while he puffed them in the great marble-paved rotunda in the centre of the house; to fill his glass from an old rusty red amphora, – these graceful occupations satisfied the young Countess.

She rode with him sometimes in the grassy shadow of aqueducts and tombs, and sometimes suffered him to show his beautiful wife at Roman dinners and balls. She played dominos with him after dinner, and carried out in a desultory way a daily scheme of reading him the newspapers. This observance was subject to fluctuations caused by the Count's invincible tendency to go to sleep, – a failing his wife never attempted to disguise or palliate. She would sit and brush the flies from him while he lay picturesquely snoozing, and, if I ventured near him, would place her finger on her lips and whisper that she thought her husband was as handsome asleep as awake. I confess I often felt tempted to reply to her that he was at least as entertaining, for the young man's happiness had not multiplied the topics on which he readily conversed. He had plenty of good sense, and his opinions on practical matters were always worth having. He would often come and sit near me while I worked at my easel and offer a friendly criticism. His taste was a little crude, but his eye was excellent, and his measurement of the resemblance between some point of my copy and the original as trustworthy as that of a mathematical instrument. But he seemed to me to have either a strange reserve or a strange simplicity; to be fundamentally unfurnished with 'ideas'. He had no beliefs nor hopes nor fears, – nothing but senses, appetites, and serenely luxurious tastes. As I watched him strolling about looking at his finger-nails, I often wondered whether he had anything that could properly be termed a soul, and whether good health and good-nature were not the sum of his advantages. 'It's lucky he's good-natured,' I used to say to myself; 'for if he were not, there is nothing in his conscience to keep him in order. If he had irritable nerves instead of quiet ones, he would strangle us as the infant Hercules strangled the poor little snakes. He's the natural man! Happily, his nature is gentle; I can mix my colours at my ease.' I wondered what he thought about and what passed through his mind in the sunny leisure which seemed to shut him in from that modern work-a-day world of which, in spite of my passion for bedaubing old panels with ineffective portraiture of mouldy statues against screens of box, I still flattered myself I was a member. I went so far as to believe that he sometimes withdrew from the world altogether. He had moods in which his consciousness seemed so remote and his mind so irresponsive and dumb, that nothing but a powerful caress or a sudden violence was likely to arouse him. Even his lavish tenderness for his wife had a quality which I but half relished. Whether or no he had a soul himself, he seemed not to suspect that she had one. I took a godfatherly interest in what it had not always seemed to me crabbed and pedantic to talk of as her moral development. I fondly believed her to be a creature susceptible of the finer spiritual emotions. But what was becoming of her spiritual life in this interminable heathenish honeymoon? Some fine day she would find herself tired of the Count's *beaux yeux*[6] and make an appeal to his mind. She had, to my knowledge, plans of study, of charity, of worthily playing her part as a Contessa Valerio, – a position as to which the family records furnished the most inspiring examples. But if the Count found the newspapers soporific, I doubted if he would turn Dante's pages very fast for his wife, or smile with much zest at the anecdotes of Vasari.[7] How could he advise her, instruct her, sustain her? And if she became a mother, how could he share her responsibilities? He doubtless would assure his little son and heir a stout pair of arms and legs and a magnificent crop of curls, and sometimes remove his cigarette to kiss a dimpled spot; but I found it hard to picture him lending his voice to teach the lusty urchin his alphabet or his prayers, or the rudiments of infant virtue. One accomplishment indeed the Count possessed which would make him an agreeable playfellow: he carried in his pocket a collection of precious fragments of antique pavement, – bits of porphyry and malachite and lapis and basalt, – disinterred on his own soil and brilliantly polished by use. With these you might see him occupied by the half-hour, playing the simple game of catch-and-toss, ranging them in a circle, tossing them in rotation, and catching them on the back of his hand. His skill was remarkable; he would send a stone five feet into the air, and pitch and catch and transpose the rest before he received it again. I watched with affectionate jealousy for the signs of a dawning sense, on Martha's part, that she was the least bit strangely mated. Once or twice, as the weeks went by, I fancied I read them, and that she looked at me with eyes which seemed to remember certain old talks of mine in which I had declared – with such verity as you please – that a Frenchman, an Italian, a Spaniard, might be a very good fellow, but that he never really respected the woman he pretended to love. For the most part, however, these dusky broodings of mine spent themselves easily in the charmed atmosphere of our romantic home. We were out of the modern world and had no business with modern scruples. The place was so bright, so still, so sacred to the silent, imperturbable past, that drowsy contentment seemed a natural law; and sometimes when, as I sat at my work, I saw my companions passing arm-in-arm across the end of one of the long-drawn vistas, and, turning back to my palette, found my colours dimmer for the radiant vision, I could easily believe that I was some loyal old chronicler of a perfectly poetical legend.

It was a help to ungrudging feelings that the Count, yielding to his wife's urgency, had undertaken a series of systematic excavations. To excavate is an expensive luxury, and neither Camillo nor his latter forefathers had possessed the means for a disinterested pursuit of archæology. But his young wife had persuaded herself that the much-trodden soil of the Villa was as full of buried treasures as a bride-cake[8] of plums, and that it would be a pretty compliment to the ancient house which had accepted her as mistress, to devote a portion of her dowry to bringing its mouldy honours to the light. I think she was not without a fancy that this liberal process would help to disinfect her Yankee dollars of the impertinent odour of trade. She took learned advice on the subject, and was soon ready to swear to you, proceeding from irrefutable premises, that a colossal gilt-bronze Minerva mentioned by Strabo[9] was placidly awaiting resurrection at a point twenty rods from the northwest angle of the house. She had a couple of grotesque old antiquaries to lunch, whom having plied with unwonted potations, she walked off their legs in the grounds; and though they agreed on nothing else in the world, they individually assured her that properly conducted researches would probably yield an unequalled harvest of discoveries. The Count had been not only indifferent, but even averse, to the scheme, and had more than once arrested his wife's complacent allusions to it by an unaccustomed acerbity of tone. 'Let them lie, the poor disinherited gods, the Minerva, the Apollo, the Ceres[10] you are so sure of finding,' he said, 'and don't break their rest. What do you want of them? We can't worship them. Would you put them on pedestals to stare and mock at them? If you can't believe in them, don't disturb them. Peace be with them!' I remember being a good deal impressed by a vigorous confession drawn from him by his wife's playfully declaring in answer to some remonstrances in this strain that he was absolutely superstitious. 'Yes, by Bacchus, I am superstitious!'[11] he cried. 'Too much so, perhaps! But I'm an old Italian, and you must take me as you find me. There have been things seen and done here which leave strange influences behind! They don't touch you, doubtless, who come of another race. But they touch me, often, in the whisper of the leaves and the odour of the mouldy soil and the blank eyes of the old statues. I can't bear to look the statues in the face. I seem to see other strange eyes in the empty sockets, and I hardly know what they say to me. I call the poor old statues ghosts. In conscience, we've enough on the place already, lurking and peering in every shady nook. Don't dig up any more, or I won't answer for my wits!'

This account of Camillo's sensibilities was too fantastic not to seem to his wife almost a joke; and though I imagined there was more in it, he made a joke so seldom that I should have been sorry to cut short the poor girl's smile. With her smile she carried her point, and in a few days arrived a kind of archæological detective, with a dozen workmen armed with pickaxes and spades. For myself, I was secretly vexed at these energetic measures; for, though fond of disinterred statues, I disliked the disinterment, and deplored the profane sounds which were henceforth to jar upon the sleepy stillness of the gardens. I especially objected to the personage who conducted the operations; an ugly little dwarfish man who seemed altogether a subterranean genius, an earthy gnome of the underworld, and went prying about the grounds with a malicious smile which suggested more delight in the money the Signor Conte was going to bury than in the expected marbles and bronzes. When the first sod had been turned, the Count's mood seemed to alter, and his curiosity got the better of his scruples. He sniffed delightedly the odour of the humid earth, and stood watching the workmen, as they struck constantly deeper, with a kindling wonder in his eyes. Whenever a pickaxe rang against a stone he would utter a sharp cry, and be deterred from jumping into the trench only by the little explorer's assurance that it was a false alarm. The near prospect of discoveries seemed to act upon his nerves, and I met him more than once strolling restlessly among his cedarn alleys, as if at last he had fallen a thinking. He took me by the arm and made me walk with him,

and discoursed ardently of the chance of a 'find'. I rather marvelled at his sudden zeal, and wondered whether he had an eye
to the past or to the future, – to the beauty of possible Miner-
vas and Apollos or to their market value. Whenever the Count
would come and denounce his little army of spadesmen for a
set of loitering vagabonds, the little explorer would glance at
me with a sarcastic twinkle which seemed to hint that excavations were a snare. We were kept some time in suspense, for
several false beginnings were made. The earth was probed in
the wrong places. The Count began to be discouraged and to
prolong his abbreviated siesta. But the little expert, who had
his own ideas, shrewdly continued his labours; and as I sat at my
easel I heard the spades ringing against the dislodged stones.
Now and then I would pause, with an uncontrollable accelera-
tion of my heart-beats. 'It *may* be,' I would say, 'that some
marble masterpiece is stirring there beneath its lightening
weight of earth! There are as good fish in the sea . . . ! I *may* be
summoned to welcome another Antinous back to fame, – a
Venus, a Faun, an Augustus!'[12]

One morning it seemed to me that I had been hearing for
half an hour a livelier movement of voices than usual; but as I
was preoccupied with a puzzling bit of work, I made no enquiries. Suddenly a shadow fell across my canvas, and I turned
round. The little explorer stood beside me, with a glittering
eye, cap in hand, his forehead bathed in perspiration. Resting
in the hollow of his arm was an earth-stained fragment of marble. In answer to my questioning glance he held it up to me,
and I saw it was a woman's shapely hand. 'Come!' he simply
said, and led the way to the excavation. The workmen were so
closely gathered round the open trench that I saw nothing till
he made them divide. Then, full in the sun and flashing it back,
almost, in spite of her dusky incrustations, I beheld, propped
up with stones against a heap of earth, a majestic marble
image. She seemed to me almost colossal, though I afterwards
perceived that she was of perfect human proportions. My
pulses began to throb, for I felt she was something great, and
that it was great to be among the first to know her. Her marvellous beauty gave her an almost human look, and her absent

eyes seemed to wonder back at us. She was amply draped, so that I saw that she was not a Venus. 'She's a Juno,'[13] said the excavator, decisively; and she seemed indeed an embodiment of celestial supremacy and repose. Her beautiful head, bound with a single band, could have bent only to give the nod of command; her eyes looked straight before her; her mouth was implacably grave; one hand, outstretched, appeared to have held a kind of imperial wand, the arm from which the other had been broken hung at her side with the most classical majesty. The workmanship was of the rarest finish; and though perhaps there was a sort of vaguely modern attempt at character in her expression, she was wrought, as a whole, in the large and simple manner of the great Greek period. She was a masterpiece of skill and a marvel of preservation. 'Does the Count know?' I soon asked, for I had a guilty sense that our eyes were taking something from her.

'The Signor Conte is at his siesta,' said the explorer, with his sceptical grin. 'We don't like to disturb him.'

'Here he comes!' cried one of the workmen, and we made way for him. His siesta had evidently been suddenly broken, for his face was flushed and his hair disordered.

'Ah, my dream – my dream was right, then!' he cried, and stood staring at the image.

'What was your dream?' I asked, as his face seemed to betray more dismay than delight.

'That they'd found a Juno; and that she rose and came and laid her marble hand on mine. Eh?' said the Count, excitedly.

A kind of awe-struck, guttural *a-ah!* burst from the listening workmen.

'This is the hand!' said the little explorer, holding up his perfect fragment. 'I've had it this half-hour, so it can't have touched you.'

'But you're apparently right as to her being a Juno,' I said. 'Admire her at your leisure.' And I turned away; for if the Count was superstitious, I wished to leave him free to relieve himself. I repaired to the house to carry the news to my god-daughter, whom I found slumbering – dreamlessly, it appeared – over a great archæological octavo. 'They've touched bottom,' I said.

'They've found a Juno of Praxiteles[14] at the very least!' She dropped her octavo, and rang for a parasol. I described the statue, but not graphically, I presume, for Martha gave a little sarcastic grimace.

'A long, fluted *peplum*?'[15] she said. 'How very odd! I don't believe she's beautiful.'

'She's beautiful enough, *figlioccia mia*,'[16] I answered, 'to make you jealous.'

We found the Count standing before the resurgent goddess in fixed contemplation, with folded arms. He seemed to have recovered from the irritation of his dream, but I thought his face betrayed a still deeper emotion. He was pale, and gave no response as his wife caressingly clasped his arm. I'm not sure, however, that his wife's attitude was not a livelier tribute to the perfection of the image. She had been laughing at my rhapsody as we walked from the house, and I had bethought myself of a statement I had somewhere seen, that women lacked the perception of the purest beauty. Martha, however, seemed slowly to measure our Juno's infinite stateliness. She gazed a long time silently, leaning against her husband, and then stepped half timidly down on the stones which formed a rough base for the figure. She laid her two rosy, ungloved hands upon the stony fingers of the goddess, and remained for some moments pressing them in her warm grasp, and fixing her living eyes upon the inexpressive brow. When she turned round her eyes were bright with an admiring tear, – a tear which her husband was too deeply absorbed to notice. He had apparently given orders that the workmen should be treated to a cask of wine, in honour of their discovery. It was now brought and opened on the spot, and the little explorer, having drawn the first glass, stepped forward, hat in hand, and obsequiously presented it to the Countess. She only moistened her lips with it and passed it to her husband. He raised it mechanically to his own; then suddenly he stopped, held it a moment aloft, and poured it out slowly and solemnly at the feet of the Juno.

'Why, it's a libation!' I cried. He made no answer, and walked slowly away.

There was no more work done that day. The labourers lay

on the grass, gazing with the native Roman relish of a fine piece of sculpture, but wasting no wine in pagan ceremonies. In the evening the Count paid the Juno another visit, and gave orders that on the morrow she should be transferred to the Casino. The Casino was a deserted garden-house, built in not ungraceful imitation of an Ionic temple, in which Camillo's ancestors must often have assembled to drink cool syrups from Venetian glasses, and listen to learned madrigals. It contained several dusty fragments of antique sculpture, and it was spacious enough to enclose that richer collection of which I began fondly to regard the Juno as but the nucleus. Here, with short delay, this fine creature was placed, serenely upright, a reversed funereal *cippus*[17] forming a sufficiently solid pedestal. The little explorer, who seemed an expert in all the offices of restoration, rubbed her and scraped her with mysterious art, removed her earthy stains, and doubled the lustre of her beauty. Her mellow substance seemed to glow with a kind of renascent purity and bloom, and, but for her broken hand, you might have fancied she had just received the last stroke of the chisel. Her fame remained no secret. Within two or three days half a dozen inquisitive *conoscenti* posted out to obtain sight of her. I happened to be present when the first of these gentlemen (a German in blue spectacles, with a portfolio under his arm) presented himself at the Villa. The Count, hearing his voice at the door, came forward and eyed him coldly from head to foot.

'Your new Juno, Signor Conte,' began the German, 'is, in my opinion, much more likely to be a certain Proserpine[18]—'

'I've neither a Juno nor a Proserpine to discuss with you,' said the Count, curtly. 'You're misinformed.'

'You've dug up no statue?' cried the German. 'What a scandalous hoax!'

'None worthy of your learned attention. I'm sorry you should have the trouble of carrying your little note-book so far.' The Count had suddenly become witty!

'But you've something, surely. The rumour is running through Rome.'

'The rumour be damned!' cried the Count, savagely. 'I've

nothing, – do you understand? Be so good as to say so to your friends.'

The answer was explicit, and the poor archæologist departed, tossing his flaxen mane. But I pitied him, and ventured to remonstrate with the Count. 'She might as well be still in the earth, if no one is to see her,' I said.

'*I*'m to see her: that's enough!' he answered with the same unnatural harshness. Then, in a moment, as he caught me eyeing him askance in troubled surprise, 'I hated his great portfolio. He was going to make some hideous drawing of her.'

'Ah, that touches me,' I said. 'I too have been planning to make a little sketch.'

He was silent for some moments, after which he turned and grasped my arm, with less irritation, but with extraordinary gravity. 'Go in there towards twilight,' he said, 'and sit for an hour and look at her. I think you'll give up your sketch. If you don't, my good old friend, – you're welcome!'

I followed his advice, and, as a friend, I gave up my sketch. But an artist is an artist, and I secretly longed to attempt one. Orders strictly in accordance with the Count's reply to our German friend were given to the servants, who, with an easy Italian conscience and a gracious Italian persuasiveness, assured all subsequent enquirers that they had been regrettably misinformed. I have no doubt, indeed, that, in default of larger opportunity, they made condolence remunerative. Further excavation was, for the present, suspended, as implying an affront to the incomparable Juno. The workmen departed, but the little explorer still haunted the premises and sounded the soil for his own entertainment. One day he came to me with his usual ambiguous grimace. 'The beautiful hand of the Juno,' he murmured; 'what has become of it?'

'I've not seen it since you called me to look at her. I remember when I went away it was lying on the grass near the excavation.'

'Where I placed it myself! After that it disappeared. *Ecco*!'[19]

'Do you suspect one of your workmen? Such a fragment as that would bring more scudi[20] than most of them ever looked at.'

'Some, perhaps, are greater thieves than the others. But if

I were to call up the worst of them and accuse him, the Count would interfere.'

'He must value that beautiful hand, nevertheless.'

The little expert in disinterment looked about him and winked. 'He values it so much that he himself purloined it. That's my belief, and I think that the less we say about it the better.'

'Purloined it, my dear sir? After all, it's his own property.'

'Not so much as that comes to! So beautiful a creature is more or less the property of every one; we've all a right to look at her. But the Count treats her as if she were a sacro-sanct image of the Madonna. He keeps her under lock and key, and pays her solitary visits. What does he do, after all? When a beautiful woman is in stone, all he can do is to look at her. And what does he do with that precious hand? He keeps it in a silver box; he has made a relic of it!' And this cynical personage began to chuckle grotesquely and walked away.

He left me musing uncomfortably, and wondering what the deuce he meant. The Count certainly chose to make a mystery of the Juno, but this seemed a natural incident of the first rapture of possession. I was willing to wait for a free access to her, and in the mean time I was glad to find that there was a limit to his constitutional apathy. But as the days elapsed I began to be conscious that his enjoyment was not communicative, but strangely cold and shy and sombre. That he should admire a marble goddess was no reason for his despising mankind; yet he really seemed to be making invidious comparisons between us. From this untender proscription his charming wife was not excepted. At moments when I tried to persuade myself that he was neither worse nor better company than usual, her face condemned my optimism. She said nothing, but she wore a constant look of pathetic perplexity. She sat at times with her eyes fixed on him with a kind of imploring curiosity, as if pitying surprise held resentment yet awhile in check. What passed between them in private, I had, of course, no warrant to enquire. Nothing, I imagined, – and that was the misery! It was part of the misery, too, that he seemed impenetrable to these mute glances, and looked over her head with an air of superb abstraction. Occasionally he noticed me looking at him in urgent deprecation, and then for a moment his heavy eye would sparkle, half, as it seemed, in defiant irony and half with a strangely stifled impulse to justify himself. But from his wife he kept his face inexorably averted; and when she approached him with some persuasive caress, he received it with an ill-concealed shudder. I inwardly protested and raged. I grew to hate the Count and everything that belonged to him. 'I was a thousand times right,' I cried; 'an Italian count may be mighty fine, but he won't *wear*! Give us some wholesome young fellow of our own blood, who'll play us none of these dusky old-world tricks. Painter as I am, I'll never recommend a picturesque husband!' I lost my pleasure in the Villa, in the purple shadows and glowing lights, the mossy marbles and the long-trailing profile of the Alban Hills.[21] My painting stood still; everything looked ugly. I sat and fumbled with my palette, and seemed to be mixing mud with my colours. My head was stuffed with dismal thoughts; an intolerable weight seemed to lie upon my heart. The Count became, to my imagination, a dark efflorescence of the evil germs which history had implanted in his line. No wonder he was foredoomed to be cruel. Was not cruelty a tradition in his race, and crime an example? The unholy passions of his forefathers stirred blindly in his untaught nature and clamoured dumbly for an issue. What a heavy heritage it seemed to me, as I reckoned it up in my melancholy musings, the Count's interminable ancestry! Back to the profligate revival of arts and vices, – back to the bloody medley of mediæval wars, – back through the long, fitfully glaring dusk of the early ages to its ponderous origin in the solid Roman state, – back through all the darkness of history it seemed to stretch, losing every feeblest claim on my sympathies as it went. Such a record was in itself a curse; and my poor girl had expected it to sit as lightly and gratefully on her consciousness as her feather on her hat! I have little idea how long this painful situation lasted. It seemed the longer from my god-daughter's continued reserve, and my inability to offer her a word of consolation. A sensitive woman, disappointed in marriage, exhausts her own ingenuity before she takes counsel. The Count's preoccupations, whatever they were, made him increasingly restless; he came and went at random, with nervous abruptness; he took long rides alone, and, as I inferred, rarely went through the form of excusing himself to his wife; and still, as time went on, he came no nearer explaining his mystery. With the lapse of time, however, I confess that my apprehensions began to be tempered with pity. If I had expected to see him propitiate his urgent ancestry by a crime, now that his native rectitude seemed resolute to deny them this satisfaction, I felt a sort of grudging gratitude. A man couldn't be so gratuitously sombre without being unhappy. He had always treated me with that antique deference to a grizzled beard for which elderly men reserve the flower of their general tenderness for waning fashions, and I thought it possible he might suffer me to lay a healing hand upon his trouble. One evening, when I had taken leave of my god-daughter and given her my useless blessing in a silent kiss, I came out and found the Count sitting in the garden in the mild starlight, and staring at a mouldy Hermes,[22] nestling in a clump of oleander. I sat down by him and informed him roundly that his conduct needed an explanation. He half turned his head, and his dark pupil gleamed an instant.

'I understand,' he said, 'you think me crazy!' And he tapped his forehead.

'No, not crazy, but unhappy. And if unhappiness runs its course too freely, of course, our poor wits are sorely tried.'

He was silent awhile, and then, 'I'm not unhappy!' he cried abruptly. 'I'm prodigiously happy. You wouldn't believe the satisfaction I take in sitting here and staring at that old weather-worn Hermes. Formerly I used to be afraid of him: his frown used to remind me of a little bushy-browed old priest who taught me Latin and looked at me terribly over the book when I stumbled in my Virgil.[23] But now it seems to me the friendliest, jolliest thing in the world, and suggests the most delightful images. He stood pouting his great lips in some old Roman's garden two thousand years ago. He saw the sandalled feet treading the alleys and the rose-crowned heads bending over the wine; he knew the old feasts and the old worship, the old

Romans and the old gods. As I sit here he speaks to me, in his own dumb way, and describes it all! No, no, my friend, I'm the happiest of men!'

I had denied that I thought he was crazy, but I suddenly began to suspect it, for I found nothing reassuring in this singular rhapsody. The Hermes, for a wonder, had kept his nose; and when I reflected that my dear Countess was being neglected for this senseless pagan block, I secretly promised myself to come the next day with a hammer and deal him such a lusty blow as would make him too ridiculous for a sentimental tête-à-tête. Meanwhile, however, the Count's infatuation was no laughing matter, and I expressed my sincerest conviction when I said, after a pause, that I should recommend him to see either a priest or a physician.

He burst into uproarious laughter. 'A priest! What should I do with a priest, or he with me? I never loved them, and I feel less like beginning than ever. A priest, my dear friend,' he repeated, laying his hand on my arm, 'don't set a priest at me, if you value *his* sanity! My confession would frighten the poor man out of his wits. As for a doctor, I never was better in my life; and unless,' he added abruptly, rising, and eyeing me askance, 'you want to poison me, in Christian charity I advise you to leave me alone.'

Decidedly, the Count *was* unsound, and I had no heart, for some days, to go back to the Villa. How should I treat him, what stand should I take, what course did Martha's happiness and dignity demand? I wandered about Rome, revolving these questions, and one afternoon found myself in the Pantheon.[24] A light spring shower had begun to fall, and I hurried for refuge into the great temple which its Christian altars have but half converted into a church. No Roman monument retains a deeper impress of ancient life, or verifies more forcibly those prodigious beliefs which we are apt to regard as dim fables. The huge dusky dome seems to the spiritual ear to hold a vague reverberation of pagan worship, as a gathered shell holds the rumour of the sea. Three or four persons were scattered before the various altars; another stood near the centre, beneath the aperture in the dome. As I drew near I perceived this was the Count. He was planted with his hands behind him, looking up first at the heavy rain-clouds, as they crossed the great bull's-eye, and then down at the besprinkled circle on the pavement. In those days the pavement was rugged and cracked and magnificently old, and this ample space, in free communion with the weather, had become as mouldy and mossy and verdant as a strip of garden soil. A tender herbage had sprung up in the crevices of the slabs, and the little microscopic shoots were twinkling in the rain. This great weather-current, through the uncapped vault, deadens most effectively the customary odours of incense and tallow, and transports one to a faith that was on friendly terms with nature. It seemed to have performed this office for the Count; his face wore an indefinable expression of ecstasy, and he was so rapt in contemplation that it was some time before he noticed me. The sun was struggling through the clouds without, and yet a thin rain continued to fall and came drifting down into our gloomy enclosure in a sort of illuminated drizzle. The Count watched it with the fascinated stare of a child watching a fountain, and then turned away, pressing his hand to his brow, and walked over to one of the ornamental altars. Here he again stood staring, but in a moment wheeled about and returned to his former place. Just then he recognized me, and perceived, I suppose, the puzzled gaze I must have fixed on him. He saluted me frankly with his hand, and at last came toward me. I fancied that he was in a kind of nervous tremor and was trying to appear calm.

'This is the best place in Rome,' he murmured. 'It's worth fifty St Peters'. But do you know I never came here till the other day? I left it to the *forestieri*.[25] They go about with their red books, and read about this and that, and think they know it. Ah! you must *feel* it, – feel the beauty and fitness of that great open skylight. Now, only the wind and the rain, the sun and the cold, come down; but of old – of old' – and he touched my arm and gave me a strange smile – 'the pagan gods and goddesses used to come sailing through it and take their places at their altars. What a procession, when the eyes of faith could see it! Those are the things they have given us instead!' And he gave a pitiful shrug. 'I should like to pull down their pictures, overturn their candlesticks, and poison their holy-water!'

'My dear Count,' I said gently, 'you should tolerate people's honest beliefs. Would you renew the Inquisition,[26] and in the interest of Jupiter and Mercury?'[27]

'People wouldn't tolerate my belief, if they guessed it!' he cried. 'There's been a great talk about the pagan persecutions; but the Christians persecuted as well, and the old gods were worshipped in caves and woods as well as the new. And none the worse for that! It was in caves and woods and streams, in earth and air and water, they dwelt. And there – and here, too, in spite of all your Christian lustrations – a son of old Italy may find them still!'

He had said more than he meant, and his mask had fallen. I looked at him hard, and felt a sudden outgush of the compassion we always feel for a creature irresponsibly excited. I seemed to touch the source of his trouble, and my relief was great, for my discovery made me feel like bursting into laughter. But I contented myself with smiling benignantly. He looked back at me suspiciously, as if to judge how far he had betrayed himself; and in his glance I read, somehow, that he had a conscience we could take hold of. In my gratitude, I was ready to thank any gods he pleased. 'Take care, take care,' I said, 'you're saying things which if the sacristan there were to hear and report—!' And I passed my hand through his arm and led him away.

I was startled and shocked, but I was also amused and comforted. The Count had suddenly become for me a delightfully curious phenomenon, and I passed the rest of the day in meditating on the strange ineffaceability of race-characteristics. A sturdy young Latin I had called Camillo; sturdier, indeed, than I had dreamed him! Discretion was now misplaced, and on the morrow I spoke to my god-daughter. She had lately been hoping, I think, that I would help her to unburden her heart, for she immediately gave way to tears and confessed that she was miserable. 'At first,' she said, 'I thought it was all fancy, and not his tenderness that was growing less, but my exactions that were growing greater. But suddenly it settled upon me like a mortal chill, – the conviction that he had ceased to care for me, that something had come between us. And the puzzling thing has been the want of possible cause in my own conduct, or of any sign that there is another woman in the case. I have racked my brain to discover what I had said or done or thought to displease him! And yet he goes about like a man too deeply injured to complain. He has never uttered a harsh word or given me a reproachful look. He has simply renounced me. I have dropped out of his life.'

She spoke with such an appealing tremor in her voice that I was on the point of telling her that I had guessed the riddle, and that this was half the battle. But I was afraid of her incredulity. My solution was so fantastic, so apparently far-fetched, so absurd, that I resolved to wait for convincing evidence. To obtain it, I continued to watch the Count, covertly and cautiously, but with a vigilance which disinterested curiosity now made intensely keen. I returned to my painting, and neglected no pretext for hovering about the gardens and the neighbourhood of the Casino. The Count, I think, suspected my designs, or at least my suspicions, and would have been glad to remember just what he had suffered himself to say to me in the Pantheon. But it deepened my interest in his extraordinary situation that, in so far as I could read his deeply brooding face, he seemed to have grudgingly pardoned me. He gave me a glance occasionally, as he passed me, in which a sort of dumb desire for help appeared to struggle with the instinct of mistrust. I was willing enough to help him, but the case was prodigiously delicate, and I wished to master the symptoms. Meanwhile I worked and waited and wondered. Ah! I wondered, you may be sure, with an interminable wonder; and, turn it over as I would, I couldn't get used to my idea. Sometimes it offered itself to me with a perverse fascination which deprived me of all wish to interfere. The Count took the form of a precious psychological study, and refined feeling seemed to dictate a tender respect for his delusion. I envied him the force of his imagination, and I used sometimes to close my eyes with a vague desire that when I opened them I might find Apollo under the opposite tree, lazily kissing his flute, or see Diana[28] hurrying with long steps down the ilex-walk. But for the most part my host seemed to me simply an unhappy young man, with an unwholesome mental twist which should be smoothed away as speedily as possible. If the remedy was to match the disease, however, it would have to be an ingenious compound!

One evening, having bidden my god-daughter good night, I had started on my usual walk to my lodgings in Rome. Five minutes after leaving the villa-gate I discovered that I had left my eye-glass – an object in constant use – behind me. I immediately remembered that, while painting, I had broken the string which fastened it round my neck, and had hooked it provisionally upon a twig of a flowering-almond tree within arm's reach. Shortly afterwards I had gathered up my things and retired, unmindful of the glass; and now, as I needed it to read the evening paper at the Caffè Greco,[29] there was no alternative but to retrace my steps and detach it from its twig. I easily found it, and lingered awhile to note the curious night-aspect of the spot I had been studying by daylight. The night was magnificent, and full-charged with the breath of the early Roman spring. The moon was rising fast and flinging her silver checkers into the heavy masses of shadow. Watching her at play, I strolled farther and suddenly came in sight of the Casino.

Just then the moon, which for a moment had been concealed, touched with a white ray a small marble figure which adorned the pediment of this rather factitious little structure. Its sudden illumination suggested that a rarer spectacle was at hand, and that the same influence must be vastly becoming to the imprisoned Juno. The door of the Casino was, as usual, locked, but the moonlight was flooding the high-placed windows so generously that my curiosity became obstinate – and inventive. I dragged a garden-seat round from the portico, placed it on end, and succeeded in climbing to the top of it and bringing myself abreast of one of the windows. The casement yielded to my pressure, turned on its hinges, and showed me what I had been looking for, – Juno visited by Diana. The beautiful image stood bathed in the radiant flood and shining with a purity which made her most persuasively divine. If by day her mellow complexion suggested faded gold, her substance now might have passed for polished silver. The effect was almost terrible; beauty so eloquent could hardly be inanimate. This was my foremost observation. I leave you to fancy whether my next was less interesting. At some distance from the foot of the statue, just out of the light, I perceived a figure lying flat on the pavement, prostrate apparently with devotion. I can hardly tell you how it completed the impressiveness of the scene. It marked the shining image as a goddess indeed, and seemed to throw a sort of conscious pride into her stony mask. I of course immediately recognized this recumbent worshipper as the Count, and while I stood gazing, as if to help me to read the full meaning of his attitude, the moonlight travelled forward and covered his breast and face. Then I saw that his eyes were closed, and that he was either asleep or swooning. Watching him attentively, I detected his even respirations, and judged there was no reason for alarm. The moonlight blanched his face, which seemed already pale with weariness. He had come into the presence of the Juno in obedience to that fabulous passion of which the symptoms had so woefully perplexed us, and, exhausted either by compliance or resistance, he had sunk down at her feet in a stupid sleep. The bright moonshine soon aroused him, however; he muttered something and raised himself, vaguely staring. Then recognizing his situation, he rose and stood for some time gazing fixedly at the glowing image with an expression which I fancied was not that of wholly unprotesting devotion. He uttered a string of broken words of which I was unable to catch the meaning, and then, after another pause and a long, melancholy moan, he turned slowly to the door. As rapidly and noiselessly as possible I descended from my post of vigilance and passed behind the Casino, and in a moment I heard the sound of the closing lock and of his departing footsteps.

The next day, meeting the little antiquarian in the grounds, I shook my finger at him with what I meant he should consider portentous gravity. But he only grinned like the malicious earth-gnome to which I had always compared him, and twisted his moustache as if my menace was a capital joke. 'If you dig any more holes here,' I said, 'you shall be thrust into the deepest of them, and have the earth packed down on top of you. We have made enough discoveries, and we want no more statues. Your Juno has almost ruined us.'

He burst out laughing. 'I expected as much,' he cried; 'I had my notions!'

'What did you expect?'

'That the Signor Conte would begin and say his prayers to her.'

'Good heavens! Is the case so common? Why did you expect it?'

'On the contrary, the case is rare. But I've fumbled so long in the monstrous heritage of antiquity, that I have learned a multitude of secrets; learned that ancient relics may work modern miracles. There's a pagan element in all of us, – I don't speak for you, *illustrissimi forestieri*,[30] – and the old gods have still their worshippers. The old spirit still throbs here and there, and the Signor Conte has his share of it. He's a good fellow, but, between ourselves, he's an impossible Christian!' And this singular personage resumed his impertinent hilarity.

'If your previsions were so distinct,' I said, 'you ought to have given me a hint of them. I should have sent your spadesmen walking.'

'Ah, but the Juno is so beautiful!'

'Her beauty be blasted! Can you tell me what has become of the Contessa's? To rival the Juno, she's turning to marble herself.'

He shrugged his shoulders. 'Ah, but the Juno is worth fifty thousand scudi!'

'I'd give a hundred thousand,' I said, 'to have her annihilated. Perhaps, after all, I shall want you to dig another hole.'

'At your service!' he answered, with a flourish; and we separated.

A couple of days later I dined, as I often did, with my host and hostess, and met the Count face to face for the first time since his prostration in the Casino. He bore the traces of it, and sat plunged in sombre distraction. I fancied that the path of the antique faith was not strewn with flowers, and that the Juno was becoming daily a harder mistress to serve. Dinner was

scarcely over before he rose from table and took up his hat. As he
did so, passing near his wife, he faltered a moment, stopped and
gave her – for the first time, I imagine – that vaguely imploring
look which I had often caught. She moved her lips in inarticulate
sympathy and put out her hands. He drew her towards him,
kissed her with a kind of angry ardour, and strode away. The
occasion was propitious, and further delay unnecessary.

'What I have to tell you is very strange,' I said to the Countess, 'very fantastic, very incredible. But perhaps you'll not find
it so bad as you feared. There *is* a woman in the case! Your
enemy is the Juno. The Count – how shall I say it? – the Count
takes her *au sérieux*.'[31] She was silent; but after a moment she
touched my arm with her hand, and I knew she meant that I
had spoken her own belief. 'You admired his antique simplicity: you see how far it goes. He has reverted to the faith of his
fathers. Dormant through the ages, that imperious statue has
silently aroused it. He believes in the pedigrees you used to
dog's-ear your School Mythology with trying to get by heart.
In a word, dear child, Camillo is a pagan!'

'I suppose you'll be terribly shocked,' she answered, 'if I say
that he's welcome to any faith, if he will only share it with me.
I'll believe in Jupiter, if he'll bid me! My sorrow's not for that:
let my husband be himself! My sorrow is for the gulf of silence
and indifference that has burst open between us. His Juno's
the reality; I'm the fiction!'

'I've lately become reconciled to this gulf of silence, and to
your fading for a while into a fiction. After the fable, the moral!
The poor fellow has but half succumbed: the other half pro-
tests. The modern man is shut out in the darkness with his
incomparable wife. How can he have failed to feel – vaguely
and grossly if it must have been, but in every throb of his
heart – that you are a more perfect experiment of nature, a
riper fruit of time, than those primitive persons for whom Juno
was a terror and Venus an example? He pays you the compliment of believing you an inconvertible modern. He has crossed
the Acheron,[32] but he has left you behind, as a pledge to the
present. We'll bring him back to redeem it. The old ancestral
ghosts ought to be propitiated when a pretty creature like you

has sacrificed the fragrance of her life. He has proved himself one of the Valerii; we shall see to it that he is the last, and yet that his decease shall leave the Conte Camillo in excellent health.'

I spoke with confidence which I had partly felt, for it seemed to me that if the Count was to be touched, it must be by the sense that his strange spiritual excursion had not made his wife detest him. We talked long and to a hopeful end, for before I went away my god-daughter expressed the desire to go out and look at the Juno. 'I was afraid of her almost from the first,' she said, 'and have hardly seen her since she was set up in the Casino. Perhaps I can learn a lesson from her, – perhaps I can guess how she charms him!'

For a moment I hesitated, with the fear that we might intrude upon the Count's devotions. Then, as something in the poor girl's face suggested that she had thought of this and felt a sudden impulse to pluck victory from the heart of danger, I bravely offered her my arm. The night was cloudy, and on this occasion, apparently, the triumphant goddess was to depend upon her own lustre. But as we approached the Casino I saw that the door was ajar, and that there was lamplight within. The lamp was suspended in front of the image, and it showed us that the place was empty. But the Count had lately been there. Before the statue stood a roughly extemporized altar, composed of a nameless fragment of antique marble, engraved with an illegible Greek inscription. We seemed really to stand in a pagan temple, and we gazed at the serene divinity with an impulse of spiritual reverence. It ought to have been deepened, I suppose, but it was rudely checked, by our observing a curious glitter on the face of the low altar. A second glance showed us it was blood!

My companion looked at me in pale horror, and turned away with a cry. A swarm of hideous conjectures pressed into my mind, and for a moment I was sickened. But at last I remembered that there is blood and blood, and the Latins were posterior to the cannibals.[33]

'Be sure it's very innocent,' I said; 'a lamb, a kid, or a sucking calf!' But it was enough for her nerves and her conscience that it was a crimson trickle, and she returned to the house in sad agitation. The rest of the night was not passed in a way to restore her to calmness. The Count had not come in, and she sat up for him from hour to hour. I remained with her and smoked my cigar as composedly as I might; but internally I wondered what in horror's name had become of him. Gradually, as the hours wore away, I shaped a vague interpretation of these dusky portents, – an interpretation none the less valid and devoutly desired for its being tolerably cheerful. The blood-drops on the altar, I mused, were the last instalment of his debt and the end of his delusion. They had been a happy necessity, for he was, after all, too gentle a creature not to hate himself for having shed them, not to abhor so cruelly insistent an idol. He had wandered away to recover himself in solitude, and he would come back to us with a repentant heart and an enquiring mind! I should certainly have believed all this more easily, however, if I could have heard his footstep in the hall. Toward dawn, scepticism threatened to creep in with the grey light, and I restlessly betook myself to the portico. Here in a few moments I saw him cross the grass, heavy-footed, splashed with mud, and evidently excessively tired. He must have been walking all night, and his face denoted that his spirit had been as restless as his body. He paused near me, and before he entered the house he stopped, looked at me a moment, and then held out his hand. I grasped it warmly, and it seemed to me to throb with all that he could not utter.

'Will you see your wife?' I asked.

He passed his hand over his eyes and shook his head. 'Not now – not yet – some time!' he answered.

I was disappointed, but I convinced her, I think, that he had cast out the devil. She felt, poor girl, a pardonable desire to celebrate the event. I returned to my lodging, spent the day in Rome, and came back to the Villa toward dusk. I was told that the Countess was in the grounds. I looked for her cautiously at first, for I thought it just possible I might interrupt the natural consequences of a reconciliation; but failing to meet her, I turned toward the Casino, and found myself face to face with the little explorer.

'Does your excellency happen to have twenty yards of stout rope about him?' he asked gravely.

'Do you want to hang yourself for the trouble you've stood sponsor to?' I answered.

'It's a hanging matter, I promise you. The Countess has given orders. You'll find her in the Casino. Sweet-voiced as she is, she knows how to make her orders understood.'

At the door of the Casino stood half a dozen of the labourers on the place, looking vaguely solemn, like outstanding dependants at a superior funeral. The Countess was within, in a position which was an answer to the surveyor's riddle. She stood with her eyes fixed on the Juno, who had been removed from her pedestal and lay stretched in her magnificent length upon a rude litter.

'Do you understand?' she said. 'She's beautiful, she's noble, she's precious, but she must go back!' And, with a passionate gesture, she seemed to indicate an open grave.

I was hugely delighted, but I thought it discreet to stroke my chin and look sober. 'She's worth fifty thousand scudi.'

She shook her head sadly. 'If we were to sell her to the Pope and give the money to the poor, it wouldn't profit us. She must go back, – she must go back! We must smother her beauty in the dreadful earth. It makes me feel almost as if she were alive; but it came to me last night with overwhelming force, when my husband came in and refused to see me, that he'll not be himself as long as she is above ground. To cut the knot we must bury her! If I had only thought of it before!'

'Not before!' I said, shaking my head in turn. 'Heaven reward our sacrifice now!'

The little surveyor, when he reappeared, seemed hardly like an agent of the celestial influences, but he was deft and active, which was more to the point. Every now and then he uttered some half-articulate lament, by way of protest against the Countess's cruelty; but I saw him privately scanning the recumbent image with an eye which seemed to foresee a malicious glee in standing on a certain unmarked spot on the turf and grinning till people stared. He had brought back an abundance of rope, and having summoned his assistants, who vigorously lifted the litter, he led the way to the original excavation, which had been left unclosed with the project of further researches. By the time we reached the edge of the grave the evening had fallen and the beauty of our marble victim was shrouded in a dusky veil. No one spoke, – if not exactly for shame, at least for regret. Whatever our plea, our performance looked, at least, monstrously profane. The ropes were adjusted and the Juno was slowly lowered into her earthy bed. The Countess took a handful of earth and dropped it solemnly on her breast. 'May it lie lightly, but for ever!' she said.

'Amen!' cried the little surveyor with a strange mocking inflection; and he gave us a bow, as he departed, which betrayed an agreeable consciousness of knowing where fifty thousand scudi were buried. His underlings had another cask of wine, the result of which, for them, was a suspension of all consciousness, and a subsequent irreparable confusion of memory as to where they had plied their spades.

The Countess had not yet seen her husband, who had again apparently betaken himself to communion with the great god Pan.[34] I was of course unwilling to leave her to encounter alone the results of her momentous deed. She wandered into the drawing-room and pretended to occupy herself with a bit of embroidery, but in reality she was bravely composing herself for an 'explanation'. I took up a book, but it held my attention as feebly. As the evening wore away I heard a movement on the threshold and saw the Count lifting the tapestried curtain which masked the door, and looking silently at his wife. His eyes were brilliant, but not angry. He had missed the Juno – and drawn a long breath! The Countess kept her eyes fixed on her work, and drew her silken stitches like an image of wifely contentment. The image seemed to fascinate him: he came in slowly, almost on tiptoe, walked to the chimney-piece, and stood there in a sort of rapt contemplation. What had passed, what was passing, in his mind, I leave to your own apprehension. My god-daughter's hand trembled as it rose and fell, and the colour came into her cheek. At last she raised her eyes and sustained the gaze in which all his returning faith seemed concentrated. He hesitated a moment, as if her very forgiveness kept the gulf open between them, and then he strode forward, fell on his two knees and buried his head in her lap. I departed as the Count had come in, on tiptoe.

He never became, if you will, a thoroughly modern man; but one day, years after, when a visitor to whom he was showing his cabinet became inquisitive as to a marble hand, suspended in one of its inner recesses, he looked grave and turned the lock on it. 'It is the hand of a beautiful creature,' he said, 'whom I once greatly admired.'

'Ah, – a Roman?' said the gentleman, with a smirk.

'A Greek,' said the Count, with a frown.

SIR EDMUND ORME

The statement appears to have been written, though the fragment is undated, long after the death of his wife, whom I take to have been one of the persons referred to. There is however nothing in the strange story to establish this point, now perhaps not of importance. When I took possession of his effects I found these pages, in a locked drawer, among papers relating to the unfortunate lady's too brief career – she died in childbirth a year after her marriage: letters, memoranda, accounts, faded photographs, cards of invitation. That's the only connexion I can point to, and you may easily, and will probably, think it too extravagant to have had a palpable basis. I can't, I allow, vouch for his having intended it as a report of real occurrence – I can only vouch for his general veracity. In any case it was written for himself, not for others. I offer it to others – having full option – precisely because of its oddity. Let them, in respect to the form of the thing, bear in mind that it was written quite for himself. I've altered nothing but the names.

If there's a story in the matter I recognize the exact moment at which it began. This was on a soft still Sunday noon in November, just after church, on the sunny Parade. Brighton[1] was full of people; it was the height of the season and the day was even more respectable than lovely – which helped to account for the multitude of walkers. The blue sea itself was decorous; it seemed to doze with a gentle snore – if that *be* decorum – while nature preached a sermon. After writing letters all the morning I had come out to take a look at it before luncheon. I leaned

over the rail dividing the King's Road from the beach, and I
think I had smoked a cigarette, when I became conscious of an
intended joke in the shape of a light walking-stick laid across
my shoulders. The idea, I found, had been thrown off by Teddy
Bostwick of the Rifles[2] and was intended as a contribution to
talk. Our talk came off as we strolled together – he always took
your arm to show you he forgave your obtuseness about his
humour – and looked at the people, and bowed to some of
them, and wondered who others were, and differed in opinion
as to the prettiness of girls. About Charlotte Marden we agreed,
however, as we saw her come toward us with her mother; and
there surely could have been no one who wouldn't have concurred. The Brighton air used of old to make plain girls pretty
and pretty girls prettier still – I don't know whether it works the
spell now. The place was at any rate rare for complexions, and
Miss Marden's was one that made people turn round. It made
us stop, heaven knows – at least it was one of the things, for we
already knew the ladies.

We turned with them, we joined them, we went where they
were going. They were only going to the end and back – they
had just come out of church. It was another manifestation of
Teddy's humour that he got immediate possession of Charlotte, leaving me to walk with her mother. However, I wasn't
unhappy; the girl was before me and I had her to talk about.
We prolonged our walk; Mrs Marden kept me and presently
said she was tired and must rest. We found a place on a
sheltered bench – we gossiped as the people passed. It had
already struck me, in this pair, that the resemblance between
mother and daughter was wonderful even among such resem-
blances, all the more that it took so little account of a difference
of nature. One often hears mature mothers spoken of as
warnings – sign-posts, more or less discouraging, of the way
daughters may go. But there was nothing deterrent in the idea
that Charlotte should at fifty-five be as beautiful, even though
it were conditioned on her being as pale and preoccupied, as
Mrs Marden. At twenty-two she had a rosy blankness and was
admirably handsome. Her head had the charming shape of her
mother's and her features the same fine order. Then there were

looks and movements and tones – moments when you could scarce say if it were aspect or sound – which, between the two appearances, referred and reminded.

These ladies had a small fortune and a cheerful little house at Brighton, full of portraits and tokens and trophies – stuffed animals on the top of bookcases and sallow varnished fish under glass – to which Mrs Marden professed herself attached by pious memories. Her husband had been 'ordered' there in ill health, to spend the last years of his life, and she had already mentioned to me that it was a place in which she felt herself still under the protection of his goodness. His goodness appeared to have been great, and she sometimes seemed to defend it from vague innuendo. Some sense of protection, of an influence invoked and cherished, was evidently necessary to her; she had a dim wistfulness, a longing for security. She wanted friends and had a good many. She was kind to me on our first meeting, and I never suspected her of the vulgar purpose of 'making up' to me – a suspicion of course unduly frequent in conceited young men. It never struck me that she wanted me for her daughter, nor yet, like some unnatural mammas, for herself. It was as if they had had a common deep shy need and had been ready to say: 'Oh be friendly to us and be trustful! Don't be afraid – you won't be expected to marry us.' 'Of course there's something about mamma: that's really what makes her such a dear!' Charlotte said to me, confidentially, at an early stage of our acquaintance. She worshipped her mother's appearance. It was the only thing she was vain of; she accepted the raised eyebrows as a charming ultimate fact. 'She looks as if she were waiting for the doctor, dear mamma,' she said on another occasion. 'Perhaps *you're* the doctor; do you think you are?' It appeared in the event that I had some healing power. At any rate when I learned, for she once dropped the remark, that Mrs Marden also held there was something 'awfully strange' about Charlotte, the relation of the two ladies couldn't but be interesting. It was happy enough, at bottom; each had the other so on her mind.

On the Parade the stream of strollers held its course, and Charlotte presently went by with Teddy Bostwick. She smiled and nodded and continued, but when she came back she stopped and spoke to us. Captain Bostwick positively declined to go in – he pronounced the occasion too jolly: might they therefore take another turn? Her mother dropped a 'Do as you like', and the girl gave me an impertinent smile over her shoulder as they quitted us. Teddy looked at me with his glass in one eye, but I didn't mind that: it was only of Miss Marden I was thinking as I laughed to my companion. 'She's a bit of a coquette, you know.'

'Don't say that – don't say that!' Mrs Marden murmured.

'The nicest girls always are – just a little,' I was magnanimous enough to plead.

'Then why are they always punished?'

The intensity of the question startled me – it had come out in a vivid flash. Therefore I had to think a moment before I put to her: 'What do you know of their punishment?'

'Well – I was a bad girl myself.'

'And were you punished?'

'I carry it through life,' she said as she looked away from me. 'Ah!' she suddenly panted in the next breath, rising to her feet and staring at her daughter, who had reappeared again with Captain Bostwick. She stood a few seconds, the queerest expression in her face; then she sank on the seat again and I saw she had blushed crimson. Charlotte, who had noticed it all, came straight up to her and, taking her hand with quick tenderness, seated herself at her other side. The girl had turned pale – she gave her mother a fixed scared look. Mrs Marden, who had had some shock that escaped our detection, recovered herself; that is she sat quiet and inexpressive, gazing at the indifferent crowd, the sunny air, the slumbering sea. My eye happened to fall nevertheless on the interlocked hands of the two ladies, and I quickly guessed the grasp of the elder to be violent. Bostwick stood before them, wondering what was the matter and asking me from his little vacant disk if *I* knew; which led Charlotte to say to him after a moment and with a certain irritation: 'Don't stand there that way, Captain Bostwick. Go away – *please* go away.'

I got up at this, hoping Mrs Marden wasn't ill; but she at

once begged we wouldn't leave them, that we would particularly stay and that we would presently come home to luncheon. She drew me down beside her and for a moment I felt her hand press my arm in a way that might have been an involuntary betrayal of distress and might have been a private signal. What she should have wished to point out to me I couldn't divine: perhaps she had seen in the crowd somebody or something abnormal. She explained to us in a few minutes that she was all right, that she was only liable to palpitations: they came as quickly as they went. It was time to move – a truth on which we acted. The incident was felt to be closed. Bostwick and I lunched with our sociable friends, and when I walked away with him he professed he had never seen creatures more completely to his taste.

Mrs Marden had made us promise to come back the next day to tea, and had exhorted us in general to come as often as we could. Yet the next day when, at five o'clock, I knocked at the door of the pretty house it was but to learn that the ladies had gone up to town. They had left a message for us with the butler: he was to say they had suddenly been called and much regretted it. They would be absent a few days. This was all I could extract from the dumb domestic. I went again three days later, but they were still away; and it was not till the end of a week that I got a note from Mrs Marden. 'We're back,' she wrote: 'do come and forgive us.' It was on this occasion, I remember – the occasion of my going just after getting the note – that she told me she had distinct intuitions. I don't know how many people there were in England at that time in that predicament, but there were very few who would have mentioned it; so that the announcement struck me as original, especially as her point was that some of these uncanny promptings were connected with myself. There were other people present – idle Brighton folk, old women with frightened eyes and irrelevant interjections – and I had too few minutes' talk with Charlotte; but the day after this I met them both at dinner and had the satisfaction of sitting next to Miss Marden. I recall this passage as the hour of its first fully coming over me that she was a beautiful liberal creature. I had seen her personality in glimpses and gleams, like a song sung in snatches, but now it was before me in a large rosy glow, as if it had been a full volume of sound. I heard the whole of the air, and it was sweet fresh music, which I was often to hum over.

After dinner I had a few words with Mrs Marden; it was at the time, late in the evening, when tea was handed about. A servant passed near us with a tray, I asked her if she would have a cup and, on her assenting, took one and offered it to her. She put out her hand for it and I gave it her, safely as I supposed; but as her fingers were about to secure it she started and faltered, so that both my frail vessel and its fine recipient dropped with a crash of porcelain and without, on the part of my companion, the usual woman's motion to save her dress. I stooped to pick up the fragments and when I raised myself Mrs Marden was looking across the room at her daughter, who returned it with lips of cheer but anxious eyes. 'Dear mamma, what on earth *is* the matter with you?' the silent question seemed to say. Mrs Marden coloured just as she had done after her strange movement on the Parade the other week, and I was therefore surprised when she said to me with unexpected assurance: 'You should really have a steadier hand!' I had begun to stammer a defence of my hand when I noticed her eyes fixed on me with an intense appeal. It was ambiguous at first and only added to my confusion; then suddenly I understood as plainly as if she had murmured 'Make believe it was you – make believe it was you.' The servant came back to take the morsels of the cup and wipe up the spilt tea, and while I was in the midst of making believe Mrs Marden abruptly brushed away from me and from her daughter's attention and went into another room. She gave no heed to the state of her dress.

I saw nothing more of either that evening, but the next morning, in the King's Road, I met the younger lady with a roll of music in her muff. She told me she had been a little way alone, to practise duets with a friend, and I asked her if she would go a little way further in company. She gave me leave to attend her to her door, and as we stood before it I enquired if I might go in. 'No, not to-day – I don't want you,' she said very straight, though not unamiably; while the words caused me to direct a wistful disconcerted gaze at one of the windows of the house. It fell on the white face of Mrs Marden, turned out at us from the drawing-room. She stood long enough to show it *was* she and not the apparition I had come near taking it for, and then she vanished before her daughter had observed her. The girl, during our walk, had said nothing about her. As I had been told they didn't want me I left them alone a little, after which certain hazards kept us still longer apart. I finally went up to London, and while there received a pressing invitation to come immediately down to Tranton, a pretty old place in Sussex belonging to a couple whose acquaintance I had lately made.

I went to Tranton from town, and on arriving found the Mardens, with a dozen other people, in the house. The first thing Mrs Marden said was 'Will you forgive me?' and when I asked what I had to forgive she answered 'My throwing my tea over you.' I replied that it had gone over herself; whereupon she said 'At any rate I was very rude – but some time I think you'll understand, and then you'll make allowances for me.' The first day I was there she dropped two or three of these references – she had already indulged in more than one – to the mystic initiation in store for me; so that I began, as the phrase is, to chaff her about it, to say I'd rather it were less wonderful and take it out at once. She answered that when it should come to me I'd have indeed to take it out – there would be little enough option. That it *would* come was privately clear to her, a deep presentiment, which was the only reason she had ever mentioned the matter. Didn't I remember she had spoken to me of intuitions? From the first of her seeing me she had been sure there were things I shouldn't escape knowing. Meanwhile there was nothing to do but wait and keep cool, not to be precipitate. She particularly wished not to become extravagantly nervous. And I was above all not to be nervous myself – one got used to everything. I returned that though I couldn't make out what she was talking of I was terribly frightened; the absence of a clue gave such a range to one's imagination. I exaggerated on purpose; for if Mrs Marden was mystifying

I can scarcely say she was alarming. I couldn't imagine what she meant, but I wondered more than I shuddered. I might have said to myself that she was a little wrong in the upper storey;[3] but that never occurred to me. She struck me as hopelessly right.

There were other girls in the house, but Charlotte the most charming; which was so generally allowed that she almost interfered with the slaughter of ground game. There were two or three men, and I was of the number, who actually preferred her to the society of the beaters.[4] In short she was recognized as a form of sport superior and exquisite. She was kind to all of us – she made us go out late and come in early. I don't know whether she flirted, but several other members of the party thought *they* did. Indeed as regards himself Teddy Bostwick, who had come over from Brighton, was visibly sure.

The third of these days was a Sunday, which determined a pretty walk to morning service over the fields. It was grey windless weather, and the bell of the little old church that nestled in the hollow of the Sussex down sounded near and domestic. We were a straggling procession in the mild damp air – which, as always at that season, gave one the feeling that after the trees were bare there was more of it, a larger sky – and I managed to fall a good way behind with Miss Marden. I remember entertaining, as we moved together over the turf, a strong impulse to say something intensely personal, something violent and important, important for *me* – such as that I had never seen her so lovely or that that particular moment was the sweetest of my life. But always, in youth, such words have been on the lips many times before they're spoken to any effect; and I had the sense, not that I didn't know her well enough – I cared little for that – but that she didn't sufficiently know *me*. In the church, a museum of old Tranton tombs and brasses, the big Tranton pew was full. Several of us were scattered, and I found a seat for Miss Marden, and another for myself beside it, at a distance from her mother and from most of our friends. There were two or three decent rustics[5] on the bench, who moved in further to make room for us, and I took my place first, to cut off my companion from our neighbours. After she was seated there was still a space left, which remained empty till service was about half over.

This at least was the moment of my noting that another person had entered and had taken the seat. When I remarked him he had apparently been for some minutes in the pew – had settled himself and put down his hat beside him and, with his hands crossed on the knob of his cane, was gazing before him at the altar. He was a pale young man in black and with the air of a gentleman. His presence slightly startled me, for Miss Marden hadn't attracted my attention to it by moving to make room for him. After a few minutes, observing that he had no prayer-book, I reached across my neighbour and placed mine before him, on the ledge of the pew; a manœuvre the motive of which was not unconnected with the possibility that, in my own destitution, Miss Marden would give me one side of *her* velvet volume to hold. The pretext however was destined to fail, for at the moment I offered him the book the intruder – whose intrusion I had so condoned – rose from his place without thanking me, stepped noiselessly out of the pew, which had no door, and, so discreetly as to attract no attention, passed down the centre of the church. A few minutes had sufficed for his devotions. His behaviour was unbecoming, his early departure even more than his late arrival; but he managed so quietly that we were not incommoded, and I found, on turning a little to look after him, that nobody was disturbed by his withdrawal. I only noticed, and with surprise, that Mrs Marden had been so affected by it as to rise, all involuntarily, in her place. She started at him as he passed, but he passed very quickly, and she as quickly dropped down again, though not too soon to catch my eye across the church. Five minutes later I asked her daughter, in a low voice, if she would kindly pass me back my prayer-book – I had waited to see if she would spontaneously perform the act. The girl restored this aid to devotion, but had been so far from troubling herself about it that she could say to me as she did so: 'Why on earth did you put it there?' I was on the point of answering her when she dropped on her knees, and at this I held my tongue. I had only been going to say: 'To be decently civil.'

After the benediction, as we were leaving our places, I was slightly surprised again to see that Mrs Marden, instead of going out with her companions, had come up the aisle to join us, having apparently something to say to her daughter. She said it, but in an instant I saw it had been a pretext – her real business was with me. She pushed Charlotte forward and suddenly breathed to me: 'Did you see him?'

'The gentleman who sat down here? How could I help seeing him?'

'Hush!' she said with the intensest excitement; 'don't *speak* to her – don't tell her!' She slipped her hand into my arm, to keep me near her, to keep me, it seemed, away from her daughter. The precaution was unnecessary, for Teddy Bostwick had already taken possession of Miss Marden, and as they passed out of church in front of me I saw one of the other men close up on her other hand. It appeared to be felt that I had had my turn. Mrs Marden released me as soon as we got out, but not before I saw she had needed my support. 'Don't speak to any one – don't tell any one!' she went on.

'I don't understand. Tell any one what?'

'Why that you saw him.'

'Surely they saw him for themselves.'

'Not one of them, not one of them.' She spoke with such passionate decision that I glanced at her – she was staring straight before her. But she felt the challenge of my eyes and stopped short, in the old brown timber porch of the church, with the others well in advance of us; where, looking at me now and in quite an extraordinary manner, 'You're the only person,' she said; 'the only person in the world.'

'But *you*, dear madam?'

'Oh me – of course. That's my curse!' And with this she moved rapidly off to join the rest of our group. I hovered at its outskirts on the way home – I had such food for rumination. Whom had I seen and why was the apparition – it rose before my mind's eye all clear again – invisible to the others? If an exception had been made for Mrs Marden why did it constitute a curse, and why was I to share so questionable a boon? This appeal, carried on in my own locked breast, kept me doubtless quiet enough at luncheon. After that repast I went out on the old terrace to smoke a cigarette, but had only taken a turn or two when I caught Mrs Marden's moulded mask at the window of one of the rooms open to the crooked flags.[6] It reminded me of the same flitting presence behind the pane at Brighton the day I met Charlotte and walked home with her. But this time my ambiguous friend didn't vanish; she tapped on the pane and motioned me to come in. She was in a queer little apartment, one of the many reception-rooms of which the ground-floor at Tranton consisted; it was known as the Indian room and had a style denominated Eastern – bamboo lounges, lacquered screens, lanterns with long fringes and strange idols in cabinets, objects not held to conduce to sociability. The place was little used, and when I went round to her we had it to ourselves. As soon as I appeared she said to me: 'Please tell me this – are you in love with my daughter?'

I really had a little to take my time. 'Before I answer your question will you kindly tell me what gives you the idea? I don't consider I've been very forward.'

Mrs Marden, contradicting me with her beautiful anxious eyes, gave me no satisfaction on the point I mentioned; she only went on strenuously: 'Did you say nothing to her on the way to church?'

'What makes you think I said anything?'

'Why the fact that you saw him.'

'Saw whom, dear Mrs Marden?'

'Oh you know,' she answered gravely, even a little reproachfully, as if I were trying to humiliate her by making her name the unnameable.

'Do you mean the gentleman who formed the subject of your strange statement in church – the one who came into the pew?'

'You saw him, you saw him!' she panted with a strange mixture of dismay and relief.

'Of course I saw him, and so did you.'

'It didn't follow. Did you feel it to be inevitable?'

I was puzzled again. 'Inevitable?'

'That you *should* see him?'

'Certainly, since I'm not blind.'

'You might have been. Every one else is.' I was wonderfully at sea and I frankly confessed it to my questioner, but the case wasn't improved by her presently exclaiming: 'I knew you would, from the moment you should be really in love with her! I knew it would be the test – what do I mean? – the proof.'

'Are there such strange bewilderments attached to that high state?' I smiled to ask.

'You can judge for yourself. You see him, you see him!' – she quite exulted in it. 'You'll see him again.'

'I've no objection, but I shall take more interest in him if you'll kindly tell me who he is.'

She avoided my eyes – then consciously met them. 'I'll tell you if you'll tell me first what you said to her on the way to church.'

'Has she told you I said anything?'

'Do I need that?' she asked with expression.

'Oh yes, I remember – your intuitions! But I'm sorry to see they're at fault this time; because I really said nothing to your daughter that was the least out of the way.'

'Are you very very sure?'

'On my honour, Mrs Marden.'

'Then you consider you're not in love with her?'

'That's another affair!' I laughed.

'You are – you *are*! You wouldn't have seen him if you hadn't been.'

'Then who the deuce *is* he, madam?' – I pressed it with some irritation.

Yet she would still only question me back. 'Didn't you at least *want* to say something to her – didn't you come very near it?'

Well, this was more to the point; it justified the famous intuitions. 'Ah "near" it as much as you like – call it the turn of a hair. I don't know what kept me quiet.'

'That was quite enough,' said Mrs Marden. 'It isn't what you say that makes the difference; it's what you feel. *That's* what he goes by.'

I was annoyed at last by her reiterated reference to an identity yet to be established, and I clasped my hands with an air of supplication which covered much real impatience, a sharper curiosity and even the first short throbs of a certain sacred dread. 'I entreat you to tell me whom you're talking about.'

She threw up her arms, looking away from me, as if to shake off both reserve and responsibility. 'Sir Edmund Orme.'

'And who may Sir Edmund Orme be?'

At the moment I spoke she gave a start. 'Hush – here they come.' Then as, following the direction of her eyes, I saw Charlotte, out on the terrace, by our own window, she added, with an intensity of warning: 'Don't notice him – *never*!'

The girl, who now had had her hands beside her eyes, peering into the room and smiling, signed to us, through the glass to admit her; on which I went and opened the long window. Her mother turned away and she came in with a laughing challenge: 'What plot in the world are you two hatching here?' Some plan – I forget what – was in prospect for the afternoon, as to which Mrs Marden's participation or consent was solicited, my own adhesion being taken for granted; and she had been half over the place in her quest. I was flurried, seeing the elder woman was – when she turned round to meet her daughter she disguised it to extravagance, throwing herself on the girl's neck and embracing her – so that, to pass it off, I overdid my gallantry.

'I've been asking your mother for your hand.'

'Oh indeed, and has she given it?' Miss Marden gaily returned.

'She was just going to when you appeared there.'

'Well, it's only for a moment – I'll leave you free.'

'Do you like him, Charlotte?' Mrs Marden asked with a candour I scarcely expected.

'It's difficult to say *before* him, isn't it?' the charming creature went on, entering into the humour of the thing, but looking at me as if she scarce liked me at all.

She would have had to say it before another person as well, for at that moment there stepped into the room from the terrace – the window had been left open – a gentleman who had come into sight, at least into mine, only within the instant. Mrs Marden had said 'Here *they* come', but he appeared to have followed her daughter at a certain distance. I recognized him at once as the personage who had sat beside us in church. This time I saw him better, saw his face and his carriage were strange. I speak of him as a personage, because one felt, indescribably, as if a reigning prince had come into the room. He held himself with something of the grand air and as if he were different from his company. Yet he looked fixedly and gravely at me, till I wondered what he expected. Did he consider that I should bend my knee or kiss his hand? He turned his eyes in the same way on Mrs Marden, but she knew what to do. After the first agitation produced by his approach she took no notice of him whatever; it made me remember her passionate adjuration to me. I had to achieve a great effort to imitate her, for though I knew nothing about him but that he was Sir Edmund Orme his presence acted as a strong appeal, almost as an oppression. He stood there without speaking – young pale handsome clean-shaven decorous, with extraordinary light blue eyes and something old-fashioned, like a portrait of years ago, in his head and in his manner of wearing his hair. He was in complete mourning – one immediately took him for very well dressed – and he carried his hat in his hand. He looked again strangely hard at me, harder than any one in the world had ever looked before; and I remember feeling rather cold and wishing he would say something. No silence had ever seemed to me so soundless. All this was of course an impression intensely rapid; but that it had consumed some instants was proved to me suddenly by the expression of countenance of Charlotte Marden, who stared from one of us to the other – he never looked at her, and she had no appearance of looking at him – and then broke out with: 'What on earth is the matter with you? You've such odd faces!' I felt the colour come back to mine, and when she went on in the same tone, 'One would think you had seen a ghost!' I was conscious I had turned very red. Sir Edmund Orme never blushed, and I was sure no embarrassment touched him. One had met people of that sort, but never any one with so high an indifference.

'Don't be impertinent, and go and tell them all that I'll join them,' said Mrs Marden with much dignity but with a tremor of voice that I caught.

'And will you come – *you*?' the girl asked, turning away. I made no answer, taking the question somehow as meant for her companion. But he was more silent than I, and when she reached the door – she was going out that way – she stopped, her hand on the knob, and looked at me, repeating it. I assented, springing forward to open the door for her, and as she passed out she exclaimed to me mockingly: 'You haven't got your wits about you – you shan't have my hand!'

I closed the door and turned round to find that Sir Edmund Orme had during the moment my back was presented to him retired by the window. Mrs Marden stood there and we looked at each other long. It had only then – as the girl flitted away – come home to me that her daughter was unconscious of what had happened. It was *that*, oddly enough, that gave me a sudden sharp shake – not my own perception of our visitor, which felt quite natural. It made the fact vivid to me that she had been equally unaware of him in church, and the two facts together – now that they were over – set my heart more sensibly beating. I wiped my forehead, and Mrs Marden broke out with a low distressful wail: 'Now you know my life – now you know my life!'

'In God's name who is he – *what* is he?'

'He's a man I wronged.'

'How did you wrong him?'

'Oh awfully – years ago.'

'Years ago? Why, he's very young.'

'Young – young?' cried Mrs Marden. 'He was born before *I* was!'

'Then why does he look so?'

She came nearer to me, she laid her hand on my arm, and there was something in her face that made me shrink a little. 'Don't you understand – don't you *feel*?' she intensely put to me.

'I feel very queer!' I laughed; and I was conscious that my note betrayed it.

'He's dead!' said Mrs Marden from her white face.

'Dead?' I panted. 'Then that gentleman was—?' I couldn't even say a word.

'Call him what you like – there are twenty vulgar names. He's a perfect presence.'

'He's a splendid presence!' I cried. 'The place is haunted, *haunted*!' I exulted in the word as if it stood for all I had ever dreamt of.

'It isn't the place – more's the pity!' she instantly returned. 'That has nothing to do with it!'

'Then it's you, dear lady?' I said as if this were still better.

'No, nor me either – I wish it were!'

'Perhaps it's me,' I suggested with a sickly smile.

'It's nobody but my child – my innocent, innocent child!' And with this Mrs Marden broke down – she dropped into a chair and burst into tears. I stammered some question – I pressed on her some bewildered appeal, but she waved me off, unexpectedly and passionately. I persisted – couldn't I help her, couldn't I intervene? 'You *have* intervened,' she sobbed; 'you're *in* it, you're *in* it.'

'I'm very glad to be in anything so extraordinary,' I boldly declared.

'Glad or not, you can't get out of it.'

'I don't want to get out of it – it's too interesting.'

'I'm glad you like it!' She had turned from me, making haste to dry her eyes. 'And now go away.'

'But I want to know more about it.'

'You'll see all you want. Go away!'

'But I want to understand what I see.'

'How can you – when I don't understand myself?' she helplessly cried.

'We'll do so together – we'll make it out.'

At this she got up, doing what more she could to obliterate her tears. 'Yes, it will be better together – that's why I've liked you.'

'Oh we'll see it through!' I returned.

'Then you must control yourself better.'

'I will, I will – with practice.'

'You'll get used to it,' said my friend in a tone I never forgot. 'But go and join them – I'll come in a moment.'

I passed out to the terrace and felt I had a part to play. So far from dreading another encounter with the 'perfect presence', as she had called it, I was affected altogether in the sense of pleasure. I desired a renewal of my luck: I opened myself wide to the impression; I went round the house as quickly as if I expected to overtake Sir Edmund Orme. I didn't overtake him just then, but the day wasn't to close without my recognizing that, as Mrs Marden had said, I should see all I wanted of him.

We took, or most of us took, the collective sociable walk which, in the English country-house, is – or was at that time – the consecrated pastime of Sunday afternoons. We were restricted to such a regulated ramble as the ladies were good for; the afternoons moreover were short, and by five o'clock we were restored to the fireside in the hall with a sense, on my part at least, that we might have done a little more for our tea. Mrs Marden had said she would join us, but she hadn't appeared; her daughter, who had seen her again before we went out, only explained that she was tired. She remained invisible all the afternoon, but this was a detail to which I gave as little heed as I had given to the circumstance of my not having Charlotte to myself, even for five minutes, during all our walk. I was too much taken up with another interest to care; I felt beneath my feet the threshold of the strange door, in my life, which had suddenly been thrown open and out of which came an air of a keenness I had never breathed and of a taste stronger than wine. I had heard all my days of apparitions, but it was a different thing to have seen one and to know that I should in all likelihood see it familiarly, as I might say, again. I was on the lookout for it as a pilot for the flash of a revolving light, and ready to generalize on the sinister subject, to answer for it to all and sundry that ghosts were much less alarming and much more amusing than was commonly supposed. There's no doubt that I was much uplifted. I couldn't get over the distinction conferred on me, the exception – in the way of mystic enlargement of vision – made in my favour. At the same time I think I did justice to Mrs Marden's absence – a commentary, when I came to think, on what she had said to me: 'Now you know my life.' She had probably been exposed to our hoverer for years, and, not having my firm fibre, had broken down under it. Her nerve was gone, though she had also been able to attest that, in a degree, one got used to it. She had got used to breaking down.

Afternoon tea, when the dusk fell early, was a friendly hour at Tranton; the firelight played into the wide white last-century hall; sympathies almost confessed themselves, lingering together, before dressing, on deep sofas, in muddy boots, for last words after walks; and even solitary absorption in the third volume of a novel that was wanted by some one else seemed a form of geniality. I watched my moment and went over to Charlotte when I saw her about to withdraw. The ladies had left the place one by one, and after I had addressed myself to her particularly the three men who had been near gradually dispersed. We had a little vague talk – she might have been a good deal preoccupied, and heaven knows *I* was – after which she said she must go: she should be late for dinner. I proved to her by book that she had plenty of time, and she objected that she must at any rate go up to see her mother, who, she feared, was unwell.

'On the contrary, she's better than she has been for a long time – I'll guarantee that,' I said. 'She has found out she can have confidence in me, and that has done her good.' Miss Marden had dropped into her chair again, I was standing before her, and she looked up at me without a smile, with a dim distress in her beautiful eyes: not exactly as if I were hurting her, but as if she were no longer disposed to treat as a joke what had passed – whatever it was, it would give at the same time no ground for the extreme of solemnity – between her mother and myself. But I could answer her enquiry in all kindness and candour, for I was really conscious that the poor lady had put off a part of her burden on me and was proportionately relieved and eased. 'I'm sure she has slept all the afternoon as she hasn't slept for years,' I went on. 'You've only to ask her.'

Charlotte got up again. 'You make yourself out very useful.'

'You've a good quarter of an hour,' I said. 'Haven't I a right to talk to you a little this way, alone, when your mother has given me your hand?'

'And is it *your* mother who has given me yours? I'm much obliged to her, but I don't want it. I think our hands are not our mothers' – they happen to be our own!' laughed the girl.

'Sit down, sit down and let me tell you!' I pleaded.

I still stood there urgently, to see if she wouldn't oblige me. She cast about, looking vaguely this way and that, as if under a compulsion that was slightly painful. The empty hall was quiet – we heard the loud ticking of the great clock. Then she slowly sank down and I drew a chair close to her. This made me face round to the fire again, and with the movement I saw disconcertedly that we weren't alone. The next instant, more strangely than I can say, my discomposure, instead of increasing, dropped, for the person before the fire was Sir Edmund Orme. He stood there as I had seen him in the Indian room, looking at me with the expressionless attention that borrowed gravity from his sombre distinction. I knew so much more about him now that I had to check a movement of recognition, an acknowledgement of his presence. When once I was aware of it, and that it lasted, the sense that we had company, Charlotte and I, quitted me: it was impressed on me on the contrary that we were but the more markedly thrown together. No influence from our companion reached her, and I made a tremendous and very nearly successful effort to hide from her that my own sensibility was other and my nerves as tense as harp-strings. I say 'very nearly', because she watched me an instant – while my words were arrested – in a way that made me fear she was going to say again, as she had said in the Indian room: 'What on earth is the matter with you?'

What the matter with me was I quickly told her, for the full knowledge of it rolled over me with the touching sight of her unconsciousness. It was touching that she became in the presence of this extraordinary portent. What was portended, danger or sorrow, bliss or bane, was a minor question; all I saw, as she sat there, was that, innocent and charming, she was close to a horror, as she might have thought it, that happened to be veiled from her but that might at any moment be disclosed. I didn't mind it now, as I found – at least more than I could bear; but nothing was more possible than she should, and if it wasn't curious and interesting it might easily be appalling. If I didn't mind it for myself, I afterwards made out, this was largely because I was so taken up with the idea of protecting her. My heart, all at once, beat high with this view; I determined to do everything I could to keep her sense sealed. What I could do might have been all obscure to me if I hadn't, as the minutes lapsed, become more aware than of anything else that I loved her. The way to save her was to love her, and the way to love her was to tell her, now and here, that I did so. Sir Edmund Orme didn't prevent me, especially as after a moment he turned his back to us and stood looking discreetly at the fire. At the end of another moment he leaned his head on his arm, against the chimney-piece, with an air of gradual dejection, like a spirit still more weary than discreet. Charlotte Marden rose with a start at what I said to her – she jumped up to escape it; but she took no offence: the feeling I expressed was too real. She only moved about the room with a deprecating murmur, and I was so busy following up any little advantage I might have obtained that I didn't notice in what manner Sir Edmund Orme disappeared. I only found his place presently vacant. This made no difference – he had been so small a hindrance; I only remember being suddenly struck with something inexorable in the sweet sad headshake Charlotte gave me.

'I don't ask for an answer now,' I said; 'I only want you to be sure – to know how much depends on it.'

'Oh I don't want to give it to you now or ever!' she replied. 'I hate the subject, please – I wish one could be let alone.' And then, since I might have found something harsh in this irrepressible artless cry of beauty beset, she added, quickly vaguely kindly, as she left the room: 'Thank you, thank you – thank you so very much!'

At dinner I was generous enough to be glad for her that, on the same side of the table with me, she hadn't me in range. Her mother was nearly opposite me, and just after we had sat down Mrs Marden gave me a long deep look that expressed, and to the utmost, our strange communion. It meant of course 'She has told me', but it meant other things beside. At any rate I know what my mute response to her conveyed: 'I've seen him again – I've seen him again!' This didn't prevent Mrs Marden from treating her neighbours with her usual scrupulous blandness. After dinner, when, in the drawing-room, the men joined the ladies and I went straight up to her to tell her how I wished we might have some quiet words, she said at once, in a low tone, looking down at her fan while she opened and shut it: 'He's here – he's here.'

'Here?' I looked round the room, but was disappointed.

'Look where *she* is,' said Mrs Marden just with the faintest asperity. Charlotte was in fact not in the main saloon, but in a smaller into which it opened and which was known as the morning-room. I took a few steps and saw her, through a doorway, upright in the middle of the room, talking with three gentlemen whose backs were practically turned to me. For a moment my quest seemed vain; then I knew one of the gentlemen – the middle one – could but be Sir Edmund Orme. This time it *was* surprising that the others didn't see him. Charlotte might have seemed absolutely to have her eyes on him and to be addressing him straight. She saw me after an instant, however, and immediately averted herself. I returned to her mother with a sharpened fear the girl might think I was watching *her*, which would be unjust. Mrs Marden had found a small sofa – a little apart – and I sat down beside her. There were some questions I had so wanted to go into that I wished we were once more in the Indian room. I presently gathered however that our privacy quite sufficed. We communicated so closely and completely now, and with such silent reciprocities, that it would in every circumstance be adequate.

'Oh yes, he's there,' I said; 'and at about a quarter-past seven he was in the hall.'

'I knew it at the time – and I was so glad!' she answered straight.

'So glad?'

'That it was your affair this time and not mine. It's a rest for me.'

'Did you sleep all the afternoon?' I then asked.

'As I haven't done for months. But how did you know that?'

'As *you* knew, I take it, that Sir Edmund was in the hall. We shall evidently each of us know things now – where the other's concerned.'

'Where *he's* concerned,' Mrs Marden amended. 'It's a blessing, the way you take it,' she added with a long mild sigh.

'I take it,' I at once returned, 'as a man who's in love with your daughter.'

'Of course – of course.' Intense as I now felt my desire for the girl to be I couldn't help laughing a little at the tone of these words; and it led my companion immediately to say: 'Otherwise you wouldn't have seen him.'

Well, I esteemed my privilege, but I saw an objection to this. 'Does every one see him who's in love with her? If so there would be dozens.'

'They're not in love with her as you are.'

I took this in and couldn't but accept it. 'I can of course only speak for myself – and I found a moment before dinner to do so.'

'She told me as soon as she saw me,' Mrs Marden replied.

'And have I any hope – any chance?'

'That you may have is what I long for, what I pray for.'

The sore sincerity of this touched me. 'Ah how can I thank you enough?' I murmured.

'I believe it will all pass – if she only loves you,' the poor woman pursued.

'It will all pass?' I was a little at a loss.

'I mean we shall then be rid of him – shall never see him again.'

'Oh if she loves me I don't care how often I see him!' I roundly returned.

'Ah you take it better than *I* could,' said my companion. 'You've the happiness not to know – not to understand.'

'I don't indeed. What on earth does he want?'

'He wants to make me suffer.' She turned her wan face upon me with it, and I saw now for the first time, and saw well, how perfectly, if this had been our visitant's design, he had done his work. 'For what I did to him,' she explained.

'And what did you do to him?'

She gave me an unforgettable look. 'I killed him.' As I had seen him fifty yards off only five minutes before, the words gave me a start. 'Yes, I make you jump; be careful. He's there still, but he killed himself. I broke his heart – he thought me awfully bad. We were to have been married, but I broke it

off – just at the last. I saw some one I liked better; I had no reason but that. It wasn't for interest or money or position or any
of that baseness. All the good things were his. It was simply
that I fell in love with Major Marden. When I saw *him* I felt
I couldn't marry any one else. I wasn't in love with Edmund
Orme; my mother and my elder, my married, sister had brought
it about. But he did love me and I knew – that is almost knew! –
how much! But I told him I didn't care – that I couldn't, that I
wouldn't ever. I threw him over, and he took something, some
abominable drug or draught that proved fatal. It was dreadful,
it was horrible, he was found that way – he died in agony. I
married Major Marden, but not for five years. I was happy,
perfectly happy – time obliterates. But when my husband died
I began to see him.'

I had listened intently, wondering. 'To see your husband?'

'Never, never – *that* way, thank God! To see *him* – and with
Chartie, always with Chartie. The first time it nearly killed
me – about seven years ago, when she first came out. Never
when I'm by myself – only with her. Sometimes not for months,
then every day for a week. I've tried everything to break the
spell – doctors and *régimes*[7] and climates; I've prayed to God
on my knees. That day at Brighton, on the Parade with you,
when you thought I was ill, that was the first for an age. And
then in the evening, when I knocked my tea over you, and the
day you were at the door with her and I saw you from the
window – each time he was there.'

'I see, I see.' I was more thrilled than I could say. 'It's an
apparition like another.'

'Like another? Have you ever seen another?' she cried.

'No, I mean the sort of thing one has heard of. It's tremendously interesting to encounter a case.'

'Do you call me a "case"?' my friend cried with exquisite
resentment.

'I was thinking of myself.'

'Oh you're the right one!' she went on. 'I was right when I
trusted you.'

'I'm devoutly grateful you did; but what made you do it?' I
asked.

'I had thought the whole thing out. I had had time to in those dreadful years while he was punishing me in my daughter.'

'Hardly that,' I objected, 'if Miss Marden never knew.'

'That has been my terror, that she *will*, from one occasion to another. I've an unspeakable dread of the effect on her.'

'She shan't, she shan't!' I engaged in such a tone that several people looked round. Mrs Marden made me rise, and our talk dropped for that evening. The next day I told her I must leave Tranton – it was neither comfortable nor considerate to remain as a rejected suitor. She was disconcerted, but accepted my reasons, only appealing to me with mournful eyes: 'You'll leave me alone then with my burden?' It was of course understood between us that for many weeks to come there would be no discretion in 'worrying poor Charlotte': such were the terms in which, with odd feminine and maternal inconsistency, she alluded to an attitude on my part that she favoured. I was prepared to be heroically considerate, but I held that even this delicacy permitted me to say a word to Miss Marden before I went. I begged her after breakfast to take a turn with me on the terrace, and as she hesitated, looking at me distantly, I let her know it was only to ask her a question and to say goodbye – I was going away for *her*.

She came out with me and we passed slowly round the house three or four times. Nothing is finer than this great airy platform, from which every glance is a sweep of the country with the sea on the furthest edge. It might have been that as we passed the windows we were conspicuous to our friends in the house, who would make out sarcastically why I was so significantly bolting. But I didn't care; I only wondered if they mightn't really this time receive the impression of Sir Edmund Orme, who joined us on one of our turns and strolled slowly on the other side of Charlotte. Of what odd essence he was made I know not; I've no theory about him – leaving that to others – any more than about such or such another of my fellow mortals (and *his* law of being) as I have elbowed in life. He was as positive, as individual and ultimate a fact as any of these. Above all he was, by every seeming, of as fine and as sensitive, of as thoroughly honourable, a mixture; so that I should no more have thought of taking a liberty, of practising an experiment, with him, of touching him, for instance, or of addressing him, since he set the example of silence, than I should have thought of committing any other social grossness. He had always, as I saw more fully later, the perfect propriety of his position – looked always arrayed and anointed, and carried himself ever, in each particular, exactly as the occasion demanded. He struck me as strange, incontestably, but somehow always struck me as right. I very soon came to attach an idea of beauty to his unrecognized presence, the beauty of an old story, of love and pain and death. What I ended by feeling was that he was on my side, watching over my interest, looking to it that no trick should be played me and that my heart at least shouldn't be broken. Oh he had taken them seriously, his own wound and his own loss – he had certainly proved this in his day. If poor Mrs Marden, responsible for these things, had, as she told me, thought the case out, I also treated it to the finest analysis I could bring to bear. It was a case of retributive just-ice, of the visiting on the children of the sins of the mothers, since not of the fathers.[8] This wretched mother was to pay, in suffering, for the suffering she had inflicted, and as the dispos-ition to trifle with an honest man's just expectations might crop up again, to my detriment, in the child, the latter young person was to be studied and watched, so that *she* might be made to suffer should she do an equal wrong. She might emulate her parent by some play of characteristic perversity not less than she resembled her in charm; and if that impulse should be determined in her, if she should be caught, that is to say, in some breach of faith or some heartless act, her eyes would on the spot, by an insidious logic, be opened suddenly and unpitiedly to the 'perfect presence', which she would then have to work as she could into her conception of a young lady's universe. I had no great fear for her, because I hadn't felt her lead me on from vanity, and I knew that if I was disconcerted it was because I had myself gone too fast. We should have a good deal of ground to get over at least before I should be in a position to be sacrificed by her. She couldn't take back what she had given before she had given rather more. Whether I

asked for more was indeed another matter, and the question I
put to her on the terrace that morning was whether I might
continue during the winter to come to Mrs Marden's house. I
promised not to come too often and not to speak to her for
three months of the issue I had raised the day before. She
replied that I might do as I liked, and on this we parted.

I carried out the vow I had made her; I held my tongue for
my three months. Unexpectedly to myself there were moments
of this time when she did strike me as capable of missing my
homage even though she might be indifferent to my happiness.
I wanted so to make her like me that I became subtle and
ingenious, wonderfully alert, patiently diplomatic. Sometimes
I thought I had earned my reward, brought her to the point of
saying: 'Well, well, you're the best of them all – you may speak
to me now.' Then there was a greater blankness than ever in
her beauty and on certain days a mocking light in her eyes, a
light of which the meaning seemed to be: 'If you don't take
care I *will* accept you, to have done with you the more effectually.' Mrs Marden was a great help to me simply by believing
in me, and I valued her faith all the more that it continued even
through a sudden intermission of the miracle that had been
wrought for me. After our visit to Tranton Sir Edmund Orme
gave us a holiday, and I confess it was at first a disappointment
to me. I felt myself by so much less designated, less involved
and connected – all with Charlotte I mean to say. 'Oh don't cry
till you're out of the wood', was her mother's comment; 'he has
let me off sometimes for six months. He'll break out again
when you least expect it – he understands his game.' For her
these weeks were happy, and she was wise enough not to talk
about me to the girl. She was so good as to assure me I was
taking the right line, that I looked as if I felt secure and that in
the long run women give way to this. She had known them do
it even when the man was a fool for that appearance, for that
confidence – a fool indeed on any terms. For herself she felt it
a good time, almost her best, a Saint Martin's summer of the
soul.[9] She was better than she had been for years, and had me to
thank for it. The sense of visitation was light on her – she wasn't
in anguish every time she looked round. Charlotte contradicted

me repeatedly, but contradicted herself still more. That winter by the old Sussex sea was a wonder of mildness, and we often sat out in the sun. I walked up and down with my young woman, and Mrs Marden, sometimes on a bench, sometimes in a Bath-chair, waited for us and smiled at us as we passed. I always looked out for a sign in her face – 'He's with you, he's with you' (she would see him before I should) but nothing came; the season had brought us as well a sort of spiritual softness. Toward the end of April the air was so like June that, meeting my two friends one night at some Brighton sociability – an evening party with amateur music – I drew the younger unresistingly out upon a balcony to which a window in one of the rooms stood open. The night was close and thick, the stars dim, and below us under the cliff we heard the deep rumble of the tide. We listened to it a little and there came to us, mixed with it from within the house, the sound of a violin accompanied by a piano – a performance that had been our pretext for escaping.

'Do you like me a little better?' I broke out after a minute. 'Could you listen to me again?'

I had no sooner spoken than she laid her hand quickly, with a certain force, on my arm. 'Hush! – isn't there some one there?' She was looking into the gloom of the far end of the balcony. This balcony ran the whole width of the house, a width very great in the best of the old houses at Brighton. We were to some extent lighted by the open window behind us, but the other windows, curtained within, left the darkness undiminished, so that I made out but dimly the figure of a gentleman standing there and looking at us. He was in evening dress, like a guest – I saw the vague sheen of his white shirt and the pale oval of his face – and he might perfectly have been a guest who had stepped out in advance of us to take the air. Charlotte took him for one at first – then evidently, even in a few seconds, saw that the intensity of his gaze was unconventional. What else she saw I couldn't determine; I was too occupied with my own impression to do more than feel the quick contact of her uneasiness. My own impression was in fact the strongest of sensations, a sensation of horror; for what could the thing mean but that the girl at last *saw*? I heard her give a sudden, gasping 'Ah!' and move quickly into the house. It was only afterwards I knew that I myself had had a totally new emotion – my horror passing into anger and my anger into a stride along the balcony with a gesture of reprobation. The case was simplified to the vision of an adorable girl menaced and terrified. I advanced to vindicate her security, but I found nothing there to meet me. It was either all a mistake or Sir Edmund Orme had vanished.

I followed her at once, but there were symptoms of confusion in the drawing-room when I passed in. A lady had fainted, the music had stopped; there was a shuffling of chairs and a pressing forward. The lady was not Charlotte, as I feared, but Mrs Marden, who had suddenly been taken ill. I remember the relief with which I learned this, for to see Charlotte stricken would have been anguish, and her mother's condition gave a channel to her agitation. It was of course all a matter for the people of the house and for the ladies, and I could have no share in attending to my friends or in conducting them to their carriage. Mrs Marden revived and insisted on going home, after which I uneasily withdrew.

I called the next morning for better news and I learnt she was more at ease, but on my asking if Charlotte would see me the message sent down was an excuse. There was nothing for me to do all day but roam with a beating heart. Toward evening however I received a line in pencil, brought by hand – 'Please come; mother wishes you.' Five minutes later I was at the door again and ushered into the drawing-room. Mrs Marden lay on the sofa, and as soon as I looked at her I saw the shadow of death in her face. But the first thing she said was that she was better, ever so much better; her poor old fluttered heart had misbehaved again, but now was decently quiet. She gave me her hand and I bent over her, my eyes on her eyes, and in this way was able to read what she didn't speak – 'I'm really very ill, but appear to take what I say exactly as I say it.' Charlotte stood there beside her, looking not frightened now, but intensely grave, and meeting no look of my own. 'She has told me – she has told me!' her mother went on.

'She has told you?' I stared from one of them to the other, wondering if my friend meant that the girl had named to her the unexplained appearance on the balcony.

'That you spoke to her again – that you're admirably faithful.'

I felt a thrill of joy at this; it showed me that memory uppermost, and also that her daughter had wished to say the thing that would most soothe her, not the thing that would alarm her. Yet I was myself now sure, as sure as if Mrs Marden had told me, that she knew and had known at the moment what her daughter had seen. 'I spoke – I spoke, but she gave me no answer,' I said.

'She will now, won't you, Chartie? I want it so, I want it!' our companion murmured with ineffable wistfulness.

'You're very good to me' – Charlotte addressed me, seriously and sweetly, but with her eyes fixed on the carpet. There was something different in her, different from all the past. She had recognized something, she felt a coercion. I could see her uncontrollably tremble.

'Ah if you would let me show you *how* good I can be!' I cried as I held out my hands to her. As I uttered the words I was touched with the knowledge that something had happened. A form had constituted itself on the other side of the couch, and the form leaned over Mrs Marden. My whole being went forth into a mute prayer that Charlotte shouldn't see it and that I should be able to betray nothing. The impulse to glance toward her mother was even stronger than the involuntary movement of taking in Sir Edmund Orme; but I could resist even that, and Mrs Marden was perfectly still. Charlotte got up to give me her hand, and then – with the definite act – she dreadfully saw. She gave, with a shriek, one stare of dismay, and another sound, the wail of one of the lost, fell at the same instant on my ear. But I had already sprung toward the creature I loved, to cover her, to veil her face, and she had as passionately thrown herself into my arms. I held her there a moment – pressing her close, given up to her, feeling each of her throbs with my own and not knowing which was which; then all of a sudden, coldly, I was sure we were alone. She released herself. The figure beside the sofa had vanished, but Mrs Marden lay in her place with closed eyes, with something in her stillness that gave us both a fresh terror. Charlotte expressed it in the cry of 'Mother, mother!' with which she flung herself down. I fell on my knees beside her – Mrs Marden had passed away.

Was the sound I heard when Chartie shrieked – the other and still more tragic sound I mean – the despairing cry of the poor lady's death-shock or the articulate sob (it was like a waft from a great storm) of the exorcized and pacified spirit? Possibly the latter, for that was mercifully the last of Sir Edmund Orme.

OWEN WINGRAVE

I

'Upon my honour you must be off your head!' cried Spencer Coyle as the young man, with a white face, stood there panting a little and repeating 'Really I've quite decided', and 'I assure you I've thought it all out.' They were both pale, but Owen Wingrave smiled in a manner exasperating to his supervisor, who however still discriminated sufficiently to feel his grimace – it was like an irrelevant leer – the result of extreme and conceivable nervousness.

'It was certainly a mistake to have gone so far; but that's exactly why it strikes me I mustn't go further,' poor Owen said, waiting mechanically, almost humbly – he wished not to swagger, and indeed had nothing to swagger about – and carrying through the window to the stupid opposite houses the dry glitter of his eyes.

'I'm unspeakably disgusted. You've made me dreadfully ill' – and Mr Coyle looked in truth thoroughly upset.

'I'm very sorry. It was the fear of the effect on you that kept me from speaking sooner.'

'You should have spoken three months ago. Don't you know your mind from one day to the other?' the elder of the pair demanded.

The young man for a moment held himself: then he quavered his plea. 'You're very angry with me and I expected it. I'm awfully obliged to you for all you've done for me. I'll do anything else for you in return, but I can't do that. Every one else will let me have it of course. I'm prepared for that – I'm prepared for everything. It's what has taken the time: to be sure I was prepared. I think it's your displeasure I feel most and regret most. But little by little you'll get over it,' Owen wound up.

'*You'll* get over it rather faster, I suppose!' the other satiri-cally exclaimed. He was quite as agitated as his young friend, and they were evidently in no condition to prolong an encoun-ter in which each drew blood. Mr Coyle was a professional 'coach'; he prepared aspirants for the army, taking only three or four at a time, to whom he applied the irresistible stimulus the possession of which was both his secret and his fortune. He hadn't a great establishment; he would have said himself that it was not a wholesale business. Neither his system, his health nor his temper could have concorded with numbers; so he weighed and measured his pupils and turned away more applicants than he passed. He was an artist in his line, caring only for picked subjects and capable of sacrifices almost pas-sionate for the individual. He liked ardent young men – there were types of facility and kinds of capacity to which he was indifferent – and he had taken a particular fancy to Owen Wingrave. This young man's particular shade of ability, to say nothing of his whole personality, almost cast a spell and at any rate worked a charm. Mr Coyle's candidates usually did won-ders, and he might have sent up a multitude. He was a person exactly of the stature of the great Napoleon,[1] with a certain flicker of genius in his light blue eye: it had been said of him that he looked like a concert-giving pianist. The tone of his favourite pupil now expressed, without intention indeed, a superior wisdom that irritated him. He hadn't at all suffered before from Wingrave's high opinion of himself, which had seemed justified by remarkable parts; but to-day, of a sudden, it struck him as intolerable. He cut short the discussion, declin-ing absolutely to regard their relations as terminated, and remarked to his pupil that he had better go off somewhere – down to Eastbourne,[2] say: the sea would bring him round – and take a few days to find his feet and come to his senses. He could afford the time, he was so well up: when Spencer Coyle remembered how well up he was he could have boxed his ears. The tall athletic young man wasn't physically a subject for simplified reasoning; but a troubled gentleness in his hand-some face, the index of compunction mixed with resolution, virtually signified that if it could have done any good he would have turned both cheeks. He evidently didn't pretend that his wisdom was superior; he only presented it as his own. It was his own career after all that was in question. He couldn't refuse to go through the form of trying Eastbourne or at least of hold-ing his tongue, though there was that in his manner which implied that if he should do so it would be really to give Mr Coyle a chance to recuperate. He didn't feel a bit overworked, but there was nothing more natural than that, with their tremendous pressure, Mr Coyle should be. Mr Coyle's own intellect would derive an advantage from his pupil's holiday. Mr Coyle saw what he meant, but controlled himself; he only demanded, as his right, a truce of three days. Owen granted it, though as fostering sad illusions this went visibly against his conscience; but before they separated the famous crammer remarked: 'All the same I feel I ought to see some one. I think you mentioned to me that your aunt had come to town?'

'Oh yes – she's in Baker Street.[3] Do go and see her,' the boy said for comfort.

His tutor sharply eyed him. 'Have you broached this folly to her?'

'Not yet – to no one. I thought it right to speak to you first.'

'Oh what you "think right"!' cried Spencer Coyle, outraged by his young friend's standards. He added that he would prob-ably call on Miss Wingrave; after which the recreant youth got out of the house.

The latter didn't, none the less, start at once for Eastbourne; he only directed his steps to Kensington Gardens,[4] from which Mr Coyle's desirable residence – he was terribly expensive and had a big house – was not far removed. The famous coach 'put up' his pupils, and Owen had mentioned to the butler that he would be back to dinner. The spring day was warm to his young blood, and he had a book in his pocket which, when he had passed into the Gardens and, after a short stroll, dropped into a chair, he took out with the slow soft sigh that finally ushers in a pleasure postponed. He stretched his long legs and began to read it; it was a volume of Goethe's poems.[5] He had been for days in a state of the highest tension, and now that the cord had snapped the relief was proportionate; only it was characteristic of him that this deliverance should take the form of an intellectual pleasure. If he had thrown up the probability of a magnificent career it wasn't to dawdle along Bond Street[6] nor parade his indifference in the window of a club. At any rate he had in a few moments forgotten everything – the tremendous pressure, Mr Coyle's disappointment and even his formidable aunt in Baker Street. If these watchers had over-taken him there would surely have been some excuse for their exasperation. There was no doubt he was perverse, for his very choice of a pastime only showed how he had got up his German.

'What the devil's the matter with him, do *you* know?' Spencer Coyle asked that afternoon of young Lechmere, who had never before observed the head of the establishment to set a fellow such an example of bad language. Young Lechmere was not only Wingrave's fellow pupil, he was supposed to be his intimate, indeed quite his best friend, and had unconsciously performed for Mr Coyle the office of making the promise of his great gifts more vivid by contrast. He was short and sturdy and as a general thing uninspired, and Mr Coyle, who found no amusement in believing in him, had never thought him less exciting than as he stared now out of a face from which you could no more guess whether he had caught an idea than you could judge of your dinner by looking at a dish-cover. Young Lechmere concealed such achievements as if they had been youthful indiscretions. At any rate he could evidently conceive no reason why it should be thought there was anything more than usual the matter with the companion of his studies; so Mr Coyle had to continue: 'He declines to go up. He chucks the whole shop!'

The first thing that struck young Lechmere in the case was the freshness, as of a forgotten vernacular, it had imparted to the governor's vocabulary. 'He doesn't want to go to Sandhurst?'

'He doesn't want to go anywhere. He gives up the army altogether. He objects,' said Mr Coyle in a tone that made young Lechmere almost hold his breath, 'to the military profession.'

'Why it has been the profession of all his family!'

'Their profession? It has been their religion! Do you know Miss Wingrave?'

'Oh yes. Isn't she awful?' young Lechmere candidly ejaculated.

His instructor demurred. 'She's formidable, if you mean that, and it's right she should be; because somehow in her very person, good maiden lady as she is, she represents the might, she represents the traditions and the exploits, of the British army. She represents the expansive property of the English name. I think his family can be trusted to come down on him, but every influence should be set in motion. I want to know what yours is. Can *you* do anything in the matter?'

'I can try a couple of rounds with him,' said young Lechmere reflectively. 'But he knows a fearful lot. He has the most extraordinary ideas.'

'Then he has told you some of them – he has taken you into his confidence?'

'I've heard him jaw by the yard,' smiled the honest youth. 'He has told me he despises it.'

'What *is* it he despises? I can't make out.'

The most consecutive of Mr Coyle's nurslings considered a moment, as if he were conscious of a responsibility. 'Why I think just soldiering, don't you know? He says we take the wrong view of it.'

'He oughtn't to talk to *you* that way. It's corrupting the youth of Athens.⁷ It's sowing sedition.'

'Oh I'm all right!' said young Lechmere. 'And he never told me he meant to chuck it. I always thought he meant to see it through, simply because he had to. He'll argue on any side you like. He can talk your head off – I will say *that* for him. But it's a tremendous pity – I'm sure he'd have a big career.'

'Tell him so then; plead with him; struggle with him – for God's sake.'

'I'll do what I can – I'll tell him it's a regular shame.'

'Yes, strike *that* note – insist on the disgrace of it.'

The young man gave Mr Coyle a queer look. 'I'm sure he wouldn't do anything dishonourable.'

'Well – it won't look right. He must be made to feel *that* – work it up. Give him a comrade's point of view – that of a brother-in-arms.'

'That's what I thought we were going to be!' young Lechmere mused romantically, much uplifted by the nature of the mission imposed on him. 'He's an awfully good sort.'

'No one will think so if he backs out!' said Spencer Coyle.

'Well, they mustn't say it to *me*!' his pupil rejoined with a flush.

Mr Coyle debated, noting his tone and aware that in the perversity of things, though this young man was a born soldier, no excitement would ever attach to *his* alternatives save perhaps on the part of the nice girl to whom at an early day he was sure to be placidly united. 'Do you like him very much – do you believe in him?'

Young Lechmere's life in these days was spent in answering terrible questions, but he had never been put through so straight a lot as these. 'Believe in him? Rather!'

'Then *save* him!'

The poor boy was puzzled, as if it were forced upon him by this intensity that there was more in such an appeal than could appear on the surface; and he doubtless felt that he was but apprehending a complex situation when after another moment, with his hands in his pockets, he replied hopefully but not pompously: 'I daresay I can bring him round!'

II

Before seeing young Lechmere Mr Coyle had determined to telegraph an enquiry to Miss Wingrave. He had prepaid the answer, which, being promptly put into his hand, brought the interview we have just related to a close. He immediately drove off to Baker Street, where the lady had said she awaited him, and five minutes after he got there, as he sat with Owen Wingrave's remarkable aunt, he repeated several times over, in his angry sadness and with the infallibility of his experience: 'He's so intelligent – he's so intelligent!' He had declared it had been a luxury to put such a fellow through.

'Of course he's intelligent; what else could he be? We've never, that I know of, had but *one* idiot in the family!' said Jane Wingrave. This was an allusion that Mr Coyle could understand, and it brought home to him another of the reasons for the disappointment, the humiliation as it were, of the good people at Paramore, at the same time that it gave an example of the conscientious coarseness he had on former occasions observed in his hostess. Poor Philip Wingrave, her late brother's eldest son, was literally imbecile and banished from view; deformed, unsocial, irretrievable, he had been relegated to a private asylum and had become among the friends of the family only a little hushed lugubrious legend. All the hopes of the house, picturesque Paramore, now unintermittently old Sir Philip's rather melancholy home – his infirmities would keep him there to the last – were therefore gathered on the second boy's head, which nature, as if in compunction for her previous botch, had, in addition to making it strikingly handsome, filled with a marked and general readiness. These two had been the only children of the old man's only son, who, like so many of his ancestors, had given up a gallant young life to the service of his country. Owen Wingrave the elder had received his death-cut, in close quarters, from an Afghan sabre;[8] the blow had come crashing across his skull. His wife, at that time in India, was about to give birth to her third child; and when the event took place, in darkness and anguish, the baby came lifeless into the world and the mother sank under the multiplication of her woes. The second of the little boys in England, who was at Paramore with his grandfather, became the peculiar charge of his aunt, the only unmarried one, and during the interesting Sunday that, by urgent invitation, Spencer Coyle, busy as he was, had, after consenting to put Owen through, spent under that roof, the celebrated crammer received a vivid impression of the influence exerted at least in intention by Miss Wingrave. Indeed the picture of this short visit remained with the observant little man a curious one – the vision of an impoverished Jacobean house, shabby and remarkably 'creepy', but full of character still and full of felicity as a setting for the distinguished figure of the peaceful old soldier. Sir Philip Wingrave, a relic rather than a celebrity, was a small brown erect octogenarian, with smouldering eyes and a studied courtesy. He liked to do the diminished honours of his house, but even when with a shaky hand he lighted a bedroom candle for a deprecating guest it was impossible not to feel him, beneath the surface, a merciless old man of blood. The eye of the imagination could glance back into his crowded Eastern past – back at episodes in which his scrupulous forms would only have made him more terrible. He had his legend – and oh there were stories about him!

Mr Coyle remembered also two other figures – a faded inoffensive Mrs Julian, domesticated there by a system of frequent visits as the widow of an officer and a particular friend of Miss Wingrave, and a remarkably clever little girl of eighteen, who was this lady's daughter and who struck the speculative visitor as already formed for other relations. She was very impertinent to Owen, and in the course of a long walk that he had taken with the young man and the effect of which, in much talk, had been to clinch his high opinion of him, he had learned – for Owen chattered confidentially – that Mrs Julian was the sister of a very gallant gentleman, Captain Hume-Walker of the Artillery, who had fallen in the Indian Mutiny[9] and between whom and Miss Wingrave (it had been that lady's one known concession) a passage of some delicacy, taking a tragic turn, was believed to have been enacted. They had been engaged to be married, but she had given way to the jealousy of her nature – had broken with him and sent him off to his fate, which had been horrible. A passionate sense of having wronged him, a hard eternal remorse had thereupon taken possession of her, and when his poor sister, linked also to a soldier, had by a still heavier blow been left almost without resources, she had devoted herself grimly to a long expiation. She had sought comfort in taking Mrs Julian to live much of the time at Paramore, where she became an unremunerated though not uncriticized housekeeper, and Spencer Coyle rather fancied it a part of this comfort that she could at leisure trample on her. The impression of Jane Wingrave was not the faintest he had gathered on that intensifying Sunday – an occasion singularly tinged for him with the sense of bereavement and mourning and memory, of names never mentioned, of the far-away plaint of widows and the echoes of battles and bad news. It was all military indeed, and Mr Coyle was made to shudder a little at the profession of which he helped to open the door to otherwise harmless young men. Miss Wingrave might moreover have made such a bad conscience worse – so cold and clear a good one looked at him out of her hard fine eyes and trumpeted in her sonorous voice.

She was a high distinguished person, angular but not awkward, with a large forehead and abundant black hair arranged like that of a woman conceiving perhaps excusably of her head as 'noble', and to-day irregularly streaked with white. If however she represented for our troubled friend the genius of a military race it was not that she had the step of a grenadier or the vocabulary of a camp-follower; it was only that such sympathies were vividly implied in the general fact to which her very presence and each of her actions and glances and tones were a constant and direct allusion – the paramount valour of her family. If she was military it was because she sprang from a military house and because she wouldn't for the world have been anything but what the Wingraves had been. She was almost vulgar about her ancestors, and if one had been tempted to quarrel with her one would have found a fair pretext in her defective sense of proportion. This temptation however said nothing to Spencer Coyle, for whom, as a strong character revealing itself in colour and sound, she was almost a 'treat' and who was glad to regard her as a force exerted on his own side. He wished her nephew had more of her narrowness instead of being almost cursed with the tendency to look at things in their relations. He wondered why when she came up to town she always resorted to Baker Street for lodgings. He had never known nor heard of Baker Street as a residence – he associated it only with bazaars and photographers. He divined in her a rigid indifference to everything that was not the passion of her life. Nothing really mattered to her but that, and she would have occupied apartments in Whitechapel[10] if they had been an item in her tactics. She had received her visitor in a large cold faded room, furnished with slippery seats and decorated with alabaster vases and wax-flowers. The only little personal comfort for which she appeared to have looked out was a fat catalogue of the Army and Navy Stores, which reposed on a vast desolate table-cover of false blue. Her clear forehead – it was like a porcelain slate, a receptacle for addresses and sums – had flushed when her nephew's crammer told her the extraordinary news; but he saw she was fortunately more angry than frightened. She had essentially, she would always have, too little imagination for fear, and the healthy habit moreover of facing everything had taught her that the occasion usually found her a quantity to reckon with. He saw that her only present fear could have been that of the failure to prevent her nephew's showing publicly for an ass, or for worse, and that to such an apprehension as this she was in fact inaccessible. Practically too she was not troubled by surprise; she recognized none of the futile, none of the subtle sentiments. If Owen had for an hour made a fool of himself she was angry; disconcerted as she would have been on learning that he had confessed to debts or fallen in love with a low girl. But there remained in any annoyance the saving fact that no one could make a fool of *her*.

'I don't know when I've taken such an interest in a young man – I think I've never done it since I began to handle them,' Mr Coyle said. 'I like him, I believe in him. It's been a delight to see how he was going.'

'Oh I know how they go!' Miss Wingrave threw back her head with an air as acquainted as if a headlong array of the generations had flashed before her with a rattle of their scabbards and spurs. Spencer Coyle recognized the intimation that she had nothing to learn from anybody about the natural carriage of a Wingrave, and he even felt convicted by her next words of being, in her eyes, with the troubled story of his check, his weak complaint of his pupil, rather a poor creature. 'If you like him,' she exclaimed, 'for mercy's sake keep him quiet!'

Mr Coyle began to explain to her that this was less easy than she appeared to imagine; but it came home to him that she really grasped little of what he said. The more he insisted that the boy had a kind of intellectual independence, the more this struck her as a conclusive proof that her nephew was a Wingrave and a soldier. It was not till he mentioned to her that Owen had spoken of the profession of arms as of something that would be 'beneath' him, it was not till her attention was arrested by this intenser light on the complexity of the problem, that she broke out after a moment's stupefied reflexion: 'Send him to see me at once!'

'That's exactly what I wanted to ask your leave to do. But I've wanted also to prepare you for the worst, to make you understand that he strikes me as really obstinate, and to suggest to you that the most powerful arguments at your command – especially if you should be able to put your hand on some intensely practical one – will be none too effective.'

'I think I've got a powerful argument' – and Miss Wingrave looked hard at her visitor. He didn't know in the least what this engine might be, but he begged her to drag it without delay into the field. He promised their young man should come to Baker Street that evening, mentioning however that he had already urged him to spend a couple of the very next days at Eastbourne. This led Jane Wingrave to enquire with surprise what virtue there might be in *that* expensive remedy, and to reply with decision when he had said 'The virtue of a little rest, a little change, a little relief to overwrought nerves', 'Ah don't coddle him – he's costing us a great deal of money! I'll talk to him and I'll take him down to Paramore; he'll be dealt with there, and I'll send him back to you straightened out.'

Spencer Coyle hailed this pledge superficially with satisfaction, but before he quitted the strenuous lady he knew he had really taken on a new anxiety – a restlessness that made him say to himself, groaning inwardly: 'Oh she *is* a grenadier at bottom, and she'll have no tact. I don't know what her powerful argument is; I'm only afraid she'll be stupid and make him worse. The old man's better – *he's* capable of tact, though he's not quite an extinct volcano. Owen will probably put him in a rage. In short it's a difficulty that the boy's the best of them.'

He felt afresh that evening at dinner that the boy was the best of them. Young Wingrave – who, he was pleased to observe, had not yet proceeded to the seaside – appeared at the repast as usual, looking inevitably a little self-conscious, but not too original for Bayswater.[11] He talked very naturally to Mrs Coyle, who had thought him from the first the most beautiful young man they had ever received; so that the person most ill at ease was poor Lechmere, who took great trouble, as if from the deepest delicacy, not to meet the eye of his misguided mate. Spencer Coyle however paid the price of his own profundity in feeling more and more worried; he could so easily see that there were all sorts of things in his young friend that the people of Paramore wouldn't understand. He began even already to react against the notion of his being harassed – to reflect that after all he had a right to his ideas – to remember that he was of a substance too fine to be handled with blunt fingers. It was in this way that the ardent little crammer, with his whimsical perceptions and complicated sympathies, was generally con-demned not to settle down comfortably either to his displeasures or to his enthusiasms. His love of the real truth never gave him a chance to enjoy them. He mentioned to Wingrave after din-ner the propriety of an immediate visit to Baker Street, and the young man, looking 'queer', as he thought – that is smiling again with the perverse high spirit in a wrong cause that he had shown in their recent interview – went off to face the ordeal. Spencer Coyle was sure he was scared – he was afraid of his aunt; but somehow this didn't strike him as a sign of pusillanimity. *He* should have been scared, he was well aware, in the poor boy's place, and the sight of his pupil marching up to the battery in spite of his terrors was a positive suggestion of the temperament of the soldier. Many a plucky youth would have funked this special exposure.

'He *has* got ideas!' young Lechmere broke out to his instructor after his comrade had quitted the house. He was bewildered and rather rueful – he had an emotion to work off. He had before dinner gone straight at his friend, as Mr Coyle had requested, and had elicited from him that his scruples were founded on an overwhelming conviction of the stupidity – the 'crass barbarism' he called it – of war. His great complaint was that people hadn't invented anything cleverer, and he was determined to show, the only way he could, that *he* wasn't so dull a brute.

'And he thinks all the great generals ought to have been shot, and that Napoleon Bonaparte in particular, the greatest, was a scoundrel, a criminal, a monster for whom language has no adequate name!' Mr Coyle rejoined, completing young Lechmere's picture. 'He favoured you, I see, with exactly the same pearls of wisdom that he produced for me. But I want to know what *you* said.'

'I said they were awful rot!' Young Lechmere spoke with emphasis and was slightly surprised to hear Mr Coyle laugh, out of tune, at this just declaration, and then after a moment continue:

'It's all very curious – I daresay there's something in it. But it's a pity!'

'He told me when it was that the question began to strike him in that light. Four or five years ago, when he did a lot of reading about all the great swells and their campaigns – Hannibal and Julius Cæsar, Marlborough and Frederick and Bonaparte.[12] He *has* done a lot of reading, and he says it opened his eyes. He says that a wave of disgust rolled over him. He talked about the "immeasurable misery" of wars, and asked me why nations don't tear to pieces the governments, the rulers that go in for them. He hates poor old Bonaparte worst of all.'

'Well, poor old Bonaparte *was* a scoundrel. He was a frightful ruffian,' Mr Coyle unexpectedly declared. 'But I suppose you didn't admit that.'

'Oh I daresay he was objectionable, and I'm very glad we laid him on his back. But the point I made to Wingrave was that his own behaviour would excite no end of remark.' And young Lechmere hung back but an instant before adding: 'I told him he must be prepared for the worst.'

'Of course he asked you what you meant by the "worst",' said Spencer Coyle.

'Yes, he asked me that, and do you know what I said? I said people would call his conscientious scruples and his wave of disgust a mere pretext. Then he asked "A pretext for what?"'

'Ah he rather had you there!' Mr Coyle returned with a small laugh that was mystifying to his pupil.

'Not a bit – for I told him.'

'What did you tell him?'

Once more, for a few seconds, with his conscious eyes in his instructor's, the young man delayed. 'Why what we spoke of a few hours ago. The appearance he'd present of not having—' The honest youth faltered afresh, but brought it out: 'The military temperament, don't you know? But do you know how he cheeked us on that?' young Lechmere went on.

'Damn the military temperament!' the crammer promptly replied.

Young Lechmere stared. Mr Coyle's tone left him uncertain if he were attributing the phrase to Wingrave or uttering his own opinion, but he exclaimed: 'Those were exactly his words!'

'He doesn't care,' said Mr Coyle.

'Perhaps not. But it isn't fair for him to abuse *us* fellows. I told him it's the finest temperament in the world, and that there's nothing so splendid as pluck and heroism.'

'Ah there you had *him*!'

'I told him it was unworthy of him to abuse a gallant, a magnificent profession. I told him there's no type so fine as that of the soldier doing his duty.'

'That's essentially *your* type, my dear boy.' Young Lechmere blushed; he couldn't make out – and the danger was naturally unexpected to him – whether at that moment he didn't exist mainly for the recreation of his friend. But he was partly reassured by the genial way this friend continued, laying a hand on his shoulder: 'Keep *at* him that way! We may do something. I'm in any case extremely obliged to you.'

Another doubt however remained unassuaged – a doubt which led him to overflow yet again before they dropped the painful subject: 'He *doesn't* care! But it's awfully odd he shouldn't!'

'So it is, but remember what you said this afternoon – I mean about your not advising people to make insinuations to *you*.'

'I believe I should knock the beggar down!' said young Lechmere. Mr Coyle had got up; the conversation had taken place while they sat together after Mrs Coyle's withdrawal from the dinner-table, and the head of the establishment administered to his candid charge, on principles that were a part of his thoroughness, a glass of excellent claret. The disciple in question, also on his feet, lingered an instant, not for another 'go', as he would have called it, at the decanter, but to wipe his microscopic moustache with prolonged and unusual care. His companion saw he had something to bring out which required a final effort, and waited for him an instant with a hand on the knob of the door. Then as young Lechmere drew nearer Spencer Coyle grew conscious of an unwonted intensity in the round and ingenuous face. The boy was nervous, but tried to behave like a man of the world. 'Of course it's between ourselves,' he stammered, 'and I wouldn't breathe such a word to any one who wasn't interested in poor Wingrave as you are. But do you think he funks it?'

Mr Coyle looked at him so hard an instant that he was visibly frightened at what he had said. 'Funks it! Funks what?'

'Why what we're talking about – the service.' Young Lechmere gave a little gulp and added with a want of active wit almost pathetic to Spencer Coyle: 'The dangers, you know!'

'Do you mean he's thinking of his skin?'

Young Lechmere's eyes expanded appealingly, and what his instructor saw in his pink face – even thinking he saw a tear – was the dread of a disappointment shocking in the degree in which the loyalty of admiration had been great.

'Is he – is he beastly *afraid*?' repeated the honest lad with a quaver of suspense.

'Dear no!' said Spencer Coyle, turning his back.

On which young Lechmere felt a little snubbed and even a little ashamed. But still more he felt relieved.

III

Less than a week after this the elder man received a note from Miss Wingrave, who had immediately quitted London with her nephew. She proposed he should come down to Paramore for the following Sunday – Owen was really so tiresome. On the spot, in that house of examples and memories and in combination with her poor dear father, who was 'dreadfully annoyed', it might be worth their while to make a last stand. Mr Coyle read between the lines of this letter that the party at Paramore had got over a good deal of ground since Miss Wingrave, in Baker Street, had treated his despair as superficial. She wasn't an insinuating woman, but she went so far as to put the question on the ground of his conferring a particular favour on an afflicted family; and she expressed the pleasure it would give them should he be accompanied by Mrs Coyle, for whom she enclosed a separate invitation. She mentioned that she was also writing, subject to Mr Coyle's approval, to young Lechmere. She thought such a nice manly boy might do her wretched nephew some good. The celebrated crammer decided to embrace this occasion; and now it was the case not so much that he was angry as that he was anxious. As he directed his answer to Miss Wingrave's letter he caught himself smiling at the thought that at bottom he was going to defend his ex-pupil rather than to give him away. He said to his wife, who was a fair fresh slow woman – a person of much more presence than himself – that she had better take Miss Wingrave at her word: it was such an extraordinary, such a fascinating specimen of an old English home. This last allusion was softly sarcastic – he had accused the good lady more than once of being in love with Owen Wingrave. She admitted that she was, she even gloried in her passion; which shows that the subject, between them, was treated in a liberal spirit. She carried out the joke by accepting the invitation with eagerness. Young Lechmere was delighted to do the same; his instructor had good-naturedly taken the view that the little break would freshen him up for his last spurt.

It was the fact that the occupants of Paramore did indeed take their trouble hard that struck our friend after he had been an hour or two in that fine old house. This very short second visit, beginning on the Saturday evening, was to constitute the strangest episode of his life. As soon as he found himself in private with his wife – they had retired to dress for dinner – they called each other's attention with effusion and almost with alarm to the sinister gloom diffused through the place. The house was admirable from its old grey front, which came forward in wings so as to form three sides of a square, but Mrs Coyle made no scruple to declare that if she had known in advance the sort of impression she was going to receive she would never have put her foot in it. She characterized it as 'uncanny' and as looking wicked and weird, and she accused her husband of not having warned her properly. He had named to her in advance some of the appearances she was to expect, but while she almost feverishly dressed she had innumerable questions to ask. He hadn't told her about the girl, the extraordinary girl, Miss Julian – that is, he hadn't told her that this young lady, who in plain terms was a mere dependant, would be in effect, and as a consequence of the way she carried herself, the most important person in the house. Mrs Coyle was already prepared to announce that she hated Miss Julian's affectations. Her husband above all hadn't told her that they should find their young charge looking five years older.

'I couldn't imagine that,' Spencer said, 'nor that the character of the crisis here would be quite so perceptible. But I suggested to Miss Wingrave the other day that they should press her nephew in real earnest, and she has taken me at my word. They've cut off his supplies – they're trying to starve him out. That's not what I meant – but indeed I don't quite *know* to-day what I meant. Owen feels the pressure, but he won't yield.' The strange thing was that, now he was there, the brooding little coach knew still better, even while half-closing his eyes to it, that his own spirit had been caught up by a wave of reaction. If he was there it was because he was on poor Owen's side. His whole impression, his whole apprehension, had on the spot become much deeper. There was something in the young fanatic's very resistance that began to charm him. When his wife, in the intimacy of the conference I have mentioned, threw off the mask and commended even with extravagance the stand his pupil had taken (he was too good to be a horrid soldier and it was noble of him to suffer for his convictions – wasn't he as upright as a young hero, even though as pale as a Christian martyr?) the good lady only expressed the sympathy which, under cover of regarding his late inmate as a rare exception, he had already recognized in his own soul.

For, half an hour ago, after they had had superficial tea in the brown old hall of the house, that searcher into the reasons of things had proposed to him, before going to dress, a short turn outside, and had even, on the terrace, as they walked together to one of the far ends, passed his hand entreatingly into his companion's arm, permitting himself thus a familiarity unusual between pupil and master and calculated to show he had guessed whom he could most depend on to be kind to him. Spencer Coyle had on his own side guessed something, so that he wasn't surprised at the boy's having a particular confidence to make. He had felt on arriving that each member of the party would want to get hold of him first, and he knew that at that moment Jane Wingrave was peering through the ancient blur of one of the windows – the house had been modernized so little that the thick dim panes were three centuries old – to see whether her nephew looked as if he were poisoning the visitor's mind. Mr Coyle lost no time therefore in reminding the youth – though careful to turn it to a laugh as he did so – that he hadn't come down to Paramore to be corrupted. He had come down to make, face to face, a last appeal, which he hoped wouldn't be utterly vain. Owen smiled sadly as they went, asking him if he thought he had the general air of a fellow who was going to knock under.

'I think you look odd – I think you look ill,' Spencer Coyle said very honestly. They had paused at the end of the terrace.

'I've had to exercise a great power of resistance, and it rather takes it out of one.'

'Ah my dear boy, I wish your great power – for you evidently possess it – were exerted in a better cause!'

Owen Wingrave smiled down at his small but erect instructor. 'I don't believe that!' Then he added, to explain why: 'Isn't what you want (if you're so good as to think well of my character) to see me exert *most* power, in whatever direction? Well, this is the way I exert most.' He allowed he had had some terrible hours with his grandfather, who had denounced him in a way to make his hair stand up on his head. He had expected them not to like it, not a bit, but had had no idea they would make such a row. His aunt was different, but she was equally insulting. Oh they had made him feel they were ashamed of him; they accused him of putting a public dishonour on their name. He was the only one who had ever backed out – he was the first for three hundred years. Every one had known he was to go up, and now every one would know him for a young hypocrite who suddenly pretended to have scruples. They talked of his scruples as you wouldn't talk of a cannibal's god. His grandfather had called him outrageous names. 'He called me – he called me—' Here Owen faltered and his voice failed him. He looked as haggard as was possible to a young man in such splendid health.

'I probably know!' said Spencer Coyle with a nervous laugh.

His companion's clouded eyes, as if following the last strange consequences of things, rested for an instant on a distant object. Then they met his own and for another moment sounded them deeply. 'It isn't true. No, it isn't. It's not *that*!'

'I don't suppose it is! But what *do* you propose instead of it?'

'Instead of what?'

'Instead of the stupid solution of war. If you take that away you should suggest at least a substitute.'

'That's for the people in charge, for governments and cabinets,' said Owen. '*They'll* arrive soon enough at a substitute, in the particular case, if they're made to understand that they'll be hanged – and also drawn and quartered – if they don't find one. Make it a capital crime; *that* will quicken the wits of ministers!' His eyes brightened as he spoke, and he looked assured and exalted. Mr Coyle gave a sigh of sad surrender – it was really a stiff obsession. He saw the moment after this when Owen was on the point of asking if he too thought him a coward; but he was relieved to be able to judge that he either didn't suspect him of it or shrank uncomfortably from putting the question to the test. Spencer Coyle wished to show confidence, but somehow a direct assurance that he didn't doubt of his courage was too gross a compliment – it would be like saying he didn't doubt of his honesty. The difficulty was presently averted by Owen's continuing: 'My grandfather can't break the entail,[13] but I shall have nothing but this place, which, as you know, is small and, with the way rents are going, has quite ceased to yield an income. He has some money – not much, but such as it is he cuts me off. My aunt does the same – she has let me know her intentions. She was to have left me her six hundred a year. It was all settled, but now what's definite is that I don't get a penny of it if I give up the army. I must add in fairness that I have from my mother three hundred a year of my own. And I tell you the simple truth when I say I don't care a rap for the loss of the money.' The young man drew the long slow breath of a creature in pain; then he added: '*That's* not what worries me!'

'What are you going to do instead then?' his friend asked without other comment.

'I don't know – perhaps nothing. Nothing great at all events. Only something peaceful!'

Owen gave a weary smile, as if, worried as he was, he could yet appreciate the humorous effect of such a declaration from a Wingrave; but what it suggested to his guest, who looked up at him with a sense that he was after all not a Wingrave for nothing and had a military steadiness under fire, was the exasperation that such a profession, made in such a way and striking them as the last word of the inglorious, might well have produced on the part of his grandfather and his aunt. 'Perhaps nothing' – when he might carry on the great tradition! Yes, he wasn't weak, and he was interesting; but there was clearly a point of view from which he was provoking. 'What *is* it then that worries you?' Mr Coyle demanded.

'Oh the house – the very air and feeling of it. There are strange voices in it that seem to mutter at me – to say dreadful things as I pass. I mean the general consciousness and responsibility of what I'm doing. Of course it hasn't been easy for me – anything rather! I assure you I don't enjoy it.' With a light in them that was like a longing for justice Owen again bent his eyes on those of the little coach; then he pursued: 'I've started up all the old ghosts. The very portraits glower at me on the walls. There's one of my great-great-grandfather (the one the extraordinary story you know is about – the old fellow who hangs on the second landing of the big staircase) that fairly stirs on the canvas, just heaves a little, when I come near it. I have to go up and down stairs – it's rather awkward! It's what my aunt calls the family circle, and they sit, ever so grimly, in judgment. The circle's all constituted here, it's a kind of awful encompassing presence, it stretches away into the past, and when I came back with her the other day Miss Wingrave told me I wouldn't have the impudence to stand in the midst of it and say such things. I *had* to say them to my grandfather; but now that I've said them it seems to me the question's ended. I want to go away – I don't care if I never come back again.'

'Oh you *are* a soldier; you must fight it out!' Mr Coyle laughed.

The young man seemed discouraged at his levity, but as they turned round, strolling back in the direction from which they had come, he himself smiled faintly after an instant and replied: 'Ah we're tainted all!'

They walked in silence part of the way to the old portico; then the elder of the pair, stopping short after having assured himself he was at a sufficient distance from the house not to be heard, suddenly put the question: 'What does Miss Julian say?'

'Miss Julian?' Owen had perceptibly coloured.

'I'm sure *she* hasn't concealed her opinion.'

'Oh it's the opinion of the family-circle, for she's a member of it of course. And then she has her own as well.'

'Her own opinion?'

'Her own family-circle.'

'Do you mean her mother – that patient lady?'

'I mean more particularly her father, who fell in battle. And her grandfather, and *his* father, and her uncles and great-uncles – they all fell in battle.'

Mr Coyle, his face now rather oddly set, took it in. 'Hasn't the sacrifice of so many lives been sufficient? Why should she sacrifice *you*?'

'Oh she *hates* me!' Owen declared as they resumed their walk.

'Ah the hatred of pretty girls for fine young men!' cried Spencer Coyle.

He didn't believe in it, but his wife did, it appeared perfectly, when he mentioned this conversation while, in the fashion that has been described, the visitors dressed for dinner. Mrs Coyle had already discovered that nothing could have been nastier than Miss Julian's manner to the disgraced youth during the half-hour the party had spent in the hall; and it was this lady's judgment that one must have had no eyes in one's head not to see that she was already trying outrageously to flirt with young Lechmere. It was a pity they had brought that silly boy: he was down in the hall with the creature at that moment. Spencer Coyle's version was different – he believed finer elements involved. The girl's footing in the house was inexplicable on any ground save that of her being predestined to Miss Wingrave's nephew. As the niece of Miss Wingrave's own unhappy intended she had been devoted early by this lady to the office of healing by a union with the hope of the race the tragic breach that had separated their elders; and if in reply to this it was to be said that a girl of spirit couldn't enjoy in such a matter having her duty cut out for her, Owen's enlightened friend was ready with the argument that a young person in Miss Julian's position would never be such a fool as really to quarrel with a capital chance. She was familiar at Paramore and she felt safe; therefore she might treat herself to the amusement of pretending she had her option. It was all innocent tricks and airs. She had a curious charm, and it was vain to pretend that the heir of that house wouldn't seem good enough to a girl, clever as she might be, of eighteen. Mrs Coyle reminded her husband that their late charge was precisely now *not* of that house: this question was among the articles that exercised their wits after the two men had taken the turn on the terrace. Spencer then mentioned to his wife that Owen was afraid of the portrait of his great-great-grandfather. He would show it to her, since she hadn't noticed it, on their way downstairs.

'Why of his great-great-grandfather more than of any of the others?'

'Oh because he's the most formidable. He's the one who's sometimes seen.'

'Seen where?' Mrs Coyle had turned round with a jerk.

'In the room he was found dead in – the White Room they've always called it.'

'Do you mean to say the house has a proved *ghost*?' Mrs Coyle almost shrieked. 'You brought me here without telling me?'

'Didn't I mention it after my other visit?'

'Not a word. You only talked about Miss Wingrave.'

'Oh I was full of the story – you've simply forgotten.'

'Then you should have reminded me!'

'If I had thought of it I'd have held my peace – for you wouldn't have come.'

'I wish indeed I hadn't!' cried Mrs Coyle. 'But what,' she immediately asked, '*is* the story?'

'Oh a deed of violence that took place here ages ago. I think it was in George the Second's time that Colonel Wingrave, one of their ancestors, struck in a fit of passion one of his children, a lad just growing up, a blow on the head of which the unhappy child died. The matter was hushed up for the hour and some other explanation put about. The poor boy was laid out in one of those rooms on the other side of the house, and amid strange smothered rumours the funeral was hurried on. The next morning, when the household assembled, Colonel Wingrave was missing; he was looked for vainly, and at last it occurred to some one that he might perhaps be in the room from which his child had been carried to burial. The seeker knocked without an answer – then opened the door. The poor man lay dead on the floor, in his clothes, as if he had reeled and fallen back, without a wound, without a mark, without anything in his appearance to indicate that he had either struggled or suffered. He was a strong sound man – there was nothing to account for such a stroke. He's supposed to have gone to the room during the night, just before going to bed, in some fit of compunction or some fascination of dread. It was only after this that the truth about the boy came out. But no one ever sleeps in the room.'

Mrs Coyle had fairly turned pale. 'I hope not indeed! Thank heaven they haven't put *us* there!'

'We're at a comfortable distance – I know the scene of the event.'

'Do you mean you've been *in*—?'

'For a few moments. They're rather proud of the place and my young friend showed it me when I was here before.'

Mrs Coyle stared. 'And what is it like?'

'Simply an empty dull old-fashioned bedroom, rather big and furnished with the things of the "period". It's panelled from floor to ceiling, and the panels evidently, years and years ago, were painted white. But the paint has darkened with time and there are three or four quaint little ancient "samplers", framed and glazed, hung on the walls.'

Mrs Coyle looked round with a shudder. 'I'm glad there are no samplers here! I never heard anything so jumpy! Come down to dinner.'

On the staircase as they went her husband showed her the portrait of Colonel Wingrave – a representation, with some force and style, for the place and period, of a gentleman with a hard handsome face, in a red coat and a peruke. Mrs Coyle pronounced his descendant old Sir Philip wonderfully like him; and her husband could fancy, though he kept it to himself, that if one should have the courage to walk the old corridors of Paramore at night one might meet a figure that resembled him roaming, with the restlessness of a ghost, hand in hand with the figure of a tall boy. As he proceeded to the drawing-room with his wife he found himself suddenly wishing he had made more of a point of his pupil's going to Eastbourne. The evening how-ever seemed to have taken upon itself to dissipate any such whimsical forebodings, for the grimness of the family-circle, as he had preconceived its composition, was mitigated by an infusion of the 'neighbourhood'. The company at dinner was recruited by two cheerful couples, one of them the vicar and his wife, and by a silent young man who had come down to fish.

This was a relief to Mr Coyle, who had begun to wonder what was after all expected of him and why he had been such a fool as to come, and who now felt that for the first hours at least the situation wouldn't have directly to be dealt with. Indeed he found, as he had found before, sufficient occupation for his ingenuity in reading the various symptoms of which the social scene that spread about him was an expression. He should probably have a trying day on the morrow: he foresaw the difficulty of the long decorous Sunday and how dry Jane Wingrave's ideas, elicited in strenuous conference, would taste. She and her father would make him feel they depended upon him for the impossible, and if they should try to associate him with too tactless a policy he might end by telling them what he thought of it – an accident not required to make his visit a depressed mistake. The old man's actual design was evidently to let their friends see in it a positive mark of their being all right. The presence of the great London coach was tantamount to a profession of faith in the results of the impending examination. It had clearly been obtained from Owen, rather to the principal visitor's surprise, that he would do nothing to interfere with the apparent concord. He let the allusions to his hard work pass and, holding his tongue about his affairs, talked to the ladies as amicably as if he hadn't been 'cut off'. When Mr Coyle looked at him once or twice across the table, catching his eye, which showed an indefinable passion, he found a puzzling pathos in his laughing face: one couldn't resist a pang for a young lamb so visibly marked for sacrifice. 'Hang him, what a pity he's such a fighter!' he privately sighed – and with a want of logic that was only superficial.

This idea however would have absorbed him more if so much of his attention hadn't been for Kate Julian, who now that he had her well before him struck him as a remarkable and even as a possibly interesting young woman. The interest resided not in any extraordinary prettiness, for if she was handsome, with her long Eastern eyes, her magnificent hair and her general unabashed originality, he had seen complexions rosier and features that pleased him more: it dwelt in a strange impression that she gave of being exactly the sort of person whom, in her position, common considerations, those of prudence and perhaps even a little those of decorum, would have enjoined on her not to be. She was what was vulgarly termed a dependant – penniless patronized tolerated; but something in all her air conveyed that if her situation was inferior her spirit, to make up for it, was above precautions or submissions. It wasn't in the least that she was aggressive – she was too indifferent for that; it was only as if, having nothing either to gain or to lose, she could afford to do as she liked. It occurred to Spencer Coyle that she might really have had more at stake than her imagination appeared to take account of; whatever this quantity might be, at any rate, he had never seen a young woman at less pains to keep the safe side. He wondered inevitably what terms prevailed between Jane Wingrave and such an inmate as this; but those questions of course were unfathomable deeps. Perhaps keen Kate lorded it even over her protectress. The other time he was at Paramore he had received an impression that, with Sir Philip beside her, the girl could fight with her back to the wall. She amused Sir Philip, she charmed him, and he liked people who weren't afraid; between him and his daughter moreover there was no doubt which was the higher in command. Miss Wingrave took many things for granted, and most of all the rigour of discipline and the fate of the vanquished and the captive.

But between their clever boy and so original a companion of his childhood what odd relation would have grown up? It couldn't be indifference, and yet on the part of happy handsome youthful creatures it was still less likely to be aversion. They weren't Paul and Virginia,[14] but they must have had their common summer and their idyll: no nice girl could have disliked such a nice fellow for anything but not liking *her*, and no nice fellow could have resisted such propinquity. Mr Coyle remembered indeed that Mrs Julian had spoken to him as if the propinquity had been by no means constant, owing to her daughter's absences at school, to say nothing of Owen's; her visits to a few friends who were so kind as to 'take' her from time to time; her sojourns in London – so difficult to manage, but still managed by God's help – for 'advantages', for drawing and singing, especially drawing, or rather painting in oils, for which she had gained high credit. But the good lady had also mentioned that the young people were quite brother and sister, which *was* a little, after all, like Paul and Virginia. Mrs Coyle had been right, and it was apparent that Virginia was doing her best to make the time pass agreeably for young Lechmere. There was no such whirl of conversation as to render it an effort for our critic to reflect on these things: the tone of the occasion, thanks principally to the other guests, was not disposed to stray – it tended to the repetition of anecdote and the discussion of rents, topics that huddled together like uneasy animals. He could judge how intensely his hosts wished the evening to pass off as if nothing had happened; and this gave him the measure of their private resentment. Before dinner was over he found himself fidgety about his second pupil. Young Lechmere, since he began to cram, had done all that might have been expected of him; but this couldn't blind his instructor to a present perception of his being in moments of relaxation as innocent as a babe. Mr Coyle had considered that the amusements of Paramore would probably give him a fillip, and the poor youth's manner testified to the soundness of the forecast. The fillip had been unmistakably administered; it had come in the form of a revelation. The light on young Lechmere's brow announced with a candour that was almost an appeal for compassion, or at least a deprecation of ridicule, that he had never seen anything like Miss Julian.

IV

In the drawing-room after dinner the girl found a chance to approach Owen's late preceptor. She stood before him a moment, smiling while she opened and shut her fan, and then said abruptly, raising her strange eyes: 'I know what you've come for, but it isn't any use.'

'I've come to look after *you* a little. Isn't *that* any use?'

'It's very kind. But I'm not the question of the hour. You won't do anything with Owen.'

Spencer Coyle hesitated a moment. 'What will *you* do with his young friend?'

She stared, looked round her. 'Mr Lechmere? Oh poor little lad! We've been talking about Owen. He admires him so.'

'So do I. I should tell you that.'

'So do we all. That's why we're in such despair.'

'Personally then you'd *like* him to be a soldier?' the visitor asked.

'I've quite set my heart on it. I adore the army and I'm awfully fond of my old playmate,' said Miss Julian.

Spencer recalled the young man's own different version of her attitude; but he judged it loyal not to challenge her. 'It's not conceivable that your old playmate shouldn't be fond of you. He must therefore wish to please you; and I don't see why – between you, such clever young people as you are! – you don't set the matter right.'

'Wish to please me!' Miss Julian echoed. 'I'm sorry to say he shows no such desire. He thinks me an impudent wretch. I've told him what I think of *him*, and he simply hates me.'

'But you think so highly! You just told me you admire him.'

'His talents, his possibilities, yes; even his personal appearance, if I may allude to such a matter. But I don't admire his present behaviour.'

'Have you had the question out with him?' Spencer asked.

'Oh yes, I've ventured to be frank – the occasion seemed to excuse it. He couldn't like what I said.'

'What did you say?'

The girl, thinking a moment, opened and shut her fan again. 'Why – as we're such good old friends – that such conduct doesn't begin to be that of a gentleman!'

After she had spoken her eyes met Mr Coyle's, who looked into their ambiguous depths. 'What then would you have said without that tie?'

'How odd for *you* to ask that – in such a way!' she returned with a laugh. 'I don't understand your position: I thought your line was to *make* soldiers!'

'You should take my little joke. But, as regards Owen Wingrave, there's no "making" needed,' he declared. 'To my

sense' – and the little crammer paused as with a consciousness
of responsibility for his paradox – 'to my sense he *is*, in a high
sense of the term, a fighting man.'

'Ah let him prove it!' she cried with impatience and turning
short off.

Spencer Coyle let her go; something in her tone annoyed
and even not a little shocked him. There had evidently been a
violent passage between these young persons, and the reflexion
that such a matter was after all none of his business but troubled him the more. It was indeed a military house, and she was
at any rate a damsel who placed her ideal of manhood –
damsels doubtless always had their ideals of manhood – in the
type of the belted warrior. It was a taste like another; but even
a quarter of an hour later, finding himself near young Lechmere, in whom this type was embodied, Spencer Coyle was still
so ruffled that he addressed the innocent lad with a certain
magisterial dryness. 'You're under no pressure to sit up late,
you know. That's not what I brought you down for.' The dinner-
guests were taking leave and the bedroom candles twinkled in
a monitory row. Young Lechmere however was too agreeably
agitated to be accessible to a snub: he had a happy preoccupation which almost engendered a grin.

'I'm only too eager for bedtime. Do you know there's an
awfully jolly room?'

Coyle debated a moment as to whether he should take the
allusion – then spoke from his general tension. 'Surely they
haven't put you there?'

'No indeed: no one has passed a night in it for ages. But
that's exactly what I want to do – it would be tremendous fun.'

'And have you been trying to get Miss Julian's leave?'

'Oh *she* can't give it she says. But she believes in it, and she
maintains that no man has ever dared.'

'No man *shall* ever!' said Spencer with decision. 'A fellow in
your critical position in particular must have a quiet night.'

Young Lechmere gave a disappointed but reasonable sigh.
'Oh all right. But mayn't I sit up for a little go at Wingrave? I
haven't had any yet.'

Mr Coyle looked at his watch. 'You may smoke *one* cigarette.'

He felt a hand on his shoulder and turned round to see his wife tilting candle-grease upon his coat. The ladies were going to bed and it was Sir Philip's inveterate hour; but Mrs Coyle confided to her husband that after the dreadful things he had told her she positively declined to be left alone, for no matter how short an interval, in any part of the house. He promised to follow her within three minutes, and after the orthodox handshakes the ladies rustled away. The forms were kept up at Paramore as bravely as if the old house had no present intensity of heartache. The only one of which Coyle noticed the drop was some salutation to himself from Kate Julian. She gave him neither a word nor a glance, but he saw her look hard at Owen. Her mother, timid and pitying, was apparently the only person from whom this young man caught an inclination of the head. Miss Wingrave marshalled the three ladies – her little procession of twinkling tapers – up the wide oaken stairs and past the watching portrait of her ill-fated ancestor. Sir Philip's servant appeared and offered his arm to the old man, who turned a perpendicular back on poor Owen when the boy made a vague movement to anticipate this office. Mr Coyle learned later that before Owen had forfeited favour it had always, when he was at home, been his privilege at bedtime to conduct his grandfather ceremoniously to rest. Sir Philip's habits were contemptuously different now. His apartments were on the lower floor and he shuffled stiffly off to them with his valet's help, after fixing for a moment significantly on the most responsible of his visitors the thick red ray, like the glow of stirred embers, that always made his eyes conflict oddly with his mild manners. They seemed to say to poor Spencer 'We'll let the young scoundrel have it to-morrow!' One might have gathered from them that the young scoundrel, who had now strolled to the other end of the hall, had at least forged a cheque. His friend watched him an instant, saw him drop nervously into a chair and then with a restless movement get up. The same movement brought him back to where Mr Coyle stood addressing a last injunction to young Lechmere.

'I'm going to bed and I should like you particularly to con-
form to what I said to you a short time ago. Smoke a single
cigarette with our host here and then go to your room. You'll
have me down on you if I hear of your having, during the
night, tried any preposterous games.' Young Lechmere, looking down with his hands in his pockets, said nothing – he only
poked at the corner of a rug with his toe; so that his fellow
visitor, dissatisfied with so tacit a pledge, presently went on to
Owen: 'I must request you, Wingrave, not to keep so sensitive
a subject sitting up – and indeed to put him to bed and turn his
key in the door.' As Owen stared an instant, apparently not
understanding the motive of so much solicitude, he added:
'Lechmere has a morbid curiosity about one of your legends –
of your historic rooms. Nip it in the bud.'

'Oh the legend's rather good, but I'm afraid the room's an
awful sell!' Owen laughed.

'You know you don't *believe* that, my boy!' young Lechmere
returned.

'I don't think he does' – Mr Coyle noticed Owen's mottled
flush.

'He wouldn't try a night there himself!' their companion
pursued.

'I know who told you that,' said Owen, lighting a cigarette
in an embarrassed way at the candle, without offering one to
either of his friends.

'Well, what if she did?' asked the younger of these gentlemen, rather red. 'Do you want them *all* yourself?' he continued
facetiously, fumbling in the cigarette-box.

Owen Wingrave only smoked quietly; then he brought out:
'Yes – what if she did? But she doesn't know,' he added.

'She doesn't know what?'

'She doesn't know anything! – I'll tuck him in!' Owen went
on gaily to Mr Coyle, who saw that his presence, now a certain
note had been struck, made the young men uncomfortable.
He was curious, but there were discretions and delicacies, with
his pupils, that he had always pretended to practise; scruples
which however didn't prevent, as he took his way upstairs, his
recommending them not to be donkeys.

At the top of the staircase, to his surprise, he met Miss Julian, who was apparently going down again. She hadn't begun to undress, nor was she perceptibly disconcerted at seeing him. She nevertheless, in a manner slightly at variance with the rigour with which she had overlooked him ten minutes before, dropped the words: 'I'm going down to look for something. I've lost a jewel.'

'A jewel?'

'A rather good turquoise, out of my locket. As it's the only *real* ornament I've the honour to possess—!' And she began to descend.

'Shall I go with you and help you?' asked Spencer Coyle.

She paused a few steps below him, looking back with her Oriental eyes. 'Don't I hear our friends' voices in the hall?'

'Those remarkable young men are there.'

'*They'll* help me.' And Kate Julian passed down.

Spencer Coyle was tempted to follow her, but remembering his standard of tact he rejoined his wife in their apartment. He delayed nevertheless to go to bed and, though he looked into his dressing-room, couldn't bring himself even to take off his coat. He pretended for half an hour to read a novel; after which, quietly, or perhaps I should say agitatedly, he stepped from the dressing-room into the corridor. He followed this passage to the door of the room he knew to have been assigned to young Lechmere and was comforted to see it closed. Half an hour earlier he had noticed it stand open; therefore he could take for granted the bewildered boy had come to bed. It was of this he had wished to assure himself, and having done so he was on the point of retreating. But at the same instant he heard a sound in the room – the occupant was doing, at the window, something that showed him he might knock without the reproach of waking his pupil up. Young Lechmere came in fact to the door in his shirt and trousers. He admitted his visitor in some surprise, and when the door was closed again the latter said: 'I don't want to make your life a burden, but I had it on my conscience to see for myself that you're not exposed to undue excitement.'

'Oh there's plenty of that!' said the ingenuous youth. 'Miss Julian came down again.'

'To look for a turquoise?'

'So she said.'

'Did she find it?'

'I don't know. I came up. I left her with poor Owen.'

'Quite the right thing,' said Spencer Coyle.

'I don't know,' young Lechmere repeated uneasily. 'I left them quarrelling.'

'What about?'

'I don't understand. They're a quaint pair!'

Spencer turned it over. He had, fundamentally, principles and high decencies, but what he had in particular just now was a curiosity, or rather, to recognize it for what it was, a sympathy, which brushed them away. 'Does it strike you that *she's* down on him?' he permitted himself to enquire.

'Rather! – when she tells him he lies!'

'What do you mean?'

'Why before *me*. It made me leave them; it was getting too hot. I stupidly brought up the question of that bad room again, and said how sorry I was I had had to promise you not to try my luck with it.'

'You can't pry about in that gross way in other people's houses – you can't take such liberties, you know!' Mr Coyle interjected.

'I'm all right – see how good I am. I don't want to go *near* the place!' said young Lechmere confidingly. 'Miss Julian said to me "Oh I daresay *you'd* risk it, but" – and she turned and laughed at poor Owen – "that's more than we can expect of a gentleman who has taken *his* extraordinary line." I could see that something had already passed between them on the subject – some teasing or challenging of hers. It may have been only chaff, but his chucking the profession had evidently brought up the question of the white feather – I mean of his pluck.'

'And what did Owen say?'

'Nothing at first; but presently he brought out very quietly: "I spent all last night in the confounded place." We both stared and cried out at this and I asked him what he had seen there. He said he had seen nothing, and Miss Julian replied that he ought to tell his story better than that – he ought to make something good of it. "It's not a story – it's a simple fact," said he; on which she jeered at him and wanted to know why, if he had done it, he hadn't told her in the morning, since he knew what she thought of him. "I know, my dear, but I don't care," the poor devil said. This made her angry, and she asked him quite seriously whether he'd care if he should know she believed him to be trying to deceive us.'

'Ah what a brute!' cried Spencer Coyle.

'She's a most extraordinary girl – I don't know what she's up to,' young Lechmere quite panted.

'Extraordinary indeed – to be romping and bandying words at that hour of the night with fast young men!'

But young Lechmere made his distinction. 'I mean because I think she likes him.'

Mr Coyle was so struck with this unwonted symptom of subtlety that he flashed out: 'And do you think he likes *her*?'

It produced on his pupil's part a drop and a plaintive sigh. 'I don't know – I give it up! – But I'm sure he *did* see something or hear something,' the youth added.

'In that ridiculous place? What makes you sure?'

'Well, because he looks as if he had. I've an idea you can tell – in such a case. He behaves as if he had.'

'Why then shouldn't he name it?'

Young Lechmere wondered and found. 'Perhaps it's too bad to mention.'

Spencer Coyle gave a laugh. 'Aren't you glad then *you're* not in it?'

'Uncommonly!'

'Go to bed, you goose,' Spencer said with renewed nervous derision. 'But before you go tell me how he met her charge that he was trying to deceive you.'

' "Take me there yourself then and lock me in!" '

'And *did* she take him?'

'I don't know – I came up.'

He exchanged a long look with his pupil. 'I don't think they're in the hall now. Where's Owen's own room?'

'I haven't the least idea.'

Mr Coyle was at a loss; he was in equal ignorance and he couldn't go about trying doors. He bade young Lechmere sink to slumber; after which he came out into the passage. He asked himself if he should be able to find his way to the room Owen had formerly shown him, remembering that in common with many of the others it had its ancient name painted on it. But the corridors of Paramore were intricate; moreover some of the servants would still be up, and he didn't wish to appear unduly to prowl. He went back to his own quarters, where Mrs Coyle soon noted the continuance of his inability to rest. As she confessed for her own part, in the dreadful place, to an increased sense of 'creepiness', they spent the early part of the night in conversation, so that a portion of their vigil was inevitably beguiled by her husband's account of his colloquy with little Lechmere and by their exchange of opinions upon it. Toward two o'clock Mrs Coyle became so nervous about their persecuted young friend, and so possessed by the fear that that wicked girl had availed herself of his invitation to put him to an abominable test, that she begged her husband to go and look into the matter at whatever cost to his own tranquillity. But Spencer, perversely, had ended, as the perfect stillness of the night settled upon them, by charming himself into a pale acceptance of Owen's readiness to face God knew what unholy strain – an exposure the more trying to excited sensibilities as the poor boy had now learned by the ordeal of the previous night how resolute an effort he should have to make. 'I hope he *is* there,' he said to his wife: 'it puts them all so hideously in the wrong!' At any rate he couldn't take on himself to explore a house he knew so little. He was inconsequent – he didn't prepare for bed. He sat in the dressing-room with his light and his novel – he waited to find himself nod. At last however Mrs Coyle turned over and ceased to talk, and at last too he fell asleep in his chair. How long he slept he only knew afterwards by computation; what he knew to begin with was that he had started up in confusion and under the shock of an appalling sound. His consciousness cleared itself fast, helped doubtless by a confirmatory cry of horror from his wife's room. But he gave no heed to his wife; he had already bounded into the passage. There the sound was repeated – it was the 'Help! help!' of a woman in agonized terror. It came from a distant quarter of the house, but the quarter was sufficiently indicated. He rushed straight before him, the sound of opening doors and alarmed voices in his ears and the faintness of the early dawn in his eyes. At a turn of one of the passages he came upon the white figure of a girl in a swoon on a bench, and in the vividness of the revelation he read as he went that Kate Julian, stricken in her pride too late with a chill of compunction for what she had mockingly done, had, after coming to release the victim of her derision, reeled away, overwhelmed, from the catastrophe that was her work – the catastrophe that the next moment he found himself aghast at on the threshold of an open door. Owen Wingrave, dressed as he had last seen him, lay dead on the spot on which his ancestor had been found. He was all the young soldier on the gained field.

THE FRIENDS OF
THE FRIENDS

I find, as you prophesied, much that's interesting, but little that helps the delicate question – the possibility of publication. Her diaries are less systematic than I hoped; she only had a blessed habit of noting and narrating. She summarized, she saved; she appears seldom indeed to have let a good story pass without catching it on the wing. I allude of course not so much to things she heard as to things she saw and felt. She writes sometimes of herself, sometimes of others, sometimes of the combination. It's under this last rubric that she's usually most vivid. But it's not, you'll understand, when she's most vivid that she's always most publishable. To tell the truth she's fearfully indiscreet, or has at least all the material for making *me* so. Take as an instance the fragment I send you after dividing it for your convenience into several small chapters. It's the contents of a thin blank-book[1] which I've had copied out and which has the merit of being nearly enough a rounded thing, an intelligible whole. These pages evidently date from years ago. I've read with the liveliest wonder the statement they so circumstantially make and done my best to swallow the prodigy they leave to be inferred.[2] These things would be striking, wouldn't they? to any reader; but can you imagine for a moment my placing such a document before the world, even though, as if she herself had desired the world should have the benefit of it, she has given her friends neither name nor initials? Have you any sort of clue to their identity? I leave her the floor.

I

I know perfectly of course that I brought it upon myself; but that doesn't make it any better. I was the first to speak of her to him – he had never even heard her mentioned. Even if I had happened not to speak some one else would have made up for it: I tried afterwards to find comfort in that reflexion. But the comfort of reflexions is thin: the only comfort that counts in life is not to have been a fool.[3] That's a beatitude I shall doubt-less never enjoy. 'Why you ought to meet her and talk it over' is what I immediately said. 'Birds of a feather flock together.' I told him who she was and that they were birds of a feather because if he had had in youth a strange adventure she had had about the same time just such another. It was well known to her friends – an incident she was constantly called on to describe. She was charming clever pretty unhappy; but it was none the less the thing to which she had originally owed her reputation.

Being at the age of eighteen somewhere abroad with an aunt she had had a vision of one of her parents at the moment of death. The parent was in England hundreds of miles away and so far as she knew neither dying nor dead. It was by day, in the museum of some great foreign town. She had passed alone, in advance of her companions, into a small room containing some famous work of art and occupied at that moment by two other persons. One of these was an old custodian; the second, before observing him, she took for a stranger, a tourist. She was merely conscious that he was bareheaded and seated on a bench. The instant her eyes rested on him however she beheld to her amazement her father, who, as if he had long waited for her, looked at her in singular distress and an impatience that was akin to reproach. She rushed to him with a bewildered cry, 'Papa, what *is* it?' but this was followed by an exhibition of still livelier feeling when on her movement he simply vanished, leaving the custodian and her relations, who were by that time at her heels, to gather round her in dismay. These persons, the official, the aunt, the cousins, were therefore in a manner witnesses of the fact – the fact at least of the impression made on her; and there was the further testimony of a doctor who was attending one of the party and to whom it was immediately afterwards communicated. He gave her a remedy for hysterics, but said to the aunt privately: 'Wait and see if something doesn't happen at home.' Something *had* happened – the poor father, suddenly and violently seized, had died that morning. The aunt, the mother's sister, received before the day was out a telegram announcing the event and requesting her to prepare her niece for it. Her niece was already prepared, and the girl's sense of this visitation remained of course indelible. We had all, as her friends, had it conveyed to us and had conveyed it creepily to each other. Twelve years had elapsed, and as a woman who had made an unhappy marriage and lived apart from her husband she had become interesting from other sources; but since the name she now bore was a name frequently borne, and since moreover her judicial separation, as things were going, could hardly count as a distinction, it was usual to qualify her as 'the one, you know, who saw her father's ghost'.

As for him, dear man, he had seen his mother's – so there you are! I had never heard of that till this occasion on which our closer, our pleasanter acquaintance led him, through some turn of the subject of our talk, to mention it and to inspire me in so doing with the impulse to let him know that he had a rival in the field – a person with whom he could compare notes. Later on his story became for him, perhaps because of my unduly repeating it, likewise a convenient worldly label; but it hadn't a year before been the ground on which he was introduced to me. He had other merits, just as she, poor thing, had others. I can honestly say that I was quite aware of them from the first – I discovered them sooner than he discovered mine. I remember how it struck me even at the time that his sense of mine was quickened by my having been able to match, though not indeed straight from my own experience, his curious anecdote. It dated, this anecdote, as hers did, from some dozen years before – a year in which, at Oxford, he had for some reason of his own been staying on into the 'Long'.[4] He had been in the August afternoon on the river. Coming back into his room while it was still distinct daylight he found his mother standing there as if her eyes had been fixed on the door. He had had a letter from her that morning out of Wales, where she was staying with her father. At the sight of him she smiled with extraordinary radiance and extended her arms to him, and then as he sprang forward and joyfully opened his own she vanished from the place. He wrote to her that night, telling her what had happened; the letter had been carefully preserved. The next morning he heard of her death. He was through this chance of our talk extremely struck with the little prodigy I was able to produce for him. He had never encountered another case. Certainly they ought to meet, my friend and he; certainly they would have something in common. I would arrange this, wouldn't I? – if *she* didn't mind; for himself he didn't mind in the least. I had promised to speak to her of the matter as soon as possible, and within the week I was able to do so. She 'minded' as little as he; she was perfectly willing to see him. And yet no meeting was to occur – as meetings are commonly understood.

II

That's just half my tale – the extraordinary way it was hindered. This was the fault of a series of accidents; but the accidents, persisting for years, became, to me and to others, a subject of mirth with either party. They were droll enough at first, then they grew rather a bore. The odd thing was that both parties were amenable: it wasn't a case of their being indifferent, much less of their being indisposed. It was one of the caprices of chance, aided I suppose by some rather settled opposition of their interests and habits. His were centred in his office, his eternal inspectorship, which left him small leisure, constantly calling him away and making him break engagements. He liked society, but he found it everywhere and took it at a run. I never knew at a given moment where he was, and there were times when for months together I never saw him.

She was on her side practically suburban: she lived at Richmond and never went 'out'.[5] She was a woman of distinction, but not of fashion, and felt, as people said, her situation. Decidedly proud and rather whimsical, she lived her life as she had planned it. There were things one could do with her, but one couldn't make her come to one's parties. One went indeed a little more than seemed quite convenient to hers, which consisted of her cousin, a cup of tea and the view. The tea was good; but the view was familiar, though perhaps not, like the cousin – a disagreeable old maid who had been of the group at the museum and with whom she now lived – offensively so. This connexion with an inferior relative, which had partly an economic motive – she proclaimed her companion a marvellous manager – was one of the little perversities we had to forgive her. Another was her estimate of the proprieties created by her rupture with her husband. That was extreme – many persons called it even morbid. She made no advances; she cultivated scruples; she suspected, or I should perhaps rather say she remembered, slights: she was one of the few women I've known whom that particular predicament had rendered modest rather than bold. Dear thing, she had some delicacy! Especially marked were the limits she had set to possible attentions from men: it was always her thought that her husband only waited to pounce on her. She discouraged if she didn't forbid the visits of male persons not senile: she said she could never be too careful.

When I first mentioned to her that I had a friend whom fate had distinguished in the same weird way as herself I put her quite at liberty to say 'Oh bring him out to see me!' I should probably have been able to bring him, and a situation perfectly innocent or at any rate comparatively simple would have been created. But she uttered no such word; she only said: 'I must meet him certainly; yes, I shall look out for him!' That caused the first delay, and meanwhile various things happened. One of them was that as time went on she made, charming as she was, more and more friends, and that it regularly befell that these friends were sufficiently also friends of his to bring him up in conversation. It was odd that without belonging, as it were, to the same world or, according to the horrid term, the same set, my baffled pair should have happened in so many cases to fall in with the same people and make them join in the droll chorus. She had friends who didn't know each other but who inevitably and punctually recommended *him*. She had also the sort of originality, the intrinsic interest, that led her to be kept by each of us as a private resource, cultivated jealously, more or less in secret, as a person whom one didn't meet in society, whom it was not for every one – whom it was not for the vulgar – to approach, and with whom therefore acquaintance was particularly difficult and particularly precious. We saw her separately, with appointments and conditions, and found it made on the whole for harmony not to tell each other. Somebody had always had a note from her still later than somebody else. There was some silly woman who for a long time, among the unprivileged, owed to three simple visits to Richmond a reputation for being intimate with 'lots of awfully clever out-of-the-way people'.

Every one has had friends it has seemed a happy thought to bring together, and every one remembers that his happiest thoughts have not been his greatest successes; but I doubt if there was ever a case in which the failure was in such direct proportion to the quantity of influence set in motion. It's really perhaps here the quantity of influence that was most remarkable. My lady and my gentleman each pronounced it to me and others quite a subject for a roaring farce. The reason first given had with time dropped out of sight and fifty better ones flourished on top of it. They were so awfully alike: they had the same ideas and tricks and tastes, the same prejudices and superstitions and heresies; they said the same things and sometimes did them; they liked and disliked the same persons and places, the same books, authors and styles; there were touches of resemblance even in their looks and features. It established much of a propriety that they were in common parlance equally 'nice' and almost equally handsome. But the great sameness, for wonder and chatter, was their rare perversity in regard to being photographed. They were the only persons ever heard of who had never been 'taken' and who had a passionate objection to it. They just *wouldn't* be – no, not for anything any one could say. I had loudly complained of this; him in particular I had so vainly desired to be able to show on my drawing-room chimney-piece in a Bond Street frame.[6] It was at any rate the very liveliest of all the reasons why they ought to know each other – all the lively reasons reduced to naught by the strange law that had made them bang so many doors in each other's face, made them the buckets in the well, the two ends of the see-saw, the two parties in the State, so that when one was up the other was down, when one was out the other was in; neither by any possibility entering a house till the other had left it or leaving it all unawares till the other was at hand. They only arrived when they had been given up, which was precisely also when they departed. They were in a word alternate and incompatible; they missed each other with an inveteracy that could be explained only by its being preconcerted. It was however so far from preconcerted that it had ended – literally after several years – by disappointing and annoying them. I don't think their curiosity was lively till it had been proved utterly vain. A great deal was of course done to help them, but it merely laid wires for them to trip. To give examples I should have to have taken notes; but I happen to remember that neither had ever been able to dine on the right occasion. The right occasion for each was the occasion that would be wrong for the other. On the wrong one they were most punctual, and there were never any but wrong ones. The very elements conspired and the constitution of man re-enforced them. A cold, a headache, a bereavement, a storm, a fog, an earthquake, a cataclysm, infallibly intervened. The whole business was beyond a joke.

Yet as a joke it had still to be taken, though one couldn't help feeling that the joke had made the situation serious, had produced on the part of each a consciousness, an awkwardness, a positive dread of the last accident of all, the only one with any freshness left, the accident that *would* bring them together. The final effect of its predecessors had been to kindle this instinct. They were quite ashamed – perhaps even a little of each other. So much preparation, so much frustration: what indeed could be good enough for it all to lead up to? A mere meeting would be mere flatness. Did I see them at the end of years, they often asked, just stupidly confronted? If they were bored by the joke they might be worse bored by something else. They made exactly the same reflexions, and each in some manner was sure to hear of the other's. I really think it was this peculiar diffidence that finally controlled the situation. I mean that if they had failed for the first year or two because they couldn't help it, they kept up the habit because they had – what shall I call it? – grown nervous. It really took some lurking volition to account for anything both so regular and so ridiculous.

III

When to crown our long acquaintance I accepted his renewed offer of marriage it was humorously said, I know, that I had made the gift of his photograph a condition. This was so far true that I had refused to give him mine without it. At any rate I had him at last, in his high distinction, on the chimney-piece, where the day she called to congratulate me she came nearer than she had ever done to seeing him. He had in being taken set her an example that I invited her to follow; he had sacrificed his perversity – wouldn't she sacrifice hers? She too must give me something on my engagement – wouldn't she give me the companion-piece? She laughed and shook her head; she had headshakes whose impulse seemed to come from as far away as the breeze that stirs a flower. The companion-piece to the portrait of my future husband was the portrait of his future wife. She had taken her stand – she could depart from it as little as she could explain it. It was a prejudice, an *entêtement*,[7] a vow – she would live and die unphotographed. Now too she was alone in that state: this was what she liked; it made her so much more original. She rejoiced in the fall of her late associate and looked a long time at his picture, about which she made no memorable remark, though she even turned it over to see the back. About our engagement she was charming – full of cordiality and sympathy. 'You've known him even longer than I've *not*,' she said, 'and that seems a very long time.' She understood how we had jogged together over hill and dale and how inevitable it was that we should now rest together. I'm definite about all this because what followed is so strange that it's a kind of relief to me to mark the point up to which our relations were as natural as ever. It was I myself who in a sudden madness altered and destroyed them. I see now that she gave me no pretext and that I only found one in the way she looked at the fine face in the Bond Street frame. How then would I have had her look at it? What I had wanted from the first was to make her care for him. Well, that was what I still wanted – up to the moment of her having promised me she would on this occasion really aid me to break the silly spell that had kept them asunder. I had arranged with him to do his part if she would as triumphantly do hers. I was on a different footing now – I was on a footing to answer for him. I would positively engage that at five on the following Saturday he should be on that spot. He was out of town on pressing business, but, pledged to keep his promise to the letter, would return on purpose and in abundant time. 'Are you perfectly sure?' I remember she asked, looking grave and considering: I thought she had turned a little pale. She was tired, she was indisposed: it was a pity he was to see her after all at so poor a moment. If he only *could* have seen her five years before! However, I replied that this time I was sure and that success therefore depended simply on herself. At five o'clock on the Saturday she would find him in a particular chair I pointed out, the one in which he usually sat and in which – though this I didn't mention – he had been sitting when, the week before, he put the question of our future to me in the way that had brought me round. She looked at it in silence, just as she had looked at the photograph, while I repeated for the twentieth time that it was too preposterous one shouldn't somehow succeed in introducing to one's dearest friend one's second self. '*Am* I your dearest friend?' she asked with a smile that for a moment brought back her beauty. I replied by pressing her to my bosom; after which she said: 'Well, I'll come. I'm extraordinarily afraid, but you may count on me.'

When she had left me I began to wonder what she was afraid

of, for she had spoken as if she fully meant it. The next day, late in the afternoon, I had three lines from her: she had found on getting home the announcement of her husband's death. She hadn't seen him for seven years, but she wished me to know it in this way before I should hear of it in another. It made however in her life, strange and sad to say, so little difference that she would scrupulously keep her appointment. I rejoiced for her – I supposed it would make at least the difference of her having more money; but even in this diversion, far from forgetting she had said she was afraid, I seemed to catch sight of a reason for her being so. Her fear, as the evening went on, became contagious, and the contagion took in my breast the form of a sudden panic. It wasn't jealousy – it just was the dread of jealousy. I called myself a fool for not having been quiet till we were man and wife. After that I should somehow feel secure. It was only a question of waiting another month – a trifle surely for people who had waited so long. It had been plain enough she was nervous, and now she was free her nervousness wouldn't be less. What was it therefore but a sharp foreboding? She had been hitherto the victim of interference, but it was quite possible she would henceforth be the source of it. The victim in that case would be my simple self. What had the interference been but the finger of Providence pointing out a danger? The danger was of course for poor *me*. It had been kept at bay by a series of accidents unexampled in their frequency; but the reign of accident was now visibly at an end. I had an intimate conviction that both parties would keep the tryst. It was more and more impressed on me that they were approaching, converging. They were like the seekers for the hidden object in the game of blindfold; they had one and the other begun to 'burn'. We had talked about breaking the spell; well, it would be effectually broken – unless indeed it should merely take another form and overdo their encounters as it had overdone their escapes. This was something I couldn't sit still for thinking of; it kept me awake – at midnight I was full of unrest. At last I felt there was only one way of laying the ghost. If the reign of accident was over I must just take up the succession. I sat down and wrote a hurried note which would meet him on his return and which as the servants had gone to bed I sallied forth bareheaded into the empty gusty street to drop into the nearest pillar-box. It was to tell him that I shouldn't be able to be at home in the afternoon as I had hoped and that he must postpone his visit till dinner-time. This was an implication that he would find me alone.

IV

When accordingly at five she presented herself I naturally felt false and base. My act had been a momentary madness, but I had at least, as they say, to live up to it. She remained an hour; he of course never came; and I could only persist in my perfidy. I had thought it best to let her come; singular as this now seems to me I held it diminished my guilt. Yet as she sat there so visibly white and weary, stricken with a sense of everything her husband's death had opened up, I felt a really piercing pang of pity and remorse. If I didn't tell her on the spot what I had done it was because I was too ashamed. I feigned astonishment – I feigned it to the end; I protested that if ever I had had confidence I had had it that day. I blush as I tell my story – I take it as my penance. There was nothing indignant I didn't say about him; I invented suppositions, attenuations; I admitted in stupefaction, as the hands of the clock travelled, that their luck hadn't turned. She smiled at this vision of their 'luck', but she looked anxious – she looked unusual: the only thing that kept me up was the fact that, oddly enough, she wore mourning – no great depths of crape, but simple and scrupulous black. She had in her bonnet three small black feathers. She carried a little muff of astrachan.[8] This put me, by the aid of some acute reflexion, a little in the right. She had written to me that the sudden event made no difference for her, but apparently it made as much difference as that. If she was inclined to the usual forms why didn't she observe that of not going the first day or two out to tea? There was some one she wanted so much to see that she couldn't wait till her husband was buried. Such a betrayal of eagerness made me hard and cruel enough to practise my

THE FRIENDS OF THE FRIENDS   131

odious deceit, though at the same time, as the hour waxed and
waned, I suspected in her something deeper still than disappointment and somewhat less successfully concealed. I mean a
strange underlying relief, the soft low emission of the breath
that comes when a danger is past. What happened as she spent
her barren hour with me was that at last she gave him up. She
let him go for ever. She made the most graceful joke of it that
I've ever seen made of anything; but it was for all that a great
date in her life. She spoke with her mild gaiety of all the other
vain times, the long game of hide-and-seek, the unprecedented
queerness of such a relation. For it *was*, or had been, a relation,
wasn't it, hadn't it? That was just the absurd part of it. When
she got up to go I said to her that it was more a relation than
ever, but that I hadn't the face after what had occurred to propose to her for the present another opportunity. It was plain
that the only valid opportunity would be my accomplished
marriage. Of course she would be at my wedding? It was even
to be hoped that *he* would.

'If *I* am, he won't be!' – I remember the high quaver and the
little break of her laugh. I admitted there might be something
in that. The thing was therefore to get us safely married first.
'That won't help us. Nothing will help us!' she said as she
kissed me farewell. 'I shall never, never see him!' It was with
those words she left me.

I could bear her disappointment as I've called it; but when
a couple of hours later I received him at dinner I discovered I
couldn't bear his. The way my manœuvre might have affected
him hadn't been particularly present to me; but the result of it
was the first word of reproach that had ever yet dropped from
him. I say 'reproach' because that expression is scarcely too
strong for the terms in which he conveyed to me his surprise
that under the extraordinary circumstances I shouldn't have
found some means not to deprive him of such an occasion. I
might really have managed either not to be obliged to go out or
to let their meeting take place all the same. They would probably have got on, in my drawing-room, well enough without
me. At this I quite broke down – I confessed my iniquity and
the miserable reason of it. I hadn't put her off and I hadn't gone

out; she had been there and, after waiting for him an hour, had departed in the belief that he had been absent by his own fault.

'She must think me a precious brute!' he exclaimed. 'Did she say of me' – and I remember the just perceptible catch of breath in his pause – 'what she had a right to say?'

'I assure you she said nothing that showed the least feeling. She looked at your photograph, she even turned round the back of it, on which your address happens to be inscribed. Yet it provoked her to no demonstration. She doesn't care so much as all that.'

'Then why are you afraid of her?'

'It wasn't of her I was afraid. It was of you.'

'Did you think I'd be so sure to fall in love with her? You never alluded to such a possibility before,' he went on as I remained silent. 'Admirable person as you pronounced her, that wasn't the light in which you showed her to me.'

'Do you mean that if it *had* been you'd have managed by this time to catch a glimpse of her? I didn't fear things then,' I added. 'I hadn't the same reason.'

He kissed me at this, and when I remembered that she had done so an hour or two before I felt for an instant as if he were taking from my lips the very pressure of hers. In spite of kisses the incident had shed a certain chill, and I suffered horribly from the sense that he had seen me guilty of a fraud. He had seen it only through my frank avowal, but I was as unhappy as if I had a stain to efface. I couldn't get over the manner of his looking at me when I spoke of her apparent indifference to his not having come. For the first time since I had known him he seemed to have expressed a doubt of my word. Before we parted I told him that I'd undeceive her – start the first thing in the morning for Richmond and there let her know he had been blameless. At this he kissed me again. I'd expiate my sin, I said; I'd humble myself in the dust; I'd confess and ask to be forgiven. At this he kissed me once more.

V

In the train the next day this struck me as a good deal for him to have consented to; but my purpose was firm enough to carry me on. I mounted the long hill to where the view begins, and then I knocked at her door. I was a trifle mystified by the fact that her blinds were still drawn, reflecting that if in the stress of my compunction I had come early I had certainly yet allowed people time to get up.

'At home, mum?' She has left home for ever.'

I was extraordinarily startled by this announcement of the elderly parlour-maid. 'She has gone away?'

'She's dead, mum, please.' Then as I gasped at the horrible word: 'She died last night.'

The loud cry that escaped me sounded even in my own ears like some harsh violation of the hour. I felt for the moment as if I had killed her; I turned faint and saw through a vagueness the woman hold out her arms to me. Of what next happened I've no recollection, nor of anything but my friend's poor stupid cousin, in a darkened room, after an interval that I suppose very brief, sobbing at me in a smothered accusatory way. I can't say how long it took me to understand, to believe and then to press back with an immense effort that pang of responsibility which, superstitiously, insanely, had been at first almost all I was conscious of. The doctor, after the fact, had been superlatively wise and clear: he was satisfied of a long-latent weakness of the heart, determined probably years before by the agitations and terrors to which her marriage had introduced her. She had had in those days cruel scenes with her husband, she had been in fear of her life. All emotion, everything in the nature of anxiety and suspense had been after that to be strongly deprecated, as in her marked cultivation of a quiet life she was evidently well aware; but who could say that any one, especially a 'real lady', might be successfully protected from *every* little rub? She had had one a day or two before in the news of her husband's death – since there were shocks of all kinds, not only those of grief and surprise. For that matter she had never dreamed of so near a release: it had looked uncommonly as if he would live as long as herself. Then in the evening, in town, she had manifestly had some misadventure: something must have happened there that it would be imperative to clear up. She had come back very late – it was past eleven o'clock, and on being met in the hall by her cousin, who was extremely anxious, had allowed she was tired and must rest a moment before mounting the stairs. They had passed together into the dining-room, her companion proposing a glass of wine and bustling to the sideboard to pour it out. This took but a moment, and when my informant turned round our poor friend had not had time to seat herself. Suddenly, with a small moan that was barely audible, she dropped upon the sofa. She was dead. What unknown 'little rub' had dealt her the blow? What concussion, in the name of wonder, *had* awaited her in town? I mentioned immediately the one thinkable ground of disturbance – her having failed to meet at my house, to which by invitation for the purpose she had come at five o'clock, the gentleman I was to be married to, who had been accidentally kept away and with whom she had no acquaintance whatever. This obviously counted for little; but something else might easily have occurred: nothing in the London streets was more possible than an accident, especially an accident in those desperate cabs. What had she done, where had she gone on leaving my house? I had taken for granted she had gone straight home. We both presently remembered that in her excursions to town she sometimes, for convenience, for refreshment, spent an hour or two at the 'Gentlewomen', the quiet little ladies' club, and I promised that it should be my first care to make at that establishment an earnest appeal. Then we entered the dim and dreadful chamber where she lay locked up in death and where, asking after a little to be left alone with her, I remained for half an hour. Death had made her, had kept her beautiful; but I felt above all, as I knelt at her bed, that it had made her, had kept her silent. It had turned the key on something I was concerned to know.

On my return from Richmond and after another duty had been performed I drove to his chambers. It was the first time, but I had often wanted to see them. On the staircase, which, as the house contained twenty sets of rooms, was unrestrictedly public, I met his servant, who went back with me and ushered me in. At the sound of my entrance he appeared in the doorway of a further room, and the instant we were alone I produced my news: 'She's dead!'

'Dead?' He was tremendously struck, and I noticed he had no need to ask whom, in this abruptness, I meant.

'She died last evening – just after leaving me.'

He stared with the strangest expression, his eyes searching mine as for a trap. 'Last evening – after leaving you?' He repeated my words in stupefaction. Then he brought out, so that it was in stupefaction I heard, 'Impossible! I saw her.'

'You "saw" her?'

'On that spot – where you stand.'

This called back to me after an instant, as if to help me to take it in, the great wonder of the warning of his youth. 'In the hour of death – I understand: as you so beautifully saw your mother.'

'Ah *not* as I saw my mother – not that way, not that way!' He was deeply moved by my news – far more moved, it was plain, than he would have been the day before: it gave me a vivid sense that, as I had then said to myself, there was indeed a relation between them and that he had actually been face to face with her. Such an idea, by its reassertion of his extraordinary privilege, would have suddenly presented him as painfully abnormal hadn't he vehemently insisted on the difference. 'I saw her living. I saw her to speak to her. I saw her as I see you now.'

It's remarkable that for a moment, though only for a moment, I found relief in the more personal, as it were, but also the more natural, of the two odd facts. The next, as I embraced this image of her having come to him on leaving me and of just what it accounted for in the disposal of her time, I demanded with a shade of harshness of which I was aware: 'What on earth did she come for?'

He had now had a minute to think – to recover himself and judge of effects, so that if it was still with excited eyes he spoke he showed a conscious redness and made an inconsequent attempt to smile away the gravity of his words. 'She came just to see me. She came – after what had passed at your house – so that we *should*, nevertheless at last meet. The impulse seemed to me exquisite, and that was the way I took it.'

I looked round the room where she had been – where *she* had been and I never had till now. 'And was the way you took it the way she expressed it?'

'She only expressed it by being here and by letting me look at her. That was enough!' he cried with an extraordinary laugh.

I wondered more and more. 'You mean she didn't speak to you?'

'She said nothing. She only looked at me as I looked at her.'

'And you didn't speak either?'

He gave me again his painful smile. 'I thought of *you*. The situation was every way delicate. I used the finest tact. But she saw she had pleased me.' He even repeated his dissonant laugh.

'She evidently "pleased" you!' Then I thought a moment. 'How long did she stay?'

'How can I say? It seemed twenty minutes, but it was probably a good deal less.'

'Twenty minutes of silence!' I began to have my definite view and now in fact quite to clutch at it. 'Do you know you're telling me a thing positively monstrous?'

He had been standing with his back to the fire; at this, with a pleading look, he came to me. 'I beseech you, dearest, to take it kindly.'

I could take it kindly, and I signified as much; but I couldn't somehow, as he rather awkwardly opened his arms, let him draw me to him. So there fell between us for an appreciable time the discomfort of a great silence.

VI

He broke it by presently saying: 'There's absolutely no doubt of her death?'

'Unfortunately none. I've just risen from my knees by the bed where they've laid her out.'

He fixed his eyes hard on the floor; then he raised them to mine. 'How does she look?'

'She looks – at peace.'

He turned away again while I watched him; but after a moment he began: 'At what hour then—?'

'It must have been near midnight. She dropped as she reached her house – from an affection of the heart which she knew herself and her physician knew her to have, but of which, patiently, bravely, she had never spoken to me.'

He listened intently and for a minute was unable to speak. At last he broke out with an accent of which the almost boyish confidence, the really sublime simplicity, rings in my ears as I write: 'Wasn't she *wonderful!*' Even at the time I was able to do it justice enough to answer that I had always told him so; but the next minute, as if after speaking he had caught a glimpse of what he might have made me feel, he went on quickly: 'You can easily understand that if she didn't get home till midnight—'

I instantly took him up. 'There was plenty of time for you to have seen her? How so,' I asked, 'when you didn't leave my house till late? I don't remember the very moment – I was pre-occupied. But you know that though you said you had lots to do you sat for some time after dinner. She, on her side, was all the evening at the "Gentlewomen", I've just come from there – I've ascertained. She had tea there; she remained a long long time.'

'What was she doing all the long long time?'

I saw him eager to challenge at every step my account of the matter; and the more he showed this the more I was moved to emphasize that version, to prefer with apparent perversity an explanation which only deepened the marvel and the mystery, but which, of the two prodigies it had to choose from, my reviving jealousy found easiest to accept. He stood there pleading with a candour that now seems to me beautiful for the privilege of having in spite of supreme defeat known the living woman; while I, with a passion I wonder at to-day, though it still smoulders in a manner in its ashes, could only reply that, through a strange gift shared by her with his mother and on her own side likewise hereditary, the miracle of his youth had been renewed for him, the miracle of hers for her. She had been to him – yes, and by an impulse as charming as he liked; but oh she hadn't been in the body! It was a simple question of evidence. I had had, I maintained, a definite statement of what she had done – most of the time – at the little club. The place was almost empty, but the servants had noticed her. She had sat motionless in a deep chair by the drawing-room fire; she had leaned back her head, she had closed her eyes, she had seemed softly to sleep.

'I see. But till what o'clock?'

'There,' I was obliged to answer, 'the servants fail me a little. The portress in particular is unfortunately a fool, even though she too is supposed to be a Gentlewoman. She was evidently at that period of the evening, without a substitute and against regulations, absent for some little time from the cage in which it's her business to watch the comings and goings. She's muddled, she palpably prevaricates; so I can't positively, from her observation, give you an hour. But it was remarked toward half-past ten that our poor friend was no longer in the club.'

It suited him down to the ground. 'She came straight here, and from here she went straight to the train.'

'She couldn't have run it so close,' I declared. 'That was a thing she particularly never did.'

'There was no need of running it close, my dear – she had plenty of time. Your memory's at fault about my having left you late: I left you, as it happens, unusually early. I'm sorry my stay with you seemed long, for I was back here by ten.'

'To put yourself into your slippers,' I retorted, 'and fall asleep in your chair. You slept till morning – you saw her in a dream!' He looked at me in silence and with sombre eyes – eyes that showed me he had some irritation to repress. Presently I went on: 'You had a visit, at an extraordinary hour, from a lady – soit:[10] nothing in the world's more probable. But there are ladies and ladies. How in the name of goodness, if she was unannounced and dumb and you had into the bargain never seen the least portrait of her – how could you identify the person we're talking of?'

'Haven't I to absolute satiety heard her described? I'll describe her for you in every particular.'

'Don't!' I cried with a promptness that made him laugh once more. I coloured at this, but I continued: 'Did your servant introduce her?'

'He wasn't here – he's always away when he's wanted. One of the features of this big house is that from the street-door the different floors are accessible practically without challenge. My servant makes love to a young person employed in the rooms above these, and he had a long bout of it last evening. When he's out on that job he leaves my outer door, on the staircase, so much ajar as to enable him to slip back without a sound. The door then only requires a push. She pushed it – that simply took a little courage.'

'A little? It took tons! And it took all sorts of impossible calculations.'

'Well, she had them – she made them. Mind you, I don't deny for a moment,' he added, 'that it was very very wonderful!'

Something in his tone kept me a time from trusting myself to speak. At last I said: 'How did she come to know where you live?'

'By remembering the address on the little label the shop-people happily left sticking to the frame I had had made for my photograph.'

'And how was she dressed?'

'In mourning, my own dear. No great depths of crape, but simple and scrupulous black. She had in her bonnet three small black feathers. She carried a little muff of astrachan. She has near the left eye,' he continued, 'a tiny vertical scar—'

I stopped him short. 'The mark of a caress from her husband.' Then I added: 'How close you must have been to her!' He made no answer to this, and I thought he blushed, observing which I broke straight off. 'Well, goodbye.'

'You won't stay a little?' He came to me again tenderly, and this time I suffered him. 'Her visit had its beauty,' he murmured as he held me, 'but yours has a greater one.'

I let him kiss me, but I remembered, as I had remembered the day before, that the last kiss she had given, as I supposed, in this world had been for the lips he touched. 'I'm life, you see,' I answered. 'What you saw last night was death.'

'It was life – it was life!'

He spoke with a soft stubbornness – I disengaged myself. We stood looking at each other hard. 'You describe the scene – so far as you describe it at all – in terms that are incomprehensible. She was in the room before you knew it?'

'I looked up from my letter-writing – at that table under the lamp I had been wholly absorbed in it – and she stood before me.'

'Then what did you do?'

'I sprang up with an ejaculation, and she, with a smile, laid her finger, ever so warningly, yet with a sort of delicate dignity, to her lips. I knew it meant silence, but the strange thing was that it seemed immediately to explain and to justify her. We at any rate stood for a time that, as I've told you, I can't calculate, face to face. It was just as you and I stand now.'

'Simply staring?'

He shook an impatient head. 'Ah! *we're* not staring!'

'Yes, but we're talking.'

'Well, *we* were – after a fashion.' He lost himself in the memory of it. 'It was as friendly as this.' I had on my tongue's end to ask if that was saying much for it, but I made the point instead that what they had evidently done was to gaze in mutual admiration. Then I asked if his recognition of her had been immediate. 'Not quite,' he replied, 'for of course I didn't expect her; but it came to me long before she went who she was – who only she could be.'

I thought a little. 'And how did she at last go?'

'Just as she arrived. The door was open behind her and she passed out.'

'Was she rapid – slow?'

'Rather quick. But looking behind her,' he smiled to add. 'I let her go, for I perfectly knew I was to take it as she wished.'

I was conscious of exhaling a long vague sigh. 'Well, you must take it now as *I* wish – you must let *me* go.'

At this he drew near me again, detaining and persuading me, declaring with all due gallantry that I was a very different matter. I'd have given anything to have been able to ask him if he had touched her, but the words refused to form themselves: I knew to the last tenth of a tone how horrid and vulgar they'd sound. I said something else – I forget exactly what; it was feebly tortuous and intended, meanly enough, to make him tell me without my putting the question. But he didn't tell me; he only repeated, as from a glimpse of the propriety of soothing and consoling me, the sense of his declaration of some minutes before – the assurance that she was indeed exquisite, as I had always insisted, but that I was his 'real' friend and his very own for ever. This led me to reassert, in the spirit of my previous rejoinder, that I had at least the merit of being alive; which in turn drew from him again the flash of contradiction I dreaded. 'Oh *she* was alive! She was, she was!'

'She was dead, she was dead!' I asseverated with an energy, a determination it should *be* so, which comes back to me now almost as grotesque. But the sound of the word as it rang out filled me suddenly with horror, and all the natural emotion the meaning of it might have evoked in other conditions gathered and broke in a flood. It rolled over me that here was a great affection quenched and how much I had loved and trusted her. I had a vision at the same time of the lonely beauty of her end. 'She's gone – she's lost to us for ever!' I burst into sobs.

'That's exactly what I feel,' he exclaimed, speaking with extreme kindness and pressing me to him for comfort. 'She's gone; she's lost to us for ever: so what does it matter now?' He bent over me, and when his face had touched mine I scarcely knew if it were wet with my tears or with his own.

VII

It was my theory, my conviction, it became, as I may say, my attitude, that they had still never 'met'; and it was just on this ground I felt it generous to ask him to stand with me at her grave. He did so very modestly and tenderly, and I assumed, though he himself clearly cared nothing for the danger, that the solemnity of the occasion, largely made up of persons who had known them both and had a sense of the long joke, would sufficiently deprive his presence of all light association. On the question of what had happened the evening of her death little more passed between us; I had been taken by a horror of the element of evidence. On either hypothesis it was gross and prying. He on his side lacked producible corroboration – everything, that is, but a statement of his house-porter, on his own admission a most casual and intermittent personage – that between the hours of ten o'clock and midnight no less than three ladies in deep black had flitted in and out of the place. This proved far too much; we had neither of us any use for three. He knew I considered I had accounted for every fragment of her time, and we dropped the matter as settled; we abstained from further discussion. What *I* knew however was that he abstained to please me rather than because he yielded to my reasons. He didn't yield – he was only indulgent; he clung to his interpretation because he liked it better. He liked it better, I held, because it had more to say to his vanity. That, in a similar position, wouldn't have been its effect on me, though I had doubtless quite as much; but these are things of individual humour and as to which no person can judge for another. I should have supposed it more gratifying to be the subject of one of those inexplicable occurrences that are chronicled in thrilling books and disputed about at learned meetings; I could conceive, on the part of a being just engulfed in the infinite and still vibrating with human emotion, of nothing more fine and pure, more high and august, than such an impulse of reparation, of admonition, or even of curiosity. *That* was beautiful, if one would, and I should in his place have thought more of myself for being so distinguished and so selected. It was public that he had already, that he had long figured in that light, and what was such a fact in itself but almost a proof? Each of the strange visitations contributed to establish the other. He had a different feeling; but he had also, I hasten to add, an unmistakable desire not to make a stand or, as they say, a fuss about it. I might believe what I liked – the more so that the whole thing was in a manner a mystery of my producing. It was an event of my history, a puzzle of my consciousness, not of his; therefore he would take about it any tone that struck me as convenient. We had both at all events other business on hand; we were pressed with preparations for our marriage.

Mine were assuredly urgent, but I found as the days went on that to believe what I 'liked' was to believe what I was more and more intimately convinced of. I found also that I didn't like it so much as that came to, or that the pleasure at all events was far from being the cause of my conviction. My obsession, as I may really call it and as I began to perceive, refused to be elbowed away, as I had hoped, by my sense of paramount duties. If I had a great deal to do I had still more to think of, and the moment came when my occupations were gravely menaced by my thoughts. I see it all now, I feel it, I live it over. It's terribly void of joy, it's full indeed to overflowing of bitterness; and yet I must do myself justice – I couldn't have been other than I was. The same strange impressions, had I to meet them again, would produce the same deep anguish, the same sharp doubts, the same still sharper certainties. Oh it's all easier to remember than to write, but even could I retrace the business hour by hour, could I find terms for the inexpressible, the ugliness and the pain would quickly stay my hand. Let me then note very simply and briefly that a week before our wedding-day, three weeks after her death, I knew in all my fibres that I had something very serious to look in the face and that if I was to make this effort I must make it on the spot and before another hour should elapse. My unextinguished jealousy – that was the Medusa-mask.[11] It hadn't died with her death, it had lividly survived, and it was fed by suspicions unspeakable. They *would* be unspeakable to-day, that is, if I hadn't felt the sharp need of uttering them at the time. This need took possession of me – to save me, as it seemed, from my fate. When once it had done so I saw – in the urgency of the case, the diminishing hours and shrinking interval – only one issue, that of absolute promptness and frankness. I could at least not do him the wrong of delaying another day; I could at least treat my difficulty as too fine for a subterfuge. Therefore very quietly, but none the less abruptly and hideously, I put it before him on a certain evening that we must reconsider our situation and recognize that it had completely altered.

He stared bravely. 'How in the world altered?'

'Another person has come between us.'

He took but an instant to think. 'I won't pretend not to know whom you mean.' He smiled in pity for my aberration, but he meant to be kind. 'A woman dead and buried!'

'She's buried, but she's not dead. She's dead for the world – she's dead for me. But she's not dead for you.'

'You hark back to the different construction we put on her appearance that evening?'

'No,' I answered, 'I hark back to nothing. I've no need of it. I've more than enough with what's before me.'

'And pray, darling, what may that be?'

'You're completely changed.'

'By that absurdity?' he laughed.

'Not so much by that one as by other absurdities that have followed it.'

'And what may *they* have been?'

We had faced each other fairly, with eyes that didn't flinch; but his had a dim strange light, and my certitude triumphed in his perceptible paleness. 'Do you really pretend,' I asked, 'not to know what they are?'

'My dear child,' he replied, 'you describe them too sketchily!'

I considered a moment. 'One may well be embarrassed to finish the picture! But from that point of view – and from the beginning – what was ever more embarrassing than your idiosyncrasy?'

He invoked his vagueness – a thing he always did beautifully. 'My idiosyncrasy?'

'Your notorious, your peculiar power.'

He gave a great shrug of impatience, a groan of overdone disdain. 'Oh my peculiar power!'

'Your accessibility to forms of life,' I coldly went on, 'your command of impressions, appearances, contacts, closed – for our gain or our loss – to the rest of us. That was originally a part of the deep interest with which you inspired me – one of the reasons I was amused, I was indeed positively proud, to know you. It was a magnificent distinction; it's a magnificent distinction still. But of course I had no prevision then of the way it would operate now; and even had that been the case I should have had none of the extraordinary way in which its action would affect me.'

'To what in the name of goodness,' he pleadingly enquired, 'are you fantastically alluding?' Then as I remained silent, gathering a tone for my charge, 'How in the world *does* it operate?' he went on; 'and how in the world are you affected?'

'She missed you for five years,' I said, 'but she never misses you now. You're making it up!'

'Making it up?' He had begun to turn from white to red.

'You see her – you see her: you see her every night!' He gave a loud sound of derision, but I felt it ring false. 'She comes to you as she came that evening,' I declared; 'having tried it she found she liked it!' I was able, with God's help, to speak without blind passion or vulgar violence; but those were the exact words – and far from 'sketchy' they then appeared to me – that I uttered. He had turned away in his laughter, clapping his hands at my folly, but in an instant he faced me again with a change of expression that struck me. 'Do you dare to deny,' I then asked, 'that you habitually see her?'

He had taken the line of indulgence, of meeting me halfway and kindly humouring me. At all events he to my astonishment suddenly said: 'Well, my dear, what if I do?'

'It's your natural right: it belongs to your constitution and to your wonderful if not perhaps quite enviable fortune. But you'll easily understand that it separates us. I unconditionally release you.'

'Release me?'

'You must choose between me and her.'

He looked at me hard. 'I see.' Then he walked away a little, as if grasping what I had said and thinking how he had best treat it. At last he turned on me afresh. 'How on earth do you know such an awfully private thing?'

'You mean because you've tried so hard to hide it? It *is* awfully private, and you may believe I shall never betray you. You've done your best, you've acted your part, you've behaved, poor dear! loyally and admirably. Therefore I've watched you in silence, playing my part too; I've noted every drop in your voice, every absence in your eyes, every effort in your indifferent hand: I've waited till I was utterly sure and miserably unhappy. How *can* you hide it when you're abjectly in love with her, when you're sick almost to death with the joy of what she gives you?' I checked his quick protest with a quicker gesture. 'You love her as you've *never* loved, and, passion for passion, she gives it straight back! She rules you, she holds you, she has you all! A woman, in such a case as mine, divines and feels and sees; she's not a dull dunce who has to be "credibly informed". You come to me mechanically, compunctiously, with the dregs of your tenderness and the remnant of your life. I can renounce you, but I can't share you: the best of you is hers, I know what it is and freely give you up to her for ever!'

He made a gallant fight, but it couldn't be patched up; he repeated his denial, he retracted his admission, he ridiculed my charge, of which I freely granted him moreover the indefensible extravagance. I didn't pretend for a moment that we were talking of common things; I didn't pretend for a moment that he and she were common people. Pray, if they *had* been, how should I ever have cared for them? They had enjoyed a rare extension of being and they had caught me up in their flight; only I couldn't breathe in such air and I promptly asked to be set down. Everything in the facts was monstrous, and most of all my lucid perception of them; the only thing allied to nature and truth was my having to act on that perception. I felt after I had spoken in this sense that my assurance was complete; nothing had been wanting to it but the sight of my effect on him. He disguised indeed the effect in a cloud of chaff, a diversion that gained him time and covered his retreat. He challenged my sincerity, my sanity, almost my humanity, and that of course widened our breach and confirmed our rupture. He did everything in short but convince me either that I was wrong or that he was unhappy: we separated and I left him to his inconceivable communion.

He never married, any more than I've done. When six years later, in solitude and silence, I heard of his death I hailed it as a direct contribution to my theory. It was sudden, it was never properly accounted for, it was surrounded by circumstances in which – for oh I took them to pieces! – I distinctly read an intention, the mark of his own hidden hand. It was the result of a long necessity, of an unquenchable desire. To say exactly what I mean, it was a response to an irresistible call.

THE TURN OF THE SCREW

The story had held us, round the fire, sufficiently breathless, but except the obvious remark that it was gruesome, as on Christmas Eve in an old house a strange tale should essentially be, I remember no comment uttered till somebody happened to note it as the only case he had met in which such a visitation had fallen on a child. The case, I may mention, was that of an apparition in just such an old house as had gathered us for the occasion – an appearance, of a dreadful kind, to a little boy sleeping in the room with his mother and waking her up in the terror of it; waking her not to dissipate his dread and soothe him to sleep again, but to encounter also herself, before she had succeeded in doing so, the same sight that had shocked him. It was this observation that drew from Douglas – not immediately, but later in the evening – a reply that had the interesting consequence to which I call attention. Some one else told a story not particularly effective, which I saw he was not following. This I took for a sign that he had himself something to produce and that we should only have to wait. We waited in fact till two nights later; but that same evening, before we scattered, he brought out what was in his mind.

'I quite agree – in regard to Griffin's ghost, or whatever it was – that its appearing first to the little boy, at so tender an age, adds a particular touch. But it's not the first occurrence of its charming kind that I know to have been concerned with a child. If the child gives the effect another turn of the screw, what do you say to *two* children—?'

'We say of course,' somebody exclaimed, 'that two children give two turns! Also that we want to hear about them.'

I can see Douglas there before the fire, to which he had got up to present his back, looking down at this converser with his hands in his pockets. 'Nobody but me, till now, has ever heard. It's quite too horrible.' This was naturally declared by several voices to give the thing the utmost price, and our friend, with quiet art, prepared his triumph by turning his eyes over the rest of us and going on: 'It's beyond everything. Nothing at all that I know touches it.'

'For sheer terror?' I remember asking.

He seemed to say it wasn't so simple as that; to be really at a loss how to qualify it. He passed his hand over his eyes, made a little wincing grimace. 'For dreadful – dreadfulness!'

'Oh how delicious!' cried one of the women.

He took no notice of her; he looked at me, but as if, instead of me, he saw what he spoke of. 'For general uncanny ugliness and horror and pain.'

'Well then,' I said, 'just sit right down and begin.'

He turned round to the fire, gave a kick to a log, watched it an instant. Then as he faced us again: 'I can't begin. I shall have to send to town.' There was a unanimous groan at this, and much reproach; after which, in his preoccupied way, he explained. 'The story's written. It's in a locked drawer – it has not been out for years. I could write to my man and enclose the key; he could send down the packet as he finds it.' It was to me in particular that he appeared to propound this – appeared almost to appeal for aid not to hesitate. He had broken a thickness of ice, the formation of many a winter; had had his reasons for a long silence. The others resented postponement, but it was just his scruples that charmed me. I adjured him to write by the first post and to agree with us for an early hearing; then I asked him if the experience in question had been his own. To this his answer was prompt. 'Oh thank God, no!'

'And is the record yours? You took the thing down?'

'Nothing but the impression. I took that *here*' – he tapped his heart. 'I've never lost it.'

'Then your manuscript—?'

'Is in old faded ink and in the most beautiful hand.' He hung fire again. 'A woman's. She has been dead these twenty years. She sent me the pages in question before she died.' They were all listening now, and of course there was somebody to be arch, or at any rate to draw the inference. But if he put the inference by without a smile it was also without irritation. 'She was a most charming person, but she was ten years older than I. She was my sister's governess,' he quietly said. 'She was the most agreeable woman I've ever known in her position; she'd have been worthy of any whatever. It was long ago, and this episode was long before. I was at Trinity, and I found her at home on my coming down the second summer. I was much there that year – it was a beautiful one; and we had, in her off-hours, some strolls and talks in the garden – talks in which she struck me as awfully clever and nice. Oh yes; don't grin: I liked her extremely and am glad to this day to think she liked me too. If she hadn't she wouldn't have told me. She had never told any one. It wasn't simply that she said so, but that I knew she hadn't. I was sure; I could see. You'll easily judge why when you hear.'

'Because the thing had been such a scare?'

He continued to fix me. 'You'll easily judge,' he repeated: '*you* will.'

I fixed him too. 'I see. She was in love.'

He laughed for the first time. 'You *are* acute. Yes, she was in love. That is she *had* been. That came out – she couldn't tell her story without its coming out. I saw it, and she saw I saw it; but neither of us spoke of it. I remember the time and the place – the corner of the lawn, the shade of the great beeches and the long hot summer afternoon. It wasn't a scene for a shudder; but oh—!' He quitted the fire and dropped back into his chair.

'You'll receive the packet Thursday morning?' I said.

'Probably not till the second post.'

'Well then; after dinner—'

'You'll all meet me here?' He looked us round again. 'Isn't anybody going?' It was almost the tone of hope.

'Everybody will stay!'

'*I* will – and *I* will!' cried the ladies whose departure had been fixed. Mrs Griffin, however, expressed the need for a little more light. 'Who was it she was in love with?'

'The story will tell,' I took upon myself to reply.

'Oh I can't wait for the story!'

'The story *won't* tell,' said Douglas; 'not in any literal vulgar way.'

'More's the pity then. That's the only way I ever understand.'

'Won't *you* tell, Douglas?' somebody else enquired.

He sprang to his feet again. 'Yes – to-morrow. Now I must go to bed. Good-night.' And, quickly catching up a candlestick, he left us slightly bewildered. From our end of the great brown hall we heard his step on the stair; whereupon Mrs Griffin spoke. 'Well, if I don't know who she was in love with I know who *he* was.'

'She was ten years older,' said her husband.

'*Raison de plus*[1] – at that age! But it's rather nice, his long reticence.'

'Forty years!' Griffin put in.

'With this outbreak at last.'

'The outbreak,' I returned, 'will make a tremendous occasion of Thursday night'; and every one so agreed with me that in the light of it we lost all attention for everything else. The last story, however incomplete and like the mere opening of a serial, had been told; we handshook and 'candlestuck',[2] as somebody said, and went to bed.

I knew the next day that a letter containing the key had, by the first post, gone off to his London apartments; but in spite of – or perhaps just on account of – the eventual diffusion of this knowledge we quite let him alone till after dinner, till such an hour of the evening in fact as might best accord with the kind of emotion on which our hopes were fixed. Then he became as communicative as we could desire, and indeed gave us his best reason for being so. We had it from him again before the fire in the hall, as we had had our mild wonders of the previous night. It appeared that the narrative he had promised to read us really required for a proper intelligence a few words of prologue. Let me say here distinctly, to have done with it, that this narrative, from an exact transcript of my own made much later, is what I shall presently give. Poor Douglas, before his death – when it was in sight – committed to me the manuscript that reached him on the third of these days and that, on the same spot, with immense effect, he began to read to our hushed little circle on the night of the fourth. The departing ladies who had said they would stay didn't, of course, thank heaven, stay: they departed, in consequence of arrangements made, in a rage of curiosity, as they professed, produced by the touches with which he had already worked us up. But that only made his little final auditory more compact and select, kept it, round the hearth, subject to a common thrill.

The first of these touches conveyed that the written statement took up the tale at a point after it had, in a manner, begun. The fact to be in possession of was therefore that his old friend, the youngest of several daughters of a poor country parson, had at the age of twenty, on taking service for the first time in the schoolroom, come up to London, in trepidation, to answer in person an advertisement that had already placed her in brief correspondence with the advertiser. This person proved, on her presenting herself for judgment at a house in Harley Street[3] that impressed her as vast and imposing – this prospective patron proved a gentleman, a bachelor in the prime of life, such a figure as had never risen, save in a dream or an old novel, before a fluttered anxious girl out of a Hampshire vicarage. One could easily fix his type; it never, happily, dies out. He was handsome and bold and pleasant, off-hand and gay and kind. He struck her, inevitably, as gallant and splendid, but what took her most of all and gave her the courage she afterwards showed was that he put the whole thing to her as a favour, an obligation he should gratefully incur. She figured him as rich, but as fearfully extravagant – saw him all in a glow of high fashion, of good looks, of expensive habits, of charming ways with women. He had for his town residence a big house filled with the spoils of travel and the trophies of the chase; but it was to his country home, an old family place in Essex, that he wished her immediately to proceed.

He had been left, by the death of his parents in India, guardian to a small nephew and a small niece,[4] children of a younger, a military brother whom he had lost two years before. These children were, by the strangest of chances for a man in his position – a lone man without the right sort of experience or a grain of patience – very heavy on his hands. It had all been a great worry and, on his own part doubtless, a series of blunders, but he immensely pitied the poor chicks and had done all he could; had in particular sent them down to his other house, the proper place for them being of course the country, and kept them there from the first with the best people he could find to look after them, parting even with his own servants to wait on them and going down himself, whenever he might, to see how they were doing. The awkward thing was that they had practically no other relations and that his own affairs took up all his time. He had put them in possession of Bly, which was healthy and secure, and had placed at the head of their little establishment – but belowstairs only – an excellent woman, Mrs Grose, whom he was sure his visitor would like and who had formerly been maid to his mother. She was now housekeeper and was also acting for the time as superintendent to the little girl, of whom, without children of her own, she was by good luck extremely fond. There were plenty of people to help, but of course the young lady who should go down as governess would be in supreme authority. She would also have, in holidays, to look after the small boy, who had been for a term at school – young as he was to be sent, but what else could be done? – and who, as the holidays were about to begin, would be back from one day to the other. There had been for the two children at first a young lady whom they had had the misfortune to lose. She had done for them quite beautifully – she was a most respectable person – till her death, the great awkwardness of which had, precisely, left no alternative but the school for little Miles. Mrs Grose, since then, in the way of manners and things, had done as she could for Flora; and there were, further, a cook, a housemaid, a dairywoman, an old pony, an old groom and an old gardener, all likewise thoroughly respectable.

So far had Douglas presented his picture when some one put a question. 'And what did the former governess die of? Of so much respectability?'

Our friend's answer was prompt. 'That will come out. I don't anticipate.'

'Pardon me – I thought that was just what you *are* doing.'

'In her successor's place,' I suggested, 'I should have wished to learn if the office brought with it—'

'Necessary danger to life?' Douglas completed my thought. 'She did wish to learn, and she did learn. You shall hear to-morrow what she learnt. Meanwhile of course the prospect struck her as slightly grim. She was young, untried, nervous: it was a vision of serious duties and little company, of really great loneliness. She hesitated – took a couple of days to consult and consider. But the salary offered much exceeded her modest measure, and on a second interview she faced the music, she engaged.' And Douglas, with this, made a pause that, for the benefit of the company, moved me to throw in –

'The moral of which was of course the seduction exercised by the splendid young man. She succumbed to it.'

He got up and, as he had done the night before, went to the fire, gave a stir to a log with his foot, then stood a moment with his back to us. 'She saw him only twice.'

'Yes, but that's just the beauty of her passion.'

A little to my surprise, on this, Douglas turned round to me. 'It *was* the beauty of it. There were others,' he went on, 'who hadn't succumbed. He told her frankly all his difficulty – that for several applicants the conditions had been prohibitive. They were somehow simply afraid. It sounded dull – it sounded strange; and all the more so because of his main condition.'

'Which was—?'

'That she should never trouble him – but never, never: neither appeal nor complain nor write about anything; only meet all questions herself, receive all moneys from his solicitor, take the whole thing over and let him alone. She promised to do this, and she mentioned to me that when, for a moment, disburdened, delighted, he held her hand, thanking her for the sacrifice, she already felt rewarded.'

'But was that all her reward?' one of the ladies asked.

'She never saw him again.'

'Oh!' said the lady; which, as our friend immediately again left us, was the only other word of importance contributed to the subject till, the next night, by the corner of the hearth, in the best chair, he opened the faded red cover of a thin old-fashioned gilt-edged album. The whole thing took indeed more nights than one, but on the first occasion the same lady put another question. 'What's your title?'

'I haven't one.'

'Oh *I* have!' I said. But Douglas, without heeding me, had begun to read with a fine clearness that was like a rendering to the ear of the beauty of his author's hand.[5]

I

I remember the whole beginning as a succession of flights and drops, a little see-saw of the right throbs and the wrong. After rising, in town, to meet his appeal I had at all events a couple of very bad days – found all my doubts bristle again, felt indeed sure I had made a mistake. In this state of mind I spent the long hours of bumping swinging coach that carried me to the stopping-place at which I was to be met by a vehicle from the house. This convenience, I was told, had been ordered, and I found, toward the close of the June afternoon, a commodious fly[6] in waiting for me. Driving at that hour, on a lovely day, through a country the summer sweetness of which served as a friendly welcome, my fortitude revived and, as we turned into the avenue, took a flight that was probably but a proof of the point to which it had sunk. I suppose I had expected, or had dreaded, something so dreary that what greeted me was a good surprise. I remember as a thoroughly pleasant impression the broad clear front, its open windows and fresh curtains and the pair of maids looking out; I remember the lawn and the bright flowers and the crunch of my wheels on the gravel and the clustered tree-tops over which the rooks circled and cawed in the golden sky. The scene had a greatness that made it a different affair from my own scant home, and there immediately appeared at the door, with a little girl in her hand, a civil person who dropped me as decent a curtsey as if I had been the mistress or a distinguished visitor. I had received in Harley Street a narrower notion of the place, and that, as I recalled it, made me think the proprietor still more of a gentleman, suggested that what I was to enjoy might be a matter beyond his promise.

I had no drop again till the next day, for I was carried triumphantly through the following hours by my introduction to the younger of my pupils. The little girl who accompanied Mrs Grose affected me on the spot as a creature too charming not to make it a great fortune to have to do with her. She was the most beautiful child I had ever seen, and I afterwards wondered why my employer hadn't made more of a point to me of this. I slept little that night – I was too much excited; and this astonished me too, I recollect, remained with me, adding to my sense of the liberality with which I was treated. The large impressive room, one of the best in the house, the great state bed, as I almost felt it, the figured full draperies, the long glasses in which, for the first time, I could see myself from head to foot, all struck me – like the wonderful appeal of my small charge – as so many things thrown in. It was thrown in as well, from the first moment, that I should get on with Mrs Grose in a relation over which, on my way, in the coach, I fear I had rather brooded. The one appearance indeed that in this early outlook might have made me shrink again was that of her being so inordinately glad to see me. I felt within half an hour that she was so glad – stout simple plain clean wholesome woman – as to be positively on her guard against showing it too much. I wondered even then a little why she should wish *not* to show it, and that, with reflexion, with suspicion, might of course have made me uneasy.

But it was a comfort that there could be no uneasiness in a connexion with anything so beatific as the radiant image of my little girl, the vision of whose angelic beauty had probably more than anything else to do with the restlessness that, before morning, made me several times rise and wander about my room to take in the whole picture and prospect; to watch from my open window the faint summer dawn, to look at such stretches of the rest of the house as I could catch, and to listen, while in the fading dusk the first birds began to twitter, for the possible recurrence of a sound or two, less natural and not without but within, that I had fancied I heard. There had been a moment when I believed I recognized, faint and far, the cry of a child; there had been another when I found myself just consciously starting as at the passage, before my door, of a light footstep. But these fancies were not marked enough not to be thrown off, and it is only in the light, or the gloom, I should rather say, of other and subsequent matters that they now come back to me. To watch, teach, 'form' little Flora would too evidently be the making of a happy and useful life. It had been agreed between us downstairs that after this first occasion I should have her as a matter of course at night, her small white bed being already arranged, to that end, in my room. What I had undertaken was the whole care of her, and she had remained just this last time with Mrs Grose only as an effect of our consideration for my inevitable strangeness and her natural timidity. In spite of this timidity – which the child herself, in the oddest way in the world, had been perfectly frank and brave about, allowing it, without a sign of uncomfortable consciousness, with the deep sweet serenity indeed of one of Raphael's holy infants,[7] to be discussed, to be imputed to her and to determine us – I felt quite sure she would presently like me. It was part of what I already liked Mrs Grose herself for, the pleasure I could see her feel in my admiration and wonder as I sat at supper with four tall candles and with my pupil, in a high chair and a bib, brightly facing me between them over bread and milk. There were naturally things that in Flora's presence could pass between us only as prodigious and gratified looks, obscure and roundabout allusions.

'And the little boy – does he look like her? Is he too so very remarkable?'

One wouldn't, it was already conveyed between us, too grossly flatter a child. 'Oh Miss, *most* remarkable. If you think well of this one!' – and she stood there with a plate in her hand, beaming at our companion, who looked from one of us to the other with placid heavenly eyes that contained nothing to check us.

'Yes; if I do—?'

'You *will* be carried away by the little gentleman!'

'Well, that, I think, is what I came for – to be carried away. I'm afraid, however,' I remember feeling the impulse to add, 'I'm rather easily carried away. I was carried away in London!'

I can still see Mrs Grose's broad face as she took this in. 'In Harley Street?'

'In Harley Street.'

'Well, Miss, you're not the first – and you won't be the last.'

'Oh I've no pretensions,' I could laugh, 'to being the only one. My other pupil, at any rate, as I understand, comes back to-morrow?'

'Not to-morrow – Friday, Miss. He arrives, as you did, by the coach, under care of the guard, and is to be met by the same carriage.'

I forthwith wanted to know if the proper as well as the pleasant and friendly thing wouldn't therefore be that on the arrival of the public conveyance I should await him with his little sister; a proposition to which Mrs Grose assented so heartily that I somehow took her manner as a kind of comforting pledge – never falsified, thank heaven! – that we should on every question be quite at one. Oh she was glad I was there!

What I felt the next day was, I suppose, nothing that could be fairly called a reaction from the cheer of my arrival; it was probably at the most only a slight oppression produced by a fuller measure of the scale, as I walked round them, gazed up at them, took them in, of my new circumstances. They had, as it were, an extent and mass for which I had not been prepared and in the presence of which I found myself, freshly, a little scared not less than a little proud. Regular lessons, in this agitation, certainly suffered some wrong; I reflected that my first duty was, by the gentlest arts I could contrive, to win the child into the sense of knowing me. I spent the day with her out of doors; I arranged with her, to her great satisfaction, that it should be she, she only, who might show me the place. She showed it step by step and room by room and secret by secret, with droll delightful childish talk about it and with the result, in half an hour, of our becoming tremendous friends. Young as she was I was struck, throughout our little tour, with her confidence and courage, with the way, in empty chambers and dull corridors, on crooked staircases that made me pause and even on the summit of an old machicolated square tower[8] that made me dizzy, her morning music, her disposition to tell me so many more things than she asked, rang out and led me on. I have not seen Bly since the day I left it, and I daresay that to my present older and more informed eyes it would show a very reduced importance. But as my little conductress, with her hair of gold and her frock of blue, danced before me round corners and pattered down passages, I had the view of a castle of romance inhabited by a rosy sprite, such a place as would somehow, for diversion of the young idea, take all colour out of story-books and fairy-tales. Wasn't it just a story-book over which I had fallen a-doze and a-dream? No; it was a big ugly antique but convenient house, embodying a few features of a building still older, half-displaced and half-utilized, in which I had the fancy of our being almost as lost as a handful of passengers in a great drifting ship. Well, I was strangely at the helm!

II

This came home to me when, two days later, I drove over with Flora to meet, as Mrs Grose said, the little gentleman; and all the more for an incident that, presenting itself the second evening, had deeply disconcerted me. The first day had been, on the whole, as I have expressed, reassuring; but I was to see it wind up to a change of note. The postbag that evening – it came late – contained a letter for me which, however, in the hand of my employer, I found to be composed but of a few words enclosing another, addressed to himself, with a seal still unbroken. 'This, I recognize, is from the head-master, and the head-master's an awful bore. Read him, please; deal with him; but mind you don't report. Not a word. I'm off!' I broke the seal with a great effort – so great a one that I was a long time coming to it; took the unopened missive at last up to my room and only attacked it just before going to bed. I had better have let it wait till morning, for it gave me a second sleepless night. With no counsel to take, the next day, I was full of distress;

and it finally got so the better of me that I determined to open myself at least to Mrs Grose.

'What does it mean? The child's dismissed his school.'

She gave me a look that I remarked at the moment; then, visibly, with a quick blankness, seemed to try to take it back. 'But aren't they all—?'

'Sent home – yes. But only for the holidays. Miles may never go back at all.'

Consciously, under my attention, she reddened. 'They won't take him?'

'They absolutely decline.'

At this she raised her eyes, which she had turned from me; I saw them fill with good tears. 'What has he done?'

I cast about; then I judged best simply to hand her my document – which, however, had the effect of making her, without taking it, simply put her hands behind her. She shook her head sadly. 'Such things are not for me, Miss.'

My counsellor couldn't read! I winced at my mistake, which I attenuated as I could, and opened the letter again to repeat it to her; then, faltering in the act and folding it up once more, I put it back in my pocket. 'Is he really *bad*?'

The tears were still in her eyes. 'Do the gentlemen say so?'

'They go into no particulars. They simply express their regret that it should be impossible to keep him. That can have but one meaning.' Mrs Grose listened with dumb emotion; she forbore to ask me what this meaning might be; so that, presently, to put the thing with some coherence and with the mere aid of her presence to my own mind, I went on: 'That he's an injury to the others.'

At this, with one of the quick turns of simple folk, she suddenly flamed up. 'Master Miles! – *him* an injury?'

There was such a flood of good faith in it that, though I had not yet seen the child, my very fears made me jump to the absurdity of the idea. I found myself, to meet my friend the better, offering it, on the spot, sarcastically. 'To his poor little innocent mates!'

'It's too dreadful,' cried Mrs Grose, 'to say such cruel things! Why he's scarce ten years old.'

'Yes, yes; it would be incredible.'

She was evidently grateful for such a profession. 'See him, Miss, first. *Then* believe it!' I felt forthwith a new impatience to see him; it was the beginning of a curiosity that, all the next hours, was to deepen almost to pain. Mrs Grose was aware, I could judge, of what she had produced in me, and she followed it up with assurance. 'You might as well believe it of the little lady. Bless her,' she added the next moment – '*look* at her!'

I turned and saw that Flora, whom, ten minutes before, I had established in the schoolroom with a sheet of white paper, a pencil and a copy of nice 'round O's', now presented herself to view at the open door. She expressed in her little way an extraordinary detachment from disagreeable duties, looking at me, however, with a great childish light that seemed to offer it as a mere result of the affection she had conceived for my person, which had rendered necessary that she should follow me. I needed nothing more than this to feel the full force of Mrs Grose's comparison, and, catching my pupil in my arms, covered her with kisses in which there was a sob of atonement.

None the less, the rest of the day, I watched for further occasion to approach my colleague, especially as, toward evening, I began to fancy she rather sought to avoid me. I overtook her, I remember, on the staircase; we went down together and at the bottom I detained her, holding her there with a hand on her arm. 'I take what you said to me at noon as a declaration that *you've* never known him to be bad.'

She threw back her head; she had clearly by this time, and very honestly, adopted an attitude. 'Oh never known him – I don't pretend *that*!'

I was upset again. 'Then you *have* known him—?'

'Yes indeed, Miss, thank God!'

On reflexion I accepted this. 'You mean that a boy who never is—?'

'Is no boy for *me*!'

I held her tighter. 'You like them with the spirit to be naughty?' Then, keeping pace with her answer, 'So do I!' I eagerly brought out. 'But not to the degree to contaminate—'

'To contaminate?' – my big word left her at a loss.

I explained it. 'To corrupt.'

She stared, taking my meaning in; but it produced in her an odd laugh. 'Are you afraid he'll corrupt *you*?' She put the question with such a fine bold humour that with a laugh, a little silly doubtless, to match her own, I gave way for the time to the apprehension of ridicule.

But the next day, as the hour for my drive approached, I cropped up in another place. 'What was the lady who was here before?'

'The last governess? She was also young and pretty – almost as young and almost as pretty, Miss, even as you.'

'Ah then I hope her youth and her beauty helped her!' I recollect throwing off. 'He seems to like us young and pretty!'

'Oh he *did*,' Mrs Grose assented: 'it was the way he liked every one!' She had no sooner spoken indeed than she caught herself up. 'I mean that's *his* way – the master's.'

I was struck. 'But of whom did you speak first?'

She looked blank, but she coloured. 'Why of *him*.'

'Of the master?'

'Of who else?'

There was so obviously no one else that the next moment I had lost my impression of her having accidentally said more than she meant; and I merely asked what I wanted to know. 'Did *she* see anything in the boy—?'

'That wasn't right? She never told me.'

I had a scruple, but I overcame it. 'Was she careful – particular?'

Mrs Grose appeared to try to be conscientious. 'About some things – yes.'

'But not about all?'

Again she considered. 'Well, Miss – she's gone. I won't tell tales.'

'I quite understand your feeling,' I hastened to reply; but I thought it after an instant not opposed to this concession to pursue: 'Did she die here?'

'No – she went off.'

I don't know what there was in this brevity of Mrs Grose's that struck me as ambiguous. 'Went off to die?' Mrs Grose looked straight out of the window, but I felt that, hypothetically, I had a right to know what young persons engaged for Bly were expected to do. 'She was taken ill, you mean, and went home?'

'She was not taken ill, so far as appeared, in this house. She left it, at the end of the year, to go home, as she said, for a short holiday, to which the time she had put in had certainly given her a right. We had then a young woman – a nursemaid who had stayed on and who was a good girl and clever; and *she* took the children altogether for the interval. But our young lady never came back, and at the very moment I was expecting her I heard from the master that she was dead.'

I turned this over. 'But of what?'

'He never told me! But please, Miss,' said Mrs Grose, 'I must get to my work.'[9]

III

Her thus turning her back on me was fortunately not, for my just preoccupations, a snub that could check the growth of our mutual esteem. We met, after I had brought home little Miles, more intimately than ever on the ground of my stupefaction, my general emotion: so monstrous was I then ready to pronounce it that such a child as had now been revealed to me should be under an interdict. I was a little late on the scene of his arrival, and I felt, as he stood wistfully looking out for me before the door of the inn at which the coach had put him down, that I had seen him on the instant, without and within, in the great glow of freshness, the same positive fragrance of purity, in which I had from the first moment seen his little sister. He was incredibly beautiful, and Mrs Grose had put her finger on it: everything but a sort of passion of tenderness for him was swept away by his presence. What I then and there took him to my heart for was something divine that I have never found to the same degree in any child – his indescribable little air of knowing nothing in the world but love. It would have been impossible to carry a bad name with a greater sweetness of innocence, and by the time I had got back to Bly with him I remained merely bewildered – so far, that is, as I was not outraged – by the sense of the horrible letter locked up in one of the drawers of my room. As soon as I could compass a private word with Mrs Grose I declared to her that it was grotesque.

She promptly understood me. 'You mean the cruel charge—?'

'It doesn't live an instant. My dear woman, *look* at him!'

She smiled at my pretension to have discovered his charm. 'I assure you, Miss, I do nothing else! What will you say then?' she immediately added.

'In answer to the letter?' I had made up my mind. 'Nothing at all.'

'And to his uncle?'

I was incisive. 'Nothing at all.'

'And to the boy himself?'

I was wonderful. 'Nothing at all.'

She gave with her apron a great wipe to her mouth. 'Then I'll stand by you. We'll see it out.'

'We'll see it out!' I ardently echoed, giving her my hand to make it a vow.

She held me there a moment, then whisked up her apron again with her detached hand. 'Would you mind, Miss, if I used the freedom—'

'To kiss me? No!' I took the good creature in my arms and after we had embraced like sisters felt still more fortified and indignant.

This at all events was for the time: a time so full that as I recall the way it went it reminds me of all the art I now need to make it a little distinct. What I look back at with amazement is the situation I accepted. I had undertaken, with my companion, to see it out, and I was under a charm apparently that could smooth away the extent and the far and difficult connexions of such an effort. I was lifted aloft on a great wave of infatuation and pity. I found it simple, in my ignorance, my confusion and perhaps my conceit, to assume that I could deal with a boy whose education for the world was all on the point of beginning. I am unable even to remember at this day what

proposal I framed for the end of his holidays and the resumption of his studies. Lessons with me indeed, that charming
summer, we all had a theory that he was to have; but I now feel
that for weeks the lessons must have been rather my own. I
learnt something – at first certainly – that had not been one of
the teachings of my small smothered life; learnt to be amused,
and even amusing, and not to think for the morrow. It was the
first time, in a manner, that I had known space and air and
freedom, all the music of summer and all the mystery of nature.
And then there was consideration – and consideration was
sweet. Oh it was a trap – not designed but deep – to my imagination, to my delicacy, perhaps to my vanity; to whatever in me
was most excitable. The best way to picture it all is to say that
I was off my guard. They gave me so little trouble – they were
of a gentleness so extraordinary. I used to speculate – but even
this with a dim disconnectedness – as to how the rough future
(for all futures are rough!) would handle them and might
bruise them. They had the bloom of health and happiness; and
yet, as if I had been in charge of a pair of little grandees, of
princes of the blood, for whom everything, to be right, would
have to be fenced about and ordered and arranged, the only
form that in my fancy the after-years could take for them was
that of a romantic, a really royal extension of the garden and
the park. It may be of course above all that what suddenly
broke into this gives the previous time a charm of stillness –
that hush in which something gathers or crouches. The change
was actually like the spring of a beast.

   In the first weeks the days were long; they often, at their finest, gave me what I used to call my own hour, the hour when,
for my pupils, tea-time and bed-time having come and gone, I
had before my final retirement a small interval alone. Much as
I liked my companions this hour was the thing in the day I
liked most; and I liked it best of all when, as the light faded –
or rather, I should say, the day lingered and the last calls of the
last birds sounded, in a flushed sky, from the old trees – I could
take a turn into the grounds and enjoy, almost with a sense of
property that amused and flattered me, the beauty and dignity
of the place. It was a pleasure at these moments to feel myself

tranquil and justified; doubtless perhaps also to reflect that by my discretion, my quiet good sense and general high propriety, I was giving pleasure – if he ever thought of it! – to the person to whose pressure I had yielded. What I was doing was what he had earnestly hoped and directly asked of me, and that I *could*, after all, do it proved even a greater joy than I had expected. I daresay I fancied myself in short a remarkable young woman and took comfort in the faith that this would more publicly appear. Well, I needed to be remarkable to offer a front to the remarkable things that presently gave their first sign.

It was plump, one afternoon, in the middle of my very hour: the children were tucked away and I had come out for my stroll. One of the thoughts that, as I don't in the least shrink now from noting, used to be with me in these wanderings was that it would be as charming as a charming story suddenly to meet some one. Some one would appear there at the turn of a path and would stand before me and smile and approve. I didn't ask more than that – I only asked that he should *know*; and the only way to be sure he knew would be to see it, and the kind light of it, in his handsome face. That was exactly present to me – by which I mean the face was – when, on the first of these occasions, at the end of a long June day, I stopped short on emerging from one of the plantations and coming into view of the house. What arrested me on the spot – and with a shock much greater than any vision had allowed for – was the sense that my imagination had, in a flash, turned real. He did stand there! – but high up, beyond the lawn and at the very top of the tower to which, on that first morning, little Flora had conducted me. This tower was one of a pair – square incongruous crenellated structures – that were distinguished, for some reason, though I could see little difference, as the new and the old. They flanked opposite ends of the house and were probably architectural absurdities, redeemed in a measure indeed by not being wholly disengaged nor of a height too pretentious, dating, in their gingerbread antiquity,[10] from a romantic revival that was already a respectable past. I admired them, had fancies about them, for we could all profit in a degree, especially when they loomed through the dusk, by the grandeur of their actual battlements; yet it was not at such an elevation that the figure I had so often invoked seemed most in place.

It produced in me, this figure, in the clear twilight, I remember, two distinct gasps of emotion, which were, sharply, the shock of my first and that of my second surprise. My second was a violent perception of the mistake of my first: the man who met my eyes was not the person I had precipitately supposed. There came to me thus a bewilderment of vision of which, after these years, there is no living view that I can hope to give. An unknown man in a lonely place is a permitted object of fear to a young woman privately bred; and the figure that faced me was – a few more seconds assured me – as little any one else I knew as it was the image that had been in my mind. I had not seen it in Harley Street – I had not seen it anywhere. The place moreover, in the strangest way in the world, had on the instant and by the very fact of its appearance become a solitude. To me at least, making my statement here with a deliberation with which I have never made it, the whole feeling of the moment returns. It was as if, while I took in, what I did take in, all the rest of the scene had been stricken with death. I can hear again, as I write, the intense hush in which the sounds of evening dropped. The rooks stopped cawing in the golden sky and the friendly hour lost for the unspeakable minute all its voice. But there was no other change in nature, unless indeed it were a change that I saw with a stranger sharpness. The gold was still in the sky, the clearness in the air, and the man who looked at me over the battlements was as definite as a picture in a frame. That's how I thought, with extraordinary quickness, of each person he might have been and that he wasn't. We were confronted across our distance quite long enough for me to ask myself with intensity who then he was and to feel, as an effect of my inability to say, a wonder that in a few seconds more became intense.

The great question, or one of these, is afterwards, I know, with regard to certain matters, the question of how long they have lasted. Well, this matter of mine, think what you will of it, lasted while I caught at a dozen possibilities, none of which made a difference for the better, that I could see, in there having been in the house – and for how long, above all? – a person of whom I was in ignorance. It lasted while I just bridled a little with the sense of how my office seemed to require that there should be no such ignorance and no such person. It lasted while this visitant, at all events – and there was a touch of the strange freedom, as I remember, in the sign of familiarity of his wearing no hat – seemed to fix me, from his position, with just the question, just the scrutiny through the fading light, that his own presence provoked. We were too far apart to call to each other, but there was a moment at which, at shorter range, some challenge between us, breaking the hush, would have been the right result of our straight mutual stare. He was in one of the angles, the one away from the house, very erect, as it struck me, and with both hands on the ledge. So I saw him as I see the letters I form on this page; then, exactly, after a minute, as if to add to the spectacle, he slowly changed his place – passed, looking at me hard all the while, to the opposite corner of the platform. Yes, it was intense to me that during this transit he never took his eyes from me, and I can see at this moment the way his hand, as he went, moved from one of the crenellations to the next. He stopped at the other corner, but less long, and even as he turned away still markedly fixed me. He turned away; that was all I knew.[11]

IV

It was not that I didn't wait, on this occasion, for more, since I was as deeply rooted as shaken. Was there a 'secret' at Bly – a mystery of Udolpho or an insane, an unmentionable relative kept in unsuspected confinement?[12] I can't say how long I turned it over, or how long, in a confusion of curiosity and dread, I remained where I had had my collision; I only recall that when I re-entered the house darkness had quite closed in. Agitation, in the interval, certainly had held me and driven me, for I must, in circling about the place, have walked three miles; but I was to be later on so much more overwhelmed that this mere dawn of alarm was a comparatively human chill. The most singular part of it in fact – singular as the rest had been – was the part I became, in the hall, aware of in meeting Mrs Grose. This picture comes back to me in the general train – the impression, as I received it on my return, of the wide white panelled space, bright in the lamplight and with its portraits and red carpet, and of the good surprised look of my friend, which immediately told me she had missed me. It came to me straightway, under her contact, that, with plain heartiness, mere relieved anxiety at my appearance, she knew nothing whatever that could bear upon the incident I had there ready for her. I had not suspected in advance that her comfortable face would pull me up, and I somehow measured the import-ance of what I had seen by my thus finding myself hesitate to mention it. Scarce anything in the whole history seems to me so odd as this fact that my real beginning of fear was one, as I may say, with the instinct of sparing my companion. On the spot, accordingly, in the pleasant hall and with her eyes on me, I, for a reason that I couldn't then have phrased, achieved an inward revolution – offered a vague pretext for my lateness and, with the plea of the beauty of the night and of the heavy dew and wet feet, went as soon as possible to my room.

Here it was another affair; here, for many days after, it was a queer affair enough. There were hours, from day to day – or at least there were moments, snatched even from clear duties – when I had to shut myself up to think. It wasn't so much yet that I was more nervous than I could bear to be as that I was remarkably afraid of becoming so; for the truth I had now to turn over was simply and clearly the truth that I could arrive at no account whatever of the visitor with whom I had been so inexplicably and yet, as it seemed to me, so intimately con-cerned. It took me little time to see that I might easily sound, without forms of enquiry and without exciting remark, any domestic complication. The shock I had suffered must have sharpened all my senses; I felt sure, at the end of three days and as the result of mere closer attention, that I had not been prac-tised upon by the servants nor made the object of any 'game'. Of whatever it was that I knew nothing was known around me. There was but one sane inference: some one had taken a liberty rather monstrous. That was what, repeatedly, I dipped into my room and locked the door to say to myself. We had been, collectively, subject to an intrusion; some unscrupulous traveller, curious in old houses, had made his way in unobserved, enjoyed the prospect from the best point of view and then stolen out as he came. If he had given me such a bold hard stare, that was but a part of his indiscretion. The good thing, after all, was that we should surely see no more of him.

This was not so good a thing, I admit, as not to leave me to judge that what, essentially, made nothing else much signify was simply my charming work. My charming work was just my life with Miles and Flora, and through nothing could I so like it as through feeling that to throw myself into it was to throw myself out of my trouble. The attraction of my small charges was a constant joy, leading me to wonder afresh at the vanity of my original fears, the distaste I had begun by entertaining for the probable grey prose of my office. There was to be no grey prose, it appeared, and no long grind; so how could work not be charming that presented itself as daily beauty? It was all the romance of the nursery and the poetry of the schoolroom. I don't mean by this of course that we studied only fiction and verse; I mean that I can express no otherwise the sort of interest my companions inspired. How can I describe that except by saying that instead of growing deadly used to them – and it's a marvel for a governess: I call the sisterhood[13] to witness! – I made constant fresh discoveries. There was one direction, assuredly, in which these discoveries stopped: deep obscurity continued to cover the region of the boy's conduct at school. It had been promptly given me, I have noted, to face that mystery without a pang. Perhaps even it would be nearer the truth to say that – without a word – he himself had cleared it up. He had made the whole charge absurd. My conclusion bloomed there with the real rose-flush of his innocence: he was only too fine and fair for the little horrid unclean school-world, and he had paid a price for it. I reflected acutely that the sense of such individual differences, such superiorities of quality, always, on the part of the majority – which could include even stupid sordid head-masters – turns infallibly to the vindictive.

Both the children had a gentleness – it was their only fault, and it never made Miles a muff[14] – that kept them (how shall I express it?) almost impersonal and certainly quite unpunishable. They were like those cherubs of the anecdote[15] who had – morally at any rate – nothing to whack! I remember feeling with Miles in especial as if he had had, as it were, nothing to call even an infinitesimal history. We expect of a small child scant enough 'antecedents', but there was in this beautiful little boy something extraordinarily sensitive, yet extraordinarily happy, that, more than in any creature of his age I have seen, struck me as beginning anew each day. He had never for a second suffered. I took this as a direct disproof of his having really been chastised. If he had been wicked he would have 'caught' it, and I should have caught it by the rebound – I should have found the trace, should have felt the wound and the dishonour.[16] I could reconstitute nothing at all, and he was therefore an angel. He never spoke of his school, never mentioned a comrade or a master; and I, for my part, was quite too much disgusted to allude to them. Of course I was under the spell, and the wonderful part is that, even at the time, I perfectly knew I was. But I gave myself up to it; it was an antidote to any pain, and I had more pains than one. I was in receipt in these days of disturbing letters from home, where things were not going well. But with this joy of my children what things in the world mattered? That was the question I used to put to my scrappy retirements. I was dazzled by their loveliness.

There was a Sunday – to get on – when it rained with such force and for so many hours that there could be no procession to church; in consequence of which, as the day declined, I had arranged with Mrs Grose that, should the evening show improvement, we would attend together the late service. The rain happily stopped, and I prepared for our walk, which, through the park and by the good road to the village, would be a matter of twenty minutes. Coming downstairs to meet my colleague in the hall, I remembered a pair of gloves that had required three stitches and that had received them – with a publicity perhaps not edifying – while I sat with the children at their tea, served on Sundays, by exception, in that cold clean temple of mahogany and brass, the 'grown-up' dining-room. The gloves had been dropped there, and I turned in to recover them. The day was grey enough, but the afternoon light still lingered, and it enabled me, on crossing the threshold, not only to recognize, on a chair near the wide window, then closed, the articles I wanted, but to become aware of a person on the other side of the window and looking straight in. One step into the room had sufficed; my vision was instantaneous; it was all there. The person looking straight in was the person who had already appeared to me. He appeared thus again with I won't say greater distinctness, for that was impossible, but with a nearness that represented a forward stride in our intercourse and made me, as I met him, catch my breath and turn cold. He was the same – he was the same, and seen, this time, as he had been seen before, from the waist up, the window, though the dining-room was on the ground floor, not going down to the terrace on which he stood. His face was close to the glass, yet the effect of this better view was, strangely, just to show me how intense the former had been. He remained but a few seconds – long enough to convince me he also saw and recognized; but it was as if I had been looking at him for years and had known him always. Something, however, happened this time that had not happened before; his stare into my face, through the glass and across the room, was as deep and hard as then, but it quitted me for a moment during which I could still watch it, see it fix successively several other things. On the spot there came to me the added shock of a certitude that it was not for me he had come. He had come for some one else.

The flash of this knowledge – for it was knowledge in the midst of dread – produced in me the most extraordinary effect, starting, as I stood there, a sudden vibration of duty and courage. I say courage because I was beyond all doubt already far gone. I bounded straight out of the door again, reached that of the house, got in an instant upon the drive and, passing along the terrace as fast as I could rush, turned a corner and came full in sight. But it was in sight of nothing now – my visitor had vanished. I stopped, almost dropped, with the real relief of this; but I took in the whole scene – I gave him time to reappear.

I call it time, but how long was it? I can't speak to the purpose
to-day of the duration of these things. That kind of measure
must have left me: they couldn't have lasted as they actually
appeared to me to last. The terrace and the whole place, the
lawn and the garden beyond it, all I could see of the park, were
empty with a great emptiness. There were shrubberies and big
trees, but I remember the clear assurance I felt that none of
them concealed him. He was there or was not there: not there
if I didn't see him. I got hold of this; then, instinctively, instead
of returning as I had come, went to the window. It was confus-
edly present to me that I ought to place myself where he had
stood. I did so; I applied my face to the pane and looked, as he
had looked, into the room. As if, at this moment, to show me
exactly what his range had been, Mrs Grose, as I had done for
himself just before, came in from the hall. With this I had the
full image of a repetition of what had already occurred. She
saw me as I had seen my own visitant; she pulled up short as I
had done; I gave her something of the shock that I had received.
She turned white, and this made me ask myself if I had blanched
as much. She stared, in short, and retreated just on *my* lines,
and I knew she had then passed out and come round to me and
that I should presently meet her. I remained where I was, and
while I waited I thought of more things than one. But there's
only one I take space to mention. I wondered why *she* should
be scared.

V

Oh she let me know as soon as, round the corner of the house,
she loomed again into view. 'What in the name of goodness is
the matter—?' She was now flushed and out of breath.

I said nothing till she came quite near. 'With me?' I must
have made a wonderful face. 'Do I show it?'

'You're as white as a sheet. You look awful.'

I considered; I could meet on this, without scruple, any degree
of innocence. My need to respect the bloom of Mrs Grose's had
dropped, without a rustle, from my shoulders, and if I wavered

for the instant it was not with what I kept back. I put out my hand to her and she took it; I held her hard a little, liking to feel her close to me. There was a kind of support in the shy heave of her surprise. 'You came for me for church, of course, but I can't go.'

'Has anything happened?'

'Yes. You must know now. Did I look very queer?'

'Through this window? Dreadful!'

'Well,' I said, 'I've been frightened.' Mrs Grose's eyes expressed plainly that *she* had no wish to be, yet also that she knew too well her place not to be ready to share with me any marked inconvenience. Oh it was quite settled that she *must* share! 'Just what you saw from the dining-room a minute ago was the effect of that. What *I* saw – just before – was much worse.'

Her hand tightened. 'What was it?'

'An extraordinary man. Looking in.'

'What extraordinary man?'

'I haven't the least idea.'

Mrs Grose gazed round us in vain. 'Then where is he gone?'

'I know still less.'

'Have you seen him before?'

'Yes – once. On the old tower.'

She could only look at me harder. 'Do you mean he's a stranger?'

'Oh very much!'

'Yet you didn't tell me?'

'No – for reasons. But now that you've guessed—'

Mrs Grose's round eyes encountered this charge. 'Ah I haven't guessed!' she said very simply. 'How can I if *you* don't imagine?'

'I don't in the very least.'

'You've seen him nowhere but on the tower?'

'And on this spot just now.'

Mrs Grose looked round again. 'What was he doing on the tower?'

'Only standing there and looking down at me.'

She thought a minute. 'Was he a gentleman?'

I found I had no need to think. 'No.' She gazed in deeper wonder. 'No.'

'Then nobody about the place? Nobody from the village?'

'Nobody – nobody. I didn't tell you, but I made sure.'

She breathed a vague relief: this was, oddly, so much to the good. It only went indeed a little way. 'But if he isn't a gentleman—'

'What *is* he? He's a horror.'

'A horror?'

'He's – God help me if I know *what* he is!'

Mrs Grose looked round once more; she fixed her eyes on the duskier distance and then, pulling herself together, turned to me with full inconsequence. 'It's time we should be at church.'

'Oh I'm not fit for church!'

'Won't it do you good?'

'It won't do *them*—!' I nodded at the house.

'The children?'

'I can't leave them now.'

'You're afraid—?'

I spoke boldly. 'I'm afraid of *him*.'

Mrs Grose's large face showed me, at this, for the first time, the far-away faint glimmer of a consciousness more acute: I somehow made out in it the delayed dawn of an idea I myself had not given her and that was as yet quite obscure to me. It comes back to me that I thought instantly of this as something I could get from her; and I felt it to be connected with the desire she presently showed to know more. 'When was it – on the tower?'

'About the middle of the month. At this same hour.'

'Almost at dark,' said Mrs Grose.

'Oh no, not nearly. I saw him as I see you.'

'Then how did he get in?'

'And how did he get out?' I laughed. 'I had no opportunity to ask him! This evening, you see,' I pursued, 'he has not been able to get in.'

'He only peeps?'

'I hope it will be confined to that!' She had now let go my

hand; she turned away a little. I waited an instant; then I brought out: 'Go to church. Goodbye. I must watch.'

Slowly she faced me again. 'Do you fear for them?'

We met in another long look. 'Don't *you*?' Instead of answering she came nearer to the window and, for a minute, applied her face to the glass. 'You see how he could see,' I meanwhile went on.

She didn't move. 'How long was he here?'

'Till I came out. I came to meet him.'

Mrs Grose at last turned round, and there was still more in her face. '*I* couldn't have come out.'

'Neither could I!' I laughed again. 'But I did come. I've my duty.'

'So have I mine,' she replied; after which she added: 'What's he like?'

'I've been dying to tell you. But he's like nobody.'

'Nobody?' she echoed.

'He has no hat.' Then seeing in her face that she already, in this, with a deeper dismay, found a touch of picture, I quickly added stroke to stroke. 'He has red hair, very red, close-curling, and a pale face, long in shape, with straight good features and little rather queer whiskers that are as red as his hair. His eyebrows are somehow darker; they look particularly arched and as if they might move a good deal. His eyes are sharp, strange – awfully; but I only know clearly that they're rather small and very fixed. His mouth's wide, and his lips are thin, and except for his little whiskers he's quite clean-shaven. He gives me a sort of sense of looking like an actor.'[17]

'An actor!' It was impossible to resemble one less, at least, than Mrs Grose at that moment.

'I've never seen one, but so I suppose them. He's tall, active, erect,' I continued, 'but never – no, never! – a gentleman.'

My companion's face had blanched as I went on; her round eyes started and her mild mouth gaped. 'A gentleman?' she gasped, confounded, stupefied: 'a gentleman *he*?'

'You know him then?'

She visibly tried to hold herself. 'But he *is* handsome?'

I saw the way to help her. 'Remarkably!'

'And dressed—?'

'In somebody's clothes. They're smart, but they're not his own.'

She broke into a breathless affirmative groan. 'They're the master's!'

I caught it up. 'You *do* know him?'

She faltered but a second. 'Quint!' she cried.

'Quint?'

'Peter Quint – his own man, his valet, when he was here!'

'When the master was?'

Gaping still, but meeting me, she pieced it all together. 'He never wore his hat, but he did wear – well, there were waist-coats missed! They were both here – last year. Then the master went, and Quint was alone.'

I followed, but halting a little. 'Alone?'

'Alone with *us*.' Then as from a deeper depth, 'In charge,' she added.

'And what became of him?'

She hung fire so long that I was still more mystified. 'He went too,' she brought out at last.

'Went where?'

Her expression, at this, became extraordinary. 'God knows where! He died.'

'Died?' I almost shrieked.

She seemed fairly to square herself, plant herself more firmly to express the wonder of it. 'Yes. Mr Quint's dead.'[18]

VI

It took of course more than that particular passage to place us together in presence of what we had now to live with as we could, my dreadful liability to impressions of the order so viv-idly exemplified, and my companion's knowledge henceforth – a knowledge half consternation and half compassion – of that liability. There had been this evening, after the revelation that left me for an hour so prostrate – there had been for either of us no attendance on any service but a little service of tears and vows, of prayers and promises, a climax to the series of mutual challenges and pledges that had straightway ensued on our retreating together to the schoolroom and shutting ourselves up there to have everything out. The result of our having everything out was simply to reduce our situation to the last rigour of its elements. She herself had seen nothing, not the shadow of a shadow, and nobody in the house but the governess was in the governess's plight; yet she accepted without directly impugning my sanity the truth as I gave it to her, and ended by showing me on this ground an awestricken tenderness, a deference to my more than questionable privilege, of which the very breath has remained with me as that of the sweetest of human charities.

What was settled between us accordingly that night was that we thought we might bear things together; and I was not even sure that in spite of her exemption it was she who had the best of the burden. I knew at this hour, I think, as well as I knew later, what I was capable of meeting to shelter my pupils; but it took me some time to be wholly sure of what my honest comrade was prepared for to keep terms with so stiff an agreement. I was queer company enough – quite as queer as the company I received; but as I trace over what we went through I see how much common ground we must have found in the one idea that, by good fortune, *could* steady us. It was the idea, the second movement, that led me straight out, as I may say, of the inner chamber of my dread. I could take the air in the court, at least, and there Mrs Grose could join me. Perfectly can I recall now the particular way strength came to me before we separated for the night. We had gone over and over every feature of what I had seen.

'He was looking for some one else, you say – some one who was not you?'

'He was looking for little Miles.' A portentous clearness now possessed me. '*That's* whom he was looking for.'

'But how do you know?'

'I know, I know, I know!' My exaltation grew. 'And *you* know, my dear!'

She didn't deny this, but I required, I felt, not even so much telling as that. She took it up again in a moment. 'What if *he* should see him?'

'Little Miles? That's what he wants!'

She looked immensely scared again. 'The child?'

'Heaven forbid! The man. He wants to appear to *them*.' That he might was an awful conception, and yet somehow I could keep it at bay; which moreover, as we lingered there, was what I succeeded in practically proving. I had an absolute certainty that I should see again what I had already seen, but something within me said that by offering myself bravely as the sole subject of such experience, by accepting, by inviting, by surmounting it all, I should serve as an expiatory victim and guard the tranquillity of the rest of the household. The children in especial I should thus fence about and absolutely save. I recall one of the last things I said that night to Mrs Grose.

'It does strike me that my pupils have never mentioned—!'

She looked at me hard as I musingly pulled up. 'His having been here and the time they were with him?'

'The time they were with him, and his name, his presence, his history, in any way. They've never alluded to it.'

'Oh the little lady doesn't remember. She never heard or knew.'

'The circumstances of his death?' I thought with some intensity. 'Perhaps not. But Miles would remember – Miles would know.'

'Ah don't try him!' broke from Mrs Grose.

I returned her the look she had given me. 'Don't be afraid.' I continued to think. 'It *is* rather odd.'

'That he has never spoken of him?'

'Never by the least reference. And you tell me they were "great friends".'

'Oh it wasn't *him*!' Mrs Grose with emphasis declared. 'It was Quint's own fancy. To play with him, I mean – to spoil him.' She paused a moment; then she added: 'Quint was much too free.'

This gave me, straight from my vision of his face – *such* a face! – a sudden sickness of disgust. 'Too free with *my* boy?'

'Too free with every one!'

I forbore for the moment to analyse this description further than by the reflexion that a part of it applied to several of the members of the household, of the half-dozen maids and men who were still of our small colony. But there was everything, for our apprehension, in the lucky fact that no discomfortable legend, no perturbation of scullions,[19] had ever, within any one's memory, attached to the kind old place. It had neither bad name nor ill fame, and Mrs Grose, most apparently, only desired to cling to me and to quake in silence. I even put her, the very last thing of all, to the test. It was when, at midnight, she had her hand on the schoolroom door to take leave. 'I *have* it from you then – for it's of great importance – that he was definitely and admittedly bad?'

'Oh not admittedly. *I* knew it – but the master didn't.'

'And you never told him?'

'Well, he didn't like tale-bearing – he hated complaints. He was terribly short with anything of that kind, and if people were all right to *him*—'

'He wouldn't be bothered with more?' This squared well enough with my impression of him: he was not a trouble-loving gentleman, nor so very particular perhaps about some of the company he himself kept. All the same, I pressed my informant. 'I promise you *I* would have told!'

She felt my discrimination. 'I daresay I was wrong. But really I was afraid.'

'Afraid of what?'

'Of things that man could do. Quint was so clever – he was so deep.'

I took this in still more than I probably showed. 'You weren't afraid of anything else? Not of his effect—?'

'His effect?' she repeated with a face of anguish and waiting while I faltered.

'On innocent little precious lives. They were in your charge.'

'No, they weren't in mine!' she roundly and distressfully returned. 'The master believed in him and placed him here because he was supposed not to be quite in health and the country air so good for him. So he had everything to say. Yes' – she let me have it – 'even about *them*.'

'Them – that creature?' I had to smother a kind of howl. 'And you could bear it?'

'No. I couldn't – and I can't now!' And the poor woman burst into tears.

A rigid control, from the next day, was, as I have said, to follow them; yet how often and how passionately, for a week, we came back together to the subject! Much as we had discussed it that Sunday night, I was, in the immediate later hours in especial – for it may be imagined whether I slept – still haunted with the shadow of something she had not told me. I myself had kept back nothing, but there was a word Mrs Grose had kept back. I was sure moreover by morning that this was not from a failure of frankness, but because on every side there were fears. It seems to me indeed, in raking it all over, that by the time the morrow's sun was high I had restlessly read into the facts before us almost all the meaning they were to receive from subsequent and more cruel occurrences. What they gave me above all was just the sinister figure of the living man – the dead one would keep a while! – and of the months he had continuously passed at Bly, which, added up, made a formidable stretch. The limit of this evil time had arrived only when, on the dawn of a winter's morning, Peter Quint was found, by a labourer going to early work, stone dead on the road from the village: a catastrophe explained – superficially at least – by a visible wound to his head; such a wound as might have been produced (and as, on the final evidence, *had* been) by a fatal slip, in the dark and after leaving the public-house, on the steepish icy slope, a wrong path altogether, at the bottom of which he lay. The icy slope, the turn mistaken at night and in liquor, accounted for much – practically, in the end and after the inquest and boundless chatter, for everything; but there had been matters in his life, strange passages and perils, secret disorders, vices more than suspected, that would have accounted for a good deal more.

I scarce know how to put my story into words that shall be a credible picture of my state of mind; but I was in these days literally able to find a joy in the extraordinary flight of heroism the occasion demanded of me. I now saw that I had been asked for a service admirable and difficult; and there would be a greatness in letting it be seen – oh in the right quarter! – that I could succeed where many another girl might have failed. It was an immense help to me – I confess I rather applaud myself as I look back! – that I saw my response so strongly and so simply. I was there to protect and defend the little creatures in the world the most bereaved and the most loveable, the appeal of whose helplessness had suddenly become only too explicit, a deep constant ache of one's own engaged affection. We were cut off, really, together; we were united in our danger. They had nothing but me, and I – well, I had *them*. It was in short a magnificent chance. This chance presented itself to me in an image richly material. I was a screen – I was to stand before them. The more I saw the less they would. I began to watch them in a stifled suspense, a disguised tension, that might well, had it continued too long, have turned to something like madness. What saved me, as I now see, was that it turned to another matter altogether. It didn't last as suspense – it was superseded by horrible proofs. Proofs, I say, yes – from the moment I really took hold.

This moment dated from an afternoon hour that I happened to spend in the grounds with the younger of my pupils alone. We had left Miles indoors, on the red cushion of a deep window-seat; he had wished to finish a book, and I had been glad to encourage a purpose so laudable in a young man whose only defect was a certain ingenuity of restlessness. His sister, on the contrary, had been alert to come out, and I strolled with her half an hour, seeking the shade, for the sun was still high and the day exceptionally warm. I was aware afresh with her, as we went, of how, like her brother, she contrived – it was the charming thing in both children – to let me alone without appearing to drop me and to accompany me without appearing to oppress. They were never importunate and yet never listless. My attention to them all really went to seeing them amuse themselves immensely without me: this was a spectacle they seemed actively to prepare and that employed me as an active admirer. I walked in a world of their invention – they had no occasion whatever to draw upon mine; so that my time

was taken only with being for them some remarkable person
or thing that the game of the moment required and that was
merely, thanks to my superior, my exalted stamp, a happy and
highly distinguished sinecure. I forget what I was on the present occasion; I only remember that I was something very
important and very quiet and that Flora was playing very hard.
We were on the edge of the lake, and, as we had lately begun
geography, the lake was the Sea of Azof.[20]

Suddenly, amid these elements, I became aware that on the
other side of the Sea of Azof we had an interested spectator.
The way this knowledge gathered in me was the strangest
thing in the world – the strangest, that is, except the very much
stranger in which it quickly merged itself. I had sat down with
a piece of work – for I was something or other that could sit –
on the old stone bench which overlooked the pond; and in this
position I began to take in with certitude and yet without direct vision the presence, a good way off, of a third person. The
old trees, the thick shrubbery, made a great and pleasant shade,
but it was all suffused with the brightness of the hot still hour.
There was no ambiguity in anything; none whatever at least in
the conviction I from one moment to another found myself
forming as to what I should see straight before me and across
the lake as a consequence of raising my eyes. They were attached
at this juncture to the stitching in which I was engaged, and I
can feel once more the spasm of my effort not to move them till
I should so have steadied myself as to be able to make up my
mind what to do. There was an alien object in view – a figure
whose right of presence I instantly and passionately questioned.
I recollect counting over perfectly the possibilities, reminding
myself that nothing was more natural for instance than the
appearance of one of the men about the place, or even of a
messenger, a postman or a tradesman's boy, from the village.
That reminder had as little effect on my practical certitude as I
was conscious – still even without looking – of its having upon
the character and attitude of our visitor. Nothing was more
natural than that these things should be the other things they
absolutely were not.

Of the positive identity of the apparition I would assure

myself as soon as the small clock of my courage should have ticked out the right second; meanwhile, with an effort that was already sharp enough, I transferred my eyes straight to little Flora, who, at the moment, was about ten yards away. My heart had stood still for an instant with the wonder and terror of the question whether she too would see; and I held my breath while I waited for what a cry from her, what some sudden innocent sign either of interest or of alarm, would tell me. I waited, but nothing came; then in the first place – and there is something more dire in this, I feel, than in anything I have to relate – I was determined by a sense that within a minute all spontaneous sounds from her had dropped; and in the second by the circumstance that also within the minute she had, in her play, turned her back to the water. This was her attitude when I at last looked at her – looked with the confirmed conviction that we were still, together, under direct personal notice. She had picked up a small flat piece of wood which happened to have in it a little hole that had evidently suggested to her the idea of sticking in another fragment that might figure as a mast and make the thing a boat. This second morsel, as I watched her, she was very markedly and intently attempting to tighten in its place. My apprehension of what she was doing sustained me so that after some seconds I felt I was ready for more. Then I again shifted my eyes – I faced what I had to face.

VII

I got hold of Mrs Grose as soon after this as I could; and I can give no intelligible account of how I fought out the interval. Yet I still hear myself cry as I fairly threw myself into her arms: 'They *know* – it's too monstrous: they know, they know!'

'And what on earth—?' I felt her incredulity as she held me.

'Why all that *we* know – and heaven knows what more besides!' Then as she released me I made it out to her, made it out perhaps only now with full coherency even to myself. 'Two hours ago, in the garden' – I could scarce articulate – 'Flora *saw*!'

Mrs Grose took it as she might have taken a blow in the stomach. 'She has told you?' she panted.

'Not a word – that's the horror. She kept it to herself! The child of eight, *that* child!' Unutterable still for me was the stupefaction of it.

Mrs Grose of course could only gape the wider. 'Then how do you know?'

'I was there – I saw with my eyes: saw she was perfectly aware.'

'Do you mean aware of *him*?'

'No – of *her*.' I was conscious as I spoke that I looked prodigious things, for I got the slow reflexion of them in my companion's face. 'Another person – this time; but a figure of quite as unmistakeable horror and evil: a woman in black, pale and dreadful – with such an air also, and such a face! – on the other side of the lake. I was there with the child – quiet for the hour; and in the midst of it she came.'

'Came how – from where?'

'From where they come from! She just appeared and stood there – but not so near.'

'And without coming nearer?'

'Oh for the effect and the feeling she might have been as close as you!'

My friend, with an odd impulse, fell back a step. 'Was she some one you've never seen?'

'Never. But some one the child has. Some one *you* have.' Then to show how I had thought it all out: 'My predecessor – the one who died.'

'Miss Jessel?'

'Miss Jessel. You don't believe me?' I pressed.

She turned right and left in her distress. 'How can you be sure?'

This drew from me, in the state of my nerves, a flash of impatience. 'Then ask Flora – *she's* sure!' But I had no sooner spoken than I caught myself up. 'No, for God's sake *don't*! She'll say she isn't – she'll lie!'

Mrs Grose was not too bewildered instinctively to protest. 'Ah how *can* you?'

'Because I'm clear. Flora doesn't want me to know.'

'It's only then to spare you.'

'No, no – there are depths, depths! The more I go over it the more I see in it, and the more I see in it the more I fear. I don't know what I *don't* see, what I *don't* fear!'

Mrs Grose tried to keep up with me. 'You mean you're afraid of seeing her again?'

'Oh no; that's nothing – now!' Then I explained. 'It's of *not* seeing her.'

But my companion only looked wan. 'I don't understand.'

'Why, it's that the child may keep it up – and that the child assuredly *will* – without my knowing it.'

At the image of this possibility Mrs Grose for a moment collapsed, yet presently to pull herself together again as from the positive force of the sense of what, should we yield an inch, there would really be to give way to. 'Dear, dear – we must keep our heads! And after all, if she doesn't mind it—!' She even tried a grim joke. 'Perhaps she likes it!'

'Like *such* things – a scrap of an infant!'

'Isn't it just a proof of her blest innocence?' my friend bravely enquired.

She brought me, for the instant, almost round. 'Oh we must clutch at *that* – we must cling to it! If it isn't a proof of what you say, it's a proof of – God knows what! For the woman's a horror of horrors.'

Mrs Grose, at this, fixed her eyes a minute on the ground; then at last raising them, 'Tell me how you know,' she said.

'Then you admit it's what she was?' I cried.

'Tell me how you know,' my friend simply repeated.

'Know? By seeing her! By the way she looked.'

'At you, do you mean – so wickedly?'

'Dear me, no – I could have borne that. She gave me never a glance. She only fixed the child.'

Mrs Grose tried to see it. 'Fixed her?'

'Ah with such awful eyes!'

She stared at mine as if they might really have resembled them. 'Do you mean of dislike?'

'God help us, no. Of something much worse.'

'Worse than dislike?' – this left her indeed at a loss.

'With a determination – indescribable. With a kind of fury of intention.'

I made her turn pale. 'Intention?'

'To get hold of her.' Mrs Grose – her eyes just lingering on mine – gave a shudder and walked to the window; and while she stood there looking out I completed my statement. '*That's* what Flora knows.'

After a little she turned round. 'The person was in black, you say?'

'In mourning – rather poor, almost shabby. But – yes – with extraordinary beauty.' I now recognized to what I had at last, stroke by stroke, brought the victim of my confidence, for she quite visibly weighed this. 'Oh handsome – very, very,' I insisted; 'wonderfully handsome. But infamous.'

She slowly came back to me. 'Miss Jessel – *was* infamous.' She once more took my hand in both her own, holding it as tight as if to fortify me against the increase of alarm I might draw from this disclosure. 'They were both infamous,' she finally said.

So for a little we faced it once more together; and I found absolutely a degree of help in seeing it now so straight. 'I appreciate,' I said, 'the great decency of your not having hitherto spoken; but the time has certainly come to give me the whole thing.' She appeared to assent to this, but still only in silence; seeing which I went on: 'I must have it now. Of what did she die? Come, there was something between them.'

'There was everything.'

'In spite of the difference—?'

'Oh of their rank, their condition' – she brought it woefully out. '*She* was a lady.'

I turned it over; I again saw. 'Yes – she was a lady.'

'And he so dreadfully below,' said Mrs Grose.

I felt that I doubtless needn't press too hard, in such company, on the place of a servant in the scale; but there was nothing to prevent an acceptance of my companion's own measure of my predecessor's abasement. There was a way to deal with that, and I dealt; the more readily for my full vision – on the evidence – of our employer's late clever good-looking 'own' man; impudent, assured, spoiled, depraved. 'The fellow was a hound.'

Mrs Grose considered as if it were perhaps a little a case for a sense of shades. 'I've never seen one like him. He did what he wished.'

'With *her*?'

'With them all.'

It was as if now in my friend's own eyes Miss Jessel had again appeared. I seemed at any rate for an instant to trace their evocation of her as distinctly as I had seen her by the pond; and I brought out with decision: 'It must have been also what *she* wished!'

Mrs Grose's face signified that it had been indeed, but she said at the same time: 'Poor woman – she paid for it!'

'Then you do know what she died of?' I asked.

'No – I know nothing. I wanted not to know; I was glad enough I didn't; and I thanked heaven she was well out of this!'

'Yet you had then your idea—'

'Of her real reason for leaving? Oh yes – as to that. She couldn't have stayed. Fancy it here – for a governess! And afterwards I imagined – and I still imagine. And what I imagine is dreadful.'

'Not so dreadful as what *I* do,' I replied; on which I must have shown her – as I was indeed but too conscious – a front of miserable defeat. It brought out again all her compassion for me, and at the renewed touch of her kindness my power to resist broke down. I burst, as I had the other time made her burst, into tears; she took me to her motherly breast, where my lamentation overflowed. 'I don't do it!' I sobbed in despair; 'I don't save or shield them! It's far worse than I dreamed. They're lost!'[21]

VIII

What I had said to Mrs Grose was true enough: there were in the matter I had put before her depths and possibilities that I lacked resolution to sound; so that when we met once more in the wonder of it we were of a common mind about the duty of resistance to extravagant fancies. We were to keep our heads if we should keep nothing else – difficult indeed as that might be in the face of all that, in our prodigious experience, seemed least to be questioned. Late that night, while the house slept, we had another talk in my room; when she went all the way with me as to its being beyond doubt that I had seen exactly what I had seen. I found that to keep her thoroughly in the grip of this I had only to ask her how, if I had 'made it up', I came to be able to give, of each of the persons appearing to me, a picture disclosing, to the last detail, their special marks – a portrait on the exhibition of which she had instantly recognized and named them. She wished, of course – small blame to her! – to sink the whole subject; and I was quick to assure her that my own interest in it had now violently taken the form of a search for the way to escape from it. I closed with her cordially on the article of the likelihood that with recurrence – for recurrence we took for granted – I should get used to my danger; distinctly professing that my personal exposure had suddenly become the least of my discomforts. It was my new suspicion that was intolerable; and yet even to this complication the later hours of the day had brought a little ease.

On leaving her, after my first outbreak, I had of course returned to my pupils, associating the right remedy for my dismay with that sense of their charm which I had already recognized as a resource I could positively cultivate and which had never failed me yet. I had simply, in other words, plunged afresh into Flora's special society and there become aware – it was almost a luxury! – that she could put her little conscious hand straight upon the spot that ached. She had looked at me in sweet speculation and then had accused me to my face of having 'cried'. I had supposed the ugly signs of it brushed away; but I could literally – for the time at all events – rejoice, under this fathomless charity, that they had not entirely disappeared. To gaze into the depths of blue of the child's eyes and pronounce their loveliness a trick of premature cunning was to be guilty of a cynicism in preference to which I naturally preferred to abjure my judgment and, so far as might be, my agitation. I couldn't abjure for merely wanting to, but I could repeat to Mrs Grose – as I did there, over and over, in the small hours – that with our small friends' voices in the air, their pressure on

one's heart and their fragrant faces against one's cheek, everything fell to the ground but their incapacity and their beauty.
It was a pity that, somehow, to settle this once for all, I had
equally to re-enumerate the signs of subtlety that, in the afternoon, by the lake, had made a miracle of my show of self-
possession. It was a pity to be obliged to re-investigate the
certitude of the moment itself and repeat how it had come to
me as a revelation that the inconceivable communion I then
surprised must have been for both parties a matter of habit. It
was a pity I should have had to quaver out again the reasons
for my not having, in my delusion, so much as questioned that
the little girl saw our visitant even as I actually saw Mrs Grose
herself, and that she wanted, by just so much as she did thus
see, to make me suppose she didn't, and at the same time,
without showing anything, arrive at a guess as to whether I
myself did! It was a pity I needed to recapitulate the portentous
little activities by which she sought to divert my attention – the
perceptible increase of movement, the greater intensity of play,
the singing, the gabbling of nonsense and the invitation to
romp.

Yet if I had not indulged, to prove there was nothing in it, in
this review, I should have missed the two or three dim elements
of comfort that still remained to me. I shouldn't for instance
have been able to asseverate to my friend that I was certain –
which was so much to the good – that *I* at least had not betrayed
myself. I shouldn't have been prompted, by stress of need, by
desperation of mind – I scarce know what to call it – to invoke
such further aid to intelligence as might spring from pushing my
colleague fairly to the wall. She had told me, bit by bit, under
pressure, a great deal; but a small shifty spot on the wrong side
of it all still sometimes brushed my brow like the wing of a bat;
and I remember how on this occasion – for the sleeping house
and the concentration alike of our danger and our watch
seemed to help – I felt the importance of giving the last jerk to
the curtain. 'I don't believe anything so horrible,' I recollect
saying; 'no, let us put it definitely, my dear, that I don't. But if
I did, you know, there's a thing I should require now, just without sparing you the least bit more – oh not a scrap, come! – to

get out of you. What was it you had in mind when, in our distress, before Miles came back, over the letter from his school,
you said, under my insistence, that you didn't pretend for him
he hadn't literally *ever* been "bad"? He has *not*, truly, "ever", in
these weeks that I myself have lived with him and so closely
watched him; he has been an imperturbable little prodigy of
delightful loveable goodness. Therefore you might perfectly
have made the claim for him if you had not, as it happened, seen
an exception to take. What was your exception, and to what
passage in your personal observation of him did you refer?'

It was a straight question enough, but levity was not our
note, and in any case I had before the grey dawn admonished
us to separate got my answer. What my friend had had in mind
proved immensely to the purpose. It was neither more nor less
than the particular fact that for a period of several months
Quint and the boy had been perpetually together. It was indeed
the very appropriate item of evidence of her having ventured to
criticize the propriety, to hint at the incongruity, of so close an
alliance, and even to go so far on the subject as a frank overture to Miss Jessel would take her. Miss Jessel had, with a very
high manner about it, requested her to mind her business, and
the good woman had on this directly approached little Miles.
What she had said to him, since I pressed, was that *she* liked to
see young gentlemen not forget their station.

I pressed again, of course, the closer for that. 'You reminded
him that Quint was only a base menial?'

'As you might say! And it was his answer, for one thing, that
was bad.'

'And for another thing?' I waited. 'He repeated your words
to Quint?'

'No, not that. It's just what he *wouldn't*!' she could still
impress on me. 'I was sure, at any rate,' she added, 'that he didn't.
But he denied certain occasions.'

'What occasions?'

'When they had been about together quite as if Quint were
his tutor – and a very grand one – and Miss Jessel only for the
little lady. When he had gone off with the fellow, I mean, and
spent hours with him.'

'He then prevaricated about it – he said he hadn't?' Her assent was clear enough to cause me to add in a moment: 'I see. He lied.'

'Oh!' Mrs Grose mumbled. This was a suggestion that it didn't matter; which indeed she backed up by a further remark. 'You see, after all, Miss Jessel didn't mind. She didn't forbid him.'

I considered. 'Did he put that to you as a justification?'

At this she dropped again. 'No, he never spoke of it.'

'Never mentioned her in connexion with Quint?'

She saw, visibly flushing, where I was coming out. 'Well, he didn't show anything. He denied,' she repeated; 'he denied.'

Lord, how I pressed her now! 'So that you could see he knew what was between the two wretches?'

'I don't know – I don't know!' the poor woman wailed.

'You do know, you dear thing,' I replied; 'only you haven't my dreadful boldness of mind, and you keep back, out of timidity and modesty and delicacy, even the impression that in the past, when you had, without my aid, to flounder about in silence, most of all made you miserable. But I shall get it out of you yet! There was something in the boy that suggested to you,' I continued, 'his covering and concealing their relation.'

'Oh he couldn't prevent—'

'Your learning the truth? I daresay! But, heavens,' I fell, with vehemence, a-thinking, 'what it shows that they must, to that extent, have succeeded in making of him!'

'Ah nothing that's not nice *now*!' Mrs Grose lugubriously pleaded.

'I don't wonder you looked queer,' I persisted, 'when I mentioned to you the letter from his school!'

'I doubt if I looked as queer as you!' she retorted with homely force. 'And if he was so bad then as that comes to, how is he such an angel now?'

'Yes indeed – and if he was a fiend at school! How, how, how? Well,' I said in my torment, 'you must put it to me again, though I shall not be able to tell you for some days. Only put it to me again!' I cried in a way that made my friend stare. 'There are directions in which I mustn't for the present let myself go.' Meanwhile I returned to her first example – the one to which she had just previously referred – of the boy's happy capacity for an occasional slip. 'If Quint – on your remonstrance at the time you speak of – was a base menial, one of the things Miles said to you, I find myself guessing, was that you were another.' Again her admission was so adequate that I continued: 'And you forgave him that?'

'Wouldn't *you*?'

'Oh yes!' And we exchanged there, in the stillness, a sound of the oddest amusement. Then I went on: 'At all events, while he was with the man—'

'Miss Flora was with the woman. It suited them all!'

It suited me too, I felt, only too well; by which I mean that it suited exactly the particular deadly view I was in the very act of forbidding myself to entertain. But I so far succeeded in checking the expression of this view that I will throw, just here, no further light on it than may be offered by the mention of my final observation to Mrs Grose. 'His having lied and been impudent are, I confess, less engaging specimens than I had hoped to have from you of the outbreak in him of the little natural man. Still,' I mused, 'they must do, for they make me feel more than ever that I must watch.'

It made me blush, the next minute, to see in my friend's face how much more unreservedly she had forgiven him than her anecdote struck me as pointing out to my own tenderness any way to do. This was marked when, at the schoolroom door, she quitted me. 'Surely you don't accuse *him*—'

'Of carrying on an intercourse that he conceals from me? Ah remember that, until further evidence, I now accuse nobody.' Then before shutting her out to go by another passage to her own place, 'I must just wait,' I wound up.

IX

I waited and waited, and the days took as they elapsed something from my consternation. A very few of them, in fact, passing, in constant sight of my pupils, without a fresh incident, sufficed to give to grievous fancies and even to odious memories a kind of brush of the sponge. I have spoken of the surrender to their extraordinary childish grace as a thing I could actively promote in myself, and it may be imagined if I neglected now to apply at this source for whatever balm it would yield. Stranger than I can express, certainly, was the effort to struggle against my new lights. It would doubtless have been a greater tension still, however, had it not been so frequently successful. I used to wonder how my little charges could help guessing that I thought strange things about them; and the circumstance that these things only made them more interesting was not by itself a direct aid to keeping them in the dark. I trembled lest they should see that they *were* so immensely more interesting. Putting things at the worst, at all events, as in meditation I so often did, any clouding of their innocence could only be – blameless and foredoomed as they were – a reason the more for taking risks. There were moments when I knew myself to catch them up by an irresistible impulse and press them to my heart. As soon as I had done so I used to wonder – 'What will they think of that? Doesn't it betray too much?' It would have been easy to get into a sad wild tangle about how much I might betray; but the real account, I feel, of the hours of peace I could still enjoy was that the immediate charm of my companions was a beguilement still effective even under the shadow of the possibility that it was studied. For if it occurred to me that I might occasionally excite suspicion by the little outbreaks of my sharper passion for them, so too I remember asking if I mightn't see a queerness in the traceable increase of their own demonstrations.

They were at this period extravagantly and preternaturally fond of me; which, after all, I could reflect, was no more than a graceful response in children perpetually bowed down over and hugged. The homage of which they were so lavish succeeded in truth for my nerves quite as well as if I never appeared to myself, as I may say, literally to catch them at a purpose in it. They had never, I think, wanted to do so many things for their poor protectress; I mean – though they got their lessons better and better, which was naturally what would please her most – in the way of diverting, entertaining, surprising her;

reading her passages, telling her stories, acting her charades, pouncing out at her, in disguises, as animals and historical characters, and above all astonishing her by the 'pieces' they had secretly got by heart and could interminably recite. I should never get to the bottom – were I to let myself go even now – of the prodigious private commentary, all under still more private correction, with which I in these days overscored their full hours. They had shown me from the first a facility for every-thing, a general faculty which, taking a fresh start, achieved remarkable flights. They got their little tasks as if they loved them; they indulged, from the mere exuberance of the gift, in the most unimposed little miracles of memory. They not only popped out at me as tigers and as Romans, but as Shakespear-eans, astronomers and navigators. This was so singularly the case that it had presumably much to do with the fact as to which, at the present day, I am at a loss for a different explan-ation: I allude to my unnatural composure on the subject of another school for Miles. What I remember is that I was con-tent for the time not to open the question, and that contentment must have sprung from the sense of his perpetually striking show of cleverness. He was too clever for a bad governess, for a parson's daughter, to spoil; and the strangest if not the bright-est thread in the pensive embroidery I just spoke of was the impression I might have got, if I had dared to work it out, that he was under some influence operating in his small intellectual life as a tremendous incitement.

If it was easy to reflect, however, that such a boy could post-pone school, it was at least as marked that for such a boy to have been 'kicked out' by a school-master was a mystification without end. Let me add that in their company now – and I was careful almost never to be out of it – I could follow no scent very far. We lived in a cloud of music and affection and success and private theatricals. The musical sense in each of the children was of the quickest, but the elder in especial had a marvellous knack of catching and repeating. The schoolroom piano broke into all gruesome fancies; and when that failed there were confabulations in corners, with a sequel of one of them going out in the highest spirits in order to 'come in' as

something new. I had had brothers myself, and it was no revelation to me that little girls could be slavish idolaters of little
boys. What surpassed everything was that there was a little
boy in the world who could have for the inferior age, sex and
intelligence so fine a consideration. They were extraordinarily
at one, and to say that they never either quarrelled or complained is to make the note of praise coarse for their quality of
sweetness. Sometimes perhaps indeed (when I dropped into
coarseness) I came across traces of little understandings between
them by which one of them should keep me occupied while the
other slipped away. There is a naïf side, I suppose, in all diplomacy; but if my pupils practised upon me it was surely with the
minimum of grossness. It was all in the other quarter that,
after a lull, the grossness broke out.

I find that I really hang back; but I must take my horrid
plunge. In going on with the record of what was hideous at Bly
I not only challenge the most liberal faith – for which I little
care; but (and this is another matter) I renew what I myself suffered, I again push my dreadful way through it to the end.[22]
There came suddenly an hour after which, as I look back, the
business seems to me to have been all pure suffering; but I have
at least reached the heart of it, and the straightest road out is
doubtless to advance. One evening – with nothing to lead up or
prepare it – I felt the cold touch of the impression that had
breathed on me the night of my arrival and which, much lighter
then as I have mentioned, I should probably have made little of
in memory had my subsequent sojourn been less agitated. I had
not gone to bed; I sat reading by a couple of candles. There was
a roomful of old books at Bly – last-century fiction some of it,
which, to the extent of a distinctly deprecated renown, but
never to so much as that of a stray specimen, had reached the
sequestered home and appealed to the unavowed curiosity of
my youth. I remember that the book I had in my hand was
Fielding's 'Amelia';[23] also that I was wholly awake. I recall further both a general conviction that it was horribly late and a
particular objection to looking at my watch. I figure finally
that the white curtain draping, in the fashion of those days, the
head of Flora's little bed, shrouded, as I had assured myself

long before, the perfection of childish rest. I recollect in short that though I was deeply interested in my author I found myself, at the turn of a page and with his spell all scattered, looking straight up from him and hard at the door of my room. There was a moment during which I listened, reminded of the faint sense I had had, the first night, of there being something undefinably astir in the house, and noted the soft breath of the open casement just move the half-drawn blind. Then, with all the marks of a deliberation that must have seemed magnificent had there been any one to admire it, I laid down my book, rose to my feet and, taking a candle, went straight out of the room and, from the passage, on which my light made little impression, noiselessly closed and locked the door.

I can say now neither what determined nor what guided me, but I went straight along the lobby, holding my candle high, till I came within sight of the tall window that presided over the great turn of the staircase. At this point I precipitately found myself aware of three things. They were practically simultaneous, yet they had flashes of succession. My candle, under a bold flourish, went out, and I perceived, by the uncovered window, that the yielding dusk of earliest morning rendered it unnecessary. Without it, the next instant, I knew that there was a figure on the stair. I speak of sequences, but I required no lapse of seconds to stiffen myself for a third encounter with Quint. The apparition had reached the landing halfway up and was therefore on the spot nearest the window, where, at sight of me, it stopped short and fixed me exactly as it had fixed me from the tower and from the garden. He knew me as well as I knew him; and so, in the cold faint twilight, with a glimmer in the high glass and another on the polish of the oak stair below, we faced each other in our common intensity. He was absolutely, on this occasion, a living detestable dangerous presence. But that was not the wonder of wonders; I reserve this distinction for quite another circumstance: the circumstance that dread had unmistakably quitted me and that there was nothing in me unable to meet and measure him.

I had plenty of anguish after that extraordinary moment, but I had, thank God, no terror. And he knew I hadn't – I found myself at the end of an instant magnificently aware of this. I felt, in a fierce rigour of confidence, that if I stood my ground a minute I should cease – for the time at least – to have him to reckon with; and during the minute, accordingly, the thing was as human and hideous as a real interview: hideous just because it *was* human, as human as to have met alone, in the small hours, in a sleeping house, some enemy, some adventurer, some criminal. It was the dead silence of our long gaze at such close quarters that gave the whole horror, huge as it was, its only note of the unnatural. If I had met a murderer in such a place and at such an hour we still at least would have spoken. Something would have passed, in life, between us; if nothing had passed one of us would have moved. The moment was so prolonged that it would have taken but little more to make me doubt if even *I* were in life. I can't express what followed it save by saying that the silence itself – which was indeed in a manner an attestation of my strength – became the element into which I saw the figure disappear; in which I definitely saw it turn, as I might have seen the low wretch to which it had once belonged turn on receipt of an order, and pass, with my eyes on the villainous back that no hunch could have more disfigured, straight down the staircase and into the darkness in which the next bend was lost.[24]

X

I remained a while at the top of the stair, but with the effect presently of understanding that when my visitor had gone, he had gone; then I returned to my room. The foremost thing I saw there by the light of the candle I had left burning was that Flora's little bed was empty; and on this I caught my breath with all the terror that, five minutes before, I had been able to resist. I dashed at the place in which I had left her lying and over which – for the small silk counterpane and the sheets were disarranged – the white curtains had been deceivingly pulled forward; then my step, to my unutterable relief, produced an answering sound: I noticed an agitation of the window-blind,

and the child, ducking down, emerged rosily from the other
side of it. She stood there in so much of her candour and so little
of her night-gown, with her pink bare feet and the golden glow
of her curls. She looked intensely grave, and I had never had
such a sense of losing an advantage acquired (the thrill of which
had just been so prodigious) as on my consciousness that she
addressed me with a reproach – 'You naughty: where *have* you
been?' Instead of challenging her own irregularity I found
myself arraigned and explaining. She herself explained, for that
matter, with the loveliest eagerest simplicity. She had known
suddenly, as she lay there, that I was out of the room, and had
jumped up to see what had become of me. I had dropped, with
the joy of her reappearance, back into my chair – feeling then,
and then only, a little faint; and she had pattered straight over
to me, thrown herself upon my knee, given herself to be held
with the flame of the candle full in the wonderful little face
that was still flushed with sleep. I remember closing my eyes an
instant, yieldingly, consciously, as before the excess of something beautiful that shone out of the blue of her own. 'You
were looking for me out of the window?' I said. 'You thought
I might be walking in the grounds?'

'Well, you know, I thought some one was' – she never
blanched as she smiled out that at me.

Oh how I looked at her now! 'And did you see any one?'

'Ah *no*!' she returned almost (with the full privilege of childish inconsequence) resentfully, though with a long sweetness in
her little drawl of the negative.

At that moment, in the state of my nerves, I absolutely
believed she lied; and if I once more closed my eyes it was
before the dazzle of the three or four possible ways in which I
might take this up. One of these for a moment tempted me
with such singular force that, to resist it, I must have gripped
my little girl with a spasm that, wonderfully, she submitted to
without a cry or a sign of fright. Why not break out at her on
the spot and have it all over? – give it to her straight in her
lovely little lighted face? 'You see, you see, you *know* that you
do and that you already quite suspect I believe it; therefore why
not frankly confess it to me, so that we may at least live with

it together and learn perhaps, in the strangeness of our fate, where we are and what it means?' This solicitation dropped, alas, as it came: if I could immediately have succumbed to it I might have spared myself – well, you'll see what. Instead of succumbing I sprang again to my feet, looked at her bed and took a helpless middle way. 'Why did you pull the curtain over the place to make me think you were still there?'

Flora luminously considered; after which, with her little divine smile: 'Because I don't like to frighten you!'

'But if I had, by your idea, gone out—?'

She absolutely declined to be puzzled; she turned her eyes to the flame of the candle as if the question were as irrelevant, or at any rate as impersonal, as Mrs Marcet[25] or nine-times-nine. 'Oh but you know,' she quite adequately answered, 'that you might come back, you dear, and that you *have*!' And after a little, when she had got into bed, I had, a long time, by almost sitting on her for the retention of her hand, to show how I recognized the pertinence of my return.

You may imagine the general complexion, from that moment, of my nights. I repeatedly sat up till I didn't know when; I selected moments when my room-mate unmistakably slept, and, stealing out, took noiseless turns in the passage. I even pushed as far as to where I had last met Quint. But I never met him there again, and I may as well say at once that I on no other occasion saw him in the house. I just missed, on the staircase, nevertheless, a different adventure. Looking down it from the top I once recognized the presence of a woman seated on one of the lower steps with her back presented to me, her body half-bowed and her head, in an attitude of woe, in her hands. I had been there but an instant, however, when she vanished without looking round at me. I knew, for all that, exactly what dreadful face she had to show; and I wondered whether, if instead of being above I had been below, I should have had the same nerve for going up that I had lately shown Quint. Well, there continued to be plenty of call for nerve. On the eleventh night after my latest encounter with that gentleman – they were all numbered now – I had an alarm that perilously skirted it and that indeed, from the particular quality of its unexpectedness, proved quite my sharpest shock.

It was precisely the first night during this series that, weary with vigils, I had conceived I might again without laxity lay myself down at my old hour. I slept immediately and, as I afterwards knew, till about one o'clock; but when I woke it was to sit straight up, as completely roused as if a hand had shaken me. I had left a light burning, but it was now out, and I felt an instant certainty that Flora had extinguished it. This brought me to my feet and straight, in the darkness, to her bed, which I found she had left. A glance at the window enlightened me further, and the striking of a match completed the picture.

The child had again got up – this time blowing out the taper, and had again, for some purpose of observation or response, squeezed in behind the blind and was peering out into the night. That she now saw – as she had not, I had satisfied myself, the previous time – was proved to me by the fact that she was disturbed neither by my re-illumination nor by the haste I made to get into slippers and into a wrap. Hidden, protected, absorbed, she evidently rested on the sill – the casement opened forward – and gave herself up. There was a great still moon to help her, and this fact had counted in my quick decision. She was face to face with the apparition we had met at the lake, and could now communicate with it as she had not then been able to do. What I, on my side, had to care for was, without disturbing her, to reach, from the corridor, some other window turned to the same quarter. I got to the door without her hearing me; I got out of it, closed it and listened, from the other side, for some sound from her. While I stood in the passage I had my eyes on her brother's door, which was but ten steps off and which, indescribably, produced in me a renewal of the strange impulse that I lately spoke of as my temptation. What if I should go straight in and march to *his* window? – what if, by risking to his boyish bewilderment a revelation of my motive, I should throw across the rest of the mystery the long halter of my boldness?

This thought held me sufficiently to make me cross to his threshold and pause again. I preternaturally listened; I figured to myself what might portentously be; I wondered if his bed were also empty and he also secretly at watch. It was a deep soundless minute, at the end of which my impulse failed. He was quiet; he might be innocent; the risk was hideous; I turned away. There was a figure in the grounds – a figure prowling for a sight, the visitor with whom Flora was engaged; but it wasn't the visitor most concerned with my boy. I hesitated afresh, but on other grounds and only a few seconds; then I had made my choice. There were empty rooms enough at Bly, and it was only a question of choosing the right one. The right one suddenly presented itself to me as the lower one – though high above the gardens – in the solid corner of the house that I have spoken of as the old tower. This was a large square chamber, arranged with some state as a bedroom, the extravagant size of which made it so inconvenient that it had not for years, though kept by Mrs Grose in exemplary order, been occupied. I had often admired it and I knew my way about in it; I had only, after just faltering at the first chill gloom of its disuse, to pass across it and unbolt in all quietness one of the shutters. Achieving this transit I uncovered the glass without a sound and, applying my face to the pane, was able, the darkness without being much less than within, to see that I commanded the right direction. Then I saw something more. The moon made the night extraordinarily penetrable and showed me on the lawn a person, diminished by distance, who stood there motionless and as if fascinated, looking up to where I had appeared – looking, that is, not so much straight at me as at something that was apparently above me. There was clearly another person above me – there was a person on the tower; but the presence on the lawn was not in the least what I had conceived and had confidently hurried to meet. The presence on the lawn – I felt sick as I made it out – was poor little Miles himself.

XI

It was not till late next day that I spoke to Mrs Grose; the rigour with which I kept my pupils in sight making it often difficult to meet her privately: the more as we each felt the importance of not provoking – on the part of the servants quite as much as on that of the children – any suspicion of a secret flurry or of a discussion of mysteries. I drew a great security in this particular from her mere smooth aspect. There was nothing in her fresh face to pass on to others the least of my horrible confidences. She believed me, I was sure, absolutely: if she hadn't I don't know what would have become of me, for I couldn't have borne the strain alone. But she was a magnificent monument to the blessing of a want of imagination, and if she could see in our little charges nothing but their beauty and amiability, their happiness and cleverness, she had no direct communication with the sources of my trouble. If they had been at all visibly blighted or battered she would doubtless have grown, on tracing it back, haggard enough to match them; as matters stood, however, I could feel her, when she surveyed them with her large white arms folded and the habit of serenity in all her look, thank the Lord's mercy that if they were ruined the pieces would still serve. Flights of fancy gave place, in her mind, to a steady fireside glow, and I had already begun to perceive how, with the development of the conviction that – as time went on without a public accident – our young things could, after all, look out for themselves, she addressed her greatest solicitude to the sad case presented by their deputy-guardian. That, for myself, was a sound simplification: I could engage that, to the world, my face should tell no tales, but it would have been, in the conditions, an immense added worry to find myself anxious about hers.

At the hour I now speak of she had joined me, under pressure, on the terrace, where, with the lapse of the season, the afternoon sun was now agreeable; and we sat there together while before us and at a distance, yet within call if we wished, the children strolled to and fro in one of their most manageable moods. They moved slowly, in unison, below us, over the lawn, the boy, as they went, reading aloud from a story-book and passing his arm round his sister to keep her quite in touch. Mrs Grose watched them with positive placidity; then I caught the suppressed intellectual creak with which she conscientiously turned to take from me a view of the back of the tapestry. I had made her a receptacle of lurid things, but there was an odd recognition of my superiority – my accomplishments and my function – in her patience under my pain. She offered her mind to my disclosures as, had I wished to mix a witch's broth and proposed it with assurance, she would have held out a large clean saucepan. This had become thoroughly her attitude by the time that, in my recital of the events of the night, I reached the point of what Miles had said to me when, after seeing him, at such a monstrous hour, almost on the very spot where he happened now to be, I had gone down to bring him in; choosing then, at the window, with a concentrated need of not alarming the house, rather that method than any noisier process. I had left her meanwhile in little doubt of my small hope of representing with success even to her actual sympathy my sense of the real splendour of the little inspiration with which, after I had got him into the house, the boy met my final articulate challenge. As soon as I appeared in the moonlight on the terrace he had come to me as straight as possible; on which I had taken his hand without a word and led him, through the dark spaces, up the staircase where Quint had so hungrily hovered for him, along the lobby where I had listened and trembled, and so to his forsaken room.

Not a sound, on the way, had passed between us, and I had wondered – oh *how* I had wondered! – if he were groping about in his dreadful little mind for something plausible and not too grotesque. It would tax his invention certainly, and I felt, this time, over his real embarrassment, a curious thrill of triumph. It was a sharp trap for any game hitherto successful. He could play no longer at perfect propriety, nor could he pretend to it; so how the deuce would he get out of the scrape? There beat in me indeed, with the passionate throb of this question, an equal dumb appeal as to how the deuce *I* should. I was confronted at last, as never yet, with all the risk attached even now to sounding my own horrid note. I remember in fact that as we pushed into his little chamber, where the bed had not been slept in at all and the window, uncovered to the moonlight, made the place so clear that there was no need of striking a match – I remember how I suddenly dropped, sank upon the edge of the bed from the force of the idea that he must know how he really, as they say, 'had' me. He could do what he liked, with all his cleverness to help him, so long as I should continue to defer to the old tradition of the criminality of those caretakers of the young who minister to superstitions and fears. He 'had' me indeed, and in a cleft stick; for who would ever absolve me, who would consent that I should go unhung, if, by the faintest tremor of an overture, I were the first to introduce into our perfect intercourse an element so dire? No, no: it was useless to attempt to convey to Mrs Grose, just as it is scarcely less so to attempt to suggest here, how, during our short stiff brush there in the dark, he fairly shook me with admiration. I was of course thoroughly kind and merciful; never, never yet had I placed on his small shoulders hands of such tenderness as those with which, while I rested against the bed, I held him there well under fire. I had no alternative but, in form at least, to put it to him.

'You must tell me now – and all the truth. What did you go out for? What were you doing there?'

I can still see his wonderful smile, the whites of his beautiful eyes and the uncovering of his clear teeth, shine to me in the dusk. 'If I tell you why, will you understand?' My heart, at this, leaped into my mouth. *Would* he tell me why? I found no sound on my lips to press it, and I was aware of answering only with a vague repeated grimacing nod. He was gentleness itself, and while I wagged my head at him he stood there more than ever a little fairy prince. It was his brightness indeed that gave me a respite. Would it be so great if he were really going to tell me? 'Well,' he said at last, 'just exactly in order that you should do this.'

'Do what?'

'Think me – for a change – *bad*!' I shall never forget the sweetness and gaiety with which he brought out the word, nor how, on top of it, he bent forward and kissed me. It was practically the end of everything. I met his kiss and I had to make, while I folded him for a minute in my arms, the most stupendous effort not to cry. He had given exactly the account of himself that permitted least my going behind it, and it was only with the effect of confirming my acceptance of it that, as I presently glanced about the room, I could say –

'Then you didn't undress at all?'

He fairly glittered in the gloom. 'Not at all. I sat up and read.'

'And when did you go down?'

'At midnight. When I'm bad I *am* bad!'

'I see, I see – it's charming. But how could you be sure I should know it?'

'Oh I arranged that with Flora.' His answers rang out with a readiness! 'She was to get up and look out.'

'Which is what she did do.' It was I who fell into the trap!

'So she disturbed you, and, to see what she was looking at, you also looked – you saw.'

'While you,' I concurred, 'caught your death in the night air!'

He literally bloomed so from this exploit that he could afford radiantly to assent. 'How otherwise should I have been bad enough?' he asked. Then, after another embrace, the incident and our interview closed on my recognition of all the reserves of goodness that, for his joke, he had been able to draw upon.

XII

The particular impression I had received proved in the morning light, I repeat, not quite successfully presentable to Mrs Grose, though I re-enforced it with the mention of still another remark that he had made before we separated. 'It all lies in half a dozen words,' I said to her, 'words that really settle the matter. "Think, you know, what I *might* do!" He threw that off to show me how good he is. He knows down to the ground what he "might do". That's what he gave them a taste of at school.'

'Lord, you do change!' cried my friend.

'I don't change – I simply make it out. The four, depend upon it, perpetually meet. If on either of these last nights you had been with either child you'd clearly have understood. The more I've watched and waited the more I've felt that if there were nothing else to make it sure it would be made so by the systematic silence of each. *Never*, by a slip of the tongue, have they so much as alluded to either of their old friends, any more than Miles has alluded to his expulsion. Oh yes, we may sit here and look at them, and they may show off to us there to their fill; but even while they pretend to be lost in their fairy-tale they're steeped in their vision of the dead restored to them. He's not reading to her,' I declared; 'they're talking of *them* – they're talking horrors! I go on, I know, as if I were crazy; and it's a wonder I'm not. What I've seen would have made *you* so; but it has only made me more lucid, made me get hold of still other things.'

My lucidity must have seemed awful, but the charming creatures who were victims of it, passing and repassing in their interlocked sweetness, gave my colleague something to hold on by; and I felt how tight she held as, without stirring in the breath of my passion, she covered them still with her eyes. 'Of what other things have you got hold?'

'Why of the very things that have delighted, fascinated and yet, at bottom, as I now so strangely see, mystified and trou-bled me. Their more than earthly beauty, their absolutely unnatural goodness. It's a game,' I went on; 'it's a policy and a fraud!'

'On the part of little darlings—?'

'As yet mere lovely babies? Yes, mad as that seems!' The very act of bringing it out really helped me to trace it – follow it all up and piece it all together. 'They haven't been good – they've only been absent. It has been easy to live with them because they're simply leading a life of their own. They're not mine – they're not ours. They're his and they're hers!'

'Quint's and that woman's?'

'Quint's and that woman's. They want to get to them.'

Oh how, at this, poor Mrs Grose appeared to study them! 'But for what?'

'For the love of all the evil that, in those dreadful days, the pair put into them. And to ply them with that evil still, to keep up the work of demons, is what brings the others back.'

'Laws!'[26] said my friend under her breath. The exclamation was homely, but it revealed a real acceptance of my further proof of what, in the bad time – for there had been a worse even than this! – must have occurred. There could have been no such justification for me as the plain assent of her experience to whatever depth of depravity I found credible in our brace of scoundrels. It was in obvious submission of memory that she brought out after a moment: 'They *were* rascals! But what can they now do?' she pursued.

'Do?' I echoed so loud that Miles and Flora, as they passed at their distance, paused an instant in their walk and looked at us. 'Don't they do enough?' I demanded in a lower tone, while the children, having smiled and nodded and kissed hands to us, resumed their exhibition. We were held by it a minute; then I answered: 'They can destroy them!' At this my companion did turn, but the appeal she launched was a silent one, the effect of which was to make me more explicit. 'They don't know as yet quite how – but they're trying hard. They're seen only across, as it were, and beyond – in strange places and on high places, the top of towers, the roof of houses, the outside of windows, the further edge of pools; but there's a deep design, on either side, to shorten the distance and overcome the obstacle: so the success of the tempters is only a question of time. They've only to keep to their suggestions of danger.'

'For the children to come?'

'And perish in the attempt!' Mrs Grose slowly got up, and I scrupulously added: 'Unless, of course, we can prevent!'

Standing there before me while I kept my seat she visibly turned things over. 'Their uncle must do the preventing. He must take them away.'

'And who's to make him?'

She had been scanning the distance, but she now dropped on me a foolish face. 'You, Miss.'

'By writing to him that his house is poisoned and his little nephew and niece mad?'[27]

'But if they *are*, Miss?'

'And if I am myself, you mean? That's charming news to be sent him by a person enjoying his confidence and whose prime undertaking was to give him no worry.'

Mrs Grose considered, following the children again. 'Yes, he do hate worry. That was the great reason—'

'Why those fiends took him in so long? No doubt, though his indifference must have been awful. As I'm not a fiend, at any rate, I shouldn't take him in.'

My companion, after an instant and for all answer, sat down again and grasped my arm. 'Make him at any rate come to you.'

I stared. 'To *me*?' I had a sudden fear of what she might do. '"Him"?'

'He ought to *be* here – he ought to help.'

I quickly rose and I think I must have shown her a queerer face than ever yet. 'You see me asking him for a visit?' No, with her eyes on my face she evidently couldn't. Instead of it even – as a woman reads another – she could see what I myself saw: his derision, his amusement, his contempt for the breakdown of my resignation at being left alone and for the fine machinery I had set in motion to attract his attention to my slighted charms. She didn't know – no one knew – how proud I had been to serve him and to stick to our terms; yet she none the less took the measure, I think, of the warning I now gave her. 'If you should so lose your head as to appeal to him for me—'

She was really frightened. 'Yes, Miss?'

'I would leave, on the spot, both him and you.'[28]

XIII

It was all very well to join them, but speaking to them proved quite as much as ever an effort beyond my strength – offered, in close quarters, difficulties as insurmountable as before. This situation continued a month, and with new aggravations and particular notes, the note above all, sharper and sharper, of the small ironic consciousness on the part of my pupils. It was not, I am as sure to-day as I was sure then, my mere infernal imagination: it was absolutely traceable that they were aware of my predicament and that this strange relation made, in a manner, for a long time, the air in which we moved. I don't mean that they had their tongues in their cheeks or did anything vulgar, for that was not one of their dangers: I do mean, on the other hand, that the element of the unnamed and untouched became, between us, greater than any other, and that so much avoidance couldn't have been made successful without a great deal of tacit arrangement. It was as if, at moments, we were perpetually coming into sight of subjects before which we must stop short, turning suddenly out of alleys that we perceived to be blind, closing with a little bang that made us look at each other – for, like all bangs, it was something louder than we had intended – the doors we had indiscreetly opened. All roads lead to Rome, and there were times when it might have struck us that almost every branch of study or subject of conversation skirted forbidden ground. Forbidden ground was the question of the return of the dead in general and of whatever, in especial, might survive, for memory, of the friends little children had lost. There were days when I could have sworn that one of them had, with a small invisible nudge, said to the other: 'She thinks she'll do it this time – but she *won't*!' To 'do it' would have been to indulge for instance – and for once in a way – in some direct reference to the lady who had prepared them for my discipline. They had a delightful endless appetite for passages in my own history to which I had again and again treated them; they were in possession of everything that had ever happened to me, had had, with every circumstance, the story of my smallest adventures and of those of my brothers and sisters and of the cat and the dog at home, as well as many particulars of the whimsical bent[29] of my father, of the furniture and arrangement of our house and of the conversation of the old women of our village. There were things enough, taking one with another, to chatter about, if one went very fast and knew by instinct when to go round. They pulled with an art of their own the strings of my invention and my memory; and nothing else perhaps, when I thought of such occasions afterwards, gave me so the suspicion of being watched from under cover. It was in any case over *my* life, *my* past and *my* friends alone that we could take anything like our ease; a state of affairs that led them sometimes without the least pertinence to break out into sociable reminders. I was invited – with no visible connexion – to repeat afresh Goody Gosling's celebrated *mot*[30] or to confirm the details already supplied as to the cleverness of the vicarage pony.

It was partly at such junctures as these and partly at quite different ones that, with the turn my matters had now taken, my predicament, as I have called it, grew most sensible. The fact that the days passed for me without another encounter ought, it would have appeared, to have done something toward soothing my nerves. Since the light brush, that second night on the upper landing, of the presence of a woman at the foot of the stair, I had seen nothing, whether in or out of the house, that one had better not have seen. There was many a corner round which I expected to come upon Quint, and many a situation that, in a merely sinister way, would have favoured the appearance of Miss Jessel. The summer had turned, the summer had gone; the autumn had dropped upon Bly and had blown out half our lights. The place, with its grey sky and withered garlands, its bared spaces and scattered dead leaves, was like a theatre after the performance – all strewn with crumpled playbills. There were exactly states of the air, conditions of sound and of stillness, unspeakable impressions of the *kind* of ministering moment, that brought back to me, long enough to catch it, the feeling of the medium in which, that June evening out of doors, I had had my first sight of Quint, and in which too, at those other instants, I had, after seeing him through the window, looked for him in vain in the circle of shrubbery. I recognized the signs, the portents – I recognized the moment, the spot. But they remained unaccompanied and empty, and I continued unmolested; if unmolested one could call a young woman whose sensibility had, in the most extraordinary fashion, not declined but deepened. I had said in my talk with Mrs Grose on that horrid scene of Flora's by the lake – and had perplexed her by so saying – that it would from that moment distress me much more to lose my power than to keep it. I had then expressed what was vividly in my mind: the truth that, whether the children really saw or not – since, that is, it was not yet definitely proved – I greatly preferred, as a safeguard, the fulness of my own exposure. I was ready to know the very worst that was to be known. What I had then had an ugly glimpse of was that my eyes might be sealed just while theirs were most opened. Well, my eyes *were* sealed, it appeared, at present – a consummation for which it seemed blasphemous not to thank God. There was, alas, a difficulty about that: I would have thanked him with all my soul had I not had in a proportionate measure this conviction of the secret of my pupils.

How can I retrace to-day the strange steps of my obsession? There were times of our being together when I would have been ready to swear that, literally, in my presence, but with my direct sense of it closed, they had visitors who were known and were welcome. Then it was that, had I not been deterred by the very chance that such an injury might prove greater than the injury to be averted, my exaltation would have broken out. 'They're here, they're here, you little wretches,' I would have cried, 'and you can't deny it now!' The little wretches denied it with all the added volume of their sociability and their tenderness, just in the crystal depths of which – like the flash of a fish in a stream – the mockery of their advantage peeped up. The shock had in truth sunk into me still deeper than I knew on the night when, looking out either for Quint or for Miss Jessel under the stars, I had seen there the boy over whose rest I watched and who had immediately brought in with him – had straightway there turned on me – the lovely upward look with which, from the battlements above us, the hideous apparition of Quint had played. If it was a question of a scare my discovery on this occasion had scared me more than any other, and it was essentially in the scared state that I drew my actual conclusions. They harassed me so that sometimes, at odd moments, I shut myself up audibly to rehearse – it was at once a fantastic relief and a renewed despair – the manner in which I might come to the point. I approached it from one side and the other while, in my room, I flung myself about, but I always broke down in the monstrous utterance of names. As they died away on my lips I said to myself that I should indeed help them to represent something infamous if by pronouncing them I should violate as rare a little case of instinctive delicacy as any schoolroom probably had ever known. When I said to myself: 'They have the manners to be silent, and you, trusted as you are, the baseness to speak!' I felt myself crimson and covered my face with my hands. After these secret scenes I chattered more than ever, going on volubly enough till one of our prodigious palpable hushes occurred – I can call them nothing else – the strange dizzy lift or swim (I try for terms!) into a stillness, a pause of all life, that had nothing to do with the more or less noise we at the moment might be engaged in making and that I could hear through any intensified mirth or quickened recitation or louder strum of the piano. Then it was that the others, the outsiders, were there. Though they were not angels they 'passed', as the French say, causing me, while they stayed, to tremble with the fear of their addressing to their younger victims some yet more infernal message or more vivid image than they had thought good enough for myself.

What it was least possible to get rid of was the cruel idea that, whatever I had seen, Miles and Flora saw *more* – things terrible and unguessable and that sprang from dreadful passages of intercourse in the past. Such things naturally left on the surface, for the time, a chill that we vociferously denied we felt; and we had all three, with repetition, got into such splendid training that we went, each time, to mark the close of the incident, almost automatically through the very same movements. It was striking of the children at all events to kiss me inveterately with a wild irrelevance and never to fail – one or the other – of the precious question that had helped us through many a peril. 'When do you think he *will* come? Don't you think we *ought* to write?' – there was nothing like that enquiry, we found by experience, for carrying off an awkwardness. 'He' of course was their uncle in Harley Street; and we lived in much profusion of theory that he might at any moment arrive to mingle in our circle. It was impossible to have given less encouragement than he had administered to such a doctrine, but if we had not had the doctrine to fall back upon we should have deprived each other of some of our finest exhibitions. He never wrote to them – that may have been selfish, but it was a part of the flattery of his trust of myself; for the way in which a man pays his highest tribute to a woman is apt to be but by the more festal celebration of one of the sacred laws of his comfort. So I held that I carried out the spirit of the pledge given not to appeal to him when I let our young friends understand that their own letters were but charming literary exercises. They were too beautiful to be posted; I kept them myself; I have them all to this hour. This was a rule indeed which only added to the satiric effect of my being plied with the supposition that he might at any moment be among us. It was exactly as if our young friends knew how almost more awkward than anything else that might be for me. There appears to me moreover as I look back no note in all this more extraordinary than the mere fact that, in spite of my tension and of their triumph, I never lost patience with them. Adorable they must in truth have been, I now feel, since I didn't in these days hate them! Would exasperation, however, if relief had longer been postponed, finally have betrayed me? It little matters, for relief arrived. I call it relief though it was only the relief that a snap brings to a strain or the burst of a thunderstorm to a day of suffocation. It was at least change, and it came with a rush.

XIV

Walking to church a certain Sunday morning, I had little Miles at my side and his sister, in advance of us and at Mrs Grose's, well in sight. It was a crisp clear day, the first of its order for some time; the night had brought a touch of frost and the autumn air, bright and sharp, made the church-bells almost gay. It was an odd accident of thought that I should have happened at such a moment to be particularly and very gratefully struck with the obedience of my little charges. Why did they never resent my inexorable, my perpetual society? Something or other had brought nearer home to me that I had all but pinned the boy to my shawl, and that in the way our companions were marshalled before me I might have appeared to provide against some danger of rebellion. I was like a gaoler with an eye to possible surprises and escapes. But all this belonged – I mean their magnificent little surrender – just to the special array of the facts that were most abysmal. Turned out for Sunday by his uncle's tailor, who had had a free hand and a notion of pretty waistcoats and of his grand little air, Miles's whole title to independence, the rights of his sex and situation, were so stamped upon him that if he had suddenly struck for freedom I should have had nothing to say. I was by the strangest of chances wondering how I should meet him when the revolution unmistakably occurred. I call it a revolution because I now see how, with the word he spoke, the curtain rose on the last act of my dreadful drama and the catastrophe was precipitated. 'Look here, my dear, you know,' he charmingly said, 'when in the world, please, am I going back to school?'

Transcribed here the speech sounds harmless enough, particularly as uttered in the sweet, high, casual pipe with which, at all interlocutors, but above all at his eternal governess, he threw off intonations as if he were tossing roses. There was something in them that always made one 'catch', and I caught at any rate now so effectually that I stopped as short as if one of the trees of the park had fallen across the road. There was something new, on the spot, between us, and he was perfectly aware I recognized it, though to enable me to do so he had no need to look a whit less candid and charming than usual. I could feel in him how he already, from my at first finding nothing to reply, perceived the advantage he had gained. I was so slow to find anything that he had plenty of time, after a minute, to continue with his suggestive but inconclusive smile: 'You know, my dear, that for a fellow to be with a lady *always*—!' His 'my dear' was constantly on his lips for me, and nothing could have expressed more the exact shade of the sentiment with which I desired to inspire my pupils than its fond familiarity. It was so respectfully easy.

But oh how I felt that at present I must pick my own phrases! I remember that, to gain time, I tried to laugh, and I seemed to see in the beautiful face with which he watched me how ugly and queer I looked. 'And always with the same lady?' I returned.

He neither blenched nor winked. The whole thing was virtually out between us. 'Ah of course she's a jolly "perfect" lady; but after all I'm a fellow, don't you see? who's – well, getting on.'

I lingered there with him an instant ever so kindly. 'Yes, you're getting on.' Oh but I felt helpless!

I have kept to this day the heartbreaking little idea of how he seemed to know that and to play with it. 'And you can't say I've not been awfully good, can you?'

I laid my hand on his shoulder, for though I felt how much better it would have been to walk on I was not yet quite able. 'No, I can't say that, Miles.'

'Except just that one night, you know—!'

'That one night?' I couldn't look as straight as he.

'Why when I went down – went out of the house.'

'Oh yes. But I forget what you did it for.'

'You forget?' – he spoke with the sweet extravagance of childish reproach. 'Why it was just to show you I could!'

'Oh yes – you could.'

'And I can again.'

I felt I might perhaps after all succeed in keeping my wits about me. 'Certainly. But you won't.'

'No, not *that* again. It was nothing.'

'It was nothing,' I said. 'But we must go on.'

He resumed our walk with me, passing his hand into my arm. 'Then when *am* I going back?'

I wore, in turning it over, my most responsible air. 'Were you very happy at school?'

He just considered. 'Oh I'm happy enough anywhere!'

'Well then,' I quavered, 'if you're just as happy here—!'

'Ah but that isn't everything! Of course *you* know a lot—'

'But you hint that you know almost as much?' I risked as he paused.

'Not half I want to!' Miles honestly professed. 'But it isn't so much that.'

'What is it then?'

'Well – I want to see more life.'

'I see; I see.' We had arrived within sight of the church and of various persons, including several of the household of Bly, on their way to it and clustered about the door to see us go in. I quickened our step; I wanted to get there before the question between us opened up much further; I reflected hungrily that he would have for more than an hour to be silent; and I thought with envy of the comparative dusk of the pew and of the almost spiritual help of the hassock on which I might bend my knees. I seemed literally to be running a race with some confusion to which he was about to reduce me, but I felt he had got in first when, before we had even entered the churchyard, he threw out –

'I want my own sort!'

It literally made me bound forward. 'There aren't many of your own sort, Miles!' I laughed. 'Unless perhaps dear little Flora!'

'You really compare me to a baby girl?'

This found me singularly weak. 'Don't you then *love* our sweet Flora?'

'If I didn't – and you too; if I didn't—!' he repeated as if retreating for a jump, yet leaving his thought so unfinished that, after we had come into the gate, another stop, which he imposed on me by the pressure of his arm, had become inevitable. Mrs Grose and Flora had passed into the church, the other worshippers had followed and we were, for the minute, alone among the old thick graves. We had paused, on the path from the gate, by a low oblong table-like tomb.

'Yes, if you didn't—?'

He looked, while I waited, about at the graves. 'Well, you know what!' But he didn't move, and he presently produced something that made me drop straight down on the stone slab as if suddenly to rest. 'Does my uncle think what *you* think?'

I markedly rested. 'How do you know what I think?'

'Ah well, of course I don't; for it strikes me you never tell me. But I mean does *he* know?'

'Know what, Miles?'

'Why the way I'm going on.'

I recognized quickly enough that I could make, to this enquiry, no answer that wouldn't involve something of a sacrifice of my employer. Yet it struck me that we were all, at Bly, sufficiently sacrificed to make that venial. 'I don't think your uncle much cares.'

Miles, on this, stood looking at me. 'Then don't you think he can be made to?'

'In what way?'

'Why by his coming down.'

'But who'll get him to come down?'

'*I* will!' the boy said with extraordinary brightness and emphasis. He gave me another look charged with that expression and then marched off alone into church.

XV

The business was practically settled from the moment I never followed him. It was a pitiful surrender to agitation, but my being aware of this had somehow no power to restore me. I only sat there on my tomb and read into what our young friend had said to me the fulness of its meaning; by the time I had grasped the whole of which I had also embraced, for absence, the pretext that I was ashamed to offer my pupils and the rest of the congregation such an example of delay. What I said to myself above all was that Miles had got something out of me and that the gage of it for him would be just this awkward collapse. He had got out of me that there was something I was much afraid of, and that he should probably be able to make use of my fear to gain, for his own purpose, more freedom. My fear was of having to deal with the intolerable question of the grounds of his dismissal from school, since that was really but the question of the horrors gathered behind. That his uncle should arrive to treat with me of these things was a solution that, strictly speaking, I ought now to have desired to bring on; but I could so little face the ugliness and the pain of it that I simply procrastinated and lived from hand to mouth. The boy, to my deep discomposure, was immensely in the right, was in a position to say to me: 'Either you clear up with my guardian the mystery of this interruption of my studies, or you cease to expect me to lead with you a life that's so unnatural for a boy.' What was so unnatural for the particular boy I was concerned with was this sudden revelation of a consciousness and a plan.

That was what really overcame me, what prevented my going in. I walked round the church, hesitating, hovering; I reflected that I had already, with him, hurt myself beyond repair. Therefore I could patch up nothing and it was too extreme an effort to squeeze beside him into the pew: he would be so much more sure than ever to pass his arm into mine and make me sit there for an hour in close mute contact with his commentary on our talk. For the first minute since his arrival I wanted to get away from him. As I paused beneath the high east window and listened to the sounds of worship I was taken with an impulse that might master me, I felt, and completely, should I give it the least encouragement. I might easily put an end to my ordeal by getting away altogether. Here was my chance; there was no one to stop me; I could give the whole thing up – turn my back and bolt. It was only a question of hurrying again, for a few preparations, to the house which the attendance at church of so many of the servants would practically have left unoccupied. No one, in short, could blame me if I should just drive desperately off. What was it to get away if I should get away only till dinner? That would be in a couple of hours, at the end of which – I had the acute prevision – my little pupils would play at innocent wonder about my non-appearance in their train.

'What *did* you do, you naughty bad thing? Why in the world, to worry us so – and take our thoughts off too, don't you know? – did you desert us at the very door?' I couldn't meet such questions nor, as they asked them, their false little lovely eyes; yet it was all so exactly what I should have to meet that, as the prospect grew sharp to me, I at last let myself go.

I got, so far as the immediate moment was concerned, away; I came straight out of the churchyard and, thinking hard, retraced my steps through the park. It seemed to me that by the time I reached the house I had made up my mind to cynical flight. The Sunday stillness both of the approaches and of the interior, in which I met no one, fairly stirred me with a sense of opportunity. Were I to get off quickly this way I should get off without a scene, without a word. My quickness would have to be remarkable, however, and the question of a conveyance was the great one to settle. Tormented, in the hall, with difficulties and obstacles, I remember sinking down at the foot of the staircase – suddenly collapsing there on the lowest step and then, with a revulsion, recalling that it was exactly where, more than a month before, in the darkness of night and just so bowed with evil things, I had seen the spectre of the most horrible of women. At this I was able to straighten myself; I went the rest of the way up; I made, in my turmoil, for the schoolroom, where there were objects belonging to me that I should have to take. But I opened the door to find again, in a flash, my eyes unsealed. In the presence of what I saw I reeled straight back upon resistance.

Seated at my own table in the clear noonday light I saw a person whom, without my previous experience, I should have taken at the first blush for some housemaid who might have stayed at home to look after the place and who, availing herself of rare relief from observation and of the schoolroom table and my pens, ink and paper, had applied herself to the considerable effort of a letter to her sweetheart. There was an effort in the way that, while her arms rested on the table, her hands, with evident weariness, supported her head; but at the moment I took this in I had already become aware that, in spite of my entrance, her attitude strangely persisted. Then it was – with the very act of its announcing itself – that her identity flared up in a change of posture. She rose, not as if she had heard me, but with an indescribable grand melancholy of indifference and detachment, and, within a dozen feet of me, stood there as my vile predecessor. Dishonoured and tragic, she was all before me; but even as I fixed and, for memory, secured it, the awful image passed away. Dark as midnight in her black dress, her haggard beauty and her unutterable woe, she had looked at me long enough to appear to say that her right to sit at my table was as good as mine to sit at hers. While these instants lasted indeed I had the extraordinary chill of a feeling that it was I who was the intruder. It was as a wild protest against it that, actually addressing her – 'You terrible miserable woman!' – I heard myself break into a sound that, by the open door, rang through the long passage and the empty house. She looked at me as if she heard me, but I had recovered myself and cleared the air. There was nothing in the room the next minute but the sunshine and the sense that I must stay.[31]

XVI

I had so perfectly expected the return of the others to be marked by a demonstration that I was freshly upset at having to find them merely dumb and discreet about my desertion. Instead of gaily denouncing and caressing me they made no allusion to my having failed them, and I was left, for the time, on perceiving that she too said nothing, to study Mrs Grose's odd face. I did this to such purpose that I made sure they had in some way bribed her to silence; a silence that, however, I would engage to break down on the first private opportunity. This opportunity came before tea: I secured five minutes with her in the housekeeper's room, where, in the twilight, amid a smell of lately-baked bread, but with the place all swept and garnished, I found her sitting in pained placidity before the fire. So I see her still, so I see her best: facing the flame from her straight chair in the dusky shining room, a large clean picture of the 'put away' – of drawers closed and locked and rest without a remedy.[32]

'Oh yes, they asked me to say nothing; and to please them – so long as they were there – of course I promised. But what had happened to you?'

'I only went with you for the walk,' I said. 'I had then to come back to meet a friend.'

She showed her surprise. 'A friend – *you*?'

'Oh yes, I've a couple!' I laughed. 'But did the children give you a reason?'

'For not alluding to your leaving us? Yes; they said you'd like it better. *Do* you like it better?'

My face had made her rueful. 'No, I like it worse!' But after an instant I added: 'Did they say why I should like it better?'

'No; Master Miles only said "We must do nothing but what she likes!"'

'I wish indeed he would! And what did Flora say?'

'Miss Flora was too sweet. She said "Oh of course, of course!" – and I said the same.'

I thought a moment. 'You were too sweet too – I can hear you all. But none the less, between Miles and me, it's now all out.'

'All out?' My companion stared. 'But what, Miss?'

'Everything. It doesn't matter. I've made up my mind. I came home, my dear,' I went on, 'for a talk with Miss Jessel.'

I had by this time formed the habit of having Mrs Grose literally well in hand in advance of my sounding that note; so that even now, as she bravely blinked under the signal of my word, I could keep her comparatively firm. 'A talk! Do you mean she spoke?'

'It came to that. I found her, on my return, in the schoolroom.'

'And what did she say?' I can hear the good woman still, and the candour of her stupefaction.

'That she suffers the torments—!'

It was this, of a truth, that made her, as she filled out my picture, gape. 'Do you mean,' she faltered '– of the lost?'

'Of the lost. Of the damned. And that's why, to share them—' I faltered myself with the horror of it.

But my companion, with less imagination, kept me up. 'To share them—?'

'She wants Flora.' Mrs Grose might, as I gave it to her, fairly have fallen away from me had I not been prepared. I still held her there, to show I was. 'As I've told you, however, it doesn't matter.'

'Because you've made up your mind? But to what?'

'To everything.'

'And what do you call "everything"?'

'Why to sending for their uncle.'

'Oh Miss, in pity do,' my friend broke out.

'Ah but I will, I *will*! I see it's the only way. What's "out", as I told you, with Miles is that if he thinks I'm afraid to – and has ideas of what he gains by that – he shall see he's mistaken. Yes, yes; his uncle shall have it here from me on the spot (and before the boy himself if necessary) that if I'm to be reproached with having done nothing again about more school—'

'Yes, Miss—' my companion pressed me.

'Well, there's that awful reason.'

There were now clearly so many of these for my poor colleague that she was excusable for being vague. 'But – a – which?'

'Why the letter from his old place.'

'You'll show it to the master?'

'I ought to have done so on the instant.'

'Oh no!' said Mrs Grose with decision.

'I'll put it before him,' I went on inexorably, 'that I can't undertake to work the question on behalf of a child who has been expelled—'

'For we've never in the least known what!' Mrs Grose declared.

'For wickedness. For what else – when he's so clever and beautiful and perfect? Is he stupid? Is he untidy? Is he infirm? Is he ill-natured? He's exquisite – so it can be only *that*; and that would open up the whole thing. After all,' I said, 'it's their uncle's fault. If he left here such people—!'

'He didn't really in the least know them. The fault's mine.' She had turned quite pale.

'Well, you shan't suffer,' I answered.

'The children shan't!' she emphatically returned.

I was silent a while; we looked at each other. 'Then what am I to tell him?'

'You needn't tell him anything. *I'll* tell him.'

I measured this. 'Do you mean you'll write—?' Remembering she couldn't, I caught myself up. 'How do you communicate?'

'I tell the bailiff. *He* writes.'

'And should you like him to write our story?'

My question had a sarcastic force that I had not fully intended, and it made her after a moment inconsequently break down. The tears were again in her eyes. 'Ah Miss, *you* write!'

'Well – to-night,' I at last returned; and on this we separated.

XVII

I went so far, in the evening, as to make a beginning. The weather had changed back, a great wind was abroad, and beneath the lamp, in my room, with Flora at peace beside me, I sat for a long time before a blank sheet of paper and listened to the lash of the rain and the batter of the gusts. Finally I went out, taking a candle; I crossed the passage and listened a minute at Miles's door. What, under my endless obsession, I had been impelled to listen for was some betrayal of his not being at rest, and I presently caught one, but not in the form I had expected. His voice tinkled out. 'I say, you there – come in.' It was gaiety in the gloom!

I went in with my light and found him in bed, very wide awake but very much at his ease. 'Well, what are *you* up to?' he asked with a grace of sociability in which it occurred to me that Mrs Grose, had she been present, might have looked in vain for proof that anything was 'out'.

I stood over him with my candle. 'How did you know I was there?'

'Why of course I heard you. Did you fancy you made no noise? You're like a troop of cavalry!' he beautifully laughed.

'Then you weren't asleep?'

'Not much! I lie awake and think.'

I had put my candle, designedly, a short way off, and then, as he held out his friendly old hand to me, had sat down on the edge of his bed. 'What is it,' I asked, 'that you think of?'

'What in the world, my dear, but *you*?'

'Ah the pride I take in your appreciation doesn't insist on that! I had so far rather you slept.'

'Well, I think also, you know, of this queer business of ours.'

I marked the coolness of his firm little hand. 'Of what queer business, Miles?'

'Why the way you bring me up. And all the rest!'

I fairly held my breath a minute, and even from my glimmering taper there was light enough to show how he smiled up at me from his pillow. 'What do you mean by all the rest?'

'Oh you know, you know!'

I could say nothing for a minute, though I felt as I held his hand and our eyes continued to meet that my silence had all the air of admitting his charge and that nothing in the whole world of reality was perhaps at that moment so fabulous as our actual relation. 'Certainly you shall go back to school,' I said, 'if it be that that troubles you. But not to the old place – we must find another, a better. How could I know it did trouble you, this question, when you never told me so, never spoke of it at all?' His clear listening face, framed in its smooth whiteness, made him for the minute as appealing as some wistful patient in a children's hospital; and I would have given, as the resemblance came to me, all I possessed on earth really to be the nurse or the sister of charity who might have helped to cure him. Well, even as it was I perhaps might help! 'Do you know you've never said a word to me about your school – I mean the old one; never mentioned it in any way?'

He seemed to wonder; he smiled with the same loveliness. But he clearly gained time; he waited, he called for guidance. 'Haven't I?' It wasn't for *me* to help him – it was for the thing I had met!

Something in his tone and the expression of his face, as I got this from him, set my heart aching with such a pang as it had never yet known; so unutterably touching was it to see his little brain puzzled and his little resources taxed to play, under the spell laid on him, a part of innocence and consistency. 'No, never – from the hour you came back. You've never mentioned to me one of your masters, one of your comrades, nor the least little thing that ever happened to you at school. Never, little Miles – no never – have you given me an inkling of anything that *may* have happened there. Therefore you can fancy how much I'm in the dark. Until you came out, that way, this morning, you had since the first hour I saw you scarce even made a reference to anything in your previous life. You seemed so perfectly to accept the present.' It was extraordinary how my absolute conviction of his secret precocity – or whatever I might call the poison of an influence that I dared but half-phrase – made him, in spite of the faint breath of his inward trouble, appear as accessible as an older person, forced me to treat him as an intelligent equal. 'I thought you wanted to go on as you are.'

It struck me that at this he just faintly coloured. He gave, at any rate, like a convalescent slightly fatigued, a languid shake of his head. 'I don't – I don't. I want to get away.'

'You're tired of Bly?'

'Oh no, I like Bly.'

'Well then—?'

'Oh *you* know what a boy wants!'

I felt I didn't know so well as Miles, and I took temporary refuge. 'You want to go to your uncle?'

Again, at this, with his sweet ironic face, he made a movement on the pillow. 'Ah you can't get off with that!'

I was silent a little, and it was I now, I think, who changed colour. 'My dear, I don't want to get off!'

'You can't even if you do. You can't, you can't!' – he lay beautifully staring. 'My uncle must come down and you must completely settle things.'

'If we do,' I returned with some spirit, 'you may be sure it will be to take you quite away.'

'Well, don't you understand that that's exactly what I'm working for? You'll have to *tell* him – about the way you've let it all drop: you'll have to tell him a tremendous lot!'

The exultation with which he uttered this helped me somehow for the instant to meet him rather more. 'And how much will *you*, Miles, have to tell him? There are things he'll ask you!'

He turned it over. 'Very likely. But what things?'

'The things you've never told me. To make up his mind what to do with you. He can't send you back—'

'I don't want to go back!' he broke in. 'I want a new field.'

He said it with admirable serenity, with positive unimpeachable gaiety; and doubtless it was that very note that most evoked for me the poignancy, the unnatural childish tragedy, of his probable reappearance at the end of three months with all this bravado and still more dishonour. It overwhelmed me now that I should never be able to bear that, and it made me let myself go. I threw myself upon him and in the tenderness of my pity I embraced him. 'Dear little Miles, dear little Miles—'

My face was close to his, and he let me kiss him, simply taking it with indulgent good humour. 'Well, old lady?'

'Is there nothing – nothing at all that you want to tell me?'

He turned off a little, facing round toward the wall and holding up his hand to look at as one had seen sick children look. 'I've told you – I told you this morning.'

Oh I was sorry for him! 'That you just want me not to worry you?'

He looked round at me now as if in recognition of my understanding him; then ever so gently, 'To let me alone,' he replied.

There was even a strange little dignity in it, something that made me release him, yet, when I had slowly risen, linger beside him. God knows *I* never wished to harass him, but I felt that merely, at this, to turn my back on him was to abandon or, to put it more truly, lose him. 'I've just begun a letter to your uncle,' I said.

'Well then, finish it!'

I waited a minute. 'What happened before?'

He gazed up at me again. 'Before what?'

'Before you came back. And before you went away.'

For some time he was silent, but he continued to meet my eyes. 'What happened?'

It made me, the sound of the words, in which it seemed to me I caught for the very first time a small faint quaver of consenting consciousness – it made me drop on my knees beside the bed and seize once more the chance of possessing him. 'Dear little Miles, dear little Miles, if you *knew* how I want to help you! It's only that, it's nothing but that, and I'd rather die than give you a pain or do you a wrong – I'd rather die than hurt a hair of you. Dear little Miles' – oh I brought it out now even if I *should* go too far – 'I just want you to help me to save you!' But I knew in a moment after this that I had gone too far.

The answer to my appeal was instantaneous, but it came in the form of an extraordinary blast and chill, a gust of frozen air and a shake of the room as great as if, in the wild wind, the casement had crashed in. The boy gave a loud high shriek which, lost in the rest of the shock of sound, might have seemed, indistinctly, though I was so close to him, a note either of jubilation or of terror. I jumped to my feet again and was conscious of darkness. So for a moment we remained, while I stared about me and saw the drawn curtains unstirred and the window still tight. 'Why the candle's out!' I then cried.

'It was I who blew it, dear!' said Miles.

XVIII

The next day, after lessons, Mrs Grose found a moment to say to me quietly: 'Have you written, Miss?'

'Yes – I've written.' But I didn't add – for the hour – that my letter, sealed and directed, was still in my pocket. There would be time enough to send it before the messenger should go to the village. Meanwhile there had been on the part of my pupils no more brilliant, more exemplary morning. It was exactly as if they had both had at heart to gloss over any recent little friction. They performed the dizziest feats of arithmetic, soaring quite out of *my* feeble range, and perpetrated, in higher spirits than ever, geographical and historical jokes. It was conspicuous of course in Miles in particular that he appeared to wish to show how easily he could let me down. This child, to my memory, really lives in a setting of beauty and misery that no words can translate; there was a distinction all his own in every impulse he revealed; never was a small natural creature, to the uninformed eye all frankness and freedom, a more ingenious, a more extraordinary little gentleman. I had perpetually to guard against the wonder of contemplation into which my initiated view betrayed me; to check the irrelevant gaze and discouraged sigh in which I constantly both attacked and renounced the enigma of what such a little gentleman could have done that deserved a penalty. Say that, by the dark prodigy I knew, the imagination of all evil *had* been opened up to him: all the justice within me ached for the proof that it could ever have flowered into an act.

He had never at any rate been such a little gentleman as when, after our early dinner on this dreadful day, he came round to me and asked if I shouldn't like him for half an hour to play to me. David playing to Saul could never have shown a finer sense of the occasion.[33] It was literally a charming exhibition of tact, of magnanimity, and quite tantamount to his saying outright: 'The true knights we love to read about never push an advantage too far. I know what you mean now: you mean that – to be let alone yourself and not followed up – you'll cease to worry and spy upon me, won't keep me so close to you, will let me go and come. Well, I "come", you see – but I don't go! There'll be plenty of time for that. I do really delight in your society and I only want to show you that I contended for a principle.' It may be imagined whether I resisted this appeal or failed to accompany him again, hand in hand, to the schoolroom. He sat down at the old piano and played as he had never played; and if there are those who think he had better have been kicking a football I can only say that I wholly agree with them. For at the end of a time that under his influence I had quite ceased to measure I started up with a strange sense of having literally slept at my post. It was after luncheon, and by the schoolroom fire, and yet I hadn't really in the least slept; I had only done something much worse – I had forgotten. Where all this time was Flora? When I put the question to Miles he played on a minute before answering, and then could only say: 'Why, my dear, how do *I* know?' – breaking moreover into a happy laugh which immediately after, as if it were a vocal accompaniment, he prolonged into incoherent extravagant song.

I went straight to my room, but his sister was not there; then, before going downstairs, I looked into several others. As she was nowhere about she would surely be with Mrs Grose, whom in the comfort of that theory I accordingly proceeded in quest of. I found her where I had found her the evening before, but she met my quick challenge with blank scared ignorance.

She had only supposed that, after the repast, I had carried off both the children; as to which she was quite in her right, for it was the very first time I had allowed the little girl out of my sight without some special provision. Of course now indeed she might be with the maids, so that the immediate thing was to look for her without an air of alarm. This we promptly arranged between us; but when, ten minutes later and in pursuance of our arrangement, we met in the hall, it was only to report on either side that after guarded enquiries we had altogether failed to trace her. For a minute there, apart from observation, we exchanged mute alarms, and I could feel with what high interest my friend returned me all those I had from the first given her.

'She'll be above,' she presently said – 'in one of the rooms you haven't searched.'

'No; she's at a distance.' I had made up my mind. 'She has gone out.'

Mrs Grose stared. 'Without a hat?'

I naturally also looked volumes. 'Isn't that woman always without one?'

'She's with *her*?'

'She's with *her*!' I declared. 'We must find them.'

My hand was on my friend's arm, but she failed for the moment, confronted with such an account of the matter, to respond to my pressure. She communed, on the contrary, where she stood, with her uneasiness. 'And where's Master Miles?'

'Oh *he*'s with Quint. They'll be in the schoolroom.'

'Lord, Miss!' My view, I was myself aware – and therefore I suppose my tone – had never yet reached so calm an assurance.

'The trick's played,' I went on; 'they've successfully worked their plan. He found the most divine little way to keep me quiet while she went off.'

' "Divine"?' Mrs Grose bewilderedly echoed.

'Infernal then!' I almost cheerfully rejoined. 'He has provided for himself as well. But come!'

She had helplessly gloomed at the upper regions. 'You leave him—?'

'So long with Quint? Yes – I don't mind that now.'

She always ended at these moments by getting possession of my hand, and in this manner she could at present still stay me. But after gasping an instant at my sudden resignation, 'Because of your letter?' she eagerly brought out.

I quickly, by way of answer, felt for my letter, drew it forth, held it up, and then, freeing myself, went and laid it on the great hall-table. 'Luke will take it,' I said as I came back. I reached the house-door and opened it; I was already on the steps.

My companion still demurred: the storm of the night and the early morning had dropped, but the afternoon was damp and grey. I came down to the drive while she stood in the doorway. 'You go with nothing on?'

'What do I care when the child has nothing? I can't wait to dress,' I cried, 'and if you must do so I leave you. Try meanwhile yourself upstairs.'

'With *them*?' Oh on this the poor woman promptly joined me![34]

XIX

We went straight to the lake, as it was called at Bly, and I daresay rightly called, though it may have been a sheet of water less remarkable than my untravelled eyes supposed it. My acquaintance with sheets of water was small, and the pool of Bly, at all events on the few occasions of my consenting, under the protection of my pupils, to affront its surface in the old flat-bottomed boat moored there for our use, had impressed me both with its extent and its agitation. The usual place of embarkation was half a mile from the house, but I had an intimate conviction that, wherever Flora might be, she was not near home. She had not given me the slip for any small adventure, and, since the day of the very great one that I had shared with her by the pond, I had been aware, in our walks, of the quarter to which she most inclined. This was why I had now given to Mrs Grose's steps so marked a direction – a direction making her, when she perceived it, oppose a resistance that showed me she was freshly mystified. 'You're going to the water, Miss? – you think she's *in*—?'

'She may be, though the depth is, I believe, nowhere very great. But what I judge most likely is that she's on the spot from which, the other day, we saw together what I told you.'

'When she pretended not to see—?'

'With that astounding self-possession! I've always been sure she wanted to go back alone. And now her brother has managed it for her.'

Mrs Grose still stood where she had stopped. 'You suppose they really *talk* of them?'

I could meet this with an assurance! 'They say things that, if we heard them, would simply appal us.'

'And if she *is* there—?'

'Yes?'

'Then Miss Jessel is?'

'Beyond a doubt. You shall see.'

'Oh thank you!' my friend cried, planted so firm that, taking it in, I went straight on without her. By the time I reached the pool, however, she was close behind me, and I knew that, whatever, to her apprehension, might befall me, the exposure of sticking to me struck her as her least danger. She exhaled a moan of relief as we at last came in sight of the greater part of the water without a sight of the child. There was no trace of Flora on that nearer side of the bank where my observation of her had been most startling, and none on the opposite edge, where, save for a margin of some twenty yards, a thick copse came down to the pond. This expanse, oblong in shape, was so narrow compared to its length that, with its ends out of view, it might have been taken for a scant river. We looked at the empty stretch, and then I felt the suggestion in my friend's eyes. I knew what she meant and I replied with a negative headshake.

'No, no; wait! She has taken the boat.'

My companion stared at the vacant mooring-place and then again across the lake. 'Then where is it?'

'Our not seeing it is the strongest of proofs. She has used it to go over, and then has managed to hide it.'

'All alone – that child?'

'She's not alone, and at such times she's not a child: she's an old, old woman.' I scanned all the visible shore while Mrs Grose took again, into the queer element I offered her, one of her plunges of submission; then I pointed out that the boat might perfectly be in a small refuge formed by one of the recesses of the pool, an indentation masked, for the hither side, by a projection of the bank and by a clump of trees growing close to the water.

'But if the boat's there, where on earth's *she*?' my colleague anxiously asked.

'That's exactly what we must learn.' And I started to walk further.

'By going all the way round?'

'Certainly, far as it is. It will take us but ten minutes, yet it's far enough to have made the child prefer not to walk. She went straight over.'

'Laws!' cried my friend again: the chain of my logic was ever too strong for her. It dragged her at my heels even now, and when we had got halfway round – a devious tiresome process, on ground much broken and by a path choked with overgrowth – I paused to give her breath. I sustained her with a grateful arm, assuring her that she might hugely help me; and this started us afresh, so that in the course of but few minutes more we reached a point from which we found the boat to be where I had supposed it. It had been intentionally left as much as possible out of sight and was tied to one of the stakes of a fence that came, just there, down to the brink and that had been an assistance to disembarking. I recognized, as I looked at the pair of short thick oars, quite safely drawn up, the prodigious character of the feat for a little girl; but I had by this time lived too long among wonders and had panted to too many livelier measures. There was a gate in the fence, through which we passed, and that brought us after a trifling interval more into the open. Then 'There she is!' we both exclaimed at once.

Flora, a short way off, stood before us on the grass and smiled as if her performance had now become complete. The next thing she did, however, was to stoop straight down and pluck – quite as if it were all she was there for – a big ugly spray of withered fern. I at once felt sure she had just come out of the copse. She waited for us, not herself taking a step, and I was conscious of the rare solemnity with which we presently approached her. She smiled and smiled, and we met; but it was all done in a silence by this time flagrantly ominous. Mrs Grose was the first to break the spell: she threw herself on her knees and, drawing the child to her breast, clasped in a long embrace the little tender yielding body. While this dumb convulsion lasted I could only watch it – which I did the more intently when I saw Flora's face peep at me over our companion's shoulder. It was serious now – the flicker had left it; but it strengthened the pang with which I at that moment envied Mrs Grose the simplicity of *her* relation. Still, all this while, nothing more passed between us save that Flora had let her foolish fern again drop to the ground. What she and I had virtually said to each other was that pretexts were useless now. When Mrs Grose finally got up she kept the child's hand, so that the two were still before me; and the singular reticence of our communion was even more marked in the frank look she addressed me. 'I'll be hanged,' it said, 'if *I'll* speak!'

It was Flora who, gazing all over me in candid wonder, was the first. She was struck with our bareheaded aspect. 'Why where are your things?'

'Where yours are, my dear!' I promptly returned.

She had already got back her gaiety and appeared to take this as an answer quite sufficient. 'And where's Miles?' she went on.

There was something in the small valour of it that quite finished me: these three words from her were in a flash like the glitter of a drawn blade the jostle of the cup that my hand for weeks and weeks had held high and full to the brim and that now, even before speaking, I felt overflow in a deluge. 'I'll tell you if you'll tell *me*—' I heard myself say, then heard the tremor in which it broke.

'Well, what?'

Mrs Grose's suspense blazed at me, but it was too late now,

and I brought the thing out handsomely. 'Where, my pet, is Miss Jessel?'

XX

Just as in the churchyard with Miles, the whole thing was upon us. Much as I had made of the fact that this name had never once, between us, been sounded, the quick smitten glare with which the child's face now received it fairly likened my breach of the silence to the smash of a pane of glass. It added to the interposing cry, as if to stay the blow, that Mrs Grose at the same instant uttered over my violence – the shriek of a creature scared, or rather wounded, which, in turn, within a few seconds, was completed by a gasp of my own. I seized my colleague's arm. 'She's there, she's there!'

Miss Jessel stood before us on the opposite bank exactly as she had stood the other time, and I remember, strangely, as the first feeling now produced in me, my thrill of joy at having brought on a proof. She was there, so I was justified; she was there, so I was neither cruel nor mad. She was there for poor scared Mrs Grose, but she was there most for Flora; and no moment of my monstrous time was perhaps so extraordinary as that in which I consciously threw out to her – with the sense that, pale and ravenous demon as she was, she would catch and understand it – an inarticulate message of gratitude. She rose erect on the spot my friend and I had lately quitted, and there wasn't in all the long reach of her desire an inch of her evil that fell short. This first vividness of vision and emotion were things of a few seconds, during which Mrs Grose's dazed blink across to where I pointed struck me as showing that she too at last saw, just as it carried my own eyes precipitately to the child. The revelation then of the manner in which Flora was affected startled me in truth far more than it would have done to find her also merely agitated, for direct dismay was of course not what I had expected. Prepared and on her guard as our pursuit had actually made her, she would repress every betrayal; and I was therefore at once shaken by my first glimpse of the particular one for which I had not allowed. To see her, without a convulsion of her small pink face, not even feign to glance in the direction of the prodigy I announced, but only, instead of that, turn at *me* an expression of hard still gravity, an expression absolutely new and unprecedented and that appeared to read and accuse and judge me – this was a stroke that somehow converted the little girl herself into a figure portentous. I gaped at her coolness even though my certitude of her thoroughly seeing was never greater than at that instant, and then, in the immediate need to defend myself, I called her passionately to witness. 'She's there, you little unhappy thing – there, there, *there*, and you know it as well as you know me!' I had said shortly before to Mrs Grose that she was not at these times a child, but an old, old woman, and my description of her couldn't have been more strikingly confirmed than in the way in which, for all notice of this, she simply showed me, without an expressional concession or admission, a countenance of deeper and deeper, of indeed suddenly quite fixed reprobation. I was by this time – if I can put the whole thing at all together – more appalled at what I may properly call her manner than at anything else, though it was quite simultaneously that I became aware of having Mrs Grose also, and very formidably, to reckon with. My elder companion, the next moment, at any rate, blotted out everything but her own flushed face and her loud shocked protest, a burst of high disapproval. 'What a dreadful turn, to be sure, Miss! Where on earth do you see anything?'

I could only grasp her more quickly yet, for even while she spoke the hideous plain presence stood undimmed and undaunted. It had already lasted a minute, and it lasted while I continued, seizing my colleague, quite thrusting her at it and presenting her to it, to insist with my pointing hand. 'You don't see her exactly as *we* see? – you mean to say you don't now – *now*? She's as big as a blazing fire! Only look, dearest woman, *look*—!' She looked, just as I did, and gave me, with her deep groan of negation, repulsion, compassion – the mixture with her pity of her relief at her exemption – a sense, touching to me even then, that she would have backed me up if she had been

able. I might well have needed that, for with this hard blow of
the proof that her eyes were hopelessly sealed I felt my own
situation horribly crumble, I felt – I *saw* – my livid predecessor
press, from her position, on my defeat, and I took the measure,
more than all, of what I should have from this instant to deal
with in the astounding little attitude of Flora. Into this attitude
Mrs Grose immediately and violently entered, breaking, even
while there pierced through my sense of ruin a prodigious
private triumph, into breathless reassurance.

'She isn't there, little lady, and nobody's there – and you
never see nothing, my sweet! How can poor Miss Jessel – when
poor Miss Jessel's dead and buried? *We* know, don't we, love?' –
and she appealed, blundering in, to the child. 'It's all a mere
mistake and a worry and a joke – and we'll go home as fast as
we can!'

Our companion, on this, had responded with a strange
quick primness of propriety, and they were again, with Mrs
Grose on her feet, united, as it were, in shocked opposition to
me. Flora continued to fix me with her small mask of disaffec-
tion, and even at that minute I prayed God to forgive me for
seeming to see that, as she stood there holding tight to our
friend's dress, her incomparable childish beauty had suddenly
failed, had quite vanished. I've said it already – she was literally, she was hideously hard; she had turned common and
almost ugly. 'I don't know what you mean. I see nobody. I see
nothing. I never *have*. I think you're cruel. I don't like you!'
Then, after this deliverance, which might have been that of a
vulgarly pert little girl in the street, she hugged Mrs Grose
more closely and buried in her skirts the dreadful little face. In
this position she launched an almost furious wail. 'Take me
away, take me away – oh take me away from *her*!'

'From *me*?' I panted.

'From you – from you!' she cried.

Even Mrs Grose looked across at me dismayed; while I had
nothing to do but communicate again with the figure that, on
the opposite bank, without a movement, as rigidly still as if
catching, beyond the interval, our voices, was as vividly there
for my disaster as it was not there for my service. The wretched

child had spoken exactly as if she had got from some outside source each of her stabbing little words, and I could therefore, in the full despair of all I had to accept, but sadly shake my head at her. 'If I had ever doubted all my doubt would at present have gone. I've been living with the miserable truth, and now it has only too much closed round me. Of course I've lost you: I've interfered, and you've seen, under *her* dictation' – with which I faced, over the pool again, our infernal witness – 'the easy and perfect way to meet it. I've done my best, but I've lost you. Goodbye.' For Mrs Grose I had an imperative, an almost frantic 'Go, go!' before which, in infinite distress, but mutely possessed of the little girl and clearly convinced, in spite of her blindness, that something awful had occurred and some collapse engulfed us, she retreated, by the way we had come, as fast as she could move.

Of what first happened when I was left alone I had no subsequent memory. I only knew that at the end of, I suppose, a quarter of an hour, an odorous dampness and roughness, chilling and piercing my trouble, had made me understand that I must have thrown myself, on my face, to the ground and given way to a wildness of grief. I must have lain there long and cried and wailed, for when I raised my head the day was almost done. I got up and looked a moment, through the twilight, at the grey pool and its blank haunted edge, and then I took, back to the house, my dreary and difficult course. When I reached the gate in the fence the boat, to my surprise, was gone, so that I had a fresh reflexion to make on Flora's extraordinary command of the situation. She passed that night, by the most tacit and, I should add, were not the word so grotesque a false note, the happiest of arrangements, with Mrs Grose. I saw neither of them on my return, but on the other hand I saw, as by an ambiguous compensation, a great deal of Miles. I saw – I can use no other phrase – so much of him that it fairly measured more than it had ever measured. No evening I had passed at Bly was to have had the portentous quality of this one; in spite of which – and in spite also of the deeper depths of consternation that had opened beneath my feet – there was literally, in the ebbing actual, an extraordinarily sweet sadness. On reaching the house I had never so much as looked for the boy; I had simply gone straight to my room to change what I was wearing and to take in, at a glance, much material testimony to Flora's rupture. Her little belongings had all been removed. When later, by the schoolroom fire, I was served with tea by the usual maid, I indulged, on the article of my other pupil, in no enquiry whatever. He had his freedom now – he might have it to the end! Well, he did have it; and it consisted – in part at least – of his coming in at about eight o'clock and sitting down with me in silence. On the removal of the tea-things I had blown out the candles and drawn my chair closer: I was conscious of a mortal coldness and felt as if I should never again be warm. So when he appeared I was sitting in the glow with my thoughts. He paused a moment by the door as if to look at me; then – as if to share them – came to the other side of the hearth and sank into a chair. We sat there in absolute stillness; yet he wanted, I felt, to be with me.[35]

XXI

Before a new day, in my room, had fully broken, my eyes opened to Mrs Grose, who had come to my bedside with worse news. Flora was so markedly feverish that an illness was perhaps at hand; she had passed a night of extreme unrest, a night agitated above all by fears that had for their subject not in the least her former but wholly her present governess. It was not against the possible re-entrance of Miss Jessel on the scene that she protested – it was conspicuously and passionately against mine. I was at once on my feet, and with an immense deal to ask; the more that my friend had discernibly now girded her loins to meet me afresh. This I felt as soon as I had put to her the question of her sense of the child's sincerity as against my own. 'She persists in denying to you that she saw, or has ever seen, anything?'

My visitor's trouble truly was great. 'Ah Miss, it isn't a matter on which I can push her! Yet it isn't either, I must say, as if I much needed to. It has made her, every inch of her, quite old.'

'Oh I see her perfectly from here. She resents, for all the world like some high little personage, the imputation on her truthfulness and, as it were, her respectability. "Miss Jessel indeed – *she*!" Ah she's "respectable", the chit! The impression she gave me there yesterday was, I assure you, the very strangest of all: it was quite beyond any of the others. I *did* put my foot in it! She'll never speak to me again.'

Hideous and obscure as it all was, it held Mrs Grose briefly silent; then she granted my point with a frankness which, I made sure, had more behind it. 'I think indeed, Miss, she never will. She do have a grand manner about it!'

'And that manner' – I summed it up – 'is practically what's the matter with her now.'

Oh that manner, I could see in my visitor's face, and not a little else besides! 'She asks me every three minutes if I think you're coming in.'

'I see – I see.' I too, on my side, had so much more than worked it out. 'Has she said to you since yesterday – except to repudiate her familiarity with anything so dreadful – a single other word about Miss Jessel?'

'Not one, Miss. And of course, you know,' my friend added, 'I took it from her by the lake that just then and there at least there *was* nobody.'

'Rather! And naturally you take it from her still.'

'I don't contradict her. What else can I do?'

'Nothing in the world! You've the cleverest little person to deal with. They've made them – their two friends, I mean – still cleverer even than nature did; for it was wondrous material to play on! Flora has now her grievance, and she'll work it to the end.'

'Yes, Miss; but to *what* end?'

'Why that of dealing with me to her uncle. She'll make me out to him the lowest creature—!'

I winced at the fair show of the scene in Mrs Grose's face; she looked for a minute as if she sharply saw them together. 'And him who thinks so well of you!'

'He has an odd way – it comes over me now,' I laughed, '– of

proving it! But that doesn't matter. What Flora wants of course
is to get rid of me.'

My companion bravely concurred. 'Never again to so much
as look at you.'

'So that what you've come to me now for,' I asked, 'is to
speed me on my way?' Before she had time to reply, however, I
had her in check. 'I've a better idea – the result of my reflexions. My going *would* seem the right thing, and on Sunday I
was terribly near it. Yet that won't do. It's *you* who must go.
You must take Flora.'

My visitor, at this, did speculate. 'But where in the world—?'

'Away from here. Away from *them*. Away, even most of all,
now, from me. Straight to her uncle.'

'Only to tell on you—?'

'No, not "only"! To leave me, in addition, with my
remedy.'

She was still vague. 'And what *is* your remedy?'

'Your loyalty, to begin with. And then Miles's.'

She looked at me hard. 'Do you think he—?'

'Won't, if he has the chance, turn on me? Yes, I venture still
to think it. At all events I want to try. Get off with his sister as
soon as possible and leave me with him alone.' I was amazed,
myself, at the spirit I had still in reserve, and therefore perhaps
a trifle the more disconcerted at the way in which, in spite of this
fine example of it, she hesitated. 'There's one thing, of course,' I
went on: 'they mustn't, before she goes, see each other for three
seconds.' Then it came over me that, in spite of Flora's presum-
able sequestration from the instant of her return from the pool,
it might already be too late. 'Do you mean,' I anxiously asked,
'that they *have* met?'

At this she quite flushed. 'Ah, Miss, I'm not such a fool as
that! If I've been obliged to leave her three or four times, it has
been each time with one of the maids, and at present, though
she's alone, she's locked in safe. And yet – and yet!' There were
too many things.

'And yet what?'

'Well, are you so sure of the little gentleman?'

'I'm not sure of anything but *you*. But I have, since last evening, a new hope. I think he wants to give me an opening. I do believe that – poor little exquisite wretch! – he wants to speak. Last evening, in the firelight and the silence, he sat with me for two hours as if it were just coming.'

Mrs Grose looked hard through the window at the grey gathering day. 'And did it come?'

'No, though I waited and waited I confess it didn't, and it was without a breach of the silence, or so much as a faint allusion to his sister's condition and absence, that we at last kissed for good-night. All the same,' I continued, 'I can't, if her uncle sees her, consent to his seeing her brother without my having given the boy – and most of all because things have got so bad – a little more time.'

My friend appeared on this ground more reluctant than I could quite understand. 'What do you mean by more time?'

'Well, a day or two – really to bring it out. He'll then be on *my* side – of which you see the importance. If nothing comes I shall only fail, and you at the worst have helped me by doing on your arrival in town whatever you may have found possible.' So I put it before her, but she continued for a little so lost in other reasons that I came again to her aid. 'Unless indeed,' I wound up, 'you really want *not* to go.'

I could see it, in her face, at last clear itself: she put out her hand to me as a pledge. 'I'll go – I'll go. I'll go this morning.'

I wanted to be very just. 'If you *should* wish still to wait I'd engage she shouldn't see me.'

'No, no: it's the place itself. She must leave it.' She held me a moment with heavy eyes, then brought out the rest. 'Your idea's the right one. I myself, Miss—'

'Well?'

'I can't stay.'

The look she gave me with it made me jump at possibilities. 'You mean that, since yesterday, you *have* seen—?'

She shook her head with dignity. 'I've *heard*—!'

'Heard?'

'From that child – horrors! There!' she sighed with tragic relief. 'On my honour, Miss, she says things—!' But at this evocation she broke down; she dropped with a sudden cry upon my sofa and, as I had seen her do before, gave way to all the anguish of it.

It was quite in another manner that I for my part let myself go. 'Oh thank God!'

She sprang up again at this, drying her eyes with a groan. ' "Thank God"?'

'It so justifies me!'

'It does that, Miss!'

I couldn't have desired more emphasis, but I just waited. 'She's so horrible?'

I saw my colleague scarce knew how to put it. 'Really shocking.'

'And about me?'

'About you, Miss – since you must have it. It's beyond everything, for a young lady; and I can't think wherever she must have picked up—'

'The appalling language she applies to me? I can then!' I broke in with a laugh that was doubtless significant enough.

It only in truth left my friend still more grave. 'Well, perhaps I ought to also – since I've heard some of it before! Yet I can't bear it,' the poor woman went on while with the same movement she glanced, on my dressing-table, at the face of my watch. 'But I must go back.'

I kept her, however. 'Ah if you can't bear it—!'

'How can I stop with her, you mean? Why just *for* that: to get her away. Far from this,' she pursued, 'far from *them*—'

'She may be different? she may be free?' I seized her almost with joy. 'Then in spite of yesterday you *believe*—'

'In such doings?' Her simple description of them required, in the light of her expression, to be carried no further, and she gave me the whole thing as she had never done. 'I believe.'

Yes, it was a joy, and we were still shoulder to shoulder: if I might continue sure of that I should care but little what else happened. My support in the presence of disaster would be the same as it had been in my early need of confidence, and if my friend would answer for my honesty I would answer for all the rest. On the point of taking leave of her, none the less, I was to some extent embarrassed. 'There's one thing of course – it occurs to me – to remember. My letter giving the alarm will have reached town before you.'

I now felt still more how she had been beating about the bush and how weary at last it had made her. 'Your letter won't have got there. Your letter never went.'

'What then became of it?'

'Goodness knows! Master Miles—'

'Do you mean *he* took it?' I gasped.

She hung fire, but she overcame her reluctance. 'I mean that I saw yesterday, when I came back with Miss Flora, that it wasn't where you had put it. Later in the evening I had the chance to question Luke, and he declared that he had neither noticed nor touched it.' We could only exchange, on this, one of our deeper mutual soundings, and it was Mrs Grose who first brought up the plumb with an almost elate 'You see!'

'Yes, I see that if Miles took it instead he probably will have read it and destroyed it.'

'And don't you see anything else?'

I faced her a moment with a sad smile. 'It strikes me that by this time your eyes are open even wider than mine.'

They proved to be so indeed, but she could still almost blush to show it. 'I make out now what he must have done at school.' And she gave, in her simple sharpness, an almost droll disillusioned nod. 'He stole!'

I turned it over – I tried to be more judicial. 'Well – perhaps.'

She looked as if she found me unexpectedly calm. 'He stole *letters*!'

She couldn't know my reasons for a calmness after all pretty shallow; so I showed them off as I might. 'I hope then it was to more purpose than in this case! The note, at all events, that I put on the table yesterday,' I pursued, 'will have given him so scant an advantage – for it contained only the bare demand for an interview – that he's already much ashamed of having gone so far for so little, and that what he had on his mind last evening was precisely the need of confession.' I seemed to myself for the instant to have mastered it, to see it all. 'Leave us, leave us' – I was already, at the door, hurrying her off. 'I'll get it out of him. He'll meet me. He'll confess. If he confesses he's saved. And if he's saved—'

'Then *you* are?' The dear woman kissed me on this, and I took her farewell. 'I'll save you without him!' she cried as she went.

XXII

Yet it was when she had got off – and I missed her on the spot – that the great pinch really came. If I had counted on what it would give me to find myself alone with Miles I quickly recognized that it would give me at least a measure. No hour of my stay in fact was so assailed with apprehensions as that of my coming down to learn that the carriage containing Mrs Grose and my younger pupil had already rolled out of the gates. Now I *was*, I said to myself, face to face with the elements, and for much of the rest of the day, while I fought my weakness, I could consider that I had been supremely rash. It was a tighter place still than I had yet turned round in; all the more that, for the first time, I could see in the aspect of others a confused reflexion of the crisis. What had happened naturally caused them all to stare; there was too little of the explained, throw out whatever we might, in the suddenness of my colleague's act. The maids and the men looked blank; the effect of which on my nerves was an aggravation until I saw the necessity of making it a positive aid. It was in short by just clutching the helm that I avoided total wreck; and I daresay that, to bear up at all, I became that morning very grand and very dry. I welcomed the consciousness that I was charged with much to do, and I caused it to be known as well that, left thus to myself, I was quite remarkably firm. I wandered with that manner, for the next hour or two, all over the place and looked, I have no doubt, as if I were ready for any onset. So, for the benefit of whom it might concern, I paraded with a sick heart.

The person it appeared least to concern proved to be, till dinner, little Miles himself. My perambulations had given me meanwhile no glimpse of him, but they had tended to make more public the change taking place in our relation as a consequence of his having at the piano, the day before, kept me, in Flora's interest, so beguiled and befooled. The stamp of publicity had of course been fully given by her confinement and departure, and the change itself was now ushered in by our non-observance of the regular custom of the schoolroom. He had already disappeared when, on my way down, I pushed open his door, and I learned below that he had breakfasted – in the presence of a couple of the maids – with Mrs Grose and his sister. He had then gone out, as he said, for a stroll; than which nothing, I reflected, could better have expressed his frank view of the abrupt transformation of my office. What he would now permit this office to consist of was yet to be settled: there was at the least a queer relief – I mean for myself in especial – in the renouncement of one pretension. If so much had sprung to the surface I scarce put it too strongly in saying that what had perhaps sprung highest was the absurdity of our prolonging the fiction that I had anything more to teach him. It sufficiently stuck out that, by tacit little tricks in which even more than myself he carried out the care for my dignity, I had had to appeal to him to let me off straining to meet him on the ground of his true capacity. He had at any rate his freedom now; I was never to touch it again: as I had amply shown, moreover, when, on his joining me in the schoolroom the previous night, I uttered, in reference to the interval just concluded, neither challenge nor hint. I had too much, from this moment, my other ideas. Yet when he at last arrived the difficulty of applying them, the accumulations of my problem, were brought straight home to me by the beautiful little presence on which what had occurred had as yet, for the eye, dropped neither stain nor shadow.

To mark, for the house, the high state I cultivated I decreed that my meals with the boy should be served, as we called it, downstairs; so that I had been awaiting him in the ponderous pomp of the room outside the window of which I had had from Mrs Grose, that first scared Sunday, my flash of something it would scarce have done to call light. Here at present I felt afresh – for I had felt it again and again – how my equilibrium depended on the success of my rigid will, the will to shut my eyes as tight as possible to the truth that what I had to deal with was, revoltingly, against nature. I could only get on at all by taking 'nature' into my confidence and my account, by treating my monstrous ordeal as a push in a direction unusual, of course, and unpleasant, but demanding after all, for a fair front, only another turn of the screw of ordinary human virtue. No attempt, none the less, could well require more tact than just this attempt to supply, one's self, *all* the nature. How could I put even a little of that article into a suppression of reference to what had occurred? How on the other hand could I make a reference without a new plunge into the hideous obscure? Well, a sort of answer, after a time, had come to me, and it was so far confirmed as that I was met, incontestably, by the quickened vision of what was rare in my little companion. It was indeed as if he had found even now – as he had so often found at lessons – still some other delicate way to ease me off. Wasn't there light in the fact which, as we shared our solitude, broke out with a specious glitter it had never yet quite worn? – the fact that (opportunity aiding, precious opportunity which had now come) it would be preposterous, with a child so endowed, to forego the help one might wrest from absolute intelligence? What had his intelligence been given him for but to save him? Mightn't one, to reach his mind, risk the stretch of a stiff arm across his character? It was as if, when we were face to face in the dining-room, he had literally shown me the way. The roast mutton was on the table and I had dispensed with attendance. Miles, before he sat down, stood a moment with his hands in his pockets and looked at the joint, on which he seemed on the point of passing some humorous judgment. But what he presently produced was: 'I say, my dear, is she really very awfully ill?'

'Little Flora? Not so bad but that she'll presently be better. London will set her up. Bly had ceased to agree with her. Come here and take your mutton.'

He alertly obeyed me, carried the plate carefully to his seat and, when he was established, went on. 'Did Bly disagree with her so terribly all at once?'

'Not so suddenly as you might think. One had seen it coming on.'

'Then why didn't you get her off before?'

'Before what?'

'Before she became too ill to travel.'

I found myself prompt. 'She's *not* too ill to travel; she only might have become so if she had stayed. This was just the moment to seize. The journey will dissipate the influence' – oh I was grand! – 'and carry it off.'

'I see, I see' – Miles, for that matter, was grand too. He settled to his repast with the charming little 'table manner' that, from the day of his arrival, had relieved me of all grossness of admonition. Whatever he had been expelled from school for, it wasn't for ugly feeding. He was irreproachable, as always, to-day; but was unmistakeably more conscious. He was discernibly trying to take for granted more things than he found, without assistance, quite easy; and he dropped into peaceful silence while he felt his situation. Our meal was of the briefest – mine a vain pretence, and I had the things immediately removed. While this was done Miles stood again with his hands in his little pockets and his back to me – stood and looked out of the wide window through which, that other day, I had seen what pulled me up. We continued silent while the maid was with us – as silent, it whimsically occurred to me, as some young couple who, on their wedding-journey, at the inn, feel shy in the presence of the waiter. He turned round only when the waiter had left us. 'Well – so we're alone!'[36]

XXIII

'Oh more or less.' I imagine my smile was pale. 'Not absolutely. We shouldn't like that!' I went on.

'No – I suppose we shouldn't. Of course we've the others.'

'We've the others – we've indeed the others,' I concurred.

'Yet even though we have them,' he returned, still with his hands in his pockets and planted there in front of me, 'they don't much count, do they?'

I made the best of it, but I felt wan. 'It depends on what you call "much"!'

'Yes' – with all accommodation – 'everything depends!' On this, however, he faced to the window again and presently reached it with his vague restless cogitating step. He remained there a while with his forehead against the glass, in contemplation of the stupid shrubs I knew and the dull things of November. I had always my hypocrisy of 'work', behind which I now gained the sofa. Steadying myself with it there as I had repeatedly done at those moments of torment that I have described as the moments of my knowing the children to be given to something from which I was barred, I sufficiently obeyed my habit of being prepared for the worst. But an extraordinary impression dropped on me as I extracted a meaning from the boy's embarrassed back – none other than the impression that I was not barred now. This inference grew in a few minutes to sharp intensity and seemed bound up with the direct perception that it was positively *he* who was. The frames and squares of the great window were a kind of image, for him, of a kind of failure. I felt that I saw him, in any case, shut in or shut out. He was admirable but not comfortable: I took it in with a throb of hope. Wasn't he looking through the haunted pane for something he couldn't see? – and wasn't it the first time in the whole business that he had known such a lapse? The first, the very first: I found it a splendid portent. It made him anxious, though he watched himself; he had been anxious all day and, even while in his usual sweet little manner he sat at table, had needed all his small strange genius to give it a gloss. When he at last turned round to meet me it was almost as if this genius had succumbed. 'Well, I think I'm glad Bly agrees with *me*!'

'You'd certainly seem to have seen, these twenty-four hours, a good deal more of it than for some time before. I hope,' I went on bravely, 'that you've been enjoying yourself.'

'Oh yes, I've been ever so far; all round about – miles and miles away. I've never been so free.'

He had really a manner of his own, and I could only try to keep up with him. 'Well, do you like it?'

He stood there smiling; then at last he put into two words – 'Do *you*?' – more discrimination than I had ever heard two words contain. Before I had time to deal with that, however, he continued as if with the sense that this was an impertinence to be softened. 'Nothing could be more charming than the way you take it, for of course if we're alone together now it's you that are alone most. But I hope,' he threw in, 'you don't particularly mind!'

'Having to do with you?' I asked. 'My dear child, how can I help minding? Though I've renounced all claim to your company – you're so beyond me – I at least greatly enjoy it. What else should I stay on for?'

He looked at me more directly, and the expression of his face, graver now, struck me as the most beautiful I had ever found in it. 'You stay on just for *that*?'

'Certainly. I stay on as your friend and from the tremendous interest I take in you till something can be done for you that may be more worth your while. That needn't surprise you.' My voice trembled so that I felt it impossible to suppress the shake. 'Don't you remember how I told you, when I came and sat on your bed the night of the storm, that there was nothing in the world I wouldn't do for you?'

'Yes, yes!' He, on his side, more and more visibly nervous, had a tone to master; but he was so much more successful than I that, laughing out through his gravity, he could pretend we were pleasantly jesting. 'Only that, I think, was to get me to do something for *you*!'

'It was partly to get you to do something,' I conceded. 'But, you know, you didn't do it.'

'Oh yes,' he said with the brightest superficial eagerness, 'you wanted me to tell you something.'

'That's it. Out, straight out. What you have on your mind, you know.'

'Ah then is *that* what you've stayed over for?'

He spoke with a gaiety through which I could still catch the finest little quiver of resentful passion; but I can't begin to express the effect upon me of an implication of surrender even so faint. It was as if what I had yearned for had come at last only to astonish me. 'Well, yes – I may as well make a clean breast of it. It was precisely for that.'

He waited so long that I supposed it for the purpose of repudiating the assumption on which my action had been founded; but what he finally said was: 'Do you mean now – here?'

'There couldn't be a better place or time.' He looked round him uneasily, and I had the rare – oh the queer! – impression of the very first symptom I had seen in him of the approach of immediate fear. It was as if he were suddenly afraid of me – which struck me indeed as perhaps the best thing to make him. Yet in the very pang of the effort I felt it vain to try sternness, and I heard myself the next instant so gentle as to be almost grotesque. 'You want so to go out again?'

'Awfully!' He smiled at me heroically, and the touching little bravery of it was enhanced by his actually flushing with pain. He had picked up his hat, which he had brought in, and stood twirling it in a way that gave me, even as I was just nearly reaching port, a perverse horror of what I was doing. To do it in *any* way was an act of violence, for what did it consist of but the obtrusion of the idea of grossness and guilt on a small helpless creature who had been for me a revelation of the possibilities of beautiful intercourse? Wasn't it base to create for a being so exquisite a mere alien awkwardness? I suppose I now read into our situation a clearness it couldn't have had at the time, for I seem to see our poor eyes already lighted with some spark of a prevision of the anguish that was to come. So we circled about with terrors and scruples, fighters not daring to close. But it was for each other we feared! That kept us a little longer suspended and unbruised. 'I'll tell you everything,' Miles said – 'I mean I'll tell you anything you like. You'll stay on with me, and we shall both be all right, and I *will* tell you – I *will*. But not now.'

'Why not now?'

My insistence turned him from me and kept him once more at his window in a silence during which, between us, you might have heard a pin drop. Then he was before me again with the air of a person for whom, outside, some one who had frankly to be reckoned with was waiting. 'I have to see Luke.'

I had not yet reduced him to quite so vulgar a lie, and I felt proportionately ashamed. But, horrible as it was, his lies made up my truth. I achieved thoughtfully a few loops of my knitting. 'Well then go to Luke, and I'll wait for what you promise. Only in return for that satisfy, before you leave me, one very much smaller request.'

He looked as if he felt he had succeeded enough to be able still a little to bargain. 'Very much smaller—?'

'Yes, a mere fraction of the whole. Tell me' – oh my work preoccupied me, and I was off-hand! – 'if, yesterday afternoon, from the table in the hall, you took, you know, my letter.'

XXIV

My grasp of how he received this suffered for a minute from something that I can describe only as a fierce split of my attention – a stroke that at first, as I sprang straight up, reduced me to the mere blind movement of getting hold of him, drawing him close and, while I just fell for support against the nearest piece of furniture, instinctively keeping him with his back to the window. The appearance was full upon us that I had already had to deal with here: Peter Quint had come into view like a sentinel before a prison. The next thing I saw was that, from outside, he had reached the window, and then I knew that, close to the glass and glaring in through it, he offered once more to the room his white face of damnation. It represents but grossly what took place within me at the sight to say that on the second my decision was made; yet I believe that no woman so overwhelmed ever in so short a time recovered her command of the *act*. It came to me in the very horror of the immediate presence that the act would be, seeing and facing what I saw and faced, to keep the boy himself unaware. The inspiration – I can call it by no other name – was that I felt how voluntarily, how transcendently, I *might*. It was like fighting with a demon for a human soul, and when I had fairly so appraised it I saw how the human soul – held out, in the tremor of my hands, at arms' length – had a perfect dew of sweat on a lovely childish forehead. The face that was close to mine was as white as the face against the glass, and out of it presently came a sound, not low nor weak, but as if from much further away, that I drank like a waft of fragrance.

'Yes – I took it.'

At this, with a moan of joy, I enfolded, I drew him close; and while I held him to my breast, where I could feel in the sudden fever of his little body the tremendous pulse of his little heart, I kept my eyes on the thing at the window and saw it move and shift its posture. I have likened it to a sentinel, but its slow wheel, for a moment, was rather the prowl of a baffled beast. My present quickened courage, however, was such that, not too much to let it through, I had to shade, as it were, my flame. Meanwhile the glare of the face was again at the window, the scoundrel fixed as if to watch and wait. It was the very confidence that I might now defy him, as well as the positive certitude, by this time, of the child's unconsciousness, that made me go on. 'What did you take it for?'

'To see what you said about me.'

'You opened the letter?'

'I opened it.'

My eyes were now, as I held him off a little again, on Miles's own face, in which the collapse of mockery showed me how complete was the ravage of uneasiness. What was prodigious was that at last, by my success, his sense was sealed and his communication stopped: he knew that he was in presence, but knew not of what, and knew still less that I also was and that I did know. And what did this strain of trouble matter when my eyes went back to the window only to see that the air was clear again and – by my personal triumph – the influence quenched? There was nothing there. I felt that the cause was mine and that I should surely get *all*. 'And you found nothing!' – I let my elation out.

He gave the most mournful, thoughtful little headshake. 'Nothing.'

'Nothing, nothing!' I almost shouted in my joy.

'Nothing, nothing,' he sadly repeated.

I kissed his forehead; it was drenched. 'So what have you done with it?'

'I've burnt it.'

'Burnt it?' It was now or never. 'Is that what you did at school?'

Oh what this brought up! 'At school?'

'Did you take letters? – or other things?'

'Other things?' He appeared now to be thinking of something far off and that reached him only through the pressure of his anxiety. Yet it did reach him. 'Did I *steal*?'

I felt myself redden to the roots of my hair as well as wonder if it were more strange to put to a gentleman such a question or to see him take it with allowances that gave the very distance of his fall in the world. 'Was it for that you mightn't go back?'

The only thing he felt was rather a dreary little surprise. 'Did you know I mightn't go back?'

'I know everything.'

He gave me at this the longest and strangest look. 'Everything?'

'Everything. Therefore *did* you—?' But I couldn't say it again. Miles could, very simply. 'No. I didn't steal.'

My face must have shown him I believed him utterly; yet my hands – but it was for pure tenderness – shook him as if to ask him why, if it was all for nothing, he had condemned me to months of torment. 'What then did you do?'

He looked in vague pain all round the top of the room and drew his breath, two or three times over, as if with difficulty. He might have been standing at the bottom of the sea and raising his eyes to some faint green twilight. 'Well – I said things.'

'Only that?'

'They thought it was enough!'

'To turn you out for?'

Never, truly, had a person 'turned out' shown so little to explain it as this little person! He appeared to weigh my question, but in a manner quite detached and almost helpless. 'Well, I suppose I oughtn't.'

'But to whom did you say them?'

He evidently tried to remember, but it dropped – he had lost it. 'I don't know!'

He almost smiled at me in the desolation of his surrender,

which was indeed practically, by this time, so complete that I ought to have left it there. But I was infatuated – I was blind with victory, though even then the very effect that was to have brought him so much nearer was already that of added separation. 'Was it to every one?' I asked.

'No; it was only to—' But he gave a sick little headshake. 'I don't remember their names.'

'Were they then so many?'

'No – only a few. Those I liked.'

Those he liked? I seemed to float not into clearness, but into a darker obscure, and within a minute there had come to me out of my very pity the appalling alarm of his being perhaps innocent. It was for the instant confounding and bottomless, for if he *were* innocent what then on earth was I? Paralysed, while it lasted, by the mere brush of the question, I let him go a little, so that, with a deep-drawn sigh, he turned away from me again; which, as he faced toward the clear window, I suffered, feeling that I had nothing now there to keep him from. 'And did they repeat what you said?' I went on after a moment.

He was soon at some distance from me, still breathing hard and again with the air, though now without anger for it, of being confined against his will. Once more, as he had done before, he looked up at the dim day as if, of what had hitherto sustained him, nothing was left but an unspeakable anxiety. 'Oh yes,' he nevertheless replied – 'they must have repeated them. To those *they* liked,' he added.

There was somehow less of it than I had expected; but I turned it over. 'And these things came round—?'

'To the masters? Oh yes!' he answered very simply. 'But I didn't know they'd tell.'

'The masters? They didn't – they've never told. That's why I ask you.'

He turned to me again his little beautiful fevered face. 'Yes, it was too bad.'

'Too bad?'

'What I suppose I sometimes said. To write home.'

I can't name the exquisite pathos of the contradiction given to such a speech by such a speaker; I only know that the next instant I heard myself throw off with homely force: 'Stuff and nonsense!' But the next after that I must have sounded stern enough. 'What *were* these things?'

My sternness was all for his judge, his executioner; yet it made him avert himself again, and that movement made *me*, with a single bound and an irrepressible cry, spring straight upon him. For there again, against the glass, as if to blight his confession and stay his answer,[37] was the hideous author of our woe – the white face of damnation. I felt a sick swim at the drop of my victory and all the return of my battle, so that the wildness of my veritable leap only served as a great betrayal. I saw him, from the midst of my act, meet it with a divination, and on the perception that even now he only guessed, and that the window was still to his own eyes free, I let the impulse flame up to convert the climax of his dismay into the very proof of his liberation. 'No more, no more, no more!' I shrieked to my visitant as I tried to press him against me.

'Is she *here*?' Miles panted as he caught with his sealed eyes the direction of my words. Then as his strange 'she' staggered me and, with a gasp, I echoed it, 'Miss Jessel, Miss Jessel!' he with sudden fury gave me back.

I seized, stupefied, his supposition – some sequel to what we had done to Flora, but this made me only want to show him that it was better still than that. 'It's not Miss Jessel! But it's at the window – straight before us. It's *there* – the coward horror, there for the last time!'

At this, after a second in which his head made the movement of a baffled dog's on a scent and then gave a frantic little shake for air and light, he was at me in a white rage, bewildered, glaring vainly over the place and missing wholly, though it now, to my sense, filled the room like the taste of poison, the wide overwhelming presence. 'It's *he*?'

I was so determined to have all my proof that I flashed into ice to challenge him. 'Whom do you mean by "he"?'

'Peter Quint – you devil!' His face gave again, round the room, its convulsed supplication. '*Where*?'

They are in my ears still, his supreme surrender of the name and his tribute to my devotion. 'What does he matter now, my own? – what will he *ever* matter? *I* have you,' I launched at the beast, 'but he has lost you for ever!' Then for the demonstration of my work, 'There, *there*!' I said to Miles.

But he had already jerked straight round, stared, glared again, and seen but the quiet day. With the stroke of the loss I was so proud of he uttered the cry of a creature hurled over an abyss, and the grasp with which I recovered him might have been that of catching him in his fall. I caught him, yes, I held him – it may be imagined with what a passion; but at the end of a minute I began to feel what it truly was that I held. We were alone with the quiet day, and his little heart, dispossessed, had stopped.

THE THIRD PERSON

I

When, a few years since, two good ladies, previously not intimate nor indeed more than slightly acquainted, found themselves domiciled together in the small but ancient town of Marr,[1] it was as a result, naturally, of special considerations. They bore the same name and were second cousins; but their paths had not hitherto crossed; there had not been coincidence of age to draw them together; and Miss Frush, the more mature, had spent much of her life abroad. She was a bland, shy, sketching person, whom fate had condemned to a monotony – triumphing over variety – of Swiss and Italian *pensions*;[2] in any one of which, with her well-fastened hat, her gauntlets and her stout boots, her camp-stool, her sketch-book, her Tauchnitz novel,[3] she would have served with peculiar propriety as a frontispiece to the natural history of the English old maid. She would have struck you indeed, poor Miss Frush, as so happy an instance of the type that you would perhaps scarce have been able to equip her with the dignity of the individual. This was what she enjoyed, however, for those brought nearer – a very insistent identity, once even of prettiness, but which now, blanched and bony, timid and inordinately queer, with its utterance all vague interjection and its aspect all eyeglass and teeth, might be acknowledged without inconvenience and deplored without reserve. Miss Amy, her kinswoman, who, ten years her junior, showed a different figure – such as, oddly enough, though formed almost wholly in English air, might have appeared much more to betray a foreign influence – Miss Amy was brown, brisk and expressive: when really young she had even been pronounced showy. She had an innocent vanity on the subject of her foot, a member which she somehow regarded as a guarantee of her wit, or at least of her good taste. Even had it not been pretty she flattered herself it would have been shod: she would never – no, never, like Susan – have given it up. Her bright brown eye was comparatively bold, and she had accepted Susan once for all as a frump. She even thought her, and silently deplored her as, a goose. But she was none the less herself a lamb.

They had benefited, this innocuous pair, under the will of an old aunt, a prodigiously ancient gentlewoman, of whom, in her later time, it had been given them, mainly by the office of others, to see almost nothing; so that the little property they came in for had the happy effect of a windfall. Each, at least, pretended to the other that she had never dreamed – as in truth there had been small encouragement for dreams in the sad character of what they now spoke of as the late lady's 'dreadful *entourage*'. Terrorised and deceived, as they considered, by her own people, Mrs Frush was scantily enough to have been counted on for an act of almost inspired justice. The good luck of her husband's nieces was that she had really outlived, for the most part, their ill-wishers and so, at the very last, had died without the blame of diverting fine Frush property from fine Frush use. Property quite of her own she had done as she liked with; but she had pitied poor expatriated Susan and had remembered poor unhusbanded Amy, though lumping them together perhaps a little roughly in her final provision. Her will directed that, should no other arrangement be more conveni- ent to her executors, the old house at Marr might be sold for their joint advantage. What befell, however, in the event, was that the two legatees, advised in due course, took an early occasion – and quite without concert – to judge their prospects on the spot. They arrived at Marr, each on her own side, and they were so pleased with Marr that they remained. So it was that they met: Miss Amy, accompanied by the office-boy of the local solicitor, presented herself at the door of the house to ask admittance of the caretaker. But when the door opened it offered to sight not the caretaker, but an unexpected, unexpecting lady in a very old waterproof, who held a long-handled eyeglass very much as a child holds a rattle. Miss Susan, already in the field, roaming, prying, meditating in the absence on an errand of the woman in charge, offered herself in this manner as in settled possession; and it was on that idea that, through the eyeglass, the cousins viewed each other with some penetration even before Amy came in. Then at last when Amy did come in it was not, any more than Susan, to go out again.

It would take us too far to imagine what might have happened had Mrs Frush made it a condition of her benevolence that the subjects of it should inhabit, should live at peace together, under the roof she left them; but certain it is that as they stood there they had at the same moment the same unprompted thought. Each became aware on the spot that the dear old house itself was exactly what she, and exactly what the other, wanted; it met in perfection their longing for a quiet harbour and an assured future; each, in short, was willing to take the other in order to get the house. It was therefore not sold; it was made, instead, their own, as it stood, with the dead lady's extremely 'good' old appurtenances not only undisturbed and undivided, but piously reconstructed and infinitely admired, the agents of her testamentary purpose rejoicing meanwhile to see the business so simplified. They might have had their private doubts – or their wives might have; might cynically have predicted the sharpest of quarrels, before three months were out, between the deluded yoke-fellows, and the dissolution of the partnership with every circumstance of recrimination. All that need be said is that such prophets would have prophesied vulgarly. The Misses Frush were not vulgar; they had drunk deep of the cup of singleness and found it prevailingly bitter; they were not unacquainted with solitude and sadness, and they recognized with due humility the supreme opportunity of their lives. By the end of three months, moreover, each knew the worst about the other. Miss Amy took her evening nap before dinner, an hour at which Miss Susan could never sleep – it was so odd; whereby Miss Susan took hers after that meal, just at the hour when Miss Amy was keenest for talk. Miss Susan, erect and unsupported, had feelings as to the way in which, in almost any posture that could pass for a seated one, Miss Amy managed to find a place in the small of her back for two out of the three sofa-cushions – a smaller place, obviously, than they had ever been intended to fit.

But when this was said all was said; they continued to have, on either side, the pleasant consciousness of a personal soil, not devoid of fragmentary ruins, to dig in. They had a theory that their lives had been immensely different, and each appeared now to the other to have conducted her career so perversely only that she should have an unfamiliar range of anecdote for her companion's ear. Miss Susan, at foreign *pensions*, had met the Russian, the Polish, the Danish, and even an occasional flower of the English, nobility, as well as many of the most extraordinary Americans, who, as she said, had made everything of her and with whom she had remained, often, in correspondence; while Miss Amy, after all less conventional, at the end of long years of London, abounded in reminiscences of literary, artistic and even – Miss Susan heard it with bated breath – theatrical society, under the influence of which she had written – there, it came out! – a novel that had been anonymously published and a play that had been strikingly type-copied.[4] Not the least charm, clearly, of this picturesque outlook at Marr would be the support that might be drawn from it for getting back, as she hinted, with 'general society' bravely sacrificed, to 'real work'. She had in her head hundreds of plots – with which the future, accordingly, seemed to bristle for Miss Susan. The latter, on her side, was only waiting for the wind to go down to take up again her sketching. The wind at Marr was often high, as was natural in a little old huddled, red-roofed, historic south-coast town which had once been in a manner mistress, as the cousins reminded each other, of the 'Channel',[5] and from which, high and dry on its hilltop though it might be, the sea had not so far receded as not to give, constantly, a taste of temper. Miss Susan came back to English scenery with a small sigh of fondness to which the consciousness of Alps and Apennines only gave more of a quaver; she had picked out her subjects and, with her head on one side and a sense that they

were easier abroad, sat sucking her water-colour brush and
nervously – perhaps even a little inconsistently – waiting and
hesitating. What had happened was that they had, each for
herself, re-discovered the country; only Miss Amy, emergent
from Bloomsbury[6] lodgings, spoke of it as primroses and
sunsets, and Miss Susan, rebounding from the Arno and the
Reuss,[7] called it, with a shy, synthetic pride, simply England.

The country was at any rate in the house with them as well
as in the little green girdle and in the big blue belt. It was in the
objects and relics that they handled together and wondered
over, finding in them a ground for much inferred importance
and invoked romance, stuffing large stories into very small
openings and pulling every faded bell-rope that might jingle
rustily into the past. They were still here in the presence, at all
events, of their common ancestors, as to whom, more than
ever before, they took only the best for granted. Was not the
best, for that matter – the best, that is, of little melancholy,
middling, disinherited Marr – seated in every stiff chair of the
decent old house and stitched into the patchwork of every
quaint old counterpane? Two hundred years of it squared
themselves in the brown, panelled parlour, creaked patiently
on the wide staircase and bloomed herbaceously in the red-
walled garden. There was nothing any one had ever done or
been at Marr that a Frush hadn't done it or been it. Yet they
wanted more of a picture and talked themselves into the fancy
of it; there were portraits – half a dozen, comparatively recent
(they called 1800 comparatively recent), and something of a
trial to a descendant who had copied Titian at the Pitti;[8] but
they were curious of detail and would have liked to people a
little more thickly their backward space, to set it up behind
their chairs as a screen embossed with figures. They threw off
theories and small imaginations, and almost conceived themselves engaged in researches; all of which made for pomp and
circumstance. Their desire was to discover something, and,
emboldened by the broader sweep of wing of her companion,
Miss Susan herself was not afraid of discovering something
bad. Miss Amy it was who had first remarked, as a warning,
that this was what it might all lead to. It was she, moreover, to

whom they owed the formula that, had anything *very* bad ever happened at Marr, they should be sorry if a Frush hadn't been in it. This was the moment at which Miss Susan's spirit had reached its highest point: she had declared, with her odd, breathless laugh, a prolonged, an alarmed or alarming gasp, that she should really be quite ashamed. And so they rested a while; not saying quite how far they were prepared to go in crime – not giving the matter a name. But there would have been little doubt for an observer that each supposed the other to mean that she not only didn't draw the line at murder, but stretched it so as to take in – well, gay deception. If Miss Susan could conceivably have asked whether Don Juan[9] had ever touched at that port, Miss Amy would, to a certainty, have wanted to know by way of answer at what port he had *not* touched. It was only unfortunately true that no one of the portraits of gentlemen looked at all like him and no one of those of ladies suggested one of his victims.

At last, none the less, the cousins had a find, came upon a box of old odds and ends, mainly documentary; partly printed matter, newspapers and pamphlets yellow and grey with time, and, for the rest, epistolary – several packets of letters, faded, scarce decipherable, but clearly sorted for preservation and tied, with sprigged ribbon of a far-away fashion, into little groups. Marr, below ground, is solidly founded – underlaid with great straddling cellars, sound and dry, that are like the groined crypts of churches and that present themselves to the meagre modern conception as the treasure-chambers of stout merchants and bankers in the old bustling days. A recess in the thickness of one of the walls had yielded up, on resolute investigation – that of the local youth employed for odd jobs and who had happened to explore in this direction on his own account – a collection of rusty superfluities among which the small chest in question had been dragged to light. It produced of course an instant impression and figured as a discovery; though indeed as rather a deceptive one on its having, when forced open, nothing better to show, at the best, than a quantity of rather illegible correspondence. The good ladies had naturally had for the moment a fluttered hope of old golden guineas – a miser's hoard; perhaps even of a hatful of those foreign coins of old-fashioned romance, ducats, doubloons, pieces of eight, as are sometimes found to have come to hiding, from over seas, in ancient ports. But they had to accept their disappointment – which they sought to do by making the best of the papers, by agreeing, in other words, to regard them as wonderful. Well, they *were*, doubtless, wonderful; which didn't prevent them, however, from appearing to be, on superficial inspection, also rather a weary labyrinth. Baffling, at any rate, to Miss Susan's unpractised eyes, the little pale-ribboned packets were, for several evenings, round the fire, while she luxuriously dozed, taken in hand by Miss Amy; with the result that on a certain occasion when, toward nine o'clock, Miss Susan woke up, she found her fellow-labourer fast asleep. A slightly irritated confession of ignorance of the Gothic character[10] was the further consequence, and the upshot of this, in turn, was the idea of appeal to Mr Patten. Mr Patten was the vicar and was known to interest himself, as such, in the ancient annals of Marr; in addition to which – and to its being even held a little that his sense of the affairs of the hour was sometimes sacrificed to such enquiries – he was a gentleman with a humour of his own, a flushed face, a bushy eyebrow and a black wide-awake[11] worn sociably askew. 'He will tell us,' said Amy Frush, 'if there's anything in them.'

'Yet if it should be,' Susan suggested, 'anything we mayn't like?'

'Well, that's just what I'm thinking of,' returned Miss Amy in her offhand way. 'If it's anything we shouldn't know—'

'We've only to tell him not to tell us? Oh, certainly,' said mild Miss Susan. She took upon herself even to give him that warning when, on the invitation of our friends, Mr Patten came to tea and to talk things over; Miss Amy sitting by and raising no protest, but distinctly promising herself that, whatever there might be to be known, and however objectionable, she would privately get it out of their initiator. She found herself already hoping that it *would* be something too bad for her cousin – too bad for any one else at all – to know, and that it most properly might remain between them. Mr Patten, at sight

of the papers, exclaimed, perhaps a trifle ambiguously, and by
no means clerically, 'My eye, what a lark!' and retired, after
three cups of tea, in an overcoat bulging with his spoil.

II

At ten o'clock that evening the pair separated, as usual, on the
upper landing, outside their respective doors, for the night; but
Miss Amy had hardly set down her candle on her dressing-
table before she was startled by an extraordinary sound, which
appeared to proceed not only from her companion's room, but
from her companion's throat. It was something she would have
described, had she ever described it, as between a gurgle and a
shriek, and it brought Amy Frush, after an interval of stricken
stillness that gave her just time to say to herself 'Some one
under her bed!' breathlessly and bravely back to the landing.
She had not reached it, however, before her neighbour, bursting in, met her and stayed her.

'There's some one in my room!'

They held each other. 'But who?'

'A man.'

'Under the bed?'

'No – just standing there.'

They continued to hold each other, but they rocked. 'Standing? Where? How?'

'Why, right in the middle – before my dressing-glass.'

Amy's blanched face by this time matched her mate's, but its
terror was enhanced by speculation. 'To look at himself?'

'No – with his back to it. To look at *me*,' poor Susan just
audibly breathed. 'To keep me off,' she quavered. 'In strange
clothes – of another age; with his head on one side.'

Amy wondered. 'On one side?'

'Awfully!' the refugee declared while, clinging together,
they sounded each other.

This, somehow, for Miss Amy, was the convincing touch;
and on it, after a moment, she was capable of the effort of dart-
ing back to close her own door. 'You'll remain then with me.'

'Oh!' Miss Susan wailed with deep assent; quite, as if, had she been a slangy person, she would have ejaculated 'Rather!' So they spent the night together; with the assumption thus marked, from the first, both that it would have been vain to confront their visitor as they didn't even pretend to each other that they would have confronted a housebreaker; and that by leaving the place at his mercy nothing worse could happen than had already happened. It was Miss Amy's approaching the door again as with intent ear and after a hush that had represented between them a deep and extraordinary interchange – it was this that put them promptly face to face with the real character of the occurrence. 'Ah,' Miss Susan, still under her breath, portentously exclaimed, 'it isn't any one—!'

'No' – her partner was already able magnificently to take her up. 'It isn't any one—'

'Who can really hurt us' – Miss Susan completed her thought. And Miss Amy, as it proved, had been so indescribably prepared that this thought, before morning, had, in the strangest, finest way, made for itself an admirable place with them. The person the elder of our pair had seen in her room was not – well, just simply was not any one in from outside. He was a different thing altogether. Miss Amy had felt it as soon as she heard her friend's cry and become aware of her commotion; as soon, at all events, as she saw Miss Susan's face. That was all – and there it was. There had been something hitherto wanting, they felt, to their small state and importance; it was present now, and they were as handsomely conscious of it as if they had previously missed it. The element in question, then, was a third person in their association, a hovering presence for the dark hours, a figure that with its head very much – too much – on one side, could be trusted to look at them out of unnatural places; yet only, it doubtless might be assumed, to look at them. They had it at last – had what was to be had in an old house where many, too many, things had happened, where the very walls they touched and floors they trod could have told secrets and named names, where every surface was a blurred mirror of life and death, of the endured, the remembered, the forgotten. Yes; the place was h—— but they stopped at sounding the word. And by morning, wonderful to say, they were used to it – had quite lived into it.

Not only this indeed, but they had their prompt theory. There was a connexion between the finding of the box in the vault and the appearance in Miss Susan's room. The heavy air of the past had been stirred by the bringing to light of what had so long been hidden. The communication of the papers to Mr Patten had had its effect. They faced each other in the morning at breakfast over the certainty that their queer roused inmate was the sign of the violated secret of these relics. No matter; for the sake of the secret they would put up with his attention; and – this, in them, was most beautiful of all – they must, though he was such an addition to their grandeur, keep him quite to themselves. Other people might hear of what was in the letters, but they should never hear of *him*. They were not afraid that either of the maids should see him – he was not a matter for maids. The question indeed was whether – should he keep it up long – they themselves would find that they could really live with him. Yet perhaps his keeping it up would be just what would make them indifferent. They turned these things over, but spent the next nights together; and on the third day, in the course of their afternoon walk, descried at a distance the vicar, who, as soon as he saw them, waved his arms violently – either as a warning or as a joke – and came more than half-way to meet them. It was in the middle – or what passed for such – of the big, bleak, blank, melancholy square of Marr; a public place, as it were, of such an absurd capacity for a crowd; with the great ivy-mantled choir and stopped transept of the nobly-planned church telling of how many centuries ago it had, for its part, given up growing.

'Why, my dear ladies,' cried Mr Patten as he approached, 'do you know what, of all things in the world, I seem to make out for you from your funny old letters?' Then as they waited, extremely on their guard now: 'Neither more nor less, if you please, than that one of your ancestors in the last century – Mr Cuthbert Frush, it would seem, by name – was hanged.'

They never knew afterwards which of the two had first found composure – found even dignity – to respond. 'And pray, Mr Patten, for what?'

'Ah, that's just what I don't yet get hold of. But if you don't mind my digging away' – and the vicar's bushy, jolly brows turned from one of the ladies to the other – 'I think I can run it to earth. They hanged, in those days, you know,' he added as if he had seen something in their faces, 'for almost any trifle!'

'Oh, I hope it wasn't for a trifle!' Miss Susan strangely tittered.

'Yes, of course one would like that, while he was about it – well, it had been, as they say,' Mr Patten laughed, 'rather for a sheep than for a lamb!'

'Did they hang at that time for a sheep?' Miss Amy wonderingly asked.

It made their friend laugh again. 'The question's whether *he* did! But we'll find out. Upon my word, you know, I quite want to myself. I'm awfully busy, but I think I can promise you that you shall hear. You *don't* mind?' he insisted.

'I think we could bear *anything*,' said Miss Amy.

Miss Susan gazed at her, on this, as for reference and appeal. 'And what is he, after all, at this time of day, *to* us?'

Her kinswoman, meeting the eyeglass fixedly, spoke with gravity. 'Oh, an ancestor's always an ancestor.'

'Well said and well felt, dear lady!' the vicar declared. 'Whatever they may have done—'

'It isn't every one,' Miss Amy replied, 'that has them to be ashamed of.'

'And we're not ashamed *yet*!' Miss Frush jerked out.

'Let me promise you then that you shan't be. Only, for I am busy,' said Mr Patten, 'give me time.'

'Ah, but we want the truth!' they cried with high emphasis as he quitted them. They were much excited now.

He answered by pulling up and turning round as short as if his professional character had been challenged. 'Isn't it just in the truth – and the truth only – that I deal?'

This they recognized as much as his love of a joke, and so they were left there together in the pleasant, if slightly overdone, void of the square, which wore at moments the air of a conscious demonstration, intended as an appeal, of the shrinkage of the population of Marr to a solitary cat. They walked on after a little, but they waited till the vicar was ever so far away before they spoke again; all the more that their doing so must bring them once more to a pause. Then they had a long look. 'Hanged!' said Miss Amy – yet almost exultantly.

This was, however, because it was not she who had seen. 'That's why his head—' but Miss Susan faltered.

Her companion took it in. 'Oh, has such a dreadful twist?'

'It *is* dreadful!' Miss Susan at last dropped, speaking as if she had been present at twenty executions.

There would have been no saying, at any rate, what it didn't evoke from Miss Amy. 'It breaks their neck,' she contributed after a moment.

Miss Susan looked away. 'That's why, I suppose, the head turns so fearfully awry. It's a most peculiar effect.'

So peculiar, it might have seemed, that it made them silent afresh. 'Well then, I hope he killed some one!' Miss Amy broke out at last.

Her companion thought. 'Wouldn't it depend on whom—?'

'No!' she returned with her characteristic briskness – a briskness that set them again into motion.

That Mr Patten was tremendously busy was evident indeed, as even by the end of the week he had nothing more to impart. The whole thing meanwhile came up again – on the Sunday afternoon; as the younger Miss Frush had been quite confident that, from one day to the other, it must. They went inveterately to evening church, to the close of which supper was postponed; and Miss Susan, on this occasion, ready the first, patiently awaited her mate at the foot of the stairs. Miss Amy at last came down, buttoning a glove, rustling the tail of a frock and looking, as her kinswoman always thought, conspicuously young and smart. There was no one at Marr, she held, who dressed like her; and Miss Amy, it must be owned, had also settled to this view of Miss Susan, though taking it in a different spirit. Dusk had gathered, but our frugal pair were always tardy lighters, and the grey close of day, in which the elder lady, on a high-backed hall chair, sat with hands patiently folded, had for all cheer the subdued glow – always subdued – of the small fire in the drawing-room, visible through a door that stood open. Into the drawing-room Miss Amy passed in search of the prayer-book she had laid down there after morning church, and from it, after a minute, without this volume, she returned to her companion. There was something in her movement that spoke – spoke for a moment so largely that nothing more was said till, with a quick unanimity, they had got themselves straight out of the house. There, before the door, in the cold, still twilight of the winter's end, while the church bells rang and the windows of the great choir showed across the empty square faintly red, they had it out again. But it was Miss Susan herself, this time, who had to bring it.

'He's there?'

'Before the fire – with his back to it.'

'Well, now you see!' Miss Susan exclaimed with elation and as if her friend had hitherto doubted her.

'Yes, I see – and what you mean.' Miss Amy was deeply thoughtful.

'About his head?'

'It *is* on one side,' Miss Amy went on. 'It makes him—' she considered. But she faltered as if still in his presence.

'It makes him awful!' Miss Susan murmured. 'The way,' she softly moaned, 'he looks at you!'

Miss Amy, with a glance, met this recognition. 'Yes – doesn't he?' Then her eyes attached themselves to the red windows of the church. 'But it means something.'

'The Lord knows what it means!' her associate gloomily sighed. Then, after an instant, 'Did he move?' Miss Susan asked.

'No – and *I* didn't.'

'Oh, I did!' Miss Susan declared, recalling to her more precipitous retreat.

'I mean I took my time. I waited.'

'To see him fade?'

Miss Amy for a moment said nothing. 'He doesn't fade. That's *it*.'

'Oh, then you did move!' her relative rejoined.

Again for a little she was silent. 'One *has* to. But I don't know what really happened. Of course I came back to you. What I mean is that I took him thoroughly in. He's young,' she added.

'But he's *bad*!' said Miss Susan.

'He's handsome!' Miss Amy brought out after a moment. And she showed herself even prepared to continue: 'Splendidly.'

' "Splendidly"! – with his neck broken and with that terrible look?'

'It's just the look that makes him so. It's the wonderful eyes. They mean something,' Amy Frush brooded.

She spoke with a decision of which Susan presently betrayed the effect. 'And what do they mean?'

Her friend had stared again at the glimmering windows of St Thomas of Canterbury. 'That it's time we should get to church.'

III

The curate that evening did duty alone; but on the morrow the vicar called and, as soon as he got into the room, let them again have it. 'He was hanged for smuggling!'

They stood there before him almost cold in their surprise and diffusing an air in which, somehow, this misdemeanour sounded out as the coarsest of all. '*Smuggling?*' Miss Susan disappointedly echoed – as if it presented itself to the first chill of their apprehension that he had then only been vulgar.

'Ah, but they hanged for it freely, you know, and I was an idiot for not having taken it, in his case, for granted. If a man swung, hereabouts, it *was* mostly for that. Don't you know it's on that we stand here to-day, such as we are – on the fact of what our bold, bad forefathers were not afraid of? It's in the floors we walk on and under the roofs that cover us. They smuggled so hard that they never had time to do anything else; and if they broke a head not their own it was only in the awkwardness of landing their brandy-kegs. I mean, dear ladies,' good Mr Patten wound up, 'no disrespect to *your* forefathers when I tell you that – as I've rather been supposing that, like all the rest of us, you were aware – they conveniently lived by it.'

Miss Susan wondered – visibly almost doubted. 'Gentlefolks?'

'It was the gentlefolks who were the worst.'

'They must have been the bravest!' Miss Amy interjected. She had listened to their visitor's free explanation with a rapid return of colour. 'And since if they lived by it they also died for it—'

'There's nothing at all to be said against them? I quite agree with you,' the vicar laughed, 'for all my cloth; and I even go so far as to say, shocking as you may think me, that we owe them, in our shabby little shrunken present, the sense of a bustling background, a sort of undertone of romance. They give us' – he humorously kept it up, verging perilously near, for his cloth, upon positive paradox – 'our little handful of legend and our small possibility of ghosts.' He paused an instant, with his lighter pulpit manner, but the ladies exchanged no look. They were in fact already, with an immense revulsion, carried quite as far away. 'Every penny in the place, really, that hasn't been earned by subtler – not nobler – arts in our own virtuous time, and though it's a pity there are not more of 'em: every penny in the place was picked up, somehow, by a clever trick, and at the risk of your neck, when the backs of the king's officers were turned. It's shocking, you know, what I'm saying to you, and I wouldn't say it to every one, but I think of some of the shabby old things about us, that represent such pickings, with a sort of sneaking kindness – as of relics of our heroic age. What are we now? We were at any rate devils of fellows then!'

Susan Frush considered it all solemnly, struggling with the spell of this evocation. 'But must we forget that they were wicked?'

'Never!' Mr Patten laughed. 'Thank you, dear friend, for reminding me. Only I'm worse than they!'

'But would you do it?'

'Murder a coastguard—?' The vicar scratched his head.

'I hope,' said Miss Amy rather surprisingly, 'you'd defend

yourself.' And she gave Miss Susan a superior glance. '*I* would!' she distinctly added.

Her companion anxiously took it up. 'Would you defraud the revenue?'

Miss Amy hesitated but a moment; then with a strange laugh, which she covered, however, by turning instantly away, 'Yes!' she remarkably declared.

Their visitor, at this, amused and amusing, eagerly seized her arm. 'Then may I count on you on the stroke of midnight to help me—?'

'To help you—?'

'To land the last new Tauchnitz.'

She met the proposal as one whose fancy had kindled, while her cousin watched them as if they had suddenly improvised a drawing-room charade. 'A service of danger?'

'Under the cliff – when you see the lugger stand in!'

'Armed to the teeth?'

'Yes – but invisibly. Your old waterproof—!'

'Mine is new. I'll take Susan's!'

This good lady, however, had her reserves. 'Mayn't one of them, all the same – here and there – have been sorry?'

Mr Patten wondered. 'For the jobs he muffed?'

'For the wrong – as it *was* wrong – he did.'

' "One" of them?' She had gone too far, for the vicar suddenly looked as if he divined in the question a reference.

They became, however, as promptly unanimous in meeting this danger, as to which Miss Susan in particular showed an inspired presence of mind. 'Two of them!' she sweetly smiled. 'May not Amy and I—?'

'Vicariously repent?' said Mr Patten. 'That depends – for the true honour of Marr – on how you show it.'

'Oh, we *sha'n't* show it!' Miss Amy cried.

'Ah, then,' Mr Patten returned, 'though atonements, to be efficient, are supposed to be public, you may do penance in secret as much as you please!'

'Well, *I* shall do it,' said Susan Frush.

Again, by something in her tone, the vicar's attention

appeared to be caught. 'Have you then in view a particular form—?'

'Of atonement?' She coloured now, glaring rather helplessly, in spite of herself, at her companion. 'Oh, if you're sincere you'll always find one.'

Amy came to her assistance. 'The way she often treats me has made her – though there's after all no harm in her – familiar with remorse. Mayn't we, at any rate,' the younger lady continued, 'now have our letters back?' And the vicar left them with the assurance that they should receive the bundle on the morrow.

They were indeed so at one as to shrouding their mystery that no explicit agreement, no exchange of vows, needed to pass between them; they only settled down, from this moment, to an unshared possession of their secret, an economy in the use and, as may even be said, the enjoyment of it, that was part of their general instinct and habit of thrift. It had been the disposition, the practice, the necessity of each to keep, fairly indeed to clutch, everything that, as they often phrased it, came their way; and this was not the first time such an influence had determined for them an affirmation of property in objects to which ridicule, suspicion, or some other inconvenience, might attach. It was their simple philosophy that one never knew of what service an odd object might *not* be; and there were days now on which they felt themselves to have made a better bargain with their aunt's executors than was witnessed in those law-papers which they had at first timorously regarded as the record of advantages taken of them in matters of detail. They had got, in short, more than was vulgarly, more than was even shrewdly supposed – such an indescribable unearned increment as might scarce more be divulged as a dread than as a delight. They drew together, old-maidishly, in a suspicious, invidious grasp of the idea that a dread of their very own – and blissfully not, of course, that of a failure of any essential supply – might, on nearer acquaintance, positively turn to a delight.

Upon some such attempted consideration of it, at all events, they found themselves embarking after their last interview

with Mr Patten, an understanding conveyed between them in
no redundancy of discussion, no flippant repetitions nor profane recurrences, yet resting on a sense of added margin, of
appropriated history, of liberties taken with time and space,
that would leave them prepared both for the worst and for the
best. The best would be that something that would turn out to
their advantage might prove to be hidden about the place; the
worst would be that they might find themselves growing to
depend only too much on excitement. They found themselves
amazingly reconciled, on Mr Patten's information, to the
particular character thus fixed on their visitor; they knew by
tradition and fiction that even the highwaymen of the same
picturesque age were often gallant gentlemen; therefore a
smuggler, by such a measure, fairly belonged to the aristocracy
of crime. When their packet of documents came back from the
vicarage Miss Amy, to whom her associate continued to leave
them, took them once more in hand; but with an effect, afresh,
of discouragement and languor – a headachy sense of faded
ink, of strange spelling and crabbed characters, of allusions
she couldn't follow and parts she couldn't match. She placed
the tattered papers piously together, wrapping them tenderly in
a piece of old figured silken stuff; then, as solemnly as if they
had been archives or statutes or title-deeds, laid them away in
one of the several small cupboards lodged in the thickness of
the wainscoted walls. What really most sustained our friends
in all ways was their consciousness of having, after all – and so
contrariwise to what appeared – a man in the house. It removed
them from that category of the manless into which no lady
really lapses till every issue is closed. Their visitor was an
issue – at least to the imagination, and they arrived finally,
under provocation, at intensities of flutter in which they felt
themselves so compromised by his hoverings that they could
only consider with relief the fact of nobody's knowing.

The real complication indeed at first was that for some weeks
after their talks with Mr Patten the hoverings quite ceased; a
circumstance that brought home to them in some degree a sense
of indiscretion and indelicacy. They hadn't mentioned him, no;
but they had come perilously near it, and they had doubtless, at

any rate, too recklessly let in the light on old buried and sheltered things, old sorrows and shames. They roamed about
the house themselves at times, fitfully and singly, when each
supposed the other out or engaged; they paused and lingered,
like soundless apparitions, in corners, doorways, passages,
and sometimes suddenly met, in these experiments, with a
suppressed start and a mute confession. They talked of him
practically never; but each knew how the other thought – all the
more that it was (oh yes, unmistakably!) in a manner different
from her own. They were together, none the less, in feeling,
while, week after week, he failed again to show, as if they had
been guilty of blowing, with an effect of sacrilege, on old gathered silvery ashes. It frankly came out for them that, possessed
as they so strangely, yet so ridiculously were, they should be able
to settle to nothing till their consciousness was yet again confirmed. Whatever the subject of it might have for them of fear or
favour, profit or loss, he had taken the taste from everything
else. He had converted *them* into wandering ghosts. At last, one
day, with nothing they could afterwards perceive to have determined it, the change came – came, as the previous splash in their
stillness had come, by the pale testimony of Miss Susan.

She waited till after breakfast to speak of it – or Miss Amy,
rather, waited to hear her; for she showed during the meal the
face of controlled commotion that her comrade already knew
and that must, with the game loyally played, serve as preface
to a disclosure. The younger of the friends really watched the
elder, over their tea and toast, as if seeing her for the first time
as possibly tortuous, suspecting in her some intention of keeping back what had happened. What had happened was that the
image of the hanged man had reappeared in the night; yet only
after they had moved together to the drawing-room did Miss
Amy learn the facts.

'I was beside the bed – in that low chair; about' – since Miss
Amy must know – 'to take off my right shoe. I had noticed
nothing before, and had had time partly to undress – had got
into my wrapper. So, suddenly – as I happened to look – there
he was. And there,' said Susan Frush, 'he stayed.'

'But where do you mean?'

'In the high-backed chair, the old flowered chintz "ear-chair"[12] beside the chimney.'

'All night? – and you in your wrapper?' Then as if this image almost challenged her credulity, 'Why didn't you go to bed?' Miss Amy enquired.

'With a – a person in the room?' her friend wonderfully asked; adding after an instant as with positive pride: 'I never broke the spell!'

'And didn't freeze to death?'

'Yes, almost. To say nothing of not having slept, I can assure you, one wink. I shut my eyes for long stretches, but whenever I opened them he was still there, and I never for a moment lost consciousness.'

Miss Amy gave a groan of conscientious sympathy. 'So that you're feeling now of course half dead.'

Her companion turned to the chimney-glass a wan, glazed eye. 'I daresay I *am* looking impossible.'

Miss Amy, after an instant, found herself still conscientious. 'You are.' Her own eyes strayed to the glass, lingering there while she lost herself in thought. 'Really,' she reflected with a certain dryness, 'if that's the kind of thing it's to be—!' there would seem, in a word, to be no withstanding it for either. Why, she afterwards asked herself in secret, should the restless spirit of a dead adventurer have addressed itself, in its trouble, to such a person as her queer, quaint, inefficient housemate? It was in *her*, she dumbly and somewhat sorely argued, that an unappeased soul of the old race should show a confidence. To this conviction she was the more directed by the sense that Susan had, in relation to the preference shown, vain and foolish complacencies. She had her idea of what, in their prodigious predicament, should be, as she called it, 'done', and that was a question that Amy from this time began to nurse the small aggression of not so much as discussing with her. She had certainly, poor Miss Frush, a new, an obscure reticence, and since she wouldn't speak first she should have silence to her fill. Miss Amy, however, peopled the silence with conjectural visions of her kinswoman's secret communion. Miss Susan, it was true, showed nothing, on any particular occasion, more than usual;

but this was just a part of the very felicity that had begun to harden and uplift her. Days and nights hereupon elapsed without bringing felicity of any order to Amy Frush. If she had no emotions it was, she suspected, because Susan had them all; and – it would have been preposterous had it not been pathetic – she proceeded rapidly to hug the opinion that Susan was selfish and even something of a sneak. Politeness, between them, still reigned, but confidence had flown, and its place was taken by open ceremonies and confessed precautions. Miss Susan looked blank but resigned; which maintained again, unfortunately, her superior air and the presumption of her duplicity. Her manner was of not knowing where her friend's shoe pinched; but it might have been taken by a jaundiced eye for surprise at the challenge of her monopoly. The unexpected resistance of her nerves was indeed a wonder: was that then the result, even for a shaky old woman, of shocks sufficiently repeated? Miss Amy brooded on the rich inference that, if the first of them didn't prostrate and the rest didn't undermine, one might keep them up as easily as – well, say an unavowed acquaintance or a private commerce of letters. She was startled at the comparison into which she fell – but what was this but an intrigue like another? And fancy Susan carrying one on! That history of the long night hours of the pair in the two chairs kept before her – for it was always present – the extraordinary measure. Was the situation it involved only grotesque – or was it quite grimly grand? It struck her as both; but that was the case with all their situations. Would it be in herself, at any rate, to show such a front? She put herself such questions till she was tired of them. A few good moments of her own would have cleared the air. Luckily they were to come.

IV

It was on a Sunday morning in April, a day brimming over with the turn of the season. She had gone into the garden before church; they cherished alike, with pottering intimacies and opposed theories and a wonderful apparatus of old gloves and trowels and spuds and little botanical cards on sticks, this feature of their establishment, where they could still differ without fear and agree without diplomacy, and which now, with its vernal promise, threw beauty and gloom and light and space, a great good-natured ease, into their wavering scales. She was dressed for church; but when Susan, who had, from a window, seen her wandering, stooping, examining, touching, appeared in the doorway to signify a like readiness, she suddenly felt her intention checked. 'Thank you,' she said, drawing near; 'I think that, though I've dressed, I won't, after all, go. Please therefore, proceed without me.'

Miss Susan fixed her. 'You're not well?'

'Not particularly. I shall be better – the morning's so perfect – here.'

'Are you really ill?'

'Indisposed; but not enough so, thank you, for you to stay with me.'

'Then it has come on but just now?'

'No – I felt not quite fit when I dressed. But it won't do.'

'Yet you'll stay out here?'

Miss Amy looked about. 'It will depend!'

Her friend paused long enough to have asked what it would depend on, but abruptly, after this contemplation, turned instead and, merely throwing over her shoulder an 'At least take care of yourself!' went rustling, in her stiffest Sunday fashion, about her business. Miss Amy, left alone, as she clearly desired to be, lingered a while in the garden, where the sense of things was somehow made still more delicious by the sweet, vain sounds from the church tower; but by the end of ten minutes she had returned to the house. The sense of things was not delicious there, for what it had at last come to was that, as they thought of each other what they couldn't say, all their contacts were hard and false. The real wrong was in what Susan thought – as to which she was much too proud and too sore to undeceive her. Miss Amy went vaguely to the drawing-room.

They sat as usual, after church, at their early Sunday dinner, face to face; but little passed between them save that Miss Amy felt better, that the curate had preached, that nobody else had stayed away, and that everybody had asked why Amy had. Amy, hereupon, satisfied everybody by feeling well enough to go in the afternoon; on which occasion, on the other hand – and for reasons even less luminous than those that had operated with her mate in the morning – Miss Susan remained within. Her comrade came back late, having, after church, paid visits; and found her, as daylight faded, seated in the drawing-room, placid and dressed, but without so much as a Sunday book – the place contained whole shelves of such reading – in her hand. She looked so as if a visitor had just left her that Amy put the question: 'Has any one called?'

'Dear, no; I've been quite alone.'

This again was indirect, and it instantly determined for Miss Amy a conviction – a conviction that, on her also sitting down just as she was and in a silence that prolonged itself, promoted in its turn another determination. The April dusk gathered, and still, without further speech, the companions sat there. But at last Miss Amy said in a tone not quite her commonest: 'This morning he came – while you were at church. I suppose it must have been really – though of course I couldn't know it – what I was moved to stay at home for.' She spoke now – out of her contentment – as if to oblige with explanations.

But it was strange how Miss Susan met her. 'You stay at home for him? *I* don't!' She fairly laughed at the triviality of the idea.

Miss Amy was naturally struck by it and after an instant even nettled. 'Then why did you do so this afternoon?'

'Oh, it wasn't for *that*!' Miss Susan lightly quavered. She made her distinction. 'I *really* wasn't well.'

At this her cousin brought it out. 'But he has been with you?'

'My dear child,' said Susan, launched unexpectedly even to herself, 'he's with me so often that if I put myself out for him—!' But as if at sight of something that showed, through the twilight, in her friend's face, she pulled herself up.

Amy, however, spoke with studied stillness. 'You've ceased then to put yourself out? You gave me, you remember, an instance of how you once did!' And she tried, on her side, a laugh.

'Oh yes – that was at first. But I've seen such a lot of him since. Do you mean *you* hadn't?' Susan asked. Then as her companion only sat looking at her: 'Has this been really the first time for you – since we last talked?'

Miss Amy for a minute said nothing. 'You've actually believed me—'

'To be enjoying on your own account what *I* enjoy? How couldn't I, at the very least,' Miss Susan cried – 'so grand and strange as you must allow me to say you've struck me?'

Amy hesitated. 'I hope I've sometimes struck you as decent!'

But it was a touch that, in her friend's almost amused preoccupation with the simple fact, happily fell short. 'You've only been waiting for what didn't come?'

Miss Amy coloured in the dusk. 'It came, as I tell you, to-day.'

'Better late than never!' And Miss Susan got up.

Amy Frush sat looking. 'It's because you thought you had ground for jealousy that *you've* been extraordinary?'

Poor Susan, at this, quite bounced about. 'Jealousy?'

It was a tone – never heard from her before – that brought Amy Frush to her feet; so that for a minute, in the unlighted room where, in honour of the spring, there had been no fire and the evening chill had gathered, they stood as enemies. It lasted, fortunately, even long enough to give one of them time suddenly to find it horrible. 'But why should we quarrel *now*?' Amy broke out in a different voice.

Susan was not too alienated quickly enough to meet it. 'It *is* rather wretched.'

'Now when we're equal,' Amy went on.

'Yes – I suppose we are.' Then, however, as if just to attenuate the admission, Susan had her last lapse from grace. 'They say, you know, that when women do quarrel it's usually about a man.'

Amy recognized it, but also with a reserve. 'Well then, let there first *be* one!'

'And don't you call *him*—?'

'No!' Amy declared and turned away, while her companion showed her a vain wonder for what she could in that case have expected. Their identity of privilege was thus established, but it is not certain that the air with which she indicated that the subject had better drop didn't press down for an instant her side of the balance. She knew that she knew most about men.

The subject did drop for the time, it being agreed between them that neither should from that hour expect from the other any confession or report. They would treat all occurrences now as not worth mentioning – a course easy to pursue from the moment the suspicion of jealousy had, on each side, been so completely laid to rest. They led their life a month or two on the smooth ground of taking everything for granted; by the end of which time, however, try as they would, they had set up no question that – while they met as a pair of gentlewomen living together only must meet – could successfully pretend to take the place of that of Cuthbert Frush. The spring softened and deepened, reached out its tender arms and scattered its shy graces; the earth broke, the air stirred, with emanations that were as touches and voices of the past; our friends bent their backs in their garden and their noses over its symptoms; they opened their windows to the mildness and tracked it in the lanes and by the hedges; yet the plant of conversation between them markedly failed to renew itself with the rest. It was not indeed that the mildness was not within them as well as without; all asperity, at least, had melted away; they were more than ever pleased with their general acquisition, which, at the winter's end, seemed to give out more of its old secrets, to hum, however faintly, with more of its old echoes, to creak, here and there, with the expiring throb of old aches. The deepest sweetness of the spring at Marr was just in its being in this way an attestation of age and rest. The place never seemed to have lived and lingered so long as when kind nature, like a maiden blessing a crone, laid rosy hands on its grizzled head. Then the new season was a light held up to show all the dignity of the years, but also all the wrinkles and scars. The good ladies in whom we are interested changed, at any rate, with the happy days, and it finally came out not only that the invidious note had dropped, but that it had positively turned to music. The whole tone of the time made so for tenderness that it really seemed as if at moments they were sad for each other. They had their grounds at last: each found them in her own consciousness; but it was as if each waited, on the other hand, to be sure she could speak without offence. Fortunately, at last, the tense cord snapped.

The old churchyard at Marr is still liberal; it does its immemorial utmost to people, with names and dates and memories and eulogies, with generations fore-shortened and confounded, the high empty table at which the grand old cripple of the church looks down over the low wall. It serves as an easy thoroughfare, and the stranger finds himself pausing in it with a sense of respect and compassion for the great maimed, ivied shoulders – as the image strikes him – of stone. Miss Susan and Miss Amy were strangers enough still to have sunk down one May morning on the sun-warmed tablet of an ancient tomb and to have remained looking about them in a sort of anxious peace. Their walks were all pointless now, as if they always stopped and turned, for an unconfessed want of interest, before reaching their object. That object presented itself at every start as the same to each, but they had come back too often without having got near it. This morning, strangely, on the return and almost in sight of their door, they were more in presence of it than they had ever been, and they seemed fairly to touch it when Susan said at last, quite in the air and with no traceable reference: 'I hope you don't mind, dearest, if I'm awfully sorry for you.'

'Oh, I know it,' Amy returned – 'I've felt it. But what does it do for us?' she asked.

Then Susan saw, with wonder and pity, how little resentment for penetration or patronage she had had to fear and out of what a depth of sentiment similar to her own her companion helplessly spoke. 'You're sorry for *me*?'

Amy at first only looked at her with tired eyes, putting out a hand that remained a while on her arm. 'Dear old girl! You might have told me before,' she went on as she took everything in; 'though, after all, haven't we each really known it?'

'Well,' said Susan, 'we've waited. We could only wait.'

'Then if we've waited together,' her friend returned, 'that *has* helped us.'

'Yes – to keep him in his place. Who would ever believe in him?' Miss Susan wearily wondered. 'If it wasn't for you and for me—'

'Not doubting of each other?' – her companion took her up: 'yes, there wouldn't be a creature. It's lucky for us,' said Miss Amy, 'that we *don't* doubt.'

'Oh, if we did we shouldn't be sorry.'

'No – except, selfishly, for ourselves. I am, I assure you, for *my* self – it has made me older. But, luckily, at any rate, we trust each other.'

'We do,' said Miss Susan.

'We do,' Miss Amy repeated – they lingered a little on that. 'But except making one feel older, what has it done for one?'

'There it is!'

'And though we've kept him in his place,' Miss Amy continued, 'he has also kept us in ours. We've lived with it,' she declared in melancholy justice. 'And we wondered at first if we could!' she ironically added. 'Well, isn't just what we feel now that we can't any longer?'

'No – it must stop. And I've my idea,' said Susan Frush.

'Oh, I assure you I've mine!' her cousin responded.

'Then if you want to act, don't mind me.'

'Because you certainly won't *me*? No, I suppose not. Well!' Amy sighed, as if, merely from this, relief had at last come. Her comrade echoed it; they remained side by side; and nothing could have had more oddity than what was assumed alike in what they had said and in what they still kept back. There would have been this at least in their favour for a questioner of their case, that each, charged dejectedly with her own experience, took, on the part of the other, the extraordinary – the ineffable, in fact – all for granted. They never named it again – as indeed it was not easy to name; the whole matter shrouded itself in personal discriminations and privacies; the comparison of notes had become a thing impossible. What was definite was that they had lived into their queer story, passed through it as through an observed, a studied, eclipse of the usual, a period of reclusion, a financial, social or moral crisis, and only desired now to live out of it again. The questioner we have been supposing might even have fancied that each, on her side, had hoped for something from it that she finally perceived it was never to give, which would have been exactly, moreover, the core of her secret and the explanation of her reserve. They at least, as the business stood, put each other to no test, and, if they were in fact disillusioned and disappointed, came together, after their long blight, solidly on that. It fully appeared between them that they felt a great deal older. When they got up from their sun-warmed slab, however, reminding each other of luncheon, it was with a visible increase of ease and with Miss Susan's hand drawn, for the walk home, into Miss Amy's arm. Thus the 'idea' of each had continued unspoken and ungrudged. It was as if each wished the other to try her own first; from which it might have been gathered that they alike presented difficulty and even entailed expense. The great questions remained. What then did he mean? what then did he want? Absolution, peace, rest, his final reprieve – merely to say *that* saw them no further on the way than they had already come. What were they at last to do for him? What could they give him that he would take? The ideas they respectively nursed still bore no fruit, and at the end of another month Miss Susan was frankly anxious about Miss Amy. Miss Amy as freely admitted that people *must* have begun to notice strange marks in them and to look for reasons. They were changed – they must change back.

V

Yet it was not till one morning at midsummer, on their meeting for breakfast, that the elder lady fairly attacked the younger's last entrenchment. 'Poor, poor Susan!' Miss Amy had said to herself as her cousin came into the room; and a moment later she brought out, for very pity, her appeal. 'What then *is* yours?'

'My idea?' It was clearly, at last, a vague comfort to Miss Susan to be asked. Yet her answer was desolate. 'Oh, it's no use!'

'But how do you know?'

'Why, I tried it – ten days ago, and I thought at first it had answered. But it hasn't.'

'He's back again?'

Wan, tired, Miss Susan gave it up. 'Back again.'

Miss Amy, after one of the long, odd looks that had now become their most frequent form of intercourse, thought it over. 'And just the same?'

'Worse.'

'Dear!' said Miss Amy, clearly knowing what that meant. 'Then what did you do?'

Her friend brought it roundly out. 'I made my sacrifice.'

Miss Amy, though still more deeply interrogative, hesitated. 'But of what?'

'Why, of my little all – or almost.'

The 'almost' seemed to puzzle Miss Amy, who, moreover, had plainly no clue to the property or attribute so described. 'Your "little all"?'

'Twenty pounds.'

'Money?' Miss Amy gasped.

Her tone produced on her companion's part a wonder as great as her own. 'What then is it yours to give?'

'My idea? It's not to *give*!' cried Amy Frush.

At the finer pride that broke out in this poor Susan's blankness flushed. 'What then is it to do?'

But Miss Amy's bewilderment outlasted her reproach. 'Do you mean he takes money?'

'The Chancellor of the Exchequer does – for "conscience".'

Her friend's exploit shone larger. 'Conscience money? You sent it to Government?' Then while, as the effect of her surprise, her mate looked too much a fool, Amy melted to kindness. 'Why, you secretive old thing!'

Miss Susan presently pulled herself more together. 'When your ancestor has robbed the revenue and his spirit walks for remorse—'

'You pay to get rid of him? I see – and it becomes what the vicar called his atonement by deputy. But what if it isn't remorse?' Miss Amy shrewdly asked.

'But it *is* – or it seemed to me so.'

'Never to me,' said Miss Amy.

Again they searched each other. 'Then, evidently, with you he's different.'

Miss Amy looked away. 'I daresay!'

'So what *is* your idea?'

Miss Amy thought. 'I'll tell you only if it works.'

'Then, for God's sake, try it!'

Miss Amy, still with averted eyes and now looking easily wise, continued to think. 'To try it I shall have to leave you. That's why I've waited so long.' Then she fully turned, and with expression: 'Can you face three days alone?'

'Oh – "alone"! I wish I ever were!'

At this her friend, as for very compassion, kissed her; for it seemed really to have come out at last – and welcome! – that poor Susan was the worse beset. 'I'll do it! But I must go up to town. Ask me no questions. All I can tell you now is—'

'Well?' Susan appealed while Amy impressively fixed her.

'It's no more remorse than *I'm* a smuggler.'

'What is it then?'

'It's bravado.'

An 'Oh!' more shocked and scared than any that, in the whole business, had yet dropped from her, wound up poor Susan's share in this agreement, appearing as it did to represent for her a somewhat lurid inference. Amy, clearly, had lights of her own. It was by their aid, accordingly, that she immediately prepared for the first separation they had had yet to suffer; of which the consequence, two days later, was that Miss Susan, bowed and anxious, crept singly, on the return from their parting, up the steep hill that leads from the station of Marr and passed ruefully under the ruined town-gate, one of the old defences, that arches over it.

But the full sequel was not for a month – one hot August night when, under the dim stars, they sat together in their little walled garden. Though they had by this time, in general, found again – as women only can find – the secret of easy speech, nothing, for the half-hour, had passed between them: Susan had only sat waiting for her comrade to wake up. Miss Amy

had taken of late to interminable dozing – as if with forfeits
and arrears to recover; she might have been a convalescent
from fever repairing tissue and getting through time. Susan
Frush watched her in the warm dimness, and the question
between them was fortunately at last so simple that she had
freedom to think her pretty in slumber and to fear that she herself, so unguarded, presented an appearance less graceful. She
was impatient, for her need had at last come, but she waited,
and while she waited she thought. She had already often done
so, but the mystery deepened to-night in the story told, as it
seemed to her, by her companion's frequent relapses. What had
been, three weeks before, the effort intense enough to leave
behind such a trail of fatigue? The marks, sure enough, had
shown in the poor girl that morning of the termination of the
arranged absence for which not three days, but ten, without
word or sign, were to prove no more than sufficient. It was at
an unnatural hour that Amy had turned up, dusty, dishevelled,
inscrutable, confessing for the time to nothing more than a
long night-journey. Miss Susan prided herself on having played
the game and respected, however tormenting, the conditions.
She had her conviction that her friend had been out of the
country, and she marvelled, thinking of her own old wanderings and her present settled fears, at the spirit with which a
person who, whatever she had previously done, had not travelled, could carry off such a flight. The hour had come at last
for this person to name her remedy. What determined it was
that, as Susan Frush sat there, she took home the fact that the
remedy was by this time not to be questioned. It had acted as
her own had not, and Amy, to all appearance, had only waited
for her to admit it. Well, she was ready when Amy woke –
woke immediately to meet her eyes and to show, after a
moment, in doing so, a vision of what was in her mind. 'What
was it now?' Susan finally said.

'My idea? Is it possible you've not guessed?'

'Oh, you're deeper, much deeper,' Susan sighed, 'than I.'

Amy didn't contradict that – seemed indeed, placidly
enough, to take it for truth; but she presently spoke as if
the difference, after all, didn't matter now. 'Happily for us

to-day – isn't it so? – our case is the same. I can speak, at any
rate, for myself. He has left me.'

'Thank God then!' Miss Susan devoutly murmured. 'For he
has left *me*.'

'Are you sure?'

'Oh, I think so.'

'But how?'

'Well,' said Miss Susan after an hesitation, 'how are *you*?'

Amy, for a little, matched her pause. 'Ah, that's what I can't
tell you. I can only answer for it that he's gone.'

'Then allow me also to prefer not to explain. The sense of
relief has for some reason grown strong in me during the last
half-hour. That's such a comfort that it's enough, isn't it?'

'Oh, plenty!' The garden-side of their old house, a window
or two dimly lighted, massed itself darkly in the summer night,
and, with a common impulse, they gave it, across the little
lawn, a long, fond look. Yes, they could be sure. 'Plenty!' Amy
repeated. 'He's gone.'

Susan's elder eyes hovered, in the same way, through her
elegant glass, at his purified haunt. 'He's gone. And how,' she
insisted, '*did* you do it?'

'Why, you dear goose' – Miss Amy spoke a little strangely – 'I
went to Paris.'

'To Paris?'

'To see what I could bring back – that I mightn't, that I
shouldn't. To do a stroke with!' Miss Amy brought out.

But it left her friend still vague. 'A stroke—?'

'To get through the Customs – under their nose.'

It was only with this that, for Miss Susan, a pale light
dawned. 'You wanted to smuggle? *That* was your idea?'

'It was *his*,' said Miss Amy. 'He wanted no "conscience
money" spent for him,' she now more bravely laughed: 'it was
quite the other way about – he wanted some bold deed done, of
the old wild kind; he wanted some big risk taken. And I took
it.' She sprang up, rebounding, in her triumph.

Her companion, gasping, gazed at her. 'Might they have
hanged you too?'

Miss Amy looked up at the dim stars. 'If I had defended

myself. But luckily it didn't come to that. What I brought in I brought' – she rang out, more and more lucid, now, as she talked – 'triumphantly. To appease him – I braved them. I chanced it, at Dover, and they never knew.'

'Then you hid it—?'

'About my person.'

With the shiver of this Miss Susan got up, and they stood there duskily together. 'It was so small?' the elder lady wonderingly murmured.

'It was big enough to have satisfied him,' her mate replied with just a shade of sharpness. 'I chose it, with much thought, from the forbidden list.'

The forbidden list hung a moment in Miss Susan's eyes, suggesting to her, however, but a pale conjecture. 'A Tauchnitz?'

Miss Amy communed again with the August stars. 'It was the *spirit* of the deed that told.'

'A Tauchnitz?' her friend insisted.

Then at last her eyes again dropped, and the Misses Frush moved together to the house. 'Well, he's satisfied.'

'Yes, and' – Miss Susan mused a little ruefully as they went – 'you got at last your week in Paris!'

THE JOLLY CORNER

I

'Every one asks me what I "think" of everything,' said Spencer Brydon; 'and I make answer as I can – begging or dodging the question, putting them off with any nonsense. It wouldn't matter to any of them really,' he went on, 'for, even were it possible to meet in that stand-and-deliver way so silly a demand on so big a subject, my "thoughts" would still be almost altogether about something that concerns only myself.' He was talking to Miss Staverton, with whom for a couple of months now he had availed himself of every possible occasion to talk; this disposition and this resource, this comfort and support, as the situation in fact presented itself, having promptly enough taken the first place in the considerable array of rather unattenuated surprises attending his so strangely belated return to America. Everything was somehow a surprise; and that might be natural when one had so long and so consistently neglected everything, taken pains to give surprises so much margin for play. He had given them more than thirty years – thirty-three, to be exact;[1] and they now seemed to him to have organized their performance quite on the scale of that licence. He had been twenty-three on leaving New York – he was fifty-six to-day: unless indeed he were to reckon as he had sometimes, since his repatriation, found himself feeling; in which case he would have lived longer than is often allotted to man. It would have taken a century, he repeatedly said to himself, and said also to Alice Staverton, it would have taken a longer absence and a more averted mind than those even of which he had been guilty, to pile up the differences, the newnesses, the queernesses, above all the big-nesses, for the better or the worse, that at present assaulted his vision wherever he looked.

The great fact all the while however had been the incalcul-ability; since he *had* supposed himself, from decade to decade, to be allowing, and in the most liberal and intelligent manner, for brilliancy of change. He actually saw that he had allowed for nothing; he missed what he would have been sure of find-ing, he found what he would never have imagined. Proportions and values were upside-down; the ugly things he had expected, the ugly things of his far-away youth, when he had too promptly waked up to a sense of the ugly – these uncanny phe-nomena placed him rather, as it happened, under the charm; whereas the 'swagger' things, the modern, the monstrous, the famous things, those he had more particularly, like thousands of ingenuous enquirers every year, come over to see, were exactly his sources of dismay. They were as so many set traps for displeasure, above all for reaction, of which his restless tread was constantly pressing the spring. It was interesting, doubtless, the whole show, but it would have been too discon-certing hadn't a certain finer truth saved the situation. He had distinctly not, in this steadier light, come over *all* for the mon-strosities; he had come, not only in the last analysis but quite on the face of the act, under an impulse with which they had nothing to do. He had come – putting the thing pompously – to look at his 'property', which he had thus for a third of a cen-tury not been within four thousand miles of; or, expressing it less sordidly, he had yielded to the humour of seeing again his house on the jolly corner, as he usually, and quite fondly, described it – the one in which he had first seen the light, in which various members of his family had lived and had died, in which the holidays of his overschooled boyhood had been passed and the few social flowers of his chilled adolescence gathered, and which, alienated then for so long a period, had, through the successive deaths of his two brothers and the termination of old arrangements, come wholly into his hands. He was the owner of another, not quite so 'good' – the jolly corner having been, from far back, superlatively extended and consecrated; and the value of the pair represented his main capital, with an income consisting, in these later years, of their respective rents which (thanks precisely to their original excellent type) had never been depressingly low. He could live in 'Europe', as he had been in the habit of living, on the product of these flourishing New York leases, and all the better since, that of the second structure, the mere number in its long row, having within a twelvemonth fallen in, renovation at a high advance had proved beautifully possible.

These were items of property indeed, but he had found himself since his arrival distinguishing more than ever between them. The house within the street, two bristling blocks westward, was already in course of reconstruction as a tall mass of flats; he had acceded, some time before, to overtures for this conversion – in which, now that it was going forward, it had been not the least of his astonishments to find himself able, on the spot, and though without a previous ounce of such experience, to participate with a certain intelligence, almost with a certain authority. He had lived his life with his back so turned to such concerns and his face addressed to those of so different an order that he scarce knew what to make of this lively stir, in a compartment of his mind never yet penetrated, of a capacity for business and a sense for construction. These virtues, so common all round him now, had been dormant in his own organism – where it might be said of them perhaps that they had slept the sleep of the just. At present, in the splendid autumn weather – the autumn at least was a pure boon in the terrible place – he loafed about his 'work' undeterred, secretly agitated; not in the least 'minding' that the whole proposition, as they said, was vulgar and sordid, and ready to climb ladders, to walk the plank, to handle materials and look wise about them, to ask questions, in fine, and challenge explanations and really 'go into' figures.

It amused, it verily quite charmed him; and, by the same stroke, it amused, and even more, Alice Staverton, though perhaps charming her perceptibly less. She wasn't however going to be better-off for it, as *he* was – and so astonishingly much: nothing was now likely, he knew, ever to make her better-off than she found herself, in the afternoon of life, as the delicately frugal possessor and tenant of the small house in Irving Place[2] to which she had subtly managed to cling through her almost unbroken New York career. If he knew the way to it now better than to any other address among the dreadful multiplied numberings which seemed to him to reduce the whole place to some vast ledger-page, overgrown, fantastic, of ruled and criss-crossed lines and figures – if he had formed, for his consolation, that habit, it was really not a little because of the charm of his having encountered and recognized, in the vast wilderness of the wholesale, breaking through the mere gross generalization of wealth and force and success, a small still scene where items and shades, all delicate things, kept the sharpness of the notes of a high voice perfectly trained, and where economy hung about like the scent of a garden. His old friend lived with one maid and herself dusted her relics and trimmed her lamps and polished her silver; she stood off, in the awful modern crush, when she could, but she sallied forth and did battle when the challenge was really to 'spirit', the spirit she after all confessed to, proudly and a little shyly, as to that of the better time, that of *their* common, their quite far-away and antediluvian social period and order. She made use of the street-cars when need be, the terrible things that people scrambled for as the panic-stricken at sea scramble for the boats; she affronted, inscrutably, under stress, all the public concussions and ordeals; and yet, with that slim mystifying grace of her appearance, which defied you to say if she were a fair young woman who looked older through trouble, or a fine smooth older one who looked young through successful indifference; with her precious reference, above all, to memories and histories into which he could enter, she was as exquisite for him as some pale pressed flower (a rarity to begin with), and, failing other sweetnesses, she was a sufficient reward of his effort. They had communities of knowledge, 'their' knowledge (this discriminating possessive was always on her lips) of presences of the other age, presences all overlaid, in his case, by the experience of a man and the freedom of a wanderer, overlaid by pleasure, by infidelity, by passages of life that were strange and dim to her, just by 'Europe' in short, but still unobscured, still exposed and cherished, under that pious visitation of the spirit from which she had never been diverted.

She had come with him one day to see how his 'apartment-house' was rising; he had helped her over gaps and explained to her plans, and while they were there had happened to have, before her, a brief but lively discussion with the man in charge, the representative of the building-firm that had undertaken his work. He had found himself quite 'standing-up' to this personage over a failure on the latter's part to observe some detail of one of their noted conditions, and had so lucidly argued his case that, besides ever so prettily flushing, at the time, for sympathy in his triumph, she had afterwards said to him (though to a slightly greater effect of irony) that he had clearly for too many years neglected a real gift. If he had but stayed at home he would have anticipated the inventor of the sky-scraper. If he had but stayed at home he would have discovered his genius in time really to start some new variety of awful architectural hare and run it till it burrowed in a goldmine. He was to remember these words, while the weeks elapsed, for the small silver ring they had sounded over the queerest and deepest of his own lately most disguised and most muffled vibrations.

It had begun to be present to him after the first fortnight, it had broken out with the oddest abruptness, this particular wanton wonderment: it met him there – and this was the image under which he himself judged the matter, or at least, not a little, thrilled and flushed with it – very much as he might have been met by some strange figure, some unexpected occupant, at a turn of one of the dim passages of an empty house. The quaint analogy quite hauntingly remained with him, when he didn't indeed rather improve it by a still intenser form: that of his opening a door behind which he would have made sure of finding nothing, a door into a room shuttered and void, and yet so coming, with a great suppressed start, on some quite erect confronting presence, something planted in the middle of the place and facing him through the dusk. After that visit to the house in construction he walked with his companion to see the other and always so much the better one, which in the eastward direction formed one of the corners, the 'jolly' one precisely, of the street now so generally dishonoured and disfigured in its westward reaches, and of the comparatively conservative Avenue. The Avenue still had pretensions, as Miss Staverton said, to decency; the old people had mostly gone, the old names were unknown, and here and there an old association seemed to stray, all vaguely, like some very aged person, out too late, whom you might meet and feel the impulse to watch or follow, in kindness, for safe restoration to shelter.

They went in together, our friends; he admitted himself with his key, as he kept no one there, he explained, preferring, for his reasons, to leave the place empty, under a simple arrangement with a good woman living in the neighbourhood and who came for a daily hour to open windows and dust and sweep. Spencer Brydon had his reasons and was growingly aware of them; they seemed to him better each time he was there, though he didn't name them all to his companion, any more than he told her as yet how often, how quite absurdly often, he himself came. He only let her see for the present, while they walked through the great blank rooms, that absolute vacancy reigned and that, from top to bottom, there was nothing but Mrs Muldoon's broomstick, in a corner, to tempt the burglar. Mrs Muldoon was then on the premises, and she loquaciously attended the visitors, preceding them from room to room and pushing back shutters and throwing up sashes – all to show them, as she remarked, how little there was to see. There was little indeed to see in the great gaunt shell where the main dispositions and the general apportionment of space, the style of an age of ampler allowances, had nevertheless for its master their honest pleading message, affecting him as some good old servant's, some lifelong retainer's appeal for a character,[3] or even for a retiring-pension; yet it was also a remark of Mrs Muldoon's that, glad as she was to oblige him by her noonday round, there was a request she greatly hoped he would never make of her. If he should wish her for any reason to come in after dark she would just tell him, if he 'plased', that he must ask it of somebody else.

The fact that there was nothing to see didn't militate for the

worthy woman against what one *might* see, and she put it
frankly to Miss Staverton that no lady could be expected to
like, could she? 'craping up to thim top storeys in the ayvil
hours'. The gas and the electric light were off the house, and
she fairly evoked a gruesome vision of her march through the
great grey rooms – so many of them as there were too! – with
her glimmering taper. Miss Staverton met her honest glare
with a smile and the profession that she herself certainly would
recoil from such an adventure. Spencer Brydon meanwhile
held his peace – for the moment; the question of the 'evil' hours
in his old home had already become too grave for him. He had
begun some time since to 'crape'. and he knew just why a
packet of candles addressed to that pursuit had been stowed
by his own hand, three weeks before, at the back of a drawer
of the fine old sideboard that occupied, as a 'fixture', the
deep recess in the dining-room. Just now he laughed at his
companions – quickly however changing the subject; for the
reason that, in the first place, his laugh struck him even at that
moment as starting the odd echo, the conscious human reso-
nance (he scarce knew how to qualify it) that sounds made
while he was there alone sent back to his ear or his fancy; and
that, in the second, he imagined Alice Staverton for the instant
on the point of asking him, with a divination, if he ever so
prowled. There were divinations he was unprepared for, and
he had at all events averted enquiry by the time Mrs Muldoon
had left them, passing on to other parts.

There was happily enough to say, on so consecrated a spot,
that could be said freely and fairly; so that a whole train of
declarations was precipitated by his friend's having herself
broken out, after a yearning look round: 'But I hope you don't
mean they want you to pull *this* to pieces!' His answer came,
promptly, with his re-awakened wrath: it was of course exactly
what they wanted, and what they were 'at' him for, daily, with
the iteration of people who couldn't for their life understand a
man's liability to decent feelings. He had found the place, just
as it stood and beyond what he could express, an interest and
a joy. There were values other than the beastly rent-values, and
in short, in short—! But it was thus Miss Staverton took him

up. 'In short you're to make so good a thing of your sky-scraper that, living in luxury on *those* ill-gotten gains, you can afford for a while to be sentimental here!' Her smile had for him, with the words, the particular mild irony with which he found half her talk suffused; an irony without bitterness and that came, exactly, from her having so much imagination – not, like the cheap sarcasms with which one heard most people, about the world of 'society', bid for the reputation of cleverness, from nobody's really having any. It was agreeable to him at this very moment to be sure that when he had answered, after a brief demur, 'Well yes: so, precisely, you may put it!' her imagination would still do him justice. He explained that even if never a dollar were to come to him from the other house he would nevertheless cherish this one; and he dwelt, further, while they lingered and wandered, on the fact of the stupefaction he was already exciting, the positive mystification he felt himself create.

He spoke of the value of all he read into it, into the mere sight of the walls, mere shapes of the rooms, mere sound of the floors, mere feel, in his hand, of the old silver-plated knobs of the several mahogany doors, which suggested the pressure of the palms of the dead; the seventy years of the past in fine that these things represented, the annals of nearly three generations, counting his grandfather's, the one that had ended there, and the impalpable ashes of his long-extinct youth, afloat in the very air like microscopic motes. She listened to everything; she was a woman who answered intimately but who utterly didn't chatter. She scattered abroad therefore no cloud of words; she could assent, she could agree, above all she could encourage, without doing that. Only at the last she went a little further than he had done himself. 'And then how do you know? You may still, after all, want to live here.' It rather indeed pulled him up, for it wasn't what he had been thinking, at least in her sense of the words. 'You mean I may decide to stay on for the sake of it?'

'Well, *with* such a home—!' But, quite beautifully, she had too much tact to dot so monstrous an *i*, and it was precisely an illustration of the way she didn't rattle. How could any one – of any wit – insist on any one else's 'wanting' to live in New York?

'Oh,' he said, 'I *might* have lived here (since I had my opportunity early in life); I might have put in here all these years. Then everything would have been different enough – and, I daresay, "funny" enough. But that's another matter. And then the beauty of it – I mean of my perversity, of my refusal to agree to a "deal" – is just in the total absence of a reason. Don't you see that if I had a reason about the matter at all it would *have* to be the other way, and would then be inevitably a reason of dollars? There are no reasons here *but* of dollars. Let us therefore have none whatever – not the ghost of one.'

They were back in the hall then for departure, but from where they stood the vista was large, through an open door, into the great square main saloon, with its almost antique felicity of brave spaces between windows. Her eyes came back from that reach and met his own a moment. 'Are you very sure the "ghost" of one doesn't, much rather, serve—?'

He had a positive sense of turning pale. But it was as near as they were then to come. For he made answer, he believed, between a glare and a grin: 'Oh ghosts – of course the place must swarm with them! I should be ashamed of it if it didn't. Poor Mrs Muldoon's right, and it's why I haven't asked her to do more than look in.'

Miss Staverton's gaze again lost itself, and things she didn't utter, it was clear, came and went in her mind. She might even for the minute, off there in the fine room, have imagined some element dimly gathering. Simplified like the death-mask of a handsome face, it perhaps produced for her just then an effect akin to the stir of an expression in the 'set' commemorative plaster. Yet whatever her impression may have been she produced instead a vague platitude. 'Well, if it were only furnished and lived in—!'

She appeared to imply that in case of its being still furnished he might have been a little less opposed to the idea of a return. But she passed straight into the vestibule, as if to leave her words behind her, and the next moment he had opened the house-door and was standing with her on the steps. He closed the door and, while he re-pocketed his key, looking up and down, they took in the comparatively harsh actuality of the Avenue, which reminded him of the assault of the outer light of the Desert on the traveller emerging from an Egyptian tomb. But he risked before they stepped into the street his gathered answer to her speech. 'For me it *is* lived in. For me it *is* furnished.' At which it was easy for her to sigh 'Ah yes—!' all vaguely and discreetly; since his parents and his favourite sister, to say nothing of other kin, in numbers, had run their course and met their end there. That represented, within the walls, ineffaceable life.

It was a few days after this that, during an hour passed with her again, he had expressed his impatience of the too flattering curiosity – among the people he met – about his appreciation of New York. He had arrived at none at all that was socially producible, and as for that matter of his 'thinking' (thinking the better or the worse of anything there) he was wholly taken up with one subject of thought. It was mere vain egoism, and it was moreover, if she liked, a morbid obsession. He found all things come back to the question of what he personally might have been, how he might have led his life and 'turned out', if he had not so, at the outset, given it up. And confessing for the first time to the intensity within him of this absurd speculation – which but proved also, no doubt, the habit of too selfishly thinking – he affirmed the impotence there of any other source of interest, any other native appeal. 'What would it have made of me, what would it have made of me? I keep forever wondering, all idiotically; as if I could possibly know! I see what it has made of dozens of others, those I meet, and it positively aches within me, to the point of exasperation, that it would have made something of me as well. Only I can't make out *what*, and the worry of it, the small rage of curiosity never to be satisfied, brings back what I remember to have felt, once or twice, after judging best, for reasons, to burn some important letter unopened. I've been sorry, I've hated it – I've never known what was in the letter. You may of course say it's a trifle—!'

'I don't say it's a trifle,' Miss Staverton gravely interrupted.

She was seated by her fire, and before her, on his feet and

restless, he turned to and fro between this intensity of his idea
and a fitful and unseeing inspection, through his single eye-
glass, of the dear little old objects on her chimney-piece. Her
interruption made him for an instant look at her harder. 'I
shouldn't care if you did!' he laughed, however; 'and it's only a
figure, at any rate, for the way I now feel. *Not* to have followed
my perverse young course – and almost in the teeth of my
father's curse, as I may say; not to have kept it up, so, "over
there", from that day to this, without a doubt or a pang; not,
above all, to have liked it, to have loved it, so much, loved it,
no doubt, with such an abysmal conceit of my own preference:
some variation from *that*, I say, must have produced some different effect for my life and for my "form". I should have stuck
here – if it had been possible; and I was too young, at twenty-
three, to judge, *pour deux sous*,[4] whether it *were* possible. If I
had waited I might have seen it was, and then I might have
been, by staying here, something nearer to one of these types
who have been hammered so hard and made so keen by their
conditions. It isn't that I admire them so much – the question
of any charm in them, or of any charm, beyond that of the
rank money-passion, exerted by their conditions *for* them, has
nothing to do with the matter: it's only a question of what fantastic, yet perfectly possible, development of my own nature I
mayn't have missed. It comes over me that I had then a strange
alter ego deep down somewhere within me, as the full-blown
flower is in the small tight bud, and that I just took the course,
I just transferred him to the climate, that blighted him for once
and for ever.'

'And you wonder about the flower,' Miss Staverton said. 'So
do I, if you want to know; and so I've been wondering these
several weeks. I believe in the flower,' she continued, 'I feel it
would have been quite splendid, quite huge and monstrous.'

'Monstrous above all!' her visitor echoed; 'and I imagine, by
the same stroke, quite hideous and offensive.'

'You don't believe that,' she returned; 'if you did you
wouldn't wonder. You'd know, and that would be enough for
you. What you feel – and what I feel *for* you – is that you'd have
had power.'

'You'd have liked me that way?' he asked.

She barely hung fire. 'How should I not have liked you?'

'I see. You'd have liked me, have preferred me, a billionaire!'

'How should I not have liked you?' she simply again asked.

He stood before her still – her question kept him motionless. He took it in, so much there was of it; and indeed his not otherwise meeting it testified to that. 'I know at least what I am,' he simply went on; 'the other side of the medal's clear enough. I've not been edifying – I believe I'm thought in a hundred quarters to have been barely decent. I've followed strange paths and worshipped strange gods; it must have come to you again and again – in fact you've admitted to me as much – that I was leading, at any time these thirty years, a selfish frivolous scandalous life. And you see what it has made of me.'

She just waited, smiling at him. 'You see what it has made of *me*.'

'Oh you're a person whom nothing can have altered. You were born to be what you are, anywhere, anyway: you've the perfection nothing else could have blighted. And don't you see how, without my exile, I shouldn't have been waiting till now—?' But he pulled up for the strange pang.

'The great thing to see,' she presently said, 'seems to me to be that it has spoiled nothing. It hasn't spoiled your being here at last. It hasn't spoiled this. It hasn't spoiled your speaking—' She also however faltered.

He wondered at everything her controlled emotion might mean. 'Do you believe then – too dreadfully! – that I *am* as good as I might ever have been?'

'Oh no! Far from it!' With which she got up from her chair and was nearer to him. 'But I don't care,' she smiled.

'You mean I'm good enough?'

She considered a little. 'Will you believe it if I say so? I mean will you let that settle your question for you?' And then as if making out in his face that he drew back from this, that he had some idea which, however absurd, he couldn't yet bargain away: 'Oh you don't care either – but very differently: you don't care for anything but yourself.'

Spencer Brydon recognized it – it was in fact what he had

absolutely professed. Yet he importantly qualified. '*He* isn't myself. He's the just so totally other person. But I do want to see him,' he added. 'And I can. And I shall.'

Their eyes met for a minute while he guessed from something in hers that she divined his strange sense. But neither of them otherwise expressed it, and her apparent understanding, with no protesting shock, no easy derision, touched him more deeply than anything yet, constituting for his stifled perversity, on the spot, an element that was like breatheable air. What she said however was unexpected. 'Well, *I've* seen him.'

'You—?'

'I've seen him in a dream.'

'Oh a "dream"—!' It let him down.

'But twice over,' she continued. 'I saw him as I see you now.'

'You've dreamed the same dream—?'

'Twice over,' she repeated. 'The very same.'

This did somehow a little speak to him, as it also gratified him. 'You dream about me at that rate?'

'Ah about *him*!' she smiled.

His eyes again sounded her. 'Then you know all about him.' And as she said nothing more: 'What's the wretch like?'

She hesitated, and it was as if he were pressing her so hard that, resisting for reasons of her own, she had to turn away. 'I'll tell you some other time!'

II

It was after this that there was most of a virtue for him, most of a cultivated charm, most of a preposterous secret thrill, in the particular form of surrender to his obsession and of address to what he more and more believed to be his privilege. It was what in these weeks he was living for – since he really felt life to begin but after Mrs Muldoon had retired from the scene and, visiting the ample house from attic to cellar, making sure he was alone, he knew himself in safe possession and, as he tacitly expressed it, let himself go. He sometimes came twice in the twenty-four hours; the moments he liked best were those of gathering dusk, of the short autumn twilight; this was the time of which, again and again, he found himself hoping most. Then he could, as seemed to him, most intimately wander and wait, linger and listen, feel his fine attention, never in his life before so fine, on the pulse of the great vague place: he preferred the lampless hour and only wished he might have prolonged each day the deep crepuscular spell. Later – rarely much before midnight, but then for a considerable vigil – he watched with his glimmering light; moving slowly, holding it high, playing it far, rejoicing above all, as much as he might, in open vistas, reaches of communication between rooms and by passages; the long straight chance or show, as he would have called it, for the revelation he pretended to invite. It was a practice he found he could perfectly 'work' without exciting remark; no one was in the least the wiser for it; even Alice Staverton, who was moreover a well of discretion, didn't quite fully imagine.

He let himself in and let himself out with the assurance of calm proprietorship; and accident so far favoured him that, if a fat Avenue 'officer' had happened on occasion to see him entering at eleven-thirty, he had never yet, to the best of his belief, been noticed as emerging at two. He walked there on the crisp November nights, arrived regularly at the evening's end; it was as easy to do this after dining out as to take his way to a club or to his hotel. When he left his club, if he hadn't been dining out, it was ostensibly to go to his hotel; and when he left his hotel, if he had spent a part of the evening there, it was ostensibly to go to his club. Everything was easy in fine; everything conspired and promoted: there was truly even in the strain of his experience something that glossed over, something that salved and simplified, all the rest of consciousness. He circulated, talked, renewed, loosely and pleasantly, old relations – met indeed, so far as he could, new expectations and seemed to make out on the whole that in spite of the career, of such different contacts, which he had spoken of to Miss Staverton as ministering so little, for those who might have watched it, to edification, he was positively rather liked than not. He was a dim secondary social success – and all with people who had truly not an idea of him. It was all mere

surface sound, this murmur of their welcome, this popping of
their corks – just as his gestures of response were the extravagant shadows, emphatic in proportion as they meant little, of
some game of *ombres chinoises*.[5] He projected himself all day,
in thought, straight over the bristling line of hard unconscious
heads and into the other, the real, the waiting life; the life that,
as soon as he had heard behind him the click of his great house-
door, began for him, on the jolly corner, as beguilingly as the
slow opening bars of some rich music follows the tap of the
conductor's wand.

He always caught the first effect of the steel point of his
stick on the old marble of the hall pavement, large black-and-
white squares that he remembered as the admiration of his
childhood and that had then made in him, as he now saw, for
the growth of an early conception of style. This effect was the
dim reverberating tinkle as of some far-off bell hung who
should say where? – in the depths of the house, of the past, of
that mystical other world that might have flourished for him
had he not, for weal or woe, abandoned it. On this impression
he did ever the same thing; he put his stick noiselessly away in
a corner – feeling the place once more in the likeness of some
great glass bowl, all precious concave crystal, set delicately
humming by the play of a moist finger round its edge. The concave crystal held, as it were, this mystical other world, and the
indescribably fine murmur of its rim was the sigh there, the
scarce audible pathetic wail to his strained ear, of all the old
baffled forsworn possibilities. What he did therefore by this
appeal of his hushed presence was to wake them into such
measure of ghostly life as they might still enjoy. They were shy,
all but unappeasably shy, but they weren't really sinister; at
least they weren't as he had hitherto felt them – before they had
taken the Form he so yearned to make them take, the Form he
at moments saw himself in the light of fairly hunting on tiptoe,
the points of his evening-shoes, from room to room and from
storey to storey.

That was the essence of his vision – which was all rank folly,
if one would, while he was out of the house and otherwise
occupied, but which took on the last verisimilitude as soon as

he was placed and posted. He knew what he meant and what he wanted; it was as clear as the figure on a cheque presented in demand for cash. His *alter ego* 'walked' – that was the note of his image of him, while his image of his motive for his own odd pastime was the desire to waylay him and meet him. He roamed, slowly, warily, but all restlessly, he himself did – Mrs Muldoon had been right, absolutely, with her figure of their 'craping'; and the presence he watched for would roam restlessly too. But it would be as cautious and as shifty; the conviction of its probable, in fact its already quite sensible, quite audible evasion of pursuit grew for him from night to night, laying on him finally a rigour to which nothing in his life had been comparable. It had been the theory of many superficially-judging persons, he knew, that he was wasting that life in a surrender to sensations, but he had tasted of no pleasure so fine as his actual tension, had been introduced to no sport that demanded at once the patience and the nerve of this stalking of a creature more subtle, yet at bay perhaps more formidable, than any beast of the forest. The terms, the comparisons, the very practices of the chase positively came again into play; there were even moments when passages of his occasional experience as a sportsman, stirred memories, from his younger time, of moor and mountain and desert, revived for him – and to the increase of his keenness – by the tremendous force of analogy. He found himself at moments – once he had placed his single light on some mantel-shelf or in some recess – stepping back into shelter or shade, effacing himself behind a door or in an embrasure, as he had sought of old the vantage of rock and tree; he found himself holding his breath and living in the joy of the instant, the supreme suspense created by big game alone.

He wasn't afraid (though putting himself the question as he believed gentlemen on Bengal tiger-shoots or in close quarters with the great bear of the Rockies had been known to confess to having put it); and this indeed – since here at least he might be frank! – because of the impression, so intimate and so strange, that he himself produced as yet a dread, produced certainly a strain, beyond the liveliest he was likely to feel. They fell for him into categories, they fairly became familiar, the signs, for his own perception, of the alarm his presence and his vigilance created; though leaving him always to remark, portentously, on his probably having formed a relation, his probably enjoying a consciousness, unique in the experience of man. People enough, first and last, had been in terror of apparitions, but who had ever before so turned the tables and become himself, in the apparitional world, an incalculable terror? He might have found this sublime had he quite dared to think of it; but he didn't too much insist, truly, on that side of his privilege. With habit and repetition he gained to an extraordinary degree the power to penetrate the dusk of distances and the darkness of corners, to resolve back into their innocence the treacheries of uncertain light, the evil-looking forms taken in the gloom by mere shadows, by accidents of the air, by shifting effects of perspective; putting down his dim luminary he could still wander on without it, pass into other rooms and, only knowing it was there behind him in case of need, see his way about, visually project for his purpose a comparative clearness. It made him feel, this acquired faculty, like some monstrous stealthy cat; he wondered if he would have glared at these moments with large shining yellow eyes, and what it mightn't verily be, for the poor hard-pressed *alter ego*, to be confronted with such a type.

He liked however the open shutters; he opened everywhere those Mrs Muldoon had closed, closing them as carefully afterwards, so that she shouldn't notice: he liked – oh this he did like, and above all in the upper rooms! – the sense of the hard silver of the autumn stars through the window-panes, and scarcely less the flare of the street-lamps below, the white electric lustre which it would have taken curtains to keep out. This was human actual social; this was of the world he had lived in, and he was more at his ease certainly for the countenance, coldly general and impersonal, that all the while and in spite of his detachment it seemed to give him. He had support of course mostly in the rooms at the wide front and the prolonged side; it failed him considerably in the central shades and the parts at the back. But if he sometimes, on his rounds, was glad of his optical reach, so none the less often the rear of the house affected him as the very jungle of his prey. The place was there more subdivided; a large 'extension' in particular, where small rooms for servants had been multiplied, abounded in nooks and corners, in closets and passages, in the ramifications especially of an ample back staircase over which he leaned, many a time, to look far down – not deterred from his gravity even while aware that he might, for a spectator, have figured some solemn simpleton playing at hide-and-seek. Outside in fact he might himself make that ironic *rapprochement*;[6] but within the walls, and in spite of the clear windows, his consistency was proof against the cynical light of New York.

It had belonged to that idea of the exasperated consciousness of his victim to become a real test for him; since he had quite put it to himself from the first that, oh distinctly! he could 'cultivate' his whole perception. He had felt it as above all open to cultivation – which indeed was but another name for his manner of spending his time. He was bringing it on, bringing it to perfection, by practice; in consequence of which it had grown so fine that he was now aware of impressions, attestations of his general postulate, that couldn't have broken upon him at once. This was the case more specifically with a phenomenon at last quite frequent for him in the upper rooms, the recognition – absolutely unmistakeable, and by a turn dating from a particular hour, his resumption of his campaign after a diplomatic drop, a calculated absence of three nights – of his being definitely followed, tracked at a distance carefully taken and to the express end that he should the less confidently, less arrogantly, appear to himself merely to pursue. It worried, it finally quite broke him up, for it proved, of all the conceivable impressions, the one least suited to his book. He was kept in sight while remaining himself – as regards the essence of his position – sightless, and his only recourse then was in abrupt turns, rapid recoveries of ground. He wheeled about, retracing his steps, as if he might so catch in his face at least the stirred air of some other quick revolution. It was indeed true that his fully dislocalized thought of these manœuvres recalled to him Pantaloon, at the Christmas farce, buffeted and tricked from

behind by ubiquitous Harlequin;[7] but it left intact the influence
of the conditions themselves each time he was re-exposed to
them, so that in fact this association, had he suffered it to
become constant, would on a certain side have but ministered
to his intenser gravity. He had made, as I have said, to create
on the premises the baseless sense of a reprieve, his three
absences; and the result of the third was to confirm the after-
effect of the second.

On his return, that night – the night succeeding his last
intermission – he stood in the hall and looked up the staircase
with a certainty more intimate than any he had yet known.
'He's *there*, at the top, and waiting – not, as in general, falling
back for disappearance. He's holding his ground, and it's the
first time – which is a proof, isn't it? that something has happened for him.' So Brydon argued with his hand on the banister
and his foot on the lowest stair; in which position he felt as
never before the air chilled by his logic. He himself turned cold
in it, for he seemed of a sudden to know what now was
involved. 'Harder pressed? – yes, he takes it in, with its thus
making clear to him that I've come, as they say, "to stay". He
finally doesn't like and can't bear it, in the sense, I mean, that
his wrath, his menaced interest, now balances with his dread.
I've hunted him till he has "turned": that, up there, is what has
happened – he's the fanged or the antlered animal brought at
last to bay.' There came to him, as I say – but determined by an
influence beyond my notation! – the acuteness of this certainty;
under which however the next moment he had broken into a
sweat that he would as little have consented to attribute to fear
as he would have dared immediately to act upon it for enter-
prise. It marked none the less a prodigious thrill, a thrill that
represented sudden dismay, no doubt, but also represented,
and with the selfsame throb, the strangest, the most joyous,
possibly the next minute almost the proudest, duplication of
consciousness.

'He has been dodging, retreating, hiding, but now, worked
up to anger, he'll fight!' – this intense impression made a single
mouthful, as it were, of terror and applause. But what was
wondrous was that the applause, for the felt fact, was so eager,

since, if it was his other self he was running to earth, this ineffable identity was thus in the last resort not unworthy of him. It bristled there – somewhere near at hand, however unseen still – as the hunted thing, even as the trodden worm of the adage *must* at last bristle;[8] and Brydon at this instant tasted probably a sensation more complex than had ever before found itself consistent with sanity. It was as if it would have shamed him that a character so associated with his own should triumphantly succeed in just skulking, should to the end not risk the open; so that the drop of this danger was, on the spot, a great lift of the whole situation. Yet with another rare shift of the same subtlety he was already trying to measure by how much more he himself might now be in peril of fear; so rejoicing that he could, in another form, actively inspire that fear, and simultaneously quaking for the form in which he might passively know it.

The apprehension of knowing it must after a little have grown in him, and the strangest moment of his adventure perhaps, the most memorable or really most interesting, afterwards, of his crisis, was the lapse of certain instants of concentrated conscious *combat*, the sense of a need to hold on to something, even after the manner of a man slipping and slipping on some awful incline; the vivid impulse, above all, to move, to act, to charge, somehow and upon something – to show himself, in a word, that he wasn't afraid. The state of 'holding-on' was thus the state to which he was momentarily reduced; if there had been anything, in the great vacancy, to seize, he would presently have been aware of having clutched it as he might under a shock at home have clutched the nearest chair-back. He had been surprised at any rate – of this he *was* aware – into something unprecedented since his original appropriation of the place; he had closed his eyes, held them tight, for a long minute, as with that instinct of dismay and that terror of vision. When he opened them the room, the other contiguous rooms, extraordinarily, seemed lighter – so light, almost, that at first he took the change for day. He stood firm, however that might be, just where he had paused; his resistance had helped him – it was as if there were something he had tided over. He knew

after a little what this was – it had been in the imminent danger of flight. He had stiffened his will against going; without
this he would have made for the stairs, and it seemed to him
that, still with his eyes closed, he would have descended them,
would have known how, straight and swiftly, to the bottom.

Well, as he had held out, here he was – still at the top, among
the more intricate upper rooms and with the gauntlet of the
others, of all the rest of the house, still to run when it should
be his time to go. He would go at his time – only at his time:
didn't he go every night very much at the same hour? He took
out his watch – there was light for that: it was scarcely a quarter past one, and he had never withdrawn so soon. He reached
his lodgings for the most part at two – with his walk of a quarter of an hour. He would wait for the last quarter – he wouldn't
stir till then; and he kept his watch there with his eyes on it,
reflecting while he held it that this deliberate wait, a wait with
an effort, which he recognized, would serve perfectly for the
attestation he desired to make. It would prove his courage –
unless indeed the latter might most be proved by his budging
at last from his place. What he mainly felt now was that, since
he hadn't originally scuttled, he had his dignities – which had
never in his life seemed so many – all to preserve and to carry
aloft. This was before him in truth as a physical image, an
image almost worthy of an age of greater romance. That
remark indeed glimmered for him only to glow the next instant
with a finer light; since what age of romance, after all, could
have matched either the state of his mind or, 'objectively', as
they said, the wonder of his situation? The only difference
would have been that, brandishing his dignities over his head
as in a parchment scroll, he might then – that is in the heroic
time – have proceeded downstairs with a drawn sword in his
other grasp.

At present, really, the light he had set down on the mantel of
the next room would have to figure his sword; which utensil,
in the course of a minute, he had taken the requisite number of
steps to possess himself of. The door between the rooms was
open, and from the second another door opened to a third.
These rooms, as he remembered, gave all three upon a common

corridor as well, but there was a fourth, beyond them, without issue save through the preceding. To have moved, to have heard his step again, was appreciably a help; though even in recognizing this he lingered once more a little by the chimney-piece on which his light had rested. When he next moved, just hesitating where to turn, he found himself considering a circumstance that, after his first and comparatively vague apprehension of it, produced in him the start that often attends some pang of recollection, the violent shock of having ceased happily to forget. He had come into sight of the door in which the brief chain of communication ended and which he now surveyed from the nearer threshold, the one not directly facing it. Placed at some distance to the left of this point, it would have admitted him to the last room of the four, the room without other approach or egress, had it not, to his intimate conviction, been closed *since* his former visitation, the matter probably of a quarter of an hour before. He stared with all his eyes at the wonder of the fact, arrested again where he stood and again holding his breath while he sounded its sense. Surely it had been *subsequently* closed – that is it had been on his previous passage indubitably open!

He took it full in the face that something had happened between – that he couldn't not have noticed before (by which he meant on his original tour of all the rooms that evening) that such a barrier had exceptionally presented itself. He had indeed since that moment undergone an agitation so extraordinary that it might have muddled for him any earlier view; and he tried to convince himself that he might perhaps then have gone into the room and, inadvertently, automatically, on coming out, have drawn the door after him. The difficulty was that this exactly was what he never did; it was against his whole policy, as he might have said, the essence of which was to keep vistas clear. He had them from the first, as he was well aware, quite on the brain: the strange apparition, at the far end of one of them, of his baffled 'prey' (which had become by so sharp an irony so little the term now to apply!) was the form of success his imagination had most cherished, projecting into it always a refinement of beauty. He had known fifty times the start of perception that had afterwards dropped; had fifty times gasped to himself 'There!' under some fond brief hallucination. The house, as the case stood, admirably lent itself; he might wonder at the taste, the native architecture of the particular time, which could rejoice so in the multiplication of doors – the opposite extreme to the modern, the actual almost complete proscription of them; but it had fairly contributed to provoke this obsession of the presence encountered telescopically, as he might say, focussed and studied in diminishing perspective and as by a rest for the elbow.

It was with these considerations that his present attention was charged – they perfectly availed to make what he saw portentous. He *couldn't*, by any lapse, have blocked that aperture; and if he hadn't, if it was unthinkable, why what else was clear but that there had been another agent? Another agent? – he had been catching, as he felt, a moment back, the very breath of him; but when he had been so close as in this simple, this logical, this completely personal act? It was so logical, that is, that one might have *taken* it for personal; yet for what did Brydon take it, he asked himself, while, softly panting, he felt his eyes almost leave their sockets. Ah this time at last they *were*, the two, the opposed projections of him, in presence; and this time, as much as one would, the question of danger loomed. With it rose, as not before, the question of courage – for what he knew the blank face of the door to say to him was 'Show us how much you have!' It stared, it glared back at him with that challenge; it put to him the two alternatives: should he just push it open or not? Oh to have this consciousness was to *think* – and to think, Brydon knew, as he stood there, was, with the lapsing moments, not to have acted! Not to have acted – that was the misery and the pang – was even still not to act; was in fact *all* to feel the thing in another, in a new and terrible way. How long did he pause and how long did he debate? There was presently nothing to measure it; for his vibration had already changed – as just by the effect of its intensity. Shut up there, at bay, defiant, and with the prodigy of the thing palpably provably *done*, thus giving notice like some stark signboard – under that accession of accent the situation itself had turned; and Brydon at last remarkably made up his mind on what it had turned to.

It had turned altogether to a different admonition; to a supreme hint, for him, of the value of Discretion! This slowly dawned, no doubt – for it could take its time; so perfectly, on his threshold, had he been stayed, so little as yet had he either advanced or retreated. It was the strangest of all things that now when, by his taking ten steps and applying his hand to a latch, or even his shoulder and his knee, if necessary, to a panel, all the hunger of his prime need might have been met, his high curiosity crowned, his unrest assuaged – it was amazing, but it was also exquisite and rare, that insistance should have, at a touch, quite dropped from him. Discretion – he jumped at that; and yet not, verily, at such a pitch, because it saved his nerves or his skin, but because, much more valuably, it saved the situation. When I say he 'jumped' at it I feel the consonance of this term with the fact that – at the end indeed of I know not how long – he did move again, he crossed straight to the door. He wouldn't touch it – it seemed now that he might *if* he would: he would only just wait there a little, to show, to prove, that he wouldn't. He had thus another station, close to the thin partition by which revelation was denied him; but with his eyes bent and his hands held off in a mere intensity of stillness. He listened as if there had been something to hear, but this attitude, while it lasted, was his own communication. 'If you won't then – good: I spare you and I give up. You affect me as by the appeal positively for pity: you convince me that for reasons rigid and sublime – what do I know? – we both of us should have suffered. I respect them then, and, though moved and privileged as, I believe, it has never been given to man, I retire, I renounce – never, on my honour, to try again. So rest for ever – and let *me*!'

That, for Brydon was the deep sense of this last demonstration – solemn, measured, directed, as he felt it to be. He brought it to a close, he turned away; and now verily he knew how deeply he had been stirred. He retraced his steps, taking up his candle, burnt, he observed, well-nigh to the socket, and marking again, lighten it as he would, the distinctness of his footfall; after which, in a moment, he knew himself at the other side of the house. He did here what he had not yet done at these hours – he opened half a casement, one of those in the front, and let in the air of the night; a thing he would have taken at any time previous for a sharp rupture of his spell. His spell was broken now, and it didn't matter – broken by his concession and his surrender, which made it idle henceforth that he should ever come back. The empty street – its other life so marked even by the great lamplit vacancy – was within call, within touch; he stayed there as to be in it again, high above it though he was still perched; he watched as for some comforting common fact, some vulgar human note, the passage of a scavenger or a thief, some night-bird however base. He would have blessed that sign of life; he would have welcomed positively the slow approach of his friend the policeman, whom he had hitherto only sought to avoid, and was not sure that if the patrol had come into sight he mightn't have felt the impulse to get into relation with it, to hail it, on some pretext, from his fourth floor.

The pretext that wouldn't have been too silly or too compromising, the explanation that would have saved his dignity and kept his name, in such a case, out of the papers, was not definite to him: he was so occupied with the thought of recording his Discretion – as an effect of the vow he had just uttered to his intimate adversary – that the importance of this loomed large and something had overtaken all ironically his sense of proportion. If there had been a ladder applied to the front of the house, even one of the vertiginous perpendiculars employed by painters and roofers and sometimes left standing overnight, he would have managed somehow, astride of the window-sill, to compass by outstretched leg and arm that mode of descent. If there had been some such uncanny thing as he had found in his room at hotels, a workable fire-escape in the form of notched cable or a canvas shoot, he would have availed himself of it as a proof – well, of his present delicacy. He nursed that sentiment, as the question stood, a little in vain, and even – at the end of he scarce knew, once more, how long – found it, as by the action on his mind of the failure of response of the outer world, sinking back to vague anguish. It seemed to him he had waited an age for some stir of the great grim hush; the life of the town was itself under a spell – so unnaturally, up and down the whole prospect of known and rather ugly objects, the blankness and the silence lasted. Had they ever, he asked himself, the hard-faced houses, which had begun to look livid in the dim dawn, had they ever spoken so little to any need of his spirit? Great builded voids, great crowded stillnesses put on, often, in the heart of cities, for the small hours, a sort of sinister mask, and it was of this large collective negation that Brydon presently became conscious – all the more that the break of day was, almost incredibly, now at hand, proving to him what a night he had made of it.

He looked again at his watch, saw what had become of his time-values (he had taken hours for minutes – not, as in other tense situations, minutes for hours) and the strange air of the streets was but the weak, the sullen flush of a dawn in which everything was still locked up. His choked appeal from his own open window had been the sole note of life, and he could but break off at last as for a worse despair. Yet while so deeply demoralized he was capable again of an impulse denoting – at least by his present measure – extraordinary resolution; of retracing his steps to the spot where he had turned cold with the extinction of his last pulse of doubt as to there being in the place another presence than his own. This required an effort strong enough to sicken him; but he had his reason, which overmastered for the moment everything else. There was the whole of the rest of the house to traverse, and how should he screw himself to that if the door he had seen closed were at present open? He could hold to the idea that the closing had practically been for him an act of mercy, a chance offered him to descend, depart, get off the ground and never again profane it. This conception held together, it worked; but what it meant for him depended now clearly on the amount of forbearance his recent action, or rather his recent inaction, had engendered. The image of the 'presence', whatever it was, waiting there for him to go – this image had not yet been so concrete for his nerves as when he stopped short of the point at which certainty would have come to him. For, with all his resolution, or more exactly with all his dread, he did stop short – he hung back from really seeing. The risk was too great and his fear too definite: it took at this moment an awful specific form.

He knew – yes, as he had never known anything – that, *should* he see the door open, it would all too abjectly be the end of him. It would mean that the agent of his shame – for his shame was the deep abjection – was once more at large and in general possession; and what glared him thus in the face was the act that this would determine for him. It would send him straight about to the window he had left open, and by that window, be long ladder and dangling rope as absent as they would, he saw himself uncontrollably insanely fatally take his way to the street. The hideous chance of this he at least could avert; but he could only avert it by recoiling in time from assurance. He had the whole house to deal with, this fact was still there; only he now knew that uncertainty alone could start him. He stole back from where he had checked himself – merely to do so was suddenly like safety – and, making blindly for the greater staircase, left gaping rooms and sounding passages behind. Here was the top of the stairs, with a fine large dim descent and three spacious landings to mark off. His instinct was all for mildness, but his feet were harsh on the floors, and, strangely, when he had in a couple of minutes become aware of this, it counted somehow for help. He couldn't have spoken, the tone of his voice would have scared him, and the common conceit or resource of 'whistling in the dark' (whether literally or figuratively) have appeared basely vulgar; yet he liked none the less to hear himself go, and when he had reached his first landing – taking it all with no rush, but quite steadily – that stage of success drew from him a gasp of relief.

The house, withal, seemed immense, the scale of space again inordinate; the open rooms, to no one of which his eyes deflected, gloomed in their shuttered state like mouths of caverns; only the high skylight that formed the crown of the deep well created for him a medium in which he could advance, but which might have been, for queerness of colour, some watery under-world. He tried to think of something noble, as that his property was really grand, a splendid possession; but this nobleness took the form too of the clear delight with which he was finally to sacrifice it. They might come in now, the build- ers, the destroyers – they might come as soon as they would. At the end of two flights he had dropped to another zone, and from the middle of the third, with only one more left, he recognized the influence of the lower windows, of half-drawn blinds, of the occasional gleam of street-lamps, of the glazed spaces of the vestibule. This was the bottom of the sea, which showed an illumination of its own and which he even saw paved – when at a given moment he drew up to sink a long look over the banisters – with the marble squares of his child- hood. By that time indubitably he felt, as he might have said in a commoner cause, better; it had allowed him to stop and draw breath, and the ease increased with the sight of the old black- and-white slabs. But what he most felt was that now surely, with the element of impunity pulling him as by hard firm hands, the case was settled for what he might have seen above had he dared that last look. The closed door, blessedly remote now, was still closed – and he had only in short to reach that of the house.

He came down further, he crossed the passage forming the access to the last flight; and if here again he stopped an instant it was almost for the sharpness of the thrill of assured escape. It made him shut his eyes – which opened again to the straight slope of the remainder of the stairs. Here was impunity still, but impunity almost excessive; inasmuch as the sidelights and the high fan-tracery of the entrance were glimmering straight into the hall; an appearance produced, he the next instant saw, by the fact that the vestibule gaped wide, that the hinged halves of the inner door had been thrown far back. Out of that again the *question* sprang at him, making his eyes, as he felt, half- start from his head, as they had done, at the top of the house, before the sign of the other door. If he had left that one open, hadn't he left this one closed, and wasn't he now in *most* imme- diate presence of some inconceivable occult activity? It was as sharp, the question, as a knife in his side, but the answer hung fire still and seemed to lose itself in the vague darkness to which the thin admitted dawn, glimmering archwise over the whole outer door, made a semicircular margin, a cold silvery nimbus that seemed to play a little as he looked – to shift and expand and contract.

It was as if there had been something within it, protected by indistinctness and corresponding in extent with the opaque surface behind, the painted panels of the last barrier to his escape, of which the key was in his pocket. The indistinctness mocked him even while he stared, affected him as somehow shrouding or challenging certitude, so that after faltering an instant on his step he let himself go with the sense that here *was* at last something to meet, to touch, to take, to know – something all unnatural and dreadful, but to advance upon which was the condition for him either of liberation or of supreme defeat. The penumbra, dense and dark, was the virtual screen of a figure which stood in it as still as some image erect in a niche or as some black-vizored sentinel guarding a treasure. Brydon was to know afterwards, was to recall and make out, the particular thing he had believed during the rest of his descent. He saw, in its great grey glimmering margin, the central vagueness diminish, and he felt it to be taking the very form toward which, for so many days, the passion of his curiosity had yearned. It gloomed, it loomed, it was something, it was somebody, the prodigy of a personal presence.

Rigid and conscious, spectral yet human, a man of his own substance and stature waited there to measure himself with his power to dismay. This only could it be – this only till he recognized, with his advance, that what made the face dim was the pair of raised hands that covered it and in which, so far from being offered in defiance, it was buried as for dark deprecation. So Brydon, before him, took him in; with every fact of him now, in the higher light, hard and acute – his planted stillness, his vivid truth, his grizzled bent head and white masking hands, his queer actuality of evening-dress, of dangling double eye-glass, of gleaming silk lappet[9] and white linen, of pearl button and gold watch-guard and polished shoe. No portrait by a great modern master could have presented him with more intensity, thrust him out of his frame with more art, as if there

had been 'treatment', of the consummate sort, in his every
shade and salience. The revulsion, for our friend, had become,
before he knew it, immense – this drop, in the act of apprehension, to the sense of his adversary's inscrutable manœuvre.
That meaning at least, while he gaped, it offered him; for he
could but gape at his other self in this other anguish, gape as a
proof that *he*, standing there for the achieved, the enjoyed, the
triumphant life, couldn't be faced in his triumph. Wasn't the
proof in the splendid covering hands, strong and completely
spread? – so spread and so intentional that, in spite of a special
verity that surpassed every other, the fact that one of these hands
had lost two fingers, which were reduced to stumps, as if accidentally shot away, the face was effectually guarded and saved.

'Saved', though, *would* it be? – Brydon breathed his wonder
till the very impunity of his attitude and the very insistence of
his eyes produced, as he felt, a sudden stir which showed the
next instant as a deeper portent, while the head raised itself,
the betrayal of a braver purpose. The hands, as he looked,
began to move, to open; then, as if deciding in a flash, dropped
from the face and left it uncovered and presented. Horror, with
the sight, had leaped into Brydon's throat, gasping there in a
sound he couldn't utter; for the bared identity was too hideous
as *his*, and his glare was the passion of his protest. The face,
that face, Spencer Brydon's? – he searched it still, but looking
away from it in dismay and denial, falling straight from
his height of sublimity. It was unknown, inconceivable, awful,
disconnected from any possibility—! He had been 'sold', he
inwardly moaned, stalking such game as this: the presence
before him was a presence, the horror within him a horror, but
the waste of his nights had been only grotesque and the success
of his adventure an irony. Such an identity fitted his at *no*
point, made its alternative monstrous. A thousand times yes,
as it came upon him nearer now – the face was the face of a
stranger. It came upon him nearer now, quite as one of those
expanding fantastic images projected by the magic lantern of
childhood; for the stranger, whoever he might be, evil, odious,
blatant, vulgar, had advanced as for aggression, and he knew
himself give ground. Then harder pressed still, sick with the

force of his shock, and falling back as under the hot breath and the roused passion of a life larger than his own, a rage of personality before which his own collapsed, he felt the whole vision turn to darkness and his very feet give way. His head went round; he was going; he had gone.

III

What had next brought him back, clearly – though after how long? – was Mrs Muldoon's voice, coming to him from quite near, from so near that he seemed presently to see her as kneeling on the ground before him while he lay looking up at her; himself not wholly on the ground, but half-raised and upheld – conscious, yes, of tenderness of support and, more particularly, of a head pillowed in extraordinary softness and faintly refreshing fragrance. He considered, he wondered, his wit but half at his service; then another face intervened, bending more directly over him, and he finally knew that Alice Staverton had made her lap an ample and perfect cushion to him, and that she had to this end seated herself on the lowest degree of the staircase, the rest of his long person remaining stretched on his old black-and-white slabs. They were cold, these marble squares of his youth; but *he* somehow was not, in this rich return of consciousness – the most wonderful hour, little by little, that he had ever known, leaving him, as it did, so gratefully, so abysmally passive, and yet as with a treasure of intelligence waiting all round him for quiet appropriation; dissolved, he might call it, in the air of the place and producing the golden glow of a late autumn afternoon. He had come back, yes – come back from further away than any man but himself had ever travelled; but it was strange how with this sense what he had come back *to* seemed really the great thing, and as if his prodigious journey had been all for the sake of it. Slowly but surely his consciousness grew, his vision of his state thus completing itself: he had been miraculously *carried* back – lifted and carefully borne as from where he had been picked up, the uttermost end of an interminable grey passage. Even with this he was suffered to rest, and what had now brought him to knowledge was the break in the long mild motion.

It had brought him to knowledge, to knowledge – yes, this was the beauty of his state; which came to resemble more and more that of a man who has gone to sleep on some news of a great inheritance, and then, after dreaming it away, after profaning it with matters strange to it, has waked up again to serenity of certitude and has only to lie and watch it grow. This was the drift of his patience – that he had only to let it shine on him. He must moreover, with intermissions, still have been lifted and borne; since why and how else should he have known himself, later on, with the afternoon glow intenser, no longer at the foot of his stairs – situated as these now seemed at that dark other end of his tunnel – but on a deep window-bench of his high saloon, over which had been spread, couch-fashion, a mantle of soft stuff lined with grey fur that was familiar to his eyes and that one of his hands kept fondly feeling as for its pledge of truth. Mrs Muldoon's face had gone, but the other, the second he had recognized, hung over him in a way that showed how he was still propped and pillowed. He took it all in, and the more he took it the more it seemed to suffice: he was as much at peace as if he had had food and drink. It was the two women who had found him, on Mrs Muldoon's having plied, at her usual hour, her latch-key – and on her having above all arrived while Miss Staverton still lingered near the house. She had been turning away, all anxiety, from worrying the vain bell-handle – her calculation having been of the hour of the good woman's visit; but the latter, blessedly, had come up while she was still there, and they had entered together. He had then lain, beyond the vestibule, very much as he was lying now – quite, that is, as he appeared to have fallen, but all so wondrously without bruise or gash; only in a depth of stupor. What he most took in, however, at present, with the steadier clearance, was that Alice Staverton had for a long unspeakable moment not doubted he was dead.

'It must have been that I *was*.' He made it out as she held him. 'Yes – I can only have died. You brought me literally to life. Only,' he wondered, his eyes rising to her, 'only, in the name of all the benedictions, how?'

It took her but an instant to bend her face and kiss him, and something in the manner of it, and in the way her hands clasped and locked his head while he felt the cool charity and virtue of her lips, something in all this beatitude somehow answered everything. 'And now I keep you,' she said.

'Oh keep me, keep me!' he pleaded while her face still hung over him: in response to which it dropped again and stayed close, clingingly close. It was the seal of their situation – of which he tasted the impress for a long blissful moment in silence. But he came back. 'Yet how did you know—?'

'I was uneasy. You were to have come, you remember – and you had sent no word.'

'Yes, I remember – I was to have gone to you at one to-day.' It caught on to their 'old' life and relation – which were so near and so far. 'I was still out there in my strange darkness – where was it, what was it? I must have stayed there so long.' He could but wonder at the depth and the duration of his swoon.

'Since last night?' she asked with a shade of fear for her possible indiscretion.

'Since this morning – it must have been: the cold dim dawn of to-day. Where have I been,' he vaguely wailed, 'where have I been?' He felt her hold him close, and it was as if this helped him now to make in all security his mild moan. 'What a long dark day!'

All in her tenderness she had waited a moment. 'In the cold dim dawn?' she quavered.

But he had already gone on piecing together the parts of the whole prodigy. 'As I didn't turn up you came straight—?'

She barely cast about. 'I went first to your hotel – where they told me of your absence. You had dined out last evening and hadn't been back since. But they appeared to know you had been at your club.'

'So you had the idea of *this*—?'

'Of what?' she asked in a moment.

'Well – of what has happened.'

'I believed at least you'd have been here. I've known, all along,' she said, 'that you've been coming.'

' "Known" it—?'

'Well, I've believed it. I said nothing to you after that talk we had a month ago – but I felt sure. I knew you *would*,' she declared.

'That I'd persist, you mean?'

'That you'd see him.'

'Ah but I didn't!' cried Brydon with his long wail. 'There's somebody – an awful beast; whom I brought, too horribly, to bay. But it's not me.'

At this she bent over him again, and her eyes were in his eyes. 'No – it's not you.' And it was as if, while her face hovered, he might have made out in it, hadn't it been so near, some particular meaning blurred by a smile. 'No, thank heaven,' she repeated – 'it's not you! Of course it wasn't to have been.'

'Ah but it *was*,' he gently insisted. And he stared before him now as he had been staring for so many weeks. 'I was to have known myself.'

'You couldn't!' she returned consolingly. And then reverting, and as if to account further for what she had herself done, 'But it wasn't only *that*, that you hadn't been at home,' she went on. 'I waited till the hour at which we had found Mrs Muldoon that day of my going with you; and she arrived, as I've told you, while, failing to bring any one to the door, I lingered in my despair on the steps. After a little, if she hadn't come, by such a mercy, I should have found means to hunt her up. But it wasn't,' said Alice Staverton, as if once more with her fine intention – 'it wasn't only that.'

His eyes, as he lay, turned back to her. 'What more then?'

She met it, the wonder she had stirred. 'In the cold dim dawn, you say? Well, in the cold dim dawn of this morning I too saw you.'

'Saw *me*—?'

'Saw *him*,' said Alice Staverton. 'It must have been at the same moment.'

He lay an instant taking it in – as if he wished to be quite reasonable. 'At the same moment?'

'Yes – in my dream again, the same one I've named to you. He came back to me. Then I knew it for a sign. He had come to you.'

At this Brydon raised himself; he had to see her better. She helped him when she understood his movement, and he sat up, steadying himself beside her there on the window-bench and with his right hand grasping her left. '*He* didn't come to me.'

'You came to yourself,' she beautifully smiled.

'Ah I've come to myself now – thanks to you, dearest. But this brute, with his awful face – this brute's a black stranger. He's none of *me*, even as I *might* have been,' Brydon sturdily declared.

But she kept the clearness that was like the breath of infallibility. 'Isn't the whole point that you'd have been different?'

He almost scowled for it. 'As different as *that*—?'

Her look again was more beautiful to him than the things of this world. 'Haven't you exactly wanted to know *how* different? So this morning,' she said, 'you appeared to me.'

'Like *him*?'

'A black stranger!'

'Then how did you know it was I?'

'Because, as I told you weeks ago, my mind, my imagination, had worked so over what you might, what you mightn't have been – to show you, you see, how I've thought of you. In the midst of that you came to me – that my wonder might be answered. So I knew,' she went on; 'and believed that, since the question held you too so fast, as you told me that day, you too would see for yourself. And when this morning I again saw I knew it would be because you had – and also then, from the first moment, because you somehow wanted me. *He* seemed to tell me of that. So why,' she strangely smiled, 'shouldn't I like him?'

It brought Spencer Brydon to his feet. 'You "like" that horror—?'

'I *could* have liked him. And to me,' she said, 'he was no horror. I had accepted him.'

' "Accepted"—?' Brydon oddly sounded.

'Before, for the interest of his difference – yes. And as *I* didn't disown him, as *I* knew him – which you at last, confronted with him in his difference, so cruelly didn't, my dear – well, he must have been, you see, less dreadful to me. And it may have pleased him that I pitied him.'

She was beside him on her feet, but still holding his hand – still with her arm supporting him. But though it all brought for him thus a dim light, 'You "pitied" him?' he grudgingly, resentfully asked.

'He has been unhappy, he has been ravaged,' she said.

'And haven't I been unhappy? Am not I – you've only to look at me! – ravaged?'

'Ah I don't say I like him *better*,' she granted after a thought. 'But he's grim, he's worn – and things have happened to him. He doesn't make shift, for sight, with your charming monocle.'

'No' – it struck Brydon: 'I couldn't have sported mine "downtown". They'd have guyed me there.'

'His great convex pince-nez – I saw it, I recognized the kind – is for his poor ruined sight. And his poor right hand—!'

'Ah!' Brydon winced – whether for his proved identity or for his lost fingers. Then, 'He has a million a year,' he lucidly added. 'But he hasn't you.'

'And he isn't – no, he isn't – *you*!' she murmured as he drew her to his breast.

NOTES

THE ROMANCE OF CERTAIN OLD CLOTHES

1. *Viola . . . Perdita*: it would have been unusual for an eighteenth-century Massachusetts gentleman to read Shakespeare for pleasure. Viola is the spirited heroine of Shakespeare's comedy *Twelfth Night* (1602) and Perdita the more serious-hearted heroine of his late romance *The Winter's Tale* (1611). Viola's name was changed to Rosalind, the name of the heroine of Shakespeare's *As You Like It*, in the 1885 version.

2. *brusquerie*: (French) bluntness, straightforwardness.

3. *of a good person*: of fine appearance.

4. *wainscoted parlour*: a parlour with panelling, usually on the lower part of the walls only, most commonly made of oak.

5. *like the ladies in the household of the Vicar of Wakefield*: in Oliver Goldsmith's novel *The Vicar of Wakefield*, published in 1766, a few years after this story is set, the vicar's daughters and wife are no strangers to the self-decorating arts.

6. *a little postern door*: a small secondary or rear door or gate.

7. *She thought he looked 'interesting'*: attractive and appealing, sympathetic.

8. *Lloyd, as I have hinted, was not a modern Petrarch*: Petrarch, the fourteenth-century Italian classical scholar and poet, wrote hundreds of poems to his unrequited love Laura during her lifetime as well as after her death. He was an early practitioner of the sonnet form.

9. *Viola's thoughts hovered lovingly about her sister's relics*: Viola, being 'tall' and 'very plump', would not have fitted into clothes made for Perdita, who is described as 'short of stature' and 'light of foot', nor could they have easily been altered.

10. *stuffs*: 'stuff' is an old-fashioned word for fabric.

THE LAST OF THE VALERII

Although 'The Last of the Valerii' does not contain an actual ghost, it
has a powerful supernatural air, which gives it the timbre of a ghost
story. I have also included it in this collection because the character of
the young Conte Valerio has an obvious correspondence with the character of Prince Amerigo in *The Golden Bowl* (1904), James's most
complex and accomplished novel. The themes of falling out of love, the
situating of nobility against money, and the collecting of artefacts are
also themes that the two works share. The character of the narrator in
'The Last of the Valerii' serves as a link between the old world of the
Count and the new world of Martha, as Bob and Fanny Assingham link
the worlds of another prince and his wife, Maggie, in *The Golden Bowl*.

1. *the familiar bust of the Emperor Caracalla*: Caracella was a
   bold and brutal Roman soldier-emperor who ruled in the early
   200s AD. The bust, made from marble, shows the emperor turning his head to the left, apparently expressing distaste or
   disapproval. An original bust made in the 200s was reinter-
   preted in the second half of the eighteenth century by the Italian
   sculptor Bartolomeo Cavaceppi (1716/1717–1799).

2. *The upholsterers were turned into it*: being too interested in upholstery in Henry James's world can be a bad sign, or an ill omen. 'He
   has a genius for upholstery,' Isabel Archer says of her unpleasant
   husband Gilbert Osmond (*The Portrait of a Lady* (1881), Ch. 38).

3. *ilex-walk*: *quercus ilex*, holm oak, is an evergreen tree native to
   the Mediterranean, similar to holly; thus a part of the grounds
   are planted lavishly with holm oak.

4. *say her prayers to the sacred Bambino at Epiphany*: pray to the
   holy infant on the holy day of Epiphany, that is, convert to
   Roman Catholicism, her husband's religion.

5. *St Peter's*: the famous renaissance basilica, the most sacred building
   of the Roman Catholic Church, in the Vatican City in Rome. In his
   1873 essay 'A Roman Holiday', collected in *Italian Hours* (1909),
   James wrote 'Taken as a walk not less than a church, St Peter's of
   course reigns alone. Even for the profane "constitutional" it serves
   where the Boulevards, where Piccadilly and Broadway, fall short . . .'

6. *beaux yeux*: (French) beautiful or fine eyes. Of Prince Amerigo
   in *The Golden Bowl*, James writes: 'His own dark blue eyes
   were of the finest, and, on occasion . . . resembled nothing so
   much as the high windows of a Roman palace.' (Book I, Ch. 2)

7. *Dante's pages ... the anecdotes of Vasari*: Dante Alighieri (*c.* 1265–1321) was a major Italian poet whose religious epic the *Divine Comedy* is considered among the greatest works of Italian literature. Giorgio Vasari (1511–74) was an Italian painter and writer, whose book *Lives of the Most Excellent Painters, Sculptors, and Architects* is considered the first important work of art history.

8. *a bride-cake*: a wedding cake.

9. *a colossal gilt-bronze Minerva mentioned by Strabo*: Minerva was the Roman goddess of wisdom. Strabo (64/63 BC–*c.* 24 AD) was a Greek philosopher, historian and geographer who wrote the *Geographica*, a vast encyclopedia of geographical knowledge.

10. *the Apollo, the Ceres*: Apollo, the son of Zeus, was a god of music and the sun in both Greek and Roman mythology. Ceres was the Roman goddess of agriculture, grain and the love a mother bears for her child.

11. *'Yes, by Bacchus, I am superstitious'*: Bacchus was the Roman god of wine and intoxication.

12. *'I may be summoned to welcome another Antinous back to fame, – a Venus, a Faun, an Augustus!'*: Antinous (*c.* 111–30) was a beautiful Bithynian Greek youth of humble origin who became a favourite of the Roman emperor Hadrian. Venus is the Roman goddess of love, beauty, sex, fertility, prosperity and desire. A Faun is a creature from Roman mythology, being half man, half goat. Augustus was the founder and first emperor of the Roman Empire, ruling from 27 BC until his death in AD 14.

13. *'She's a Juno'*: the Roman goddess Juno was the daughter of Saturn, both wife and sister of Jupiter, and mother of Mars and Vulcan, as well as protector of the state and of Rome's women.

14. *Juno of Praxiteles*: Praxiteles was the most famous and skilled of the Greek sculptors of the fourth century BC, few if any of whose works survive, but who was famous for his nude sculpture of Aphrodite, though not for a Juno (or, by her Greek name, Hera).

15. *peplum*: a shallow, decorative slip or frill of fabric, sometimes gathered, extending round the waist of a woman's garment. In the case of the statue, the peplum would have been represented in marble.

16. *figlioccia mia*: (Italian) my god-daughter.

17. *cippus*: a small, low pillar, square or round, commonly having an inscription, used here as a plinth.

18. *Proserpine*: an ancient Roman goddess whose cult was based on those of Greek Persephone and her mother Demeter, the Greek goddess of grain and agriculture.

19. *Ecco!*: (Italian) a mild, variously used exclamation meaning 'well now', or 'there you are'.

20. *Scudi*: the Roman *scudo* (plural: *scudi*) was the currency of the Papal States until 1866.

21. *the Alban Hills*: an area of extinct volcanoes twelve miles south-east of Rome; a favourite summer resort for Romans because of its coolness and beauty.

22. *Hermes*: the Greek god of commerce, and also the messenger of the gods.

23. *Virgil*: (70–19 BC) an ancient Roman poet of the Augustan period.

24. *the Pantheon*: a Roman temple, built in 27 BC, dedicated to all the gods of pagan Rome. It burnt down, twice, and the present building was built during Hadrian's reign (AD 117–138). James wrote to his sister Alice from Rome in 1869 that the Pantheon was so beautiful 'It makes you profoundly regret that you are not a pagan suckled in the creed outworn that produced it. It's the most conclusive example I have yet seen of the simple sublime.' (*Henry James Letters*, ed. Leon Edel (Cambridge, MA: Harvard University Press, 1974–1984), vol. 1, p. 161–64)

25. *forestieri*: (Italian) foreigners, tourists.

26. *the Inquisition*: an ecclesiastical tribunal established by Pope Gregory IX in the thirteenth century for the suppression of heresy. It was notorious for the use of torture.

27. *Jupiter and Mercury*: Jupiter, in Roman mythology, is the king of all the gods. Mercury is the god of communication, boundaries, merchandise and merchants, commonly associated with the Greek god Hermes.

28. *Diana*: the Roman goddess of chastity, hunting and the moon. James in the 1870s was preoccupied by the figure of Diana: in the 1874 story 'Adina' (whose heroine's name is an anagram of the goddess's), in 'Longstaff's Marriage' (1878), where the heroine is Diana Belfield, and in *The Portrait of a Lady* (1881) where Isabel Archer's last name suggests the goddess's bow and arrow.

29. *Caffè Greco*: the oldest café and bar in Rome, opened in 1760 on Via dei Condotti, it remains there to this day. Keats and Byron sat at its marble tables.

30. *illustrissimi forestieri*: (Italian) distinguished foreigners.

31. *au sérieux*: (French) seriously.

32. *the Acheron*: in ancient Greek mythology, the Acheron was one of the five rivers of the underworld, known as the 'river of woe'.

33. *the Latins were posterior to the cannibals*: the Romans came after the cannibals.

34. *Pan*: the Greek god of the wild, who appeared as a faun, half
    man and half goat.

SIR EDMUND ORME

1. *Brighton*: a famous, fashionable south-coast English seaside
    town with a reputation for romance. Beale Farange marries Mai-
    sie's governess Miss Overmore in Brighton in *What Maisie Knew*
    and it is also where Adam Verver proposes marriage to Charlotte
    Stant in *The Golden Bowl*. In that same novel Paris is referred to
    as 'Brighton at a hundred-fold higher pitch' (Book second, ch.7).
2. *of the Rifles*: the Rifle Brigade was a regiment of the British
    army distinguished for the part it played in creating the notion
    of the modern infantryman.
3. *a little wrong in the upper storey*: unbalanced, a bit mad.
4. *she almost interfered with the slaughter of ground game . . .
    preferred her to the society of the beaters*: such was Charlotte's
    charm that some men preferred her company to taking part in
    the shoot. Beaters are hired men who help out on a shoot by
    using sticks and shouting to rouse and scare birds into flight so
    that they can be killed.
5. *decent rustics*: respectable country people.
6. *flags*: flagstones (of the paved terrace).
7. *régimes*: (French) diets, special exercises.
8. *It was a case of retributive justice, of the visiting on the chil-
    dren of the sins of the mothers, since not of the fathers*: this is a
    reference to the Old Testament Book of Exodus 20:5, 'I the
    Lord thy God am a jealous God, visiting the iniquity of the
    fathers upon the children.'
9. *a Saint Martin's summer of the soul*: a St Martin's Summer is a
    period of unusually warm weather in late autumn, St Martin's
    Day being 11 November; thus a feeling of wellbeing, a late
    blooming for Mrs Marden in the autumn of her life.

OWEN WINGRAVE

1. *exactly of the stature of the great Napoleon*: Napoleon Bonaparte
    (1769–1821), the first Emperor of France and a great military
    commander, was thought to be of short stature at five foot two

inches. More recent research asserts that his actual height was closer to five foot seven – at a time when the average height in France was five foot five – and thus that he was not short at all.

2.   *Eastbourne*: a seaside town in Sussex, quieter and more refined than the Brighton of 'Sir Edmund Orme'. Eastbourne is twenty miles west along the coast from Rye, where Henry James lived at Lamb House from 1898 to 1916.

3.   *Baker Street*: a long street in the Marylebone area of central London, laid out in the eighteenth century. A prosperous, lively thoroughfare, extended in 1921 to include York Place and again in 1930 to take in Upper Baker Street, its most famous residents were William Pitt the younger, Arnold Bennett, and H.G. Wells. James associated it with the Victorian novelist William Makepeace Thackeray: in his childhood, 'as I trod the vast length of Baker Street, the Thackerayan vista of other days, I throbbed with the pride of a vastly enlarged acquaintance.' (*Henry James: Autobiographies*, ed. Philip Horne (New York: Library of America, 2016), p. 183). The fictional detective Sherlock Holmes also 'lived' there at 221b.

4.   *Kensington Gardens*: a large public park in West London near the handsome stuccoed villas of Kensington and Knightsbridge. James lived nearby at 34 De Vere Gardens from 1886 to 1898.

5.   *a volume of Goethe's poems*: the German poet, playwright, novelist, critic and statesman Johann Wolfgang von Goethe (1749–1832) was born in Frankfurt and the author of the verse-drama *Faust* (1808) and the two-part novel *Wilhelm Meister* (1795–6; 1821). In March 1864, James wrote a letter to Thomas Sargent Perry, imagining himself dead, in jest, and writing a 'spiritual, supernatural message' from an afterlife in which he found himself consorting with Shakespeare, Goethe and Charles Lamb. 'I am lucky in having Goethe all to myself, for I am the only one who speaks German.' (*Henry James Letters*, ed. Leon Edel (Cambridge, MA: Harvard University Press, 1974–1984), vol. 1, p. 49–51)

6.   *dawdle along Bond Street*: behave like a wealthy man of leisure or fashion, a playboy even, the opposite of a serious military person, strolling on one of the grandest and most expensive shopping streets in London.

7.   *It's corrupting the youth of Athens*: in section 24b of Plato's *Apology* (399 BC), the Greek philosopher Socrates says he has been accused of being a 'wrongdoer because he corrupts the youth and does not believe in the gods the state believes in'.

8. *Afghan sabre*: Owen Wingrave's father Owen was killed in a war
    in Afghanistan. The British fought wars there in 1839–42 and
    in 1878–80, with the second war being the most likely refer-
    ence here as this story appears to be set in the present or near
    present.

9. *the Indian Mutiny*: in 1857 there was a widespread but largely
    unsuccessful rebellion by the Indian army against British colo-
    nial rule.

10. *Whitechapel*: a district of East London, not far from the city
    centre, notorious throughout the nineteenth century for pov-
    erty, over-crowding, poor sanitation, high mortality rates
    (including, just before this tale, the 'Whitechapel Murders',
    1888–91, by 'Jack the Ripper') and prostitution; therefore an
    extraordinarily unlikely habitat for Miss Wingrave.

11. *Bayswater*: a respectable but unremarkable central London
    residential district. It includes the area of Lancaster Gate where
    Kate Croy's Aunt Maud attempts to work her magic in *The
    Wings of the Dove*.

12. *Hannibal and Julius Cæsar, Marlborough and Frederick and
    Bonaparte*: Hannibal (247–183/2 BC) was a Carthaginian mili-
    tary commander, generally considered one of the greatest
    military commanders in history. Julius Caesar (100–44 BC) was
    a reforming politician and military general of the late Roman
    Republic, who greatly extended the Roman dominions by con-
    quest, before seizing power and making himself dictator of
    Rome, paving the way for the imperial system. The greatest
    achievement of the first Duke of Marlborough, John Churchill
    (1650–1722), was almost single-handedly preventing a Bourbon
    super-state from dominating Europe. 'He bore a greater burden,
    military and political, than any British commander before or
    since, and of him alone could it be said that he never besieged a
    town he did not take, or fought a battle he did not win,' writes
    his most recent biographer Richard Holmes in *Marlborough:
    England's Fragile Genius* (2008). Frederick the Great (1712–
    86), King of Prussia 1740–86, was notable for his successful
    reorganization of Prussian armies and his final success against
    great odds in the Seven Years' War. Napoleon Bonaparte (see
    also note 1) rose to prominence during the French Revolution
    and led several successful campaigns during the Revolutionary
    Wars. Napoleon dominated European and world affairs for
    more than a decade, building a large empire that ruled over con-
    tinental Europe.

13. *entail*: a restrictive settlement of the inheritance of property to certain heirs over a number of generations so that it cannot be bequeathed in a different way, or sold.

14. *Paul and Virginia*: *Paul et Virginia* is a tragic novel by Jacques-Henri Bernardin de Saint-Pierre (1737–1814), first published in 1788. The novel's eponymous characters, Rousseauesque children of nature, are friends since birth who grow up on a tropical island and fall in love.

THE FRIENDS OF THE FRIENDS

1. *It's the contents of a thin blank-book*: a notebook with blank pages, modest in contrast with the 'faded red cover of a thin old-fashioned gild-edged album' in which the story has been written down in 'The Turn of the Screw'.

2. *done my best to swallow the prodigy they leave to be inferred*: done my best to absorb the extraordinary situation given in these pages.

3. *the only comfort that counts in life is not to have been a fool*: this wounded, world-weary style is unusual in a Henry James character and contrasts with the delicate sensibility of the man and the woman who see the ghosts in this tale.

4. *the 'Long'*: the long vacation, the summer holidays.

5. *'out'*: out into society, to parties and organized social occasions.

6. *a Bond Street frame*: an expensive picture-frame. (See also note 6 to 'Owen Wingrave'.)

7. *entêtement*: (French) stubbornness.

8. *astrachan*: dark, curly fleece of lambs from Astrakhan in Russia, or fabric resembling it.

9. *mum*: a common corruption of Ma'am, which is itself a shortening of Madam.

10. *soit*: (French) so be it.

11. *the Medusa-mask*: a mask like the face of the mythical Greek monster Medusa. Medusa's hair was made of venomous serpents and her face was considered so hideous that all who looked at her were turned to stone.

THE TURN OF THE SCREW

1. *Raison de plus*: (French) all the more reason.

2. *'candlestuck'*: set a candle in a candlestick.

3. *Harley Street*: a long prosperous thoroughfare of mainly Geor-
    gian houses in central London, popular with the upper classes;
    records show the street had twenty medical practices by 1860,
    though its reputation as the main street for British medical
    knowledge came later. Florence Nightingale worked in a hos-
    pital for 'sick gentlewomen' in Upper Harley Street in 1853–4.
4. *He had been left, by the death of his parents in India, guardian to
    a small nephew and a small niece*: these lines carry the strong sug-
    gestion, seldom mentioned, that the children may well have moved
    continents as well as having suffered multiple bereavements.
5. End of the first of twelve instalments of 'The Turn of the Screw' that
    ran in the magazine *Collier's Weekly* from January 1898.
6. *a commodious fly*: a spacious one-horse carriage.
7. *deep sweet serenity indeed of one of Raphael's holy infants*:
    Raffaello Sanzio da Urbino (1483–1520) was one of the most
    important painters of the Renaissance. Among his religious
    works featuring children are the *Canigiani Madonna* in Munich
    (1507) and *The Holy Family of Francis I* (1518), in the Louvre.
8. *an old machicolated square tower*: a square tower in the fash-
    ion of a castle turret, with battlements.
9. End of the second *Weekly* instalment in *Collier's*.
10. *gingerbread antiquity*: old-fashioned fairy-tale appearance.
11. Third instalment and 'Part First' of the serialisation ended here.
12. *a mystery of Udolpho or an insane, an unmentionable relative
    kept in unsuspected confinement*: *The Mysteries of Udolpho*
    (1794) is a novel written by Anne Radcliffe featuring ghosts
    (which turn out not to be real) and a heroine carried off to a
    lonely castle. It is gently satirized by Jane Austen in *Northanger
    Abbey* (1817). In Charlotte Brontë's *Jane Eyre* (1847), Mr Roch-
    ester keeps 'an unmentionable relative', his distressed wife
    Bertha Mason, 'in unsuspected confinement' in his attic ('in
    unsuspected confinement'). These references show that the gov-
    erness has literary heroines, in peril, on her mind from the start.
13. *the sisterhood*: the word 'sisterhood' occurs five times in James's
    novel about feminism, *The Bostonians*, first published as a serial in
    1885–86.
14. *a muff*: a person who lacks skill or aptitude.
15. *those cherubs of the anecdote*: cherubs were often represented
    in painting and statues as having a head and wings but no body.
    In his diary, Henry Crabb Robinson recalls a memory that
    Lamb had of Coleridge. Hearing of the death of one of their
    Christ's Hospital school masters, who had been 'a severe

disciplinarian', Coleridge said 'he hoped his soul was in heaven [. . .] borne there by a host of cherubs, all face and wing, and without anything to excite his whipping propensities!' (Henry Crabb Robinson, *Diary, Reminiscences, and Correspondence* (London: Macmillan and Co., 1869) vol. 2, p. 36)

16. *I should have found the trace, should have felt the wound and the dishonour*: in all versions of the tale before the New York Edition this sentence ends with the word 'trace'.

17. *He gives me a sort of sense of looking like an actor*: in the popular imagination, actors were far removed from the notion of respectability. It is, however, surprising that the governess compares Quint to an actor as she also says later on the same page that she has 'never seen one'. The later reference to playbills on page 200 is also notable for this reason. James himself had just emerged from the bruising experience of having his play *Guy Domville* poorly received on the London stage.

18. End of fourth instalment in *Collier's Weekly*.

19. *scullions*: servants employed to do menial kitchen tasks.

20. *Sea of Azof*: a shallow northern extension of the Black Sea, located on the southern coastlines of Russia and Ukraine.

21. Fifth instalment and 'Part Second' ended here.

22. *I find that I really hang back; but I must take my horrid plunge . . . push my dreadful way through it to the end*: in this passage the words 'horrid' and dreadful' only appear in the New York Edition of the tale.

23. *'Amelia'*: by Henry Fielding (1707–54), a popular novel, published in 1751, tracing the vicissitudes of the eponymous heroine's marriage, which has to overcome a succession of challenges financial, sexual and emotional.

24. End of sixth weekly instalment.

25. *Mrs Marcet*: Jane Marcet (1769–1858), a writer of popular introductory books, particularly on science and economics, under the general title 'Conversations', taking the form of a dialogue between two pupils and their teacher.

26. *Laws!*: an exclamation of astonishment or indignation, derived from 'Lord', or 'Lordy me', itself a corruption of 'Lord help me'.

27. *By writing to him that his house is poisoned and his little nephew and niece mad?*: in the *Collier's Weekly* serial this sentence read: 'By writing to him that I have the honor to inform him that they see the dead come back?'

28. Seventh instalment and 'Part Third' of the serialization ended here after seven further sentences that were cut in the transition to publication in book form.

29. *whimsical bent*: this was 'eccentric habits' in *Collier's Weekly* and 'eccentric nature' in the first book edition, *The Two Magics*.

30. *Goody Gosling's celebrated mot*: this may refer to a joke or fine phrase by one of the governess's former neighbours ('Goody' is an archaic abbreviation of 'Goodwife', a term of respect for an older woman, usually married, often of the servant class); or perhaps to a Mother Goose-style nursery rhyme enjoyed by the children.

31. Eighth weekly instalment ended here.

32. *a large clean picture of the 'put away' – of drawers closed and locked and rest without a remedy*: In the *Collier's Weekly* serial this passage read 'a large, clean image of cupboards closed and diligence vaguely baffled'.

33. *David playing to Saul could never have shown a finer sense of the occasion*: a reference, to 1 Samuel 16:14–23: 'David took an harp, and played with his hand; so Saul was refreshed, and was well, and the evil spirit departed from him (v. 23).' In his 1984 Penguin English Library edition of *The Aspern Papers and The Turn of the Screw*, Anthony Curtis notes that 'Oscar Cargill and others . . . have produced this reference as conclusive evidence of James's intention that the governess's condition was pathological.'

34. Ninth weekly instalment and 'Part Fourth', ended here.

35. Tenth instalment ended here.

36. Eleventh instalment ended here.

37. *stay his answer*: prevent his answer.

THE THIRD PERSON

1. *Marr*: a fictional town based on Rye in East Sussex, where Henry James lived from 1898, and which had formerly been notorious for smuggling.

2. *pensions*: (French) small hotels, inns.

3. *her Tauchnitz novel*: the Tauchnitz 'Collection of British Authors' started in 1842 and continued for almost exactly one hundred years, running to over 5,300 volumes and covering almost all the most important and interesting English literature over that period. They were only for sale in continental Europe,

so they would have been regarded as contraband in England, a detail which becomes important later in the story.

4. *strikingly type-copied*: typed on a typewriter; 'strikingly' serves very well to show the cousins' excitement about the play while giving a sense of fingers hitting typewriter keys.

5. *the 'Channel'*: the English Channel, what the French call *La Manche* (the sleeve), is the stretch of sea running between the south coast of England and the north coast of France.

6. *Bloomsbury*: an area of central London, not especially fashionable at this time and notable for its large formal squares and green spaces and also as the location of much of London University, and the British Museum. It had not yet established itself as the home of the influential artists and writers who came to be known as the Bloomsbury Group; indeed Rye, the town in which Henry James lived from 1898, with a number of notable writers in the area, has been thought of as a pre-Bloomsbury Bloomsbury.

7. *the Arno and the Reuss*: the Arno is a river in Italy which flows through Florence, descending 150 miles from the Tuscan Apennines to the Ligurian Sea. The Reuss is the fourth largest river in Switzerland. The upper Reuss forms the main valley of the canton of Uri. The lower Reuss runs from Lake Lucerne to the confluence with the Aare at Brugg.

8. *Titian at the Pitti*: Titian (Tiziano Vecellio) is commonly considered to be the greatest painter of sixteenth-century Venice. James wrote to his brother William from Rome on New Year's Day 1870 that he was in Florence and 'took a turn yesterday thro' the Uffizi & the Pitti. All my old friends there stood forth & greeted me with a splendid good-grace. The lustrissimo [splendid] Tiziano in especial gave me a glorious Venetian welcome.' (*Henry James Letters*, ed. Leon Edel (Cambridge, MA: Harvard University Press, 1974–1989), pp. 179–189) The museum at the Pitti Palace, which was formerly the residence of the Grand Dukes of Tuscany and later of the King of Italy, houses several important collections of art.

9. *Don Juan*: the legendary, fictional Spanish libertine might have been known to the cousins from the poem of the same title (1819–24) by Byron, or Molière's 1665 play *Don Juan*. In his 1888 essay on Robert Louis Stevenson, published in the *Century* magazine, xxxv (pp. 137–74), James wrote that Stevenson's style 'is eminently conscious of its responsibilities, and meets them with a kind of gallantry – as if language were a pretty

woman, and a person who proposes to handle it had of necessity to be something of a Don Juan.'

10. *Gothic character*: an old-fashioned Germanic style of lettering.

11. *wide-awake*: a soft, low-crowned felt hat, usually brown or black, also known as a Quaker hat. Rembrandt wears a type of wide-awake hat in his 1632 self-portrait.

12. *ear-chair*: a high-backed upholstered armchair with side pieces projecting from near the top of the back, what we would now term a wing chair.

THE JOLLY CORNER

1. *He had given them more than thirty years – thirty-three, to be exact*: Henry James himself left America to live in Paris in 1875, moving to England the following year. He returned only twice to the United States during the next twenty-nine years. 'The Jolly Corner' was written following visits to New York in 1904–5, his long absence mirroring that of Spencer Brydon.

2. *Irving Place*: named after the American writer Washington Irving (1783–1859), author of 'Rip Van Winkle' (1819). A short street running between 14th and 20th streets in New York City, a block east of Union Square, it lies in the district of the city where James lived as a child (1847–55).

3. *a character*: a character reference.

4. *pour deux sous*: (French) for two coins of very little value, for two cents, thus: I was too young, at twenty-three, to judge even in the smallest way.

5. *ombres chinoises*: (French, literally 'Chinese shadows') shadow theatre.

6. *rapprochement*: (French) connection.

7. *Pantaloon . . . Harlequin*: characters from the Italian *commedia dell'arte*, a popular form of entertainment from the sixteenth to the eighteenth century. Pantaloon was a Venetian merchant, rich, greedy and naïve; and Harlequin a light-hearted, clever servant in chequered costume. These characters continued into the English pantomime tradition, still popular at Christmas.

8. *even as the trodden worm of the adage must at last bristle*: 'the smallest worm will turn being trodden on, / And doves will peck in safeguard of their brood.' *Henry VI, Part III*, act II, scene 2.

9. *lappet*: a decorative flap or fold of fabric or lace attached to a head-dress or formal garment, sometimes scarf-like, framing the face.

PENGUIN CLASSICS

DAISY MILLER
HENRY JAMES

'I'm a fearful, frightful flirt! Did you ever hear of a nice girl that was not?'

Travelling in Europe with her family, Daisy Miller, an exquisitely beautiful young American woman, presents her fellow-countryman Winterbourne with a dilemma he cannot resolve. Is she deliberately flouting social conventions in the way she talks and acts, or is she simply ignorant of them? When she strikes up an intimate friendship with an urbane young Italian, her flat refusal to observe the codes of respectable behaviour leaves her perilously exposed. In *Daisy Miller* Henry James brilliantly dramatized the conflict between old-world manners and nouveau riche tourists, and created his first great portrait of an enigmatic and independent American woman.

Part of a series of new Penguin Classics editions of Henry James's works, this edition contains a chronology, further reading, notes and a wide-ranging introduction by David Lodge discussing the genesis of the tale, its huge success and James's controversial revision of the text for his New York Edition. Appendices include Henry James's Preface from the New York Edition and a note on James's adaptation of his story as a play.

'A small masterpiece' Leon Edel

Edited with an introduction and notes by David Lodge
Series editor Philip Horne

PENGUIN CLASSICS

THE AMBASSADORS
HENRY JAMES

> 'I've come, you know, to make you break with everything,
> neither more nor less, and take you straight home'

Concerned that her son Chad may have become involved with a woman of dubious reputation, the formidable Mrs Newsome sends her 'ambassador' Strether from Massachusetts to Paris to extricate him. Strether's mission, however, is gradually undermined as he falls under the spell of the city and finds Chad refined rather than corrupted by its influence and that of his charming companion, the Comtesse de Vionnet. As the summer wears on, Mrs Newsome comes to the conclusion that she must send another envoy to Paris to confront the errant Chad, and a Strether whose view of the world has changed profoundly. James's favourite novel and one of the greatest of his late works, *The Ambassadors* is a subtle and often witty exploration of different American responses to a European environment.

In his introduction, Harry Levin discusses the novel's depiction of the significance of Paris to the American mind and the late awakening of a sensitive and open-minded man. This edition also contains notes on the text.

Edited with an introduction by Harry Levin

PENGUIN CLASSICS

THE BOSTONIANS
HENRY JAMES

> 'There was nothing weak about Miss Olive,
> she was a fighting woman, and she would fight him to the death'

Basil Ransom, an attractive young Mississippi lawyer, is on a visit to his cousin
Olive, a wealthy feminist, in Boston when he accompanies her to a meeting on
the subject of women's emancipation. One of the speakers is Verena Tarrant,
and although he disapproves of all she claims to stand for, Basil is immediately
captivated by her and sets about 'reforming' her with his traditional views. But
Olive has already made Verena her protégée, and soon a battle is under way for
exclusive possession of her heart and mind. The Bostonians is one of James's most
provocative and astute portrayals of a world caught between old values and the lure
of progress.

Richard Lansdown's introduction discusses *The Bostonians* as James's most
successful political work and his funniest novel. This edition contains extracts from
Tocqueville and from James's 'The American Scene', which illuminate the novel's
social context. There are also notes and a bibliography.

Edited with an introduction by Richard Lansdown